JOAN JOHNSTON

INVINCIBLE

Recycling programs for this product may not exist in your area.

ISBN-13: 978-0-7783-2757-8

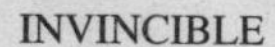

INVINCIBLE

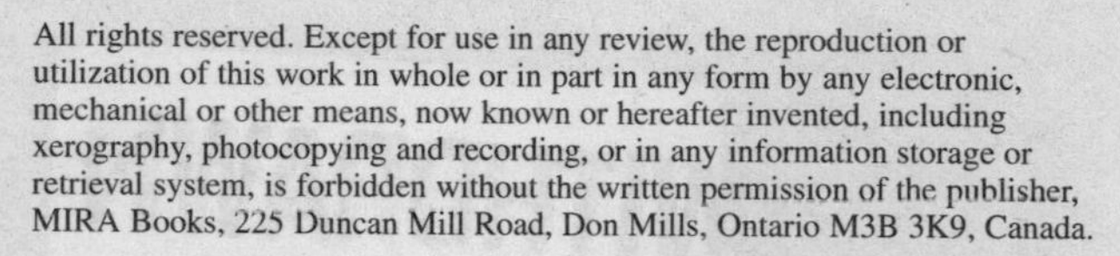

For questions and comments about the quality of this book please contact us at Customer_eCare@Harlequin.ca.

www.MIRABooks.com

Printed in U.S.A.

For Donna Hayes, Loriana Sacilotto,
Margaret O'Neill Marbury, Valerie Gray and Linda McFall.
A writer couldn't ask for a better support team.

Prologue

How hard could it be to find spouses for her five grown children before she died? Bella supposed it depended on how long it took for her failing heart to give out. No one had ever accused the five Benedict children of being easy to handle. All of them over twenty-five, and not one of them ever engaged, let alone married.

That might have something to do with the lives they led as members of British royalty. Bella was actually Isabella Wharton Benedict, Duchess of Blackthorne. She certainly had her work cut out for her finding mates for four British-American lords and a lady. Bella corrected herself. Make that four gentlemen rogues and a spoiled rotten lady.

Could she do it? Did she dare try?

Bella stared out the window from her hospital bed at the University of Virginia Medical Center in Charlottesville, wondering where to start. She ran a brush through her shoulder-length black hair, which was threaded with more silver every day. She might be in the autumn of her life, but here in Virginia it was spring, when love blossomed.

Cardinals flirted in the flowering dogwood trees. Blue-and-black-and-yellow butterflies cavorted in the daffodils. Squirrels chattered at each other and played tag, tails flying. With any luck, her titled offspring would find themselves equally vulnerable to romance during this fertile season.

She threw the engraved silver brush onto the bedside table and turned her attention back to the doctor standing at the foot of her hospital bed. "What's the verdict?"

"You're still at about thirty percent heart function."

That was actually good news. At least she hadn't lost function since her last checkup. She could live—for a while, maybe years—with that little heart function. But the point was, her heart was dying, and she was dying along with it.

That's what she got for insisting she could ski down an icy slope in the Alps. She'd survived the blunt force trauma to her heart when she'd lost control and gone over a cliff. But the injury had caused scarring that had resulted in reduced heart function and continuing heart failure.

"How long do I have?" she asked.

"The new meds I gave you should keep you up and running for a while."

"Running?" Bella said with a quirk of her lips.

"Figuratively," the doctor qualified. "You should certainly be exercising regularly to keep what's left of your heart muscle healthy. And take your meds!"

Bella eyed the numerous bottles of pills she needed to keep her heart functioning. She hated depending on all those pills, but they allowed her an almost-normal life. ACE inhibitors. Beta blockers. Aldosterone antagonist drugs. She couldn't begin to name the individual prescriptions. The problem was, at some point—in the not too distant future—her heart was still going to fail.

"How long do I have?" Bella asked again.

"Can't say," the doctor replied.

"Guess."

The doctor shrugged. "A year for sure. Maybe two. Three if you take care of yourself—and you're lucky. Or you could have a heart attack tomorrow. We just can't predict these things."

Bella shivered. That wasn't much of a future.

"I do have some good news," the doctor said.

"I'll take what I can get."

"We've been making enormous strides in stem cell therapy. Stay alive long enough and we may be able to rejuvenate that heart of yours with your own stem cells."

"How long is long enough?" Bella asked.

The doctor focused on the medical chart in his hands. "Can't say."

"And if my heart continues to fail?"

"Heart transplant is a possibility down the line. Unfortunately, it won't be easy finding a heart for you, Bella. B-negative donors aren't thick on the ground."

Bella smiled. Her doctor was young, a prodigy whose bedside manner left a lot to be desired. She appreciated his honesty. Knowing how much—or rather, how little—time she had left allowed her to plan how to use it wisely.

But a year? Two years? Three, if she was lucky? She had even less time than she'd hoped to get her children wed. With so little time, some of those marriages might have to be arranged without her offspring's cooperation. It had to be marriage, she'd decided. Nothing less would do. Her marriage to Bull Benedict had been her salvation.

It had started badly, with blackmail on her side. Her aunt had threatened twenty-nine-year-old billionaire financier Jonathan "Bull" Benedict with charges of statutory rape if he didn't marry destitute seventeen-year-old Isabella Wharton, Duchess of Blackthorne. Bull had sworn he'd hate her forever if she forced him into marriage.

She'd bit her lip and gone along with her aunt's wishes in order to save her hereditary home, Blackthorne Abbey. And to give her unborn child a name. It was only later that Bull questioned whether he was the father of their first child. Only later that he learned Oliver was some other man's son.

Because they were bound by law, they'd been forced to deal with one another's lies. Because they were husband and wife, they'd scratched their bloody way through the tangled thorns of deceit to a love that healed all wounds.

Bella wanted her children bound to someone they could love by vows made before God. She was certain the moral commitment created by the spoken words, words pledging love and faith to one another, would give the young lovers the perseverance necessary to work through any differences that threatened their happiness.

She didn't want her children wandering the world alone after she was gone, believing that love was a false thing. That love couldn't be trusted. That was the lesson she feared they'd learned from the wickedness—the malicious trickery—that had finally torn her marriage apart.

"Of course, Bella, if you do end up with a new heart—or a rejuvenated one—you'll be good to go for another fifty years," the doctor said, interrupting her thoughts.

"Thanks a lot," Bella said with a wry laugh. She was fifty-two. Reaching a hundred and two sounded pretty ambitious. And lonely, unless she could find a way to win her husband's forgiveness. Bella felt hopeless about any sort of reconciliation with Bull. Especially when she considered how little she could tell him—certainly not the truth—about the event that had caused their bitter separation ten years ago, after twenty-five years of marriage.

They were still legally wed, but it was a marriage in name only. They lived separate lives. Every day for the past ten years, she'd feared Bull would come to her and ask for a divorce. It had never happened. She wondered if he was clinging to a fragile thread of hope, as she was, that someday they would find their way back to each other. Or whether he simply wanted to preserve his fortune. A fortune which, thanks to an ironclad prenuptial agreement, would only have to be shared with her if they stayed married for twenty-five years. They'd reached that mark a month before their separation.

Bella sighed inwardly. The chances of "love conquering all" seemed slim, considering how little time she had left. She needed to focus on her children's happiness. When the end came would be soon enough to make peace with Bull.

"When can I get out of here?" she asked.

"Today, if you promise to follow my orders," the doctor replied. "Make sure you exercise, Bella. Take your meds. And avoid stress. Otherwise…" He drew a finger across his neck, hung his head sideways and made a dying sound.

Bella grimaced at his antics. Maybe she could get Oliver, Riley, Payne, Max and Lydia to come to her, instead of having to go to the four corners of the earth to find them. Without revealing her precarious health, of course. Mother's Day was coming up. That would make a good excuse to summon them to The Seasons, the Benedict family estate near Richmond, a former tobacco plantation her estranged husband's family had owned since colonial days.

The doctor turned to Bella's personal assistant, a quiet, intelligent, almost homely girl Bella had hired three years ago when she first began taking medication for her ailing heart, and ordered, "I don't want her out partying till the wee hours, Emily. Bella needs rest if she's going to stay alive until we can repair her heart—or find her a new one."

"Of course, Doctor," Emily replied. "I'll take good care of Her Grace."

Twenty-eight-year-old Emily Sheldon was nothing if not dutiful, Bella thought. The young Englishwoman refused to address Bella by name, instead referring to her in clipped British tones as "Your Grace," an honor to which Bella was entitled by virtue of her aristocratic rank.

The refined, straitlaced young woman, who'd become as dear to her as another daughter, would follow the doctor's orders to the letter. If Bella didn't want to find herself being hounded by her assistant, she was going to have to involve Emily in her matchmaking plans.

When the doctor was gone, Emily began fussing with the sheets, pulling them up around Bella's pale blue silk robe and smoothing them down. "I urge you to consider the consequences if you disobey the doctor's orders, Your Grace. I'll do my best to help you—"

Bella put a hand on her assistant's delicate wrist and said, "Please sit down, Emily. I have something to discuss that's going to require your entire attention—our entire attention—for the foreseeable future."

1

"Hello, Princess."

Kristin Lassiter's heart skipped a beat. Without warning, she found herself facing a man she'd prayed never to see again. "Max?" Her voice broke because her throat had suddenly swollen closed. "What are you doing here?"

"Close the door, Agent Lassiter," Max said.

Kristin had been ordered to report to the Special Agent in Charge of the FBI's Miami Field Office. She was just going back on duty in the field with a new partner, following the disastrous shooting incident she'd been involved in four months ago. So she wasn't surprised her boss wanted to see her. But Rudy wasn't in his office. This man was. With *man* being the operative word.

The last time she'd seen Max Benedict, he'd been a boy of eighteen. She'd been sixteen. They'd been best friends for three years. And lovers for one night. They hadn't seen or spoken to each other since.

The troubled boy she'd known had been lithe and

fit and tanned. This tall, broad-shouldered man looked powerful. And dangerous.

Kristin felt a spurt of alarm that bordered on panic. Why was he here? Had he come to find out why she'd run from him all those years ago?

"Why are you here, Max?"

"I have a proposition for you."

Before she could open her mouth to protest he said, "A *business* proposition."

So, he wasn't here for personal reasons. She slowly exhaled, careful not to sigh audibly with relief. He was acting like they were old friends. But they hadn't been friends for a very long time. She'd been vulnerable to him once. Had adored him with all the luminous passion one devoted to a first love. Seeing him in the flesh, seeing the promise of the boy revealed in the virile man standing before her, stirred all those unwanted feelings to life.

Max couldn't possibly believe she'd want anything to do with him now. Ten years had gone by since he'd used and discarded her. He must know her bitter feelings toward him hadn't changed. Nor would they ever. So what was this boy from her past—turned dangerous man—doing here?

"Close the door, Agent Lassiter," Max repeated.

This time, it wasn't a request, it was a command, spoken in Max's brisk British accent. She knew he could as easily have issued the order in French or Spanish or Italian or Russian, or even Portuguese, a result of his attendance at a series of elite British, American and

European boarding schools. He'd honed his talent by conversing with the many foreign players on the junior tennis tour, where she'd first met Max all those years ago.

But the Max she'd known was long gone. The man standing before her was a stranger. His once Caribbean-warm blue eyes looked cold and remote. The playful dimple in his right cheek was gone, replaced by a nose and cheekbones and chin that looked carved from granite. There was no sign of the soft lips she'd kissed. His mouth was pressed into a flat, unrelenting line.

When she'd known Max in the past, he'd been dressed most often in tennis shorts and a sleeveless cutoff T-shirt that revealed an impressive set of biceps and six-pack abs. She felt certain the powerful, corded muscles were still there. But they were concealed by a perfectly tailored wool-and-silk suit that likely equaled the cost of a first-class ticket to London and a white Egyptian cotton shirt and Armani tie that probably matched her monthly food budget.

The fact Max had called her *Agent Lassiter* suggested he was here on official business. But his tailored suit was at odds with the rest of his appearance. A dark, two-day-old beard made his rugged features look disreputable. And the straight black hair he'd kept short on the tennis court had grown long enough that a shaggy lock of black hair had slipped onto his brow.

He looked like one of the bad guys.

But Kristin knew that Max Benedict, youngest son of the infamous billionaire banker Jonathan "Bull"

Benedict and his estranged wife, Bella, the Duchess of Blackthorne, was nothing more than a wealthy, care-for-nothing playboy. His expensive clothing—and the fact he badly needed a haircut and a shave—convinced her of that.

Instead of closing the door as he'd ordered, she said, "Where's Rudy?"

Max shoved papers out of the way and perched on the edge of Rudy's cluttered mahogany desk before replying, "Your boss knows why I'm here. He let me use his office for this meeting."

Kristin snorted. It was an inelegant, rude sound, revealing just how ridiculous she thought his statement was.

He made a disgusted sound in his throat, rose and crossed past her to shut the door. She'd expected him to slam it, but the quiet click told her even more certainly that she was now caged with a feral predator. She felt the urge to flee, but resisted it.

She turned to face him, stuck her balled fists on her hips and said, "What's going on, Max?"

Irritation rolled off him in waves. She realized that he wasn't any happier to be in the same room with her than she'd been to find him in her boss's office.

He leaned back against the door, his arms crossed over his chest. It appeared her way out was blocked. But she'd been trained in self-defense. And she had a Glock 27 concealed beneath her suit jacket.

"I told them this wouldn't work," he muttered.

"Since I don't know who you're talking about, or why you're here, I can't respond to that," she retorted.

"Foster Benedict sent me," he said.

Kristin's brows rose in surprise. "Isn't Foster your uncle?"

Max nodded curtly.

"Your *uncle* sent you here?" she asked incredulously.

"My uncle, the advisor to the president on matters of terrorism, sent me here," he clarified.

Kristin took three steps and dropped into one of the two brass-studded saddle-brown leather chairs in front of Rudy's desk. "I really have fallen down the rabbit hole," she murmured, shaking her head.

Max strode across the room to stare out the window. The FBI's concrete-and-glass Miami Field Office was nowhere near the palm trees, white-sand beaches and marine-blue waters of Miami Beach. Instead, the view from Rudy's fourth-floor window in North Miami Beach revealed a network of superhighways leading into, out of and around Miami.

Max turned back to her and asked, "How much tennis are you playing these days?"

The question, coming out of the blue, surprised her into replying, "I usually play on weekends with the kids who attend my dad's tennis academy."

"You look fit enough." Max crossed and perched once again on the corner of the desk in front of her. He proceeded with a perusal of her body that left her feeling flushed. And indignant.

"Would you like me to undress so you can take a better look?"

He met her gaze, then slowly, seductively, looked her up and down again. "Since I've already seen what's underneath that cheap blue suit, my imagination can fill in the blanks."

She shoved herself out of the chair and stalked over to look out the window herself. Having just noted all the improvements in his physique over the years, it was humiliating to be told he still saw the underdeveloped body of a sixteen-year-old girl. It was true her bosom had never been anything to shout about. But he'd seemed more than pleased with her small breasts during the one night they'd spent together.

At sixteen, she'd been a world-class athlete. Her body had been toned and firm. It still was. The flyaway blond curls she'd worn in a ponytail on the tennis court were captured ruthlessly in a bun at her nape, although stray curls always seemed to escape. She reached up self-consciously to tuck one behind her ear.

Max seemed to have grown an inch or two taller, to perhaps 6'3", but she was the same 5'9" she'd been at sixteen. She wore no more makeup now to flatter her blue eyes or conceal her freckled complexion than she had then. And her bosom had stayed as small and trim as the rest of her.

"You look even more beautiful now than you did ten years ago, Princess," he said softly.

Kristin realized he was standing right behind her, so close she could feel the warmth of his breath on her neck.

She hated the fact that his compliment pleased her so much. At the same time, she wondered how he'd managed to cross the room without her hearing a sound.

He blew softly on a stray curl that lay against her throat.

She felt a frisson of desire run down her spine and jerked herself away from him. "Stop that!"

She saw the knowing smile on his face and felt her flush deepen. She deflected his attempt at seduction by saying, "Who is it you're here to see, Max? Some once-upon-a-time princess? Or Agent Lassiter? Make up your mind."

"Right," he said. "Down to business." He met her gaze and said, "I have a job for you."

"I already have a job," she snapped.

"Your boss has agreed to give you leave to perform a special mission."

"A special mission?" she parroted back, adding a scalding dose of sarcasm.

"There's been an assassination threat against President Taylor."

That sounded real. That sounded ominous. Andrea Taylor wasn't a particularly popular president because of actions she'd taken to end the ongoing war in the Middle East. "How could you possibly know something like that?"

"Interpol intercepted email traffic—source never identified—that suggested someone is planning to take advantage of the president's seating proximity to the tennis courts to kill her during the U.S. Open tennis event over the Labor Day weekend in New York. The president is a huge fan of the game and always attends the tournament at Flushing Meadows."

"Interpol? So how did you get this information? Don't the Secret Service and Homeland Security have primary responsibility for protecting—"

"Interpol sent its information to the Central Intelligence Agency," he interrupted. "Tennis is an international sport, with players and coaches from a lot of nations with grudges against the United States, and presumably someone who might want to kill the president. The CIA decided the threat deserved investigation, so they contacted me. I work for them on occasion."

Kristin felt like laughing, but there was nothing amusing about Max's stony expression. "On occasion? So you're what? A private investigator or something?"

"A covert operative," he said.

"A spy?" she asked incredulously.

He nodded curtly.

Then she did laugh. "That's crazy, Max. I don't believe you. Show me some credentials."

"I work undercover. I don't carry credentials. Or a gun," he added, anticipating her next question.

"Why would the CIA hire you? I mean, you're just a rich playboy."

He raised a sardonic brow. "Who better to hobnob with wealthy drug czars playing polo in Argentina or attending the Carnival in Rio. Or munitions dealers gambling in Monte Carlo, or Arab terrorists playing tennis in Dubai?

"I have infamous parents. Outrageous siblings. I'm a peer of the realm, Lord Maxwell, youngest son of the Duchess of Blackthorne and her cruel—or is it crazy?—billionaire husband. Who would ever suspect me of spying? Which is why I'm so good at what I do."

His explanation made surprising sense. She asked the next obvious question. "Why me?"

"Short answer? You're a world-class tennis player who also happens to be a trained FBI agent."

"I still don't get it," Kristin said.

"Foster drew the logical inference that if an attack was going to be made at a tennis locale in the States, the attacker might have some connection to tennis. He—or she—might be a coach, a player or someone working for a player or in a player's family. He figured we might intercept the assassin if we send someone undercover to another tennis venue in advance of the U.S. Open. After some discussion, Wimbledon was selected over the French Open."

That also made sense, Kristin conceded. The French Open was at the end of the month, which didn't leave much time for planning.

"The CIA figured since I have a tennis background, and I live in London, I'm the logical person to infiltrate the professional tennis locker rooms at Wimbledon and listen for what I might hear about an assassination attempt on the president."

Kristin made a face. "I haven't played professional tennis for the past ten years."

"Neither have I," Max replied. "Which is why the CIA

arranged with Scotland Yard—and the cooperation of the All England Lawn Tennis Club—for an exhibition mixed doubles match to be played prior to opening day at Wimbledon. Since Foster knew you and I were friends when we played junior tennis, he suggested you as my doubles partner."

"I didn't know your uncle knew we were friends."

Max didn't reply to her non sequitur. He rubbed a hand across his nape and said, "I told him this was a bad idea."

"Because I haven't played tennis for ten years?"

"That. And because of what happened between us."

There it was. The elephant in the room. Kristin said nothing, because she had no idea what to say.

He eyed her and said into the silence, "I knew it would be hard—maybe impossible—for us to work together. But I couldn't very well explain why to my CIA boss or my uncle. Especially since I'm not quite sure myself what happened."

He'd contacted her in every way he could after their one night of love. One night of *sex,* she amended. But she'd refused to communicate with him. It was all water under the bridge. There was no going back. So why speak of it now? Especially since he was right. It would be impossible for them to work together. So why put them both through the agony of trying?

"I presume you're hoping I'll get you off the hook by refusing your offer," she said at last.

He nodded. "I was pretty sure you'd refuse. But I was obliged to bring you the offer."

"Who will you get if I say no?"

He shrugged. "I don't know. I'll find someone."

Kristin had a pretty good idea who that someone might be. A woman she disliked intensely. But she didn't say the name, because she didn't want to discuss what had happened ten years ago. Better to let sleeping dogs lie.

"Well? What's your answer, Princess?" Max said. "Want to play spy with me?"

Trust Max to make a joke of the whole thing. She wasn't laughing. She met his gaze and said, "You're off the hook, Max. My answer to your generous offer is no."

"But—"

"Not just no," she amended. "But hell no."

2

Kristin was feeling frantic. Was her daughter a passenger on the flight from Switzerland that had landed at Miami International Airport an hour ago? Or had Felicity found some way to elude her chaperon before the plane took off? Would she be seeing Flick in a few minutes, when she cleared customs? Or had her precocious child managed to run away again?

Kristin paced impatiently at the waiting area for friends and family of arriving American Airlines passengers clearing customs. With any luck, her nine-year-old daughter had gotten on AA Flight 87 from London, which had connected with AA Flight 6485 from Zurich, Switzerland, where Flick had been enrolled in boarding school. The headmistress hadn't wanted to wait until Kristin could come get her daughter. She'd insisted on putting Flick on the first available flight back to the States with a chaperon from the school.

Apparently, Flick had gotten into a fight with another girl. The headmistress's decision had been final: Flick was no longer welcome at the school.

It was one more disaster to add to a growing list. How different—how much worse—her life was just seven days after she'd refused Max's offer!

Over the past week since she'd met with Max Benedict, Kristin had lost weight from her already slender frame, so her cheeks looked gaunt. She had dark circles under her eyes from too many sleepless nights. A glimpse of herself reflected in the glass windows leading outside showed a heart-shaped face that looked haunted.

I should have gone to London, she thought. But making that choice wouldn't have erased all the problems facing her now. She had to believe she'd made the right choice refusing Max, although his visit had left her feeling slightly anxious and surprisingly sad.

Several of those waiting for family to clear customs watched her warily, despite the fact she didn't fit any sort of terrorist profile. As usual, her naturally curly blond hair was pinned up tight, although bothersome wisps had escaped. She wore a professional-looking collared white cotton blouse, crisp with extra starch from the dry cleaner, along with navy blue trousers. The matching navy blue jacket hid the Glock 27 she wore in a belt holster and had an inside pocket where she kept her FBI badge.

Although it was questionable whether either gun or badge would still be in her possession after her meeting with the FBI's Shooting Incident Review Team (SIRT), an FBI version of Internal Affairs, later this afternoon.

Kristin's glance darted from one individual to the next, automatically surveilling the waiting area. She focused intently on a suspicious-looking man who fit a profile the government wasn't supposed to be using. His thick black eyebrows rose in alarm before he reached for a giggling two-year-old with black-button eyes and lifted her into his lap, holding her close to protect her from the crazy-looking lady.

So, probably not a terrorist, Kristin thought. *Although he likely thinks you might be one. Get a grip. Be cool.*

The last thing she wanted was for someone to point her out to airport authorities as a possible threat. That would be all she'd need to make her day perfect.

Why did Felicity have to pick *now* to get herself kicked out of that Swiss boarding school? Her daughter had refused to tell the headmistress what had provoked the fight. But there was no question of Flick staying after she'd blackened the left eye and broken the left front tooth of the Spanish ambassador's daughter.

Kristin had faced not one, not two, but three serious traumas over the past week and managed to stay calm and collected. But Flick's misbehavior, which had resulted in her ejection from school, had just handed Kristin the straw that might break the proverbial camel's back.

On such short notice, she hadn't been able to find a nanny or housekeeper she liked to take care of Felicity after school and on weekends while she was on the job. She was going to have to take time off work until she could get the help she needed. Which she didn't want to do.

She didn't want the Miami SAC to think she wasn't

able to handle the fallout from the shooting four days ago, which had come too closely on the heels of the shooting four months ago. And been equally disastrous.

You're invincible, Kristin. Nothing can beat you.

How many times had her father spoken those words to her and her sister on the tennis court growing up? A hundred thousand maybe. She'd never quite believed him. Especially after her older sister, Stephanie, had died in a tragic auto accident at seventeen, leaving Kristin, four years younger, to bear the burden of her sister's promise as a rising tennis star.

Their mother had long since left their father, because he ate, slept and lived tennis. Kristin had no choice but to try to please her father on the tennis court or be left out of his life altogether.

She hadn't been as tall as Stephanie. Or as strong. And she didn't have her sister's fluid grace. Facts which caused her father endless frustration when he coached her. He was often disappointed in her performance and demanded that she practice to the point of exhaustion.

Which reminded her of the first time she'd met Max.

She'd been thirteen and had qualified to play at Wimbledon in the Girls' Singles competition. She'd already won her first match, but her father wasn't happy with her ground strokes. She had a day off between matches, so he'd insisted she spend time after her match practicing with a male hitting partner.

Her exercise clothes were sweat-soaked, despite the cool evening air. Her curly blond hair was bedraggled.

She could barely swing her right arm to hit the ball. But until her father was satisfied, she couldn't leave the court.

"Do it again, Kristin," he ordered from the sideline. "This time, push through the ball with your whole body."

"I'm doing the best I can," she retorted as she slammed a ball down the line.

"That's out!" he shouted. "By an inch. Keep the ball in the court, Kristin."

She'd checked her grip and hit three more balls as hard as she could down the line. Every one landed just past the baseline.

"Damn it, Kristin. What's the matter with you?"

"I'm tired, Daddy."

"You stay here and work until you can get the ball in the court." He stomped off and left her there.

Her hitting partner shrugged his shoulders and said, "Why don't we call it quits?"

"You heard him," she said. "I need to practice."

"I didn't plan to be here all night. You'll have to find someone else to hit with you," he said as he stuffed his racquet back into his bag.

Kristin stared at the teenage boy in disbelief. "My father is paying you—"

"Not enough," the kid said. "See you tomorrow morning."

Kristin stood on the court, her shoulders slumped, knowing she couldn't head back to the locker room for at least another hour without getting grounded. That was her father's favorite punishment, and it worked because she hated being confined indoors in some motel or hotel while on the road.

She heard someone behind her say, "Hey, kid. I'll hit with you."

She turned around and saw an older boy, with the most beautiful blue eyes she'd ever seen, standing on the opposite side of the court. It took her a moment to recognize him. "I know you. You're—"

"In need of some hitting practice," he said with a grin. He retrieved a racquet from his bag and dropped the bag on the sideline. "I was practicing my serve on the next court over. I couldn't help overhearing your coach. Sounded like he was a little tough on you."

"My dad just wants me to be the best I can be," she said. "Aren't you—"

A tennis ball was coming at her fast and with a lot of spin. She interrupted herself to hit it back. When the ball was on his side of the court she finished "—Max Benedict?"

"That's me," he said, whipping the ball back at her. "What's your name?"

She could hardly believe she was hitting with one of the top five male players on the junior tour. A fifteen-year-old! She took a small backswing and slammed the ball back at him. Max Benedict was also a hunk.

"My name's Kristin Lassiter," she blurted. She felt a blush starting at her throat at just the thought of a boy as good-looking as Max being romantically interested in her. Which she knew was ridiculous. He dated older women. As opposed to barely teenage girls, like her.

"You've got great strokes, K," he said as he tried to lob her.

She backed up to get the ball that had been hit high into the air and slammed it back down at him. "My name's Kristin, not Kay," she corrected.

"The letter K's easier to say," he replied as he ran for her overhead and snapped it back down at her.

Kristin struggled to get out of the way, so she could return the ball, but she was tired and her feet wouldn't move. "Ah!" she cried as she swung and missed.

"Finally!" he said as he trotted to the net. "I was beginning to think you'd never miss."

She crossed to the net, shoving flyaway curls off her face. "I miss plenty. Just ask my father."

"You're great, kid. Don't let anyone tell you different."

"You're just saying that."

"Why would I lie?"

She eyed him askance. "I don't know. Why are you playing with me? I mean, you're really a great player. And you're two years older than me." She flushed at having revealed that she knew his age.

"You remind me of my younger sister, Lydia," he said, tucking a curl behind her ear. "She's thirteen, too. I couldn't imagine Lydia putting up with a tenth of what your dad put you through tonight. I've had my own problems with well-intentioned parents. I guess I wanted to help."

Kristin rose to her father's defense. "He just wants me to win."

"There are more important things than winning," Max said.

"Name one thing," she challenged.

"Having fun. Enjoying the game," he replied.

"It wouldn't be much fun if I didn't win," she pointed out.

"Wouldn't it?"

She made a face. "I don't know. I've never thought about it much. I've been too focused on winning."

"Next time you play, think about having a good time. And winning," he said with a grin. "I'm sure you'll do just fine. Gotta go." He winked at her and waved a hand at someone behind her.

When she turned to look, she saw a female player—someone on the women's tour, rather than the junior tour—waiting for him on the sideline. He dumped his racquet in his bag, stalked over to the woman and kissed her on the lips.

He never looked back.

That was all it had taken for Max Benedict to capture her heart. A few minutes hitting tennis balls together. A considerate word of encouragement. A stray curl tucked behind her ear. A wink as he walked off the court. She'd loved him from that moment on.

Kristin grunted with disgust, then realized she was standing in an airport waiting area full of people who might wonder what she found so disgusting. She grimaced and crossed to stare out the windows at the traffic crawling by. What a fool she'd been all those years ago. She'd been well aware her feelings of love weren't mutual. To Max, she'd been a substitute for the little sister he apparently missed while traveling on the tour.

He'd often come to hit with her on the practice court during that summer at Wimbledon, at times when her father wasn't around.

Max made her believe in herself. He made her believe she could have fun on the tennis court. He made her believe she could win.

She became invincible.

She won the Girls' Singles Championship that summer at Wimbledon and the next two years, as well. She won at Roland Garros in Paris. And she was the Girls' Singles U.S. Open Champion at thirteen, fourteen and fifteen. She was the bright future of American tennis. The public was fascinated by the tall, honey-blonde phenom, a killer without mercy on the tennis court—who looked like an angel off of it.

Her tennis career ended abruptly at age sixteen, when she lost in the Wimbledon Girls' Singles Championship match to the rival she'd beaten the previous two years. When she'd discovered, with frightening, daunting clarity, that she wasn't so invincible after all.

Kristin heard a commotion and turned around.

"Mom?" Felicity burst into tears as she bolted out of the doorway from customs.

Kristin barely had time to take two steps and open her arms before her daughter threw herself into them. She could feel Flick trembling and felt her insides clench at the sound of her daughter's wrenching sobs. She tightened her grip to offer comfort. Why was Flick so distraught? What was going on?

"Mrs. Lassiter?" the chaperon who'd accompanied Flick through customs inquired. The elderly woman was small and compact and wore a tailored wool suit that might have been comfortable in Switzerland but looked out of place in Miami.

"I'm Special Agent Lassiter," Kristin said, to avoid having to explain that it was Ms. not Mrs., since she'd never been married.

"There was an incident on the plane—"

"It wasn't my fault!" Flick protested. "I told them I didn't want anything to eat, but they wouldn't believe me." Flick was tall for her age, and because her vocabulary was so grandiloquent—Flick's own description of her *extravagantly colorful* speech—she was often mistaken for a child far older than she was.

Kristin could imagine the rest. "I'll be glad to pay for any damages."

"The flight attendant had some difficulty calming the woman sitting next to Felicity," the chaperon said. "She wants her silk blouse replaced."

"I'll take care of it," Kristin said.

The chaperon handed her a card. "Here's her personal information. You might want to be gone when she exits customs," she said with a sympathetic smile.

"Thanks. And thanks for bringing my daughter home."

Kristin put her arm around Flick's narrow shoulders, looked around and said, "Where's your luggage, Flick?"

"She didn't check any bags," the chaperon said. "I have a flight home to catch, so I'll leave you two to sort this out."

Kristin frowned as she watched the chaperon hurry away, then turned to her daughter and said, "Why didn't you bring anything with you?"

"The headmistress is packing everything up. She's going to ship it to me," Flick explained. "She said she didn't trust me in the dormitory."

Good lord! She'd wondered why Flick was still wearing her school uniform. If she wasn't mistaken, there was a spot of blood on the collar of Flick's white blouse, above the red V-neck wool sweater she wore with a blue-red-and-green-plaid wool pleated skirt. "All right. Let's go home."

Flick stopped dead in her tracks and looked up at Kristin, her blue eyes brimming with tears. "I don't want to go home, Mom. I want to go see Gramps in the hospital."

Kristin stared at her daughter in shock. "How did you know—? How could you possibly—? Who told you Gramps is in the hospital?"

"I'm not stupid, Mom. Gramps emailed me every day—until last Wednesday. Nothing Thursday or Friday or Saturday or Sunday. I knew something was wrong. So I tried calling him. Which got me in trouble with Mrs.

Fortin. But he didn't call me back. So I knew something was wrong.

"Then I called you and asked why Gramps didn't call me back and you said—"

"I said he wasn't feeling well. But that doesn't mean he's in the hospital, Flick."

"But he is, isn't he?" her daughter challenged. "Because if he wasn't, Gramps would have called me back, no matter how sick he was. What's wrong with him, Mom? How bad is he hurt? Was he in a car accident, or what?"

Kristin felt trapped. She'd hoped to shield Flick from the truth for long enough to let her father regain more of his faculties. But that obviously wasn't possible now. "He's had a stroke, Flick."

"A stroke? What's that?"

"A blood vessel broke in his brain."

"Is he dying?" Flick cried.

"No, but the stroke caused some of his brain not to work right. That's why Gramps hasn't called you back. The stroke affected his speech, so he can't talk very well yet."

"Yet?" Flick said, looking, as she always did, for the loophole that allowed her to escape anything she found unpleasant.

"With therapy, he should get much better. But, Flick…"

Kristin cupped her hands gently on either side of her daughter's anxious face and said, "His right side is paralyzed. He can't walk or write—"

"Or type," Flick interjected, pulling free. "So he couldn't email me back."

"That's right."

"Then it's a good thing I got myself kicked out of that ludicrous school," Flick said, her eyes narrowed in fierce determination. "Gramps is going to need my help to get better."

Ludicrous: Worthy of scorn as absurdly inept, false or foolish.

It was the first time Kristin had heard Flick use the word. It seemed her daughter's vocabulary had grown in the four months since she'd seen her at Christmas. It wasn't always an advantage having a child who was so smart. Like now, when her daughter had manipulated her world to arrive home, instead of being at school where she belonged.

Kristin put an arm around Flick and walked toward the airport garage where she'd left her car, listening attentively as her daughter talked a mile a minute about everything that had happened since she'd last seen her mother.

Kristin heard a word—*superfluous*—that she didn't know and realized she was going to have to look it up when she got home. She'd spent more time practicing on the tennis courts as a child than she had studying. She'd been homeschooled and had done the least work she could to get a high school diploma.

It was only after Flick was born that she'd realized she was going to need a college degree. She'd gone to the University of Miami and received a B.A. in

Communications, figuring she could use the public relations and promotional writing courses to help Harry promote his tennis academy. After 9/11 everything changed, and she decided to join the FBI.

Flick, on the other hand, had started reading at four. By the time she was seven, Kristin had resorted to parenting books to try and figure out how to manage her brilliant daughter. One night, she'd caught Flick reading her most recent parenting book under the covers. It was a toss-up who was learning to manage whom.

But despite her intelligence, Flick was still a child. Kristin had kept her daughter in the dark about her grandfather's stroke early last week, the day after Max's visit, in fact, in an attempt to shield Flick from the worst of it. She'd hoped her father would be well on the road to physical recovery before Flick saw him again.

Her father's face—eye, cheek and mouth—sagged on the right side, giving him a frightening appearance, which worsened when he tried to speak. Her nine-year-old daughter might be intellectually ready to help her grandfather. But Kristin wondered how she would react when she saw him in his hospital bed.

"Please, Mom," Flick pleaded. "Let's go see Gramps."

Kristin was torn. "Flick, I'm not sure—"

"Please, Mom!"

Kristin realized that if she didn't take Flick to see her grandfather, her creative daughter would find some way to get to the hospital on her own. "He's very sick, honey. I'm afraid seeing you will upset him." *And you.*

"I won't upset him, Mom," the girl promised. "I just want to talk to him."

Talk to him? He can't talk! Kristin knew her daughter didn't comprehend the seriousness of her grandfather's illness. But there was no keeping the two of them apart.

Harry Lassiter had been a part of Flick's life from the day she was born, a surrogate father. No wonder her daughter was so desperate to see him. And Flick's appearance might turn out to be a blessing in disguise.

Kristin's father, a man who'd kept himself in excellent physical condition his entire life, was infuriated by his helplessness after the unexpected stroke. Harry had resisted the idea of physical therapy that could only promise improvement, rather than perfect health. Maybe Flick's presence would encourage him to try harder to get back on his feet, even if he needed help walking from now on.

Kristin studied her daughter's eager face. The bright blue eyes, strong chin and straight black hair from her father. The high cheekbones and uptilted nose from her mother. When she set her mind to something, the nine-year-old was a force to be reckoned with.

Harry Lassiter was as helpless to deny this extraordinary child whatever she wanted as Kristin was herself. Hopefully, her father would be swept up by the whirlwind that was her daughter. By the time he came down again, he'd be standing on his own two feet.

For the first time in a very long time, Kristin smiled. Maybe things were finally going to turn around. "Come on, Flick. Let's go see Gramps."

3

Kristin perched on the edge of her father's bed at Jackson Memorial Hospital and said, "Dad, I have a surprise for you. You have a visitor."

"On ahn un," her father replied.

Don't want one.

Kristin knew what he'd said only because she knew how her proud father felt about anyone seeing him like he was now. "I know you don't want to see anyone. You don't have a choice."

His gray eyes blazed with anger, and one cheek lifted as the side of his mouth turned down in a snarl. "No!"

That was clear enough. But Flick was waiting in the visitors' lounge down the hall. God knew how long the inquisitive nine-year-old could last in a hospital waiting room without getting into trouble. Kristin had warned Flick to behave herself and hurried to her father's room to prepare him for seeing his granddaughter. She didn't have a lot of time to argue with him.

Her stomach knotted as she watched the once-invincible Harry Lassiter visibly struggle to say, "I ih e ere?"

Why is she here?

Kristin had debated whether to tell her father that Flick had gotten herself thrown out of school. It was one more thing he didn't need to worry about. But she didn't want to set a bad example by asking Flick to lie, and Flick would likely blurt it out anyway.

"Flick was worried when you stopped emailing. She got herself thrown out of school so she could come find out what happened to you."

Kristin thought she saw the flicker of a smile cross half her father's face. If so, it was the first since his stroke.

He sighed audibly. "Aw igh."

"Well, all right," Kristin said with a smile of her own, relieved that he'd given in so easily. "I'll be right back. I left her—"

"Gramps!"

Kristin turned to find Flick poised in the doorway, a look of horror on her face.

"Ow! Ow! Ow!" her father howled, creating a gargoyle face that caused Flick to whimper, before he turned away with a sound of anguish, flailing with his one good hand under the sheet.

Out! Out! Out!

Kristin fought the urge to grab Flick and run—from her father, from her job, from her self-destructing life. But she stood her ground. Because in her head she heard: *Never run from a challenge. Remember, you're invincible.*

"You're scaring Flick, Dad," Kristin said in a firm voice. "Flick, come here," she said in an equally firm voice.

Flick tore fearful eyes from her grandfather's supine body and stared dazed at her mother.

"Come here," Kristin repeated, holding out her hand to her daughter. "I know Gramps looks different. I would have prepared you, if you'd waited in the lounge. Because of his stroke, the right side of his face droops. That's why he looks so…funny. So…weird. So…odd," Kristin finished, after searching for the right word and never finding it.

"Dad, look at us," she commanded her father. "I want Flick to see your face in repose." His face would still look strange, but not so horrible as it had when he'd howled. Kristin kept a reassuring hand on Flick's shoulder, to stop her in case she was tempted to run.

Kristin caught the stab of betrayal in her father's eyes as he slowly turned back to face his granddaughter.

Grandfather and granddaughter stared at each other somberly for a full thirty seconds before her father said, "Iz oo, ik."

"I missed you, too, Gramps," Flick said.

"Air oo, uh?"

"Yeah," Flick agreed. "You scared me pretty bad."

Kristin barely managed to avoid rolling her eyes. Trust Flick to be totally honest.

"I'm okay now," Flick continued. She left the security

of Kristin's side and crossed to her grandfather, bracing her hands on the bed to lift herself up and plop her rump down next to his hips. "But your face does look bizarre."

Bizarre: Strikingly out of the ordinary. That was the word Kristin had been seeking. Trust Flick to root it out of her enormous vocabulary.

Kristin glanced at her watch, a twenty-five-dollar Timex with a brown leather band that Flick had given her for Christmas, which lit in the dark and kept perfect time. If she didn't leave soon she was going to be late for her meeting with SIRT. "Dad, I've got a meeting. We have to leave, but—"

"Ik an ay ere."

Flick can stay here.

"I don't know, Dad," Kristin said, staring worriedly at her daughter.

"I'll be fine, Mom," Flick said. "Visiting hours aren't over till four. I checked."

"You're sure it won't be too much for you, Dad?"

"Gramps, you need to comb your hair," Flick said, eyeing his tousled blond hair with her head tilted. "It's a mess. Where's your comb?"

"No om. Us."

No comb. Brush.

Flick hopped down and rummaged through the drawer in the small metal chest beside the bed. She found a boar-bristle hairbrush, set it on the bed, then climbed back up beside him. "Where do you want your part?"

He turned relieved eyes to Kristin and said, "O. I ine."

Go. I'm fine.

Kristin hurried from the room before she could reconsider. She couldn't miss her investigative meeting with SIRT. And maybe, if Flick had enough trouble communicating with her grandfather, he'd reconsider the speech therapy he'd been refusing.

Kristin headed east from Jackson Memorial on the Dolphin Expressway and kept her fingers crossed as she merged onto I-95 North toward the Miami Field Office. On paper, the MFO was only a seventeen-minute drive straight up the Interstate from the hospital. But all it took was one fender bender to turn I-95 into a parking lot in the middle of the day.

She exhaled when she found traffic moving freely. But she hadn't driven more than a mile before she found herself slowing to a crawl. "Come on!" she muttered, pounding the steering wheel of her Camry. She checked her watch. She'd given herself an extra twenty minutes to get there, just in case, and it looked like she was going to need every second of it.

She turned the radio to a station that played upbeat Latin music and imagined herself sitting on a warm beach under a colorful umbrella with an ice-cold mojito in hand. She was doing a lot of imagining these days, because her life kept shifting out of her control.

During the past week, she had been asked to spy in London, called 911 to come get her father after his stroke, been involved in another shooting incident at work, in which her partner was seriously wounded, and picked up her errant daughter at the airport after she'd been thrown out of school.

Kristin felt like she'd hit her limit of bad news for one week. Except she now had to face the Shooting Incident Review Team, which held her fate in its hands. What if the board decided to suspend her? Or fire her? She felt a knot forming in the pit of her stomach.

Breathe, Kristin. This, too, shall pass.

But where would she be when it did?

It took fifteen minutes before she passed a two-car accident, which wasn't even blocking the lane, but which motorists had slowed down to ogle. She made fast time the rest of the way to the exit for North Miami Beach, but she could almost feel the minutes ticking away.

The concrete-and-glass MFO building took up an entire city block and more. The FBI had set up shop in Miami as far back as 1924, and there were still enough criminals—and violations of the rights of American citizens in Mexico, the Caribbean and Central and South America—to keep the MFO hopping.

Kristin heard a clap of thunder and eyed the dark clouds overhead. "Do not rain," she muttered. "Do not rain." It had been unseasonably hot the entire month of April and unseasonably rainy, as well. She drove as fast as she dared around the enormous MFO parking lot searching for a spot, anxious to get inside before the downpour started.

She started jogging when the first large raindrops hit her cheeks and eyelashes, but before she reached the door, the heavens let go. Kristin was breathing hard by the time she got inside and stood dripping—and swearing under her breath—at the security checkpoint.

"You look like a drowned rat, Lassiter."

Kristin turned and saw her boss, Special Agent in Charge Rudy Rodriguez, ready to exit the building, umbrella in hand. In the four years since she'd come to Miami from the FBI Academy at Quantico, Kristin had never seen the Miami SAC caught unprepared.

Rudy was several inches under six feet, big-chested, with a thick waist and dark, sharp eyes. The SAC brushed his receding black hairline straight back from his brow with a palm and said, "I thought your meeting with SIRT was at 3:00."

"It is." Kristin had never gotten used to the SAC's gravelly voice, the result of being nearly strangled to death in an undercover drug operation gone bad.

Rudy glanced at his watch, then reached into his suit coat pocket and came out with a neatly ironed white handkerchief, which he handed to her. "You might want to dry off a little before you head upstairs."

She took the monogrammed cotton cloth, dabbed at her forehead, cheeks and chin, brushed off the shoulders and lapels of her suit jacket, and handed it back. "Thanks."

She noticed Rudy didn't offer advice about what she should say at the hearing. Or console her for having to go through the process of being questioned by SIRT again.

"Good luck," he said. Then he was gone.

Kristin cleared security as quickly as she could, then took the elevator up to the office of Supervisory Special Agent Roberta Harrison, who was in charge of the MFO's Office of Professional Responsibility. The OPR was charged with ensuring that agents conducted themselves with the highest level of integrity and professionalism. SSA Harrison did everything by the book, which made her good at her job.

But Harrison had never worked in the field, so she had very little idea how quickly decisions had to be made in moments of extreme duress. And therefore little—make that *no*—tolerance for honest mistakes.

Which was what the shooting incident Kristin had been involved in four months ago had been. Kristin was aware of how much it had irked SSA Harrison that no disciplinary action had been mandated by the Shooting Incident Review Team in that instance.

Unfortunately, there was no way to excuse what Kristin had done four days ago as an honest mistake. It was dereliction of duty, at the very least. Agent Harrison was finally going to get her pound of flesh. And maybe Kristin's badge and gun.

Kristin's crisply ironed shirt had been wilted by the rain, but she squared her shoulders anyway as she was ushered into the hearing room by a civil service secretary. Because she'd so recently been examined—interrogated—by SIRT, she knew what was coming.

Her heartbeat ratcheted up another notch and she took a calming breath to try to slow it down. Her stomach made a rumbling sound and she realized she hadn't eaten lunch. Maybe that was the reason she felt so nauseous. Or maybe it was the result of a life rocketing out of her control.

"Sit down, please, Agent Lassiter," SSA Harrison said. Technically, Agent Harrison wasn't part of SIRT, but she'd apparently decided to attend the meeting.

Kristin seated herself and looked from one sober face on the SIRT panel to the next seated across from her. Three of the four FBI special agents on the Shooting Incident Review Team identified themselves as being from the Criminal Investigative Division, Training Division (Ballistics) and the Office of General Counsel.

"We've met," the fourth special agent reminded her. "I'm Todd Akers, Inspector in Charge of this investigation." Akers reminded her he was from the Inspection Division.

Kristin surreptitiously wiped her sweaty palms on the front of her trousers under the conference table as she eyed her inquisitors. No one on the Shooting Incident Review Team looked sympathetic.

She didn't blame them. The charges against her were serious. She and her partner had been ambushed inside a home in Liberty City while they were questioning the occupants about an armed bank robbery. Because she'd hesitated before drawing her weapon—and then hesitated too long before firing it—her partner had been shot and seriously wounded. And because she'd fallen apart after her partner was wounded, the suspected bank robbers had escaped.

"I wondered whether SIRT was letting you off too

lightly the last time, Agent Lassiter," Roberta Harrison said. "I thought at the time you were acting with reckless disregard for human life when you shot that sixteen-year-old boy. You were lucky the local authorities decided not to prosecute."

"I believed he had a gun." Kristin felt her face flushing with the heat of anger. She'd been cleared of any wrongdoing in the previous shooting incident by SIRT, and here was Roberta Harrison, who wasn't even part of the review team, trying her all over again.

"That poor boy didn't even have a gun, did he?" Harrison said. "It was a cell phone. You shot an unarmed sixteen-year-old."

"He matched the description of a suspect in an armed bank robbery. I identified myself as FBI. I told him to keep his hands where I could see them. Instead, he reached into his jacket pocket."

"You didn't wait to see whether he had a weapon. You just shot him."

"If I'd waited, I might have been killed. Or seriously wounded, as my partner was when I failed to shoot quickly enough four days ago."

"So, you admit you failed to back up your partner?" Harrison said triumphantly.

Kristin let out a shaky breath. How easily she'd fallen into the trap Harrison had laid for her. She looked toward the Agent in Charge of the review team, who wouldn't meet her gaze.

The truth was, her failure to draw her weapon—and to shoot it—was almost predictable. She'd been warned by the psychiatrist she'd been required to see after the shooting four months ago that she might hesitate to shoot in the future.

She'd been on administrative duty for months. After she completed counseling, she'd been asked if she thought she could go back to work and fire her weapon without hesitation. She'd said yes.

She'd been wrong.

"I hesitated before drawing my weapon. And I hesitated before firing—to make sure the suspect had a weapon. By the time I realized he had a gun, he'd already shot George." Her brand-new partner, who was busy manhandling another suspect, who was unarmed.

"In fact, the suspect shot Agent Parker twice before you fired your weapon, isn't that true?" Harrison said.

Kristin nodded curtly. "I fired, but the suspect darted around the corner out of the kitchen, and I missed. Once George was down, the suspect he was cuffing took off. He was unarmed, so I didn't shoot. He knocked me down and fled, along with the other suspect, through the back door. I could tell George was seriously wounded, so I stayed with him."

"Rather than pursuing the suspects, even though one of them had shot your partner."

"Yes, ma'am," Kristin said. "I thought we had enough information to find them again. And I wanted to render all the aid I could to my partner."

She'd visited George in the hospital yesterday, where he was in serious but stable condition. He didn't blame her, but he no longer wanted to be her partner.

"You've got a problem, Lassiter," one of the SIRT panel members interjected. "Better get it fixed, or no one will want to work with you."

Most FBI agents didn't draw their weapons during their entire careers. She'd drawn hers twice, with disastrous results both times. She'd shot too fast. Then she'd shot too slow. She supposed the fear was, the next time she'd be afraid even to draw her weapon.

Kristin wasn't sure herself what she would do if the situation arose again. Which explained why Harrison seemed so determined to pin her wings to the wall like a butterfly in a lab experiment. Harry Lassiter's invincible little girl was looking pretty damned vulnerable right about now.

"Do you have anything you'd like to say on your own behalf?" the SIRT Agent in Charge asked.

It could have happened to anyone, Kristin thought. But that argument wasn't going to do her much good. Or maybe, *After what happened last time, you can understand why I had to be* sure *he had a gun before I fired.*

She didn't make either argument. Nothing could excuse her behavior. So she simply said, "No, sir. I have nothing to add."

"SIRT will consider the evidence and inform you of what disciplinary action it deems necessary—if any—within the next few weeks," Akers said. "Until then, Agent Lassiter, keep your nose clean."

Kristin rose and realized her legs felt shaky. She steadied herself and headed for the door.

"Oh, one more thing," SSA Harrison said, stopping Kristin at the door.

She turned and waited for whatever barb Harrison had saved for a parting shot.

"You need to see Rebecca in the information office downstairs. The MFO wants to issue a press release about your lawsuit."

Kristin stared at the SSA blankly. "Lawsuit? I'm not involved in any lawsuit."

"A reporter from the *Miami Herald* has already contacted the bureau. I assumed you'd received the paperwork. After this second shooting incident, the parents of the boy you killed are suing you in civil court for wrongful death. Better get yourself a lawyer, Lassiter."

A lawyer? She couldn't afford a lawyer, not on top of the expenses for her father's hospital stay and his rehabilitation and the cost of a nanny for Flick. Her father would hate the publicity a lawsuit would bring, and it would make Flick's life a nightmare. Not to mention her own. What if she ended up suspended without pay? Or lost her job. That was a distinct possibility, considering how badly the hearing had gone. Then what?

Kristin felt her knees threaten to buckle. She curled her hands into fists and stiffened her legs. A lawsuit was just one more straw. One tiny little straw.

You can do it. Remember, you're invincible.

To hell with that. Kristin yanked the door to the hearing room open and headed for the stairwell. She realized she wasn't going to make it. There were no private offices on this floor, just cubicles connected with a lot of other cubicles in a large room. There was nowhere to hide and lick her wounds.

She felt the choking knot building in her throat. Her nose burned with the threat of tears. She blinked to clear her blurring vision. She wasn't going to break down. She refused to give SSA Roberta Harrison the satisfaction. She felt a tear hit her cheek and angrily brushed it away. But she was losing the battle against the sob growing in her chest.

There was only one place she could hope for any privacy. She hurried around the corner and shoved her way into the ladies' room, searching for feet under the stalls. With a lack of trust she'd learned from the bureau, she smacked open each stall door, letting the metal slam against the opposite wall, as though she were clearing a house.

When Kristin was absolutely certain no one else was in the room, she let the sob break free.

4

The knock on the door came at a very inopportune moment.

Max had just eased the last button free on his date's blouse and was sliding the black silk off her shoulders. After his meeting with Kristin in Miami, he'd been irritated to discover that he was having difficulty getting her out of his mind. This seduction—of another woman—was an attempt to remove her entirely.

He ignored the knock.

Despite orders from his uncle, he hadn't yet found a replacement for Kristin on the tennis court. As ridiculous as it sounded, he kept hoping she'd change her mind. He hadn't wanted her as his partner, but once she'd refused him, no one else would do.

He kept wondering what he'd done wrong all those years ago to make her hate him so much. Considering everything, it was no surprise she'd said no to playing spy. He was lucky she had. He didn't need her complicating his life—or the risky assignment he'd been given.

But he couldn't help comparing the porcelain skin

he was kissing with Kristin's freckled shoulder. K had been self-conscious about her freckles. He'd loved kidding her about them. And kissing each and every one of them. Which had taken the better part of the one night they'd spent together.

"Max?" The perturbed female voice saying his name woke him from his reverie.

He realized he'd stopped caressing his date and was staring out the tall, mullioned windows of the bedroom in the north wing of Blackthorne Abbey where he'd brought her. The room, supposedly slept in by Henry II, had once been the lair of the Beast of Blackthorne. Not a real beast, of course, but the younger brother of the sixth Duke of Blackthorne, a soldier whose face had been badly scarred at the Battle of Waterloo.

K had loved that story, which also involved a fair maiden, a duke with amnesia and twin eight-year-old girls lost in the hidden passageways of the Abbey leading to the dungeon.

"Max?"

He realized he'd drifted off again. *Damn and blast, K. What are you doing to me?*

"Where was I?" he said with a rueful grin.

"Making me feel beautiful and desired."

Max didn't see the feline smile that accompanied the words, because he was lost again in the past.

"You make me feel so beautiful."

Those were the words K had said when he'd looked at her naked for the first time. She'd been surprisingly bold—taking his dare when he'd shown up at her hotel room one afternoon unannounced, two years after they'd first met—dropping the hotel's white terry cloth robe, which she'd donned after her shower, and standing before him in all her glory. Especially since he'd still been dressed in sweaty tennis clothes. He'd been so startled by what she'd done, he hadn't said anything for a moment. She'd lowered her gaze, suddenly a shy fifteen-year-old again.

He'd quickly taken the few steps to bring him close, lifted her chin with a forefinger, looked into her eyes and said, "You are so beautiful."

That was when she'd said the words that had thrilled and enthralled him. *"You make me feel so beautiful."* He could see it was true. She blossomed like a flower before him, her eyes full of joy and her smile wide and happy. It was the most wonderful, most powerful feeling he'd ever had in seventeen years of living—the ability to bring another human being utter joy.

And he'd only looked at her.

That precious moment had been interrupted when her father knocked on the door and called out to her. Max had raced for the hotel closet and hidden there while K grabbed the robe she'd discarded and anxiously tied it tight at her waist. Her father had wanted to discuss tactics for the next day's match, so Max had spent an uncomfortable hour fending off a bunch of empty hangers.

When Harry had finally gone, K's playful mood had left along with him. She'd pleaded fatigue and apologized. Max had left without touching her, without even kissing her. But he'd been entranced with her from that moment on. To say he'd wanted her would be to understate the matter. He'd craved her.

Because of their separate tennis schedules, the opportunity to finish what she'd started didn't come for almost a year. When he'd finally convinced her to sleep with him, he'd been so impatient to be inside her—and so ignorant of the true state of her innocence—that he'd hurt her. And disappointed her. Despite only wanting to love her, he'd somehow made her hate him.

K had kept him at arm's length forever after. Or at least until he'd been forced by his uncle to approach her and ask her to work with him.

It had been an awful lesson to learn about human nature. You couldn't make a person love you, no matter how much you loved them. What had happened with K was exactly what had happened with his mother. Once he'd let her in, she'd shut him out. The pain the second time was terrible enough to cure him of the disease.

Love was for fools and idiots.

"Max, would you rather we didn't do this?"

Max was startled to discover he'd been neglecting his date again. He'd spent a great deal of time talking Veronica Granville, a reporter for the *Times* of London, into spending the weekend with him at Blackthorne Abbey, his family's hereditary castle—complete with moat—in Kent. He'd arranged her seduction carefully, and it was proceeding according to plan. Or had been, until that knock had interrupted them.

And thoughts of that infuriating female from my past.

Max made himself focus on pressing kisses against

the throat of the woman in his arms, but as he brushed aside Veronica's long, straight blond hair, memories of Kristin intruded. He remembered ribbing K about her corkscrew curls, which she hated. And shoving K's lush blond curls out of the way to kiss her nape as he lay beside her. He remembered how she'd shivered with pleasure in his arms. And how good it had felt to finally press his naked flesh against hers.

He supposed it was K's lack of sexual experience that had made kissing her and caressing her so memorable. He couldn't help smiling as he recalled how amazed she'd looked when he'd kissed the tip of her small breast.

"I'm glad to see you're enjoying yourself," Veronica said as she turned in his embrace.

The smile disappeared as he acknowledged how totally Kristin Lassiter had been dominating his thoughts.

The knock came again.

The statuesque blonde in his arms stared at the thick, wooden-planked door, with its enormous black wrought-iron hinges and said, "I thought you said we were the only guests at the Abbey."

"We are." He'd told the reporter he was a distant cousin of the Duchess of Blackthorne's estranged husband, and that the duchess had offered to let him stay as a guest at the Abbey. He'd learned from bitter experience that he couldn't trust a woman's feelings when she knew from the outset that he was the youngest son of the infamous Bella and Bull.

Max blessed his mother for the diligence she'd used in keeping photos of her children out of the papers and off the internet. With some fancy footwork during his brief junior tennis career that included refusing to pose for photos or turning his head when the cameras flashed during the trophy presentation, he'd remained virtually invisible both in print and online. There were pictures, but not good ones.

"I heard you tell the butler we didn't want to be disturbed," Veronica said. "Who could it be?"

"Ignore it," he murmured, brushing aside her silky blond hair and teasing her ear with his teeth, determined, this time, to banish K from his thoughts.

The knock came again, cracking like thunder.

And he bit Veronica's ear.

"Ouch!" Veronica grabbed her ear as she pulled away and shrugged her blouse back onto her shoulders. "Answer the damned door, Max," she snapped, turning her back as she rebuttoned her blouse.

Since she was dressed again, he sighed and headed for the door. When he opened it, he found the Blackthorne butler, whose forebears had worked at the Abbey since medieval times, wearing formal clothes and holding a silver platter containing a blue-tinged white envelope. The word *TELEGRAM*, framed by four red stripes, was written in blue on the upper left hand corner.

"I presume that's for me, Smythe," Max said quietly.

"Yes, your lordship," the butler replied, just as quietly. "It was delivered by personal messenger."

It was impossible to get Smythe to call him Max. He'd been trying since he was a boy of six. It was Lord

Maxwell, or your lordship, as though they were living a century or two in the past. Considering the English laws of succession, there was no way he should be a lord. It was Smythe who'd explained to him how, thanks to his courageous ancestors—and an act of Parliament—he remained fourth in line to inherit the Blackthorne dukedom.

It was a pretty good story, actually. One of K's favorites, back in the days when they were speaking to each other.

When all the male Blackthorne heirs had died heroically during the Battle of Britain in the Second World War, Parliament had amended the Letters Patent creating the Dukedom of Blackthorne so the title would pass "to all and every other issue male *and female,* lineally descending of or from the said Duke of Blackthorne, to be held by them severally and successively, the elder and the descendants of every elder issue to be preferred before the younger of such issue."

Which meant that either males *or females* could inherit the dukedom. This prevented the title from being extinguished by the death of the last male Blackthorne during the war. It was the first time such a thing had been done since the Dukedom of Marlborough was preserved in the same way for similar reasons in 1706.

As the elder of twin sisters, his mother was the current holder of the title. Max's eldest brother, Oliver, would succeed her as the next Duke of Blackthorne. As the eldest son, Oliver currently held one of the Duke of

Blackthorne's lesser titles, Earl of Courtland, and was often referred to simply as Courtland.

Max stared at the note on the silver platter and said, "This couldn't wait, Smythe?"

"It is a missive from Her Grace."

Max knew that as far as anyone at the Abbey was concerned, communication from the duchess was like word from on high. He thought back to the last time his mother had gotten in touch with him. It was six months ago, when she'd emailed to ask if he was coming home to Blackthorne Abbey for Christmas. He wasn't.

He was only here now because his mother was not. And because he'd hoped the exotic locale would help him seduce Veronica—and forget K.

He'd failed miserably on both counts.

"Thank you, Smythe," he said, taking the note from the tray.

The butler bowed, then took an arthritic step back, before turning and limping away. As he retreated, his uneven cadence echoed off the high stone ceilings in the hall.

The instant the door was closed, Max crushed the missive, dropped it onto an ivory-inlaid chess table and said, "Where were we?"

But Veronica the Reporter was curious. She crossed the Aubusson carpet to the table, picked up the crushed paper and pressed it flat across the front of her skirt. "It's a telegram. From America." She turned to Max and asked, "Why would anyone send a telegram in this day and age? I mean, why not phone or fax, or text or email?"

It wasn't until she pointed it out that Max realized just how odd his mother's missive was. He took the telegram from Veronica and tore it open. He crossed to the windows edged with ivy on the outside and hung with gold brocade curtains on the inside and held the note up where it could catch the last rays of daylight.

Veronica followed him. "What is it, Max? Who's it from?"

Max let out a sigh of relief, crushed the note once more and tossed it onto an ancient oak chest that ran below the mullioned windows. "It's nothing."

"Mind if I look?" She didn't wait for permission, just picked up the discarded paper, straightened it out for a second time and began to read.

Max grimaced, knowing what was coming.

She gasped and turned to stare at him. "The Duchess of Blackthorne is your *mother?*"

He met her gaze and shrugged. "It's no big deal."

"Don't try using those innocent baby blues on me," she said sharply. "Your mother's not just famous, Max. She's infamous."

Which was why he never mentioned the connection. "So?"

"So? *So?*" she repeated incredulously.

Max knew exactly what was running through her mind. He'd lived through some of it and heard stories all his life about the rest. Seventeen-year-old Lady Isabella's fairy-tale romance and rocky marriage to twenty-nine-year-old American banking heir Bull Benedict had been tabloid fodder for years.

First, Bella had stolen Bull away from her twenty-one-year-old second cousin, Lady Regina Delaford, daughter of the Marquess of Tenby, whom Bull had been courting. To add insult to injury, Bull and Bella had married barely a month after they'd met. The poverty-stricken duchess had even agreed to sign a prenuptial agreement to prove she wasn't marrying the banking heir for his billions.

Eyebrows rose at the birth of their first child a mere eight months later. The public gasped each time Bella showed up at some charity function wearing the priceless jewels—each with a legend attached—that Bull had given to his wife during their marriage: rubies, pearls, sapphires, emeralds and diamonds.

Last, but not least, the public had devoured news of Bull and Bella's antagonistic separation after twenty-five years of marriage. Gossip said Bull hadn't divorced his wife because after twenty-five years of marriage, the prenup became null and void, and Bella could lay claim to as much as the English courts decided to give her of Bull's tremendous fortune.

Even though they were separated, they continued to show up at the same charity, political and business functions in England, Europe and America, providing more delicious tidbits for the gossips.

As though to goad her husband, Bella never failed to wear one of the fabulous jewels Bull had given her during their marriage as a sign of his enduring love—when she walked in on the arm of another man.

"Are you going to America for Mother's Day?" Veronica asked as she crossed to him.

"Maybe. Maybe not."

She pressed her abdomen against his as she slid her arms around his neck. She played with the straight black hair at his nape, sending a shiver down his spine.

It seemed his seduction of the reporter was back on track.

Max leaned forward to kiss the beautiful woman in his arms but hesitated when she whispered, "I can't believe I'm kissing the Duchess of Blackthorne's son."

He lifted his head and stared down at her with the cynicism he always felt when someone seemed awed by who he was. Or rather, who his mother was. No one knew the real Max Benedict.

Except K. She'd known exactly who he was.

And rejected you.

The boy. She'd rejected the boy. He was a man now. Would K see that if she got to know him again? Would she be able to love him again? Did he want her to love him again? The thought was dizzying. Intriguing. And terrifying. He'd simply have to be sure this time, if it came to it, that he was the one doing the rejecting.

Even K—Agent Lassiter—had believed the carefully cultivated common belief that he was a care-for-nothing playboy, a reckless rogue who'd learned his hedonism from Bull and Bella in their heyday. Despite what K might think of his behavior, the deception made him a very good spy.

Not that he worked all the time. Or even every time the CIA—or some other American governmental organization identifying itself with capital letters—asked. But he was a valuable asset.

As he'd pointed out to K, by virtue of his pedigree, he had access to the very wealthy, which included drug czars and their sons and daughters, and munitions dealers and their sons and daughters, and of course, wealthy Arab potentates who might be funding terrorist activities and their sons, if not their daughters.

It was amazing how much information was dropped over a drink after a game of polo. Or during one of his seductions.

The sad thing was, Max hadn't wanted information from Veronica Granville. He'd simply liked the way she looked. He'd liked how bright she was, how witty she'd been at the bar where they'd crossed paths. He'd hoped for some good sex, along with some intelligent company.

Now she had stars in her eyes, put there by his mother's infamy. From now on, he would question whether her interest in him wasn't really interest in getting closer to his mother.

But he wasn't going to turn down the sex just because it might come with a few strings attached.

"Max," she whispered in his ear. "If you go to America, will you take me with you?"

"We can talk about that later," he said, used to

negotiations where he promised nothing but the promise of something that might be offered in the future. "We have more important things to focus on right now."

Max captured her mouth with his as he pulled her close. She rubbed herself against him like a cat drunk on catnip. He felt a little sad when he realized he didn't trust her enthusiastic response.

He cleared his mind and focused on sensations. The softness of her breasts against his chest. The sweet taste of her mouth. The heat that surged through his veins, causing almost instant rock-hard arousal. The throbbing need he would soon slake inside her hot, wet, willing body.

Insidious thoughts crept back in. Of K lecturing him on how lucky he was to have a mother. And how if she still had a mother, she'd treasure every day she had with her. He'd argued that his situation was different. That the duchess hadn't been a mother for many years. Just like K's mother, when Bella had left his father, she'd left her children, as well.

So why, after all these years, had the duchess invited him to spend Mother's Day at The Seasons? He had boyhood memories of holidays spent there with his brothers and his four male cousins, Nash, Ben, Carter and Rhett, Foster's sons with his first wife, Abigail.

When Foster had divorced Abby, they'd divided their four sons between them. Foster got Ben and Carter. Abby got Nash and Rhett. Both parents had remarried and had more kids. Max and his brothers hadn't been back to The

Seasons since his parents had separated ten years ago. So what was his mother's invitation all about?

"Max? Is something wrong?"

Max realized he'd stopped kissing Veronica and was once again staring out the window over her shoulder.

Damn you, Mother. You're worse than K. Why can't you stay the hell out of my life!

Max let go of the reporter and took a step back. "I'm sorry, Veronica. Maybe we can do this another time."

"What?"

He could see she was annoyed. He didn't blame her. He was more than a little annoyed himself at the distraction K—and his mother's telegram—had created.

"I'll drive you back to London." He was glad now he'd decided to make the hour drive south on the M20 motorway from London, rather than taking the train with Veronica from Victoria Station.

Her hands shot to her hips. "I thought we were going to spend the weekend here, Max. Why the sudden change in plans?"

She would have done better kissing him again, Max reflected. He didn't have much tolerance for female indignation. Although, he supposed she had a right to be upset.

She narrowed her eyes and said, "It's that telegram, isn't it? Is something going on with the duchess? I could use a scoop, Max. What do you know? Or think you know?"

"There's nothing going on with my mother except a desire to keep all her lambs in the fold," Max shot back.

"What mother wouldn't want her children with her on Mother's Day?" Veronica pointed out.

"Mine."

Max didn't elaborate. He wasn't about to tell a reporter from the *Times* how seldom he'd seen his mother since his parents had split up. How visits with her, from the age of seven onward—when he'd been shipped off to boarding school—had been prized, because they'd been so few and far between. And how often those visits had been canceled.

He and his brothers had spent their lives in one English or European or American boarding school after another. There had been so many because whenever one or another of them had done something to get himself thrown out, the others had refused to stay where they weren't all welcome. As the youngest, Max had created his own share of the carnage.

None of them had held a candle to Oliver. Oliver had a gift. He could destroy as easily with words as with a blow.

But, of course, Oliver had a greater burden to bear than any of the rest of them.

Max had heard the rumors about who'd really sired his eldest brother, who had dark brown eyes, rather than blue or gray, like both of their parents and the rest of his siblings. Max wasn't sure what he believed. But he'd more than once defended both his mother's—and his brother's—honor.

Max had been lonely at the end, because he was five years younger than his next older brother, Payne. His brothers had all gone on to university—or not—and he'd been left behind. Sometimes he wondered how Lydia had managed. Being the only girl, and nearly two years younger than he was, she'd been all alone from the start.

"You're not being fair, Max," Veronica said with a petulant pout that made him realize how much he would have enjoyed having that mouth, with those full lips, taking full advantage of his body.

"I'll make it up to you," he said.

"Promise you'll bring me back here?" she said, moving close again.

Rather than reply in words, he took her in his arms and kissed her, giving the effort his full attention. And comparing the kiss, inevitably, with kissing K. He and K definitely had unfinished business. Whether she came to work with him or not, he hadn't seen her for the last time. He realized the woman he held in his arms wasn't the one he wanted to be kissing and let her go.

"You won't forget me, Max," Veronica said in a breathy voice when he released her.

"Believe me, Veronica, you're unforgettable," Max said with a teasing wink. He would never forget how difficult it had been to concentrate on this woman when he was thinking about another.

Veronica smiled and he watched her shoulders relax.

"Excuse me while I visit the powder room," she said. She turned and he realized she had no idea where it was.

He pointed her in the right direction. "In there."

He almost groaned with regret as he watched the sexy sway of her hips as she walked away. He was sure she had the sexual sophistication to please him a great deal in bed. Veronica turned to glance at him over her shoulder, her long blond hair swinging free, and smiled. The invitation remained.

He should take advantage of it. He should cross the room and take her in his arms and finish what he had, by God, started.

But there was no way he could enjoy partaking of such delicious fruit until he'd settled things one way or the other with K. He was going to have to talk with her again. He was going to have to convince her to work with him. If for no other reason than to prove to himself that the woman wouldn't—simply couldn't—live up to his memories of her.

Maybe he ought to go to America for Mother's Day. He could stop by The Seasons and find out what the hell his mother wanted.

More importantly, he'd be on the same continent as K. He could take a flight down to Miami and talk some sense into her. Because he wasn't going to have any peace until he did.

5

"Another gift has arrived, Your Grace, along with a note declining your invitation."

Bella growled with frustration, then put a hand to her heart, which was beating hard enough from anxiety to hurt. What if none of her children showed up? She couldn't bear the thought. Did they despise her so much? Or were they truly as busy as they claimed to be?

Bella forced herself to take a deep, calming breath as she settled onto a rock-hard horsehair Victorian sofa. The sofa had survived firc and plague and pestilence over the centuries, which was why the uncomfortable thing still stood in the parlor at The Seasons.

She took several more deep breaths but didn't feel the least bit calmed. Oliver, Riley and Payne had already rejected her invitation, citing business commitments. "Who sent the latest gift?" she asked her assistant. "Lydia or Max?"

"It's from Lady Lydia," Emily said.

"So Max might still come."

"We can always hope, Your Grace."

Bella eyed the young woman. “But you don’t believe he’ll show.”

“We can always hope,” Emily repeated. “You know how busy everyone is. According to the report from Warren & Warren Investigations, Courtland—I mean, the earl—Oliver—is purchasing ranch land in Argentina. Lord Riley is negotiating for oil tankers in Hong Kong. And Lord Payne…” A thoughtful frown wrinkled her forehead before she said, “Oh, yes. Mr. Warren reported that Lord Riley is on a ship somewhere in the Aegean, researching an underwater archeological find.”

“And Lydia’s excuse?” Bella asked.

“According to the note that came with your gift, she’s in Venice. She mentioned something about hunting down a stolen painting.”

Bella picked up a needlepointed pillow from the sofa and threw it across the room toward the elaborately carved white marble fireplace. It fell short. She hissed with fury.

“Are you all right, Your Grace?” Emily asked, rushing to her side.

“I’m fine, Emily,” Bella said with irritation. “There’s nothing wrong with my heart. Go back to your knitting.”

Emily reluctantly crossed the room, picked up a pair of knitting needles and a partially completed blue wool sweater from a silk-brocade-covered wing chair, and sat down.

“You know what I hate most about what’s happening here?” Bella said.

Over the clack of her knitting needles Emily asked, "What's that, Your Grace?"

"The smug look I'm going to see on my brother-in-law's face when only one of my children shows up here today." Bella heard footsteps on the creaky, carpeted wooden *Gone-With-the-Wind* staircase in the central hallway of the nearly four-century-old home. She glanced over her shoulder and found Foster Benedict, Bull's younger brother—and her nemesis—standing in the doorway to the parlor. "Speak of the devil," she muttered.

"Good morning, Bella," he said with surprising cordiality.

Bella watched as Foster crossed to a breakfront where a silver coffee service and a selection of pastries had been set out by the butler. Foster had been incensed when she'd told him she intended to have her children visit her for Mother's Day at The Seasons. He'd already made plans to have his children meet their mother there. He'd ordered her to go somewhere else.

Bella had refused. Since she was still Bull's wife, she was entitled to use of The Seasons. Instead, she'd suggested Foster have his family join hers, as they had during holidays in years gone by. Given no other choice, he'd agreed.

"It seems it won't be as crowded here this weekend as I feared," Foster said.

Bella saw the superior look on his face in the gilded mirror behind the breakfront. And heard the satisfaction in his voice. Foster expected five of his seven children—two of his four sons and his three teenage daughters—to bc on hand today. He must be aware that at least four of her five children would not.

"I wouldn't look so smug if I were you," Bella said.

"Why not?" Foster said.

"Your children are making their way here from a few miles up the road. It's understandable if mine aren't able to come from halfway around the world. And I'm expecting Max to turn up at any moment."

"One out of five," Foster mused. "Frankly, one more than I expected."

"You've always been a son of a bitch, Foster."

"You're the bitch incarnate," Foster shot back.

"How dare you!" Emily said, rising from her chair to confront Foster. "Take that back."

Foster laughed viciously. "Take it back?" He turned to Bella and said, "Tell your minion to back off, Bella. Or I'll have *her* for breakfast."

Emily looked flustered, but she stood her ground.

"Sit down, Emily," Bella said in an even voice. Then she focused her narrowed eyes on Foster and said, "Don't threaten Emily again, or I'll have to retaliate in a way you won't like."

"What would that be?"

"Use your imagination," Bella said. "You know I make good on my promises."

The last time they'd locked horns Bella had arranged for Foster to lose an extraordinary amount of money on one of his investments. Foster understood the power of money.

His mouth turned down in a sour look. "Like I said. You're a bitch."

He turned back to the silver coffeepot and continued his recitation as though their altercation had never happened. "Just so you know, Ben brought his fiancée, Anna," he said as he poured coffee into a china teacup. "Carter's home on leave from duty in Iraq, so he invited his girl, Sloan, to come for the day."

He added a spoonful of sugar, then turned to her with china cup in hand. "I'm surprising Patsy by having Amanda and Bethany and Camille flown in on the family jet from that French boarding school they attend. I pick them up in Richmond before lunch."

"I'm sure Patsy will enjoy having her daughters here," Bella said neutrally. She was willing to be just exactly as polite as Foster was. Besides, she'd never had any enmity for Patsy or her three daughters. The elder two girls were twins with curly blond hair who resembled their mother. The younger had dark hair like her father.

To be perfectly honest, Bella liked Patsy Benedict. Foster's second wife would never be called thin or chic, but Patsy had warm hazel eyes and had always been extraordinarily kind to her.

But from the beginning, there had never been any love lost between her and her brother-in-law. The first time Foster had met her, he'd called her "a conniving bitch." He was the one who'd insisted on the prenup. This was the first time they'd come in contact with one another in ten years. It seemed Foster's animosity had survived her separation from Bull intact.

Which caused her to reply to his recitation with just a little satisfaction of her own, "I'm sure it will be nice to have most of your children here for Mother's Day. But I can't help wondering, where is their mother?"

Foster cleared his throat uncomfortably. "She'll be here."

"Why didn't Patsy come with you from Washington?"

Bella knew that Foster, a retired four-star general, currently served as an advisor to the president on terrorism. He and Patsy had a brick home in the Fan District of Richmond, but Foster spent most of his time in another large home they owned in Chevy Chase, Maryland, just outside Washington, D.C.

"Patsy's been staying at her father's ranch in Texas the past few months," Foster said. "Her father's been ill."

"Then it's nice you'll have a chance to get together today. When is she arriving? Are you picking her up at the airport, too?"

Foster cleared his throat again. "She said she'd make her own travel arrangements."

Bella knew more about the situation between Foster and his second wife than she'd let on. She had enough social contacts in the Capitol to hear the rumors that Patsy and Foster had separated several months ago. Bella wasn't sure of the exact problem, but it must have been something serious, since the couple had been together for nearly twenty years. She could understand why Foster didn't want her around, if he was attempting a reconciliation with his wife.

Well, Bella wouldn't get in his way. For Patsy's sake, if not his. Besides, she had enough problems of her own. How was she going to get her sons married off before she died, if they were determined to avoid her company?

Bella had employed Warren & Warren Investigations, with its main offices in Dallas, Texas, often over the years to keep tabs on her children. Sam Warren's information had always been reliable. She rarely interfered in her children's lives, but once or twice, as they were growing up, she'd come to the rescue of one or another of her sons without his knowledge.

She'd helped anonymously, because she'd known none of them would want or appreciate her help. Lydia had remained loyal to her mother after the separation, but she knew the boys blamed her for breaking up their once-happy family.

It was *your fault. You're guilty as charged.*

There were circumstances she'd never had a chance to explain that might have excused her behavior, if only Bull had been willing to listen. He'd been too angry to hear reason. And she'd felt too betrayed to explain.

She'd stood shocked and heartbroken as Foster tried to goad his brother into divorcing her. His diatribe was indelibly etched in her memory.

"She was a bitch when you met her, and she hasn't changed one iota in the twenty-five years you've been married to her. I say cut your losses and get the hell out while you can."

Bella wasn't sure she would ever be able to forgive Bull for refusing to listen to her. Although, at this point, it didn't really matter, did it? She was running out of time to tell Bull the truth. Running out of chances to make amends before her heart failed.

When Foster spoke, it was as though he'd been reading her mind. "I called Bull at his office in Paris and mentioned this little visit of yours to The Seasons. I wondered if he might have some idea why you decided to come here, considering the fact you haven't been to The Seasons once since your separation."

"Oh?" Bella said warily. "What did he say?"

"He was ready to get on a plane and come here himself. I didn't think that was a good idea, considering everything."

Of course you didn't.

He arched a brow and said, "I told him that if you'd wanted him here, you would have invited him."

And you heard me tell Bull when we ended up brangling at the Heart Association Ball in February, that I would rather die than lay eyes on him again.

"You know Bull," Foster continued. "He does what he wants. If he comes, he'll be on the jet from Paris with my girls. He thought it would be a good chance to see all the kids."

Bella heard the rest of Foster's thought without it being spoken: *He's not coming here to see you. Bull Benedict wouldn't spit on you if you were on fire.* It wasn't exaggerating to say that she and Bull had fought their own Revolutionary War during the ten years they'd been separated.

"The condition his European banks are in with this

crazy global economy, I doubt he can get away." Foster set down his coffee cup. "I'd better get going, or I'll be late."

Bella exhaled audibly when Foster left the room. She glanced at Emily, who was eyeing her worriedly, and shook her head to indicate she was fine. The young woman was acting like a mother hen with one chick. Bella didn't bother repeating that she was fine. She simply rose and headed for the stairs. Climbing that enormous staircase was great exercise. And she needed time alone in her room to think.

If she and Bull were going to be in the same room again, she should take advantage of the opportunity to explain what she'd kept secret for so many years.

Maybe, at long last, she would.

6

"Hello, Bull."

"Hello, Duchess."

Bella felt her heart flutter when Bull called her Duchess. It had been his pet name for her during their marriage, spoken with tenderness and love. He'd rarely used it after they'd separated. Right now it sounded…so very good. She waited for thc snide or snarly comment that usually followed, turning their post-separation encounters into a cat and dog fight.

It didn't come.

She eased back into the Adirondack chair situated on the sunny bank of the James River, where both families had gathered for a Mother's Day picnic, and gestured him into the chair beside her. "Would you like to join me?"

"How are you?" he asked as he stooped under a colorful umbrella and slid into the slatted wooden lawn chair beside her.

Such an innocent question. How should she answer it? She felt the tension gather in her shoulders just from sitting so close to Bull. Felt her heart begin the ridiculous pitty-pat that proximity to this masterful, passionate man always caused. She looked into his sky-blue eyes and opened her mouth to tell him the truth. What came out was, "I'm fine."

His gaze roamed her face. "You look a little pale. I didn't see you at Cote D'Azur or Saint-Jean-Cap-Ferrat over the winter. What have you been doing with yourself?"

I skipped a holiday on the French Riviera this year because I was getting a lot of medical tests. You see, my heart is failing. I'm slowly—but surely—dying.

Bella thought the words. They never made it out of her mouth. She'd heard the subtle insinuation in Bull's voice. The mocking suggestion that she'd been hiding out with yet another lover. The truth stuck in her throat.

Lies came so much easier. At the beginning of their marriage, lies had been necessary. The truth would have destroyed everything.

Unfortunately, lying had become the easy way to keep peace between them. It was difficult to believe she could tell the truth now and not have it turned against her. But she'd already lost Bull. When the most important thing in her life was gone, what did she have to lose?

"To be honest, Bull, I'm—"

Before she could finish her sentence, she was interrupted by Foster's three teenage girls. They rushed up to her Adirondack chair and grabbed her hands and arms, pulling her to her feet.

"Come and join us, Aunt Bella," one of the twins urged. "We're going canoeing."

Bella was already standing by the time she said, "No, thank you, girls. I prefer to enjoy the James River from its banks, rather than by paddling through it. You go ahead."

The twins turned their attention to Bull, who'd risen to his feet when the girls pulled her upright. "Come with us, Uncle Bull," one twin pleaded. "We hardly ever see you anymore."

"Please come," the second twin urged. "There are three of us, so if we take two canoes we need another paddler."

"What about your dad?" Bull asked. "Have you asked him?"

"Daddy said he needs to talk to Mom," the youngest of the three girls said.

"We think that's a good idea," one of the twins said. Three worried glances slid to their parents, who were following an old wagon trail along the river bank. Foster and Patsy walked along separate tracks in the dirt road. The conversation seemed heated.

"What about one of your older brothers?" Bull asked.

"Ben and Carter already took their girlfriends out on the Chris-Craft," one of the twins replied.

"C'mon, Uncle Bull. *Pleeeeeze,*" the youngest girl begged, latching onto his arm with both her hands. "Otherwise, I can't go."

Bull glanced in Bella's direction. "I hoped to spend some time talking with your aunt."

Bella wondered what he had in mind. They'd rarely spoken cordially during their separation. They hadn't spoken at all since February. And yet, before it was too late, she hoped to explain things she'd left unexplained.

Time was running out.

She was seized with a sudden fear. Once she told Bull the truth, there would be no turning back. Whatever chance they might have had for some sort of reconciliation before she died might be gone. There was still a great deal of the day left. Maybe, if she had more time to think, she could find a better way to say what had to be said.

She glanced toward Camille's crestfallen face and said, "Go ahead, Bull. We can talk when you get back."

"All right," he said, his gaze intent on her. "I'm going to hold you to that."

Bella watched as Camille slid her arm through Bull's and hauled him off toward the boathouse, talking his ear off as he strode away. The twins ran ahead. Their matching pink bikini bathing suits revealed just how grown-up they'd become in the years since she'd last seen them.

The sun was hot, and Bella settled back into the umbrella-shaded Adirondack. Foster's second family was almost grown and would soon be leading lives apart from their parents. Meaning Patsy might feel more free to walk away from her husband. Which would be too bad. She didn't like Foster, but she hated to see another family broken up.

Bella's gaze naturally sought out the riverbank again, where Patsy and Foster were walking together. Or rather, walking in the same direction. Their body language made it clear they weren't "together." They stopped and faced each other.

Patsy's chin jutted, and she perched balled fists on her hips. Foster locked his hands behind his head, then dropped them to his sides as he took a step toward Patsy. She took a step back, maintaining the distance between them.

The sharp sound of Patsy's voice carried to Bella, but not the words she spoke. The wind caught Foster's intense masculine tones and carried them in her direction, as well, without revealing what he'd said.

Bella wished she knew more about what had caused the rift between them in the first place. She'd always envied the fact that, after he divorced his first wife, Foster had found another woman to love. In the years since she and Bull had separated, Bella had never found another man who could inspire anything close to the feelings Bull had. Lord knew—and the gossip columns had reported endlessly—how hard she'd tried.

It was little comfort to know that Bull hadn't found anyone either. He, at least, had gone through several long-term liaisons. In each case, she'd held her breath waiting to hear him ask her for a divorce. But the relationships had always ended.

With the days of her life numbered, Bella knew how foolish she'd been to walk away from the one man she'd ever truly loved. All those wasted years! Regret seemed futile, but she felt it all the same. She wanted Bull's arms around her again before it was too late. She needed to tell him the truth. She just hoped he would be able to forgive her.

"Your Grace?"

Bella turned and felt her heart sink when she saw what Emily was holding. Her assistant had stayed at the main house to await news from the one child who hadn't yet replied to her invitation.

"Lord Maxwell won't be coming," Emily said as she handed a floral card to Bella. "He sent flowers—your favorite, hyacinths—along with the note."

"Thank you, Emily," Bella said as she took the note. She opened it and read:

Dear Mother,

Sorry I can't be with you to celebrate. I'm sure you'll have plenty of company without me. I'll see you when you return home.

Max

The note sounded cold to Bella. It was certainly missing any sort of affection. Not *Love, Max* or even *Your loving son, Max*. Just *Max*. No XXXs or OOOs—no kisses or hugs.

Bella felt her throat swell with emotion. She swallowed over the painful lump that formed. She couldn't remember the last time she'd hugged or kissed one of her children. They'd been gone at school so much. That had been her choice, of course. It had seemed safer to keep them out of the line of fire while she and Bull were lobbing verbal grenades in the years before they'd finally moved into separate homes.

But the war had gone on for far too long. When she'd finally brought her sons home to Blackthorne Abbey on holiday, she'd found them aloof. And nothing she'd said or done had been able to melt the wall of ice that had grown between them.

The younger boys had followed Oliver's lead. Because of the rumors that had surrounded her eldest son's birth, Oliver had learned early how to fight back. He won the battle against the gossips by not caring what others thought…or felt.

Consequently, her eldest son had a ruthless streak that ran deep. Oliver wasn't entirely heartless. He clearly loved his younger brothers and sister. But he was unforgiving. And he could be cold-blooded, as he had been when he'd refused her invitation for Mother's Day without a stitch of Riley's politeness or Payne's tact or Max's apology or Lydia's kindness.

Her eldest son was a bitter man. Perhaps it was time to tell him who his father was. And how he had been conceived. Then his rancor toward the world could be aimed where it truly belonged.

Was that really fair? Would the truth make her son's

life better? Or a hundred times worse? By unburdening herself, wouldn't she be adding to the malignant weight her son had carried all his life?

"Your Grace? Are you feeling well?" Emily asked.

Bella realized her heart was pounding. "I'm fine," she said. "Sit down, Emily. Get out of the sun."

Emily smiled and said. "I like the sun, Your Grace. There's too little of it in England."

Bella waved her away. "You should be off canoeing with the girls."

"My place is here with you."

"Then sit down," she said. "I don't like to have you hovering."

Emily looked guilty. And uncomfortable. She hesitated, then settled into the Adirondack Bull had vacated.

Bella felt awful for making her assistant feel self-conscious. Staying in one's place out of respect was one thing, but the girl took it too far. Emily was another person she was determined to see well-settled before the end. The woman deserved to be happy. Although, it was hard to imagine Emily being attracted to—or, unfortunately, attractive to—a man.

"Do you have a boyfriend, Emily?" she asked.

Emily's mouth dropped into an O of surprise. "Why, no, Your Grace."

"Is there some man you fancy?"

Emily turned beet red. It wasn't an attractive color on her.

"I didn't mean to embarrass you," Bella said. "I was merely curious."

"There is a man, Your Grace, but..."

"But you're stuck traveling around the world with me."

"It isn't that, Your Grace. I love spending time with you."

"Then what is it, Emily?"

The young woman twisted her hands in her lap. At long last, she met Bella's gaze and said, "I've loved him from the moment I met him. But he doesn't even know I'm alive."

"Oh." That was a sad state of affairs. One Bella would have to rectify. Just as soon as she managed to get her own large brood married off.

"Are you sure you're all right, Your Grace?" Emily asked.

Bella realized she was twisting the large diamond she still wore on the third finger of her left hand in painful circles on her swollen finger. She laid her hands in her lap and said, "I'm disappointed about what's happened this weekend, if you want to know the truth."

"Very understandable, Your Grace. Your children are—"

"Ungrateful monsters? Spoiled brats? Renegades without a conscience?"

"Oh, no, Your Grace," Emily protested. "I would never—"

"I've said it for you," Bella soothed. And yet, she felt

frustrated by the result of her first attempt at making amends with both husband and children.

Was it hope that made her feel so agitated? Or fear? Whatever she was going to do, whether it was trying to win back her husband, or finding spouses for her children, she'd better get started doing it.

She'd tell Bull the truth today, she decided. As for the other task she'd given herself... It wasn't going to be easy arranging romantic liaisons for her sons and daughter if she couldn't even get them to come see her for a special occasion like Mother's Day. She was simply going to have to intrude on their lives, whether they liked it or not.

But where to begin?

Max was in London. He'd even agreed to see her when she got home. She knew the perfect woman for her youngest son. She should have done something long ago to get the two of them together. Now, at long last, she hoped to make things right. It made sense to start matchmaking with Max.

"Emily, I need you to make some travel arrangements for us."

"Certainly, Your Grace. Where are we going?"

"Home. But first we're going to—"

Foster descended on Bella like a blustery winter wind. "This is all your fault!"

Foster's unexpected attack frightened Bella enough to make her heart jump. She put a hand against her chest and shot a warning look at Emily, to keep her from revealing the existence of her heart condition.

"I have many sins for which I will have to answer," Bella answered as languidly as she could. "I doubt any of them have much to do with you."

"My wife sees you flitting around the world without a thought in your head and—"

"Flitting?" Bella interrupted, arching a disdainful brow.

"Wandering, traipsing, gadding about," Foster interjected, furiously. "And she starts thinking life in one place is too confining."

"Are you sure it's not life with *one man* she finds too confining?" Bella said in a silky voice.

Foster braced his hands on the arms of her Adirondack and leaned in so close she could feel his breath on her face. "You're not the one to be talking. At least my children showed up here today. You're reaping what you've sowed, Bella," he said viciously.

"I hardly think—"

"You sent those poor kids of yours off to boarding schools their whole lives while you partied your way around the world." He sneered down at her. "What did you expect? You treated them like dirt. They're just paying you back."

"That's quite enough," Bella said quietly.

Foster stood up, but he didn't step back. "I've barely gotten started, lady. You had to come here when you knew I was trying to mend things with my wife. You've been a bad seed from the start. You insinuated yourself between Bull and the woman he was courting. You teased him and taunted him and stole him away from the caring person—the lady—he should have married. It's a shame Bull couldn't see what I did."

"I loved your brother." *I still love him!* Bella wanted to cry. But that would be setting fire to gasoline, considering Foster's rage.

"You don't know what love is!" Foster said with a sneer. "You tricked my brother into marrying you. Christ, you threatened him with jail if he didn't."

"I had nothing to do with that," Bella protested. Her aunt, who'd stood in for her dead parents, had threatened to go to the police and have Bull charged with statutory rape if he didn't marry her. "Bull wasn't innocent," Bella pointed out. "He did have sex with a seventeen-year-old."

"But some other guy got there first, didn't he, Bella?" Foster snarled. "Because Oliver isn't Bull's son. For God's sake, his eyes are brown!"

Bella's face blanched. Both Bella and Bull had blue eyes. Which made Oliver's brown eyes a genetic impossibility. Some other man had to be his father. The truth had been there all along, but Foster had ever spoken it aloud. Until now.

"You love those detestable diamonds and rubies and pearls my brother lavished on you more than you ever loved him or any of those kids," Foster ranted. "You're a lying, cheating bitch, Bella. Just stay the hell away from me and my brother!"

Bella pressed a fist against her heart and leaned forward, struggling to breathe. "I won't bother you…for much…"

"It's her heart!" Emily cried, rising from her Adirondack.

Foster jerked his head around and searched the horizon. "Bull!" he yelled. "Get over here. Bella's having a heart attack!"

7

"You had me worried, Duchess."

Bella sat up straighter in her Richmond hospital bed. "I'm sorry, Bull." The quiet apology should have been spoken years ago for the two great wrongs she'd done to the man standing beside her bed. Bella felt genuinely contrite, sorry enough to finally confess the lies she'd allowed to stand. If only she could find the courage to reveal the truth. About everything.

Yet, she put it off a moment longer. "You heard the doctor. It wasn't anything serious."

Bull snorted. "A panic attack? Horseshit. You've been an ice queen since the day I met you. What's really going on, Duchess? Is there something wrong with your heart?"

The use of her nickname—and Bull's pugnacious tone—suggested the gloves had come off. He was so close to the truth, Bella felt her weakened heart wrench with fear. She didn't want Bull taking her back because she was dying. She didn't want his pity. She'd sworn the doctor to secrecy and ordered him to give her husband a less serious reason for her fainting spell. He wasn't buying it.

"Bull, I—"

"You're awake," Foster said as he shoved open the door without knocking and entered Bella's hospital room. "Good."

Patsy followed him inside, smiling at Bella as they crossed to the opposite side of the bed from Bull. "Good morning, Bella. You're looking much better than you did on the ride to the hospital yesterday."

Since it would have taken the same time for an ambulance to arrive at The Seasons as it took for them to drive to Richmond, Foster and Patsy had sat in the front seat of Foster's Mercedes while Bull held Bella in his arms in the backseat. They'd made it to the emergency room at Levinson Heart Hospital, on the Chippenham Campus of CJW Medical Center, in record time.

Bella just wished she'd been awake for more of the trip.

"I don't think I've ever seen Bull in such a state," Patsy said with a teasing wink. "He didn't stop pacing at the emergency room door until the doctor told him you'd regained consciousness."

Bella shot a quick glance at Bull. Did that mean he still cared? Could he possibly still love her? The thought gave her pause. And hope.

"Bull was worried how the kids would feel if you kicked the bucket on Mother's Day when none of them had shown up to see you," Foster said.

Patsy shot her husband a look that expressed Bella's feelings about her brother-in-law's comment exactly.

"That was unkind, Foster," Patsy said.

To Bella's surprise, Foster responded to his wife's criticism by turning to Bella and saying, "Excuse me. That was uncalled-for."

Foster was rewarded with a smile from Patsy. Bella realized the two of them must have made up. It seemed Foster wasn't going to chance offending his wife again, even if it meant making nice with a woman he regularly wished to the devil.

"I wanted to be sure you were feeling better this morning," Patsy said, brushing a hand across Bella's shoulder. "We'll leave the two of you to talk."

Bella took another look at Bull and realized he must have spent the entire night at the hospital. He hadn't shaved. The gray and black stubble gave his face a rugged look. He was wearing the same docksiders, jeans and V-necked gray cashmere sweater over a white T-shirt that he'd worn to the picnic.

"Thank you, Patsy," Bella said. "I am feeling better. And thank you, too, Foster, for getting me to the hospital."

Foster didn't say *you're welcome.*

Bella was sure he would rather she'd expired on the spot. Or in the car on the way to the hospital. Or in the hospital after she'd arrived.

Instead, Foster said to Patsy, "We'd better get going, honey. The girls need to get back to school. The jet's scheduled to leave at noon." He turned to his older brother and said, "Should we wait for you, Bull? Or do you want to catch a cab to the airport?"

Bella felt a jolt of surprise. She hadn't realized the girls were going back to school so soon. Or that Bull might be traveling back to Europe with them.

"I'll get my own ride," Bull replied.

Bella noticed he hadn't said he wasn't returning to Paris with his nieces. It was time to confess. If she was ever going to confess.

She suddenly felt breathless, but not because her heart wasn't pumping enough oxygen.

Once Foster and Patsy were gone, Bull crossed and sat on the edge of her bed. "Are you going to tell me the truth, Duchess?"

"About what?" Bella asked warily.

"About what put you in that bed."

"The doctor already told you—"

"What you told him to tell me," Bull interrupted. "I want the truth, Bella. By God, I deserve the truth."

Yes, he did. There was no going forward without going back. It was time he heard the truth…about the night he'd found her in bed with another man.

"There's something I have to tell you, first," she said. "The night you found me in bed with—"

"Don't go there, Bella," he warned.

"You wouldn't let me explain then, or even later, but—"

"There's no excuse for what you did."

He was doing it again. Condemning her without allowing her to explain.

"The point is—" she began.

"The point is, you slept with another man. In our bed. End of discussion."

Bella felt her cheeks heating, felt her heart thumping and put a knotted hand against her painful chest. She was going to die of a broken heart, all right. Broken by this stubborn man who wouldn't listen. Who hadn't trusted. Who'd believed the worst and never allowed her to explain. She'd felt every bit as betrayed by his lack of trust as he had by what he thought he'd seen.

"Bull, you're going to listen to my explanation or—"

He stood abruptly and said, "Keep your damned secrets, then, Bella. I don't give a damn if your heart stops. I swear I don't. I thought…I hoped…"

He rubbed a hand across the back of his neck, then dropped it and shook his head.

"Thought what?" she asked softly. "Hoped what?"

"I thought I could forget what happened. I hoped…" He looked up and met her gaze. "Damn it, I can't forget. Or forgive. I forgave you for Oliver. You promised you'd never betray me again. You lied, Bella. You cheated on me once too often."

He turned on his heel and was out the door while her mouth was still open to protest.

"You fool!" she cried as the door closed behind him. "It wasn't me! It wasn't *me!*"

Tears pooled in her eyes and slid down her cheeks as she made her explanation to the empty room. "It was my twin, you stupid man. It was Alicia. She tricked you into sleeping with her at the start of our marriage. When I found out, I told her to leave the Abbey, to get out of my life forever. She said she'd leave, but I'd be sorry for choosing you over her."

Her sister had wreaked a terrible vengeance.

"She made sure you found her—*pretending to be me*—in your bed with another man."

Bella had never been unfaithful to Bull. She'd loved him—still loved him—more than life. She'd never told him about Alicia's impersonation of her—and the fact he'd been duped into having sex with her jealous twin sister—because she'd been ashamed of, and appalled by, Alicia's behavior. So he'd believed he was seeing Bella impaled on another man's shaft.

Alicia had smirked in triumph when she'd admitted to Bella what she'd done. "Let's see if your precious husband will have anything to do with you now!" she'd taunted.

Bull was gone for three days before he'd returned to confront her. When she'd tried to explain what Alicia had done, he'd demanded, "Was that him? Was that Oliver's father? I have to know. Tell me the truth, Bella."

The problem was, somehow Alicia had chosen Oliver's father with whom to commit her supposedly adulterous act. It had been impossible to tell Bull the truth about Alicia without revealing the truth about Oliver's father.

And that was a story she would never, never, ever tell.

Bella moaned. Ruined. Everything was ruined.

Emily stuck her head in the doorway, then came hurrying across the room. “Your Grace? What’s wrong?”

Bella quickly swiped the tears off her cheeks, then grabbed a tissue from a box on the side table and dabbed at the mascara that had smudged at the corners of her eyes. “Nothing that hasn’t been wrong for a very long time. I have matchmaking to do and not much time to do it. Have you spoken with the appropriate parties in London?”

“Yes, Your Grace.”

“Have you gathered all the information on the young woman?”

“Yes, Your Grace.”

“Have you finished making our travel arrangements?”

“Your doctor said—”

“Yes or no. Have you made the arrangements, Emily?”

Emily sighed. “Yes, Your Grace. Our flight to Miami leaves first thing tomorrow morning.”

“Good. It’s time I started playing cupid.”

8

Kristin had just gotten the bad news from the Miami SAC. Rudy was sympathetic but there was nothing he could do. The Miami OPR—heavily influenced, Kristin was sure, by SSA Harrison—had decided Kristin should be suspended until SIRT came back with its recommendation for action on her second shooting incident.

"What am I supposed to do?" she asked.

"Get your daughter into school," Rudy said. "Spend some time with your father. See the shrink, so you're ready to come back when the time comes."

"So you think I will be coming back?"

"Not my call," Rudy said. "What about that assignment with the CIA?"

Kristin frowned. "I thought you'd hate the idea."

Rudy lifted a brow. "I'm not crazy about loaning out my agents, but this is a serious threat, Agent Lassiter. How about it? I understand you're a world-class tennis player. Sounds like you're the right woman for the job."

At least it would be a job. The one she had seemed to be in jeopardy. "I'll think about it."

"Be sure to turn in your badge and gun before you leave the building," Rudy said.

That sounded more than a little final. Kristin left Rudy's office in a daze. *What if I lose my job? How will I survive?*

She felt even more shaken when she dropped off her credentials and the weapon that had replaced the gun that had been sent to the FBI's ballistics lab at Quantico after the first shooting. She hadn't been without badge or gun for four years. They'd become a part of her identity. Who would she be without them?

More to the point, how was she going to survive the several financial catastrophes she was facing without her job. Maybe she could borrow some money at the bank while she still had her job. Perhaps get a home equity line of credit. Except she already had a second mortgage. And the banks weren't loaning money these days without months and months of paperwork. She needed money now. And she needed lots of it.

You could always rob a bank.

Kristin snickered. Which was better than sobbing.

She'd taken a few precious days of her vacation allowance to deal with Flick's appearance and her father's stroke. She didn't have many more left. Then what?

Her father had recently mortgaged his tennis facility to expand and improve it, so he was cash poor. He had assistants to help, but players came to the Lassiter Tennis Academy to be coached by Harry Lassiter. She had to figure out a way to keep the academy running until Harry could at least come back and supervise players from a wheelchair.

Harry had been so fit, he'd never bought health insurance. His bills at the hospital were mounting astronomically. She didn't want to imagine what physical therapy—and perhaps a nurse at home—were going to cost.

Kristin was still in shock when she left the MFO. She felt frightened. She'd worried that she might be put on administrative duty again, but she hadn't imagined being suspended. The reality of the situation came crashing down on her.

I could be fired.

She made it to her car before her knees buckled. She sat in the hot sun, trembling as though it were bitter cold. She'd left Flick with her father when she'd come in to see Rudy and promised she'd be back within a couple of hours. She needed to go pick up her daughter.

Then what, Kristin? Then what?

The offer from Max was looking a lot more attractive. Assuming the CIA was still willing to use her when she was on suspension from the FBI. Of course, there were her "special qualifications" for the job in London. Maybe if she helped find an assassin, it would influence the FBI to keep her.

Kristin suddenly realized she had no idea how to contact Max. He hadn't given her a business card. Of course, neither playboys nor spies needed business cards. She knew Max was living in London. But would a spy have a listed telephone number?

She could always contact his mother. But as much as Max hated the duchess, would she be likely to know where he could be found?

Kristin used the trip south on I-95 to Jackson Memorial to compose herself. She mentally worked out the exact wording she would use to explain how she'd gotten time off from work. No sense upsetting her father or Flick, both of whom had an uncanny ability to tell when she was troubled. And no sense worrying herself, until she knew for sure she'd been fired.

In the parking garage, she added some lipstick and tucked a stray curl behind her ear. She took a deep, calming breath and let it out. Then she put a smile on her face. She grimaced at how phony it looked in the rearview mirror and tried again. Better. She was as ready as she would ever be to face her family without revealing the chaos that threatened them all.

One thing at a time. One day at a time. That's how she'd survived when she was sixteen and her world had fallen apart. It wasn't so very different now that she was twenty-six. With a little thought—and a lot of luck—she was certain she could figure out a way to turn all these bitter lemons into sweet, icy-cold lemonade.

Kristin stepped off the elevator at Jackson Memorial onto the floor where her father was recuperating and stopped dead when she saw who was sitting alone in the visitors' lounge.

"Good morning, Ms. Lassiter."

Kristin's heart skipped a beat as she eyed the elegantly dressed woman in the waiting room. Bella Benedict had eyes that were almost violet in hue and barely a wrinkle on her face. Her black hair was parted on the side, cut to shoulder length and threaded with silver that set off her ivory complexion and made her look ethereally beautiful.

She was wearing a beige silk suit, with a necklace of pearls—clearly not the famous one Kristin had heard about—hanging in ropes across the silk blouse beneath it. Her crossed legs revealed a pair of leopard-spotted Jimmy Choos or Manolo Blahniks or some other exclusive brand of heels that were higher than anything Kristin had ever owned.

The duchess was wearing the exquisite square-cut diamond ring her husband had given her on their engagement. It sparkled like polar ice in the sunlight. Was it eight carats? Eight-point-five, she remembered Max telling her. The duchess had kept it on her ring finger all through her separation from Max's father. Max had suggested she wore it in defiance of her husband, while she entertained her many lovers.

Kristin couldn't imagine a single reason—except for one, which was a well-kept secret—why the Duchess of Blackthorne had come calling. "To say I'm surprised to see you here would be a massive understatement," she said at last.

The duchess smiled. "I'm a bit surprised to be here myself."

Kristin felt the hairs on the back of her neck hackle,

like an animal that senses threat. She didn't trust the woman. Bella Benedict's reputation—as someone who put her own interests first—preceded her. "What do you want?"

"Please, sit down," the duchess said, gesturing to an upholstered chair angled toward the durable leather couch where she sat. "We need to talk."

"I have nothing to say to you," Kristin replied.

"I'm sure that's true," the duchess conceded. "But I know you need money. I'd like to help."

Kristin felt her cheeks heat with shame and anger. "I don't want your help."

"I've gone about this all wrong," the duchess said with a moue of distress. "Please, won't you sit down? I only want what's best for my granddaughter, Felicity."

The blood drained from Kristin's face.

"I believe you call her Flick." And in case Kristin had any doubt that the cat was out of the bag, the duchess continued, "My son Max's nine-year-old daughter."

Kristin's heart was threatening to beat its way out of her chest. "Does Max know?"

The duchess shook her head. "I didn't think it was my place to tell him."

"Thank God." Kristin had kept Flick's birth father a secret for ten years. Her first thought, her greatest fear, when Max had shown up in Rudy's office, was that he'd somehow found out about Flick. But he hadn't given any indication that he knew about his daughter. If the duchess was telling the truth, he was still oblivious to the fact he was a father.

So why had the duchess come? Not for any good reason, she was sure. The deep friendship that had grown between her and Max during the three years before she'd left the tour had flourished in great part because of Max's frustrating relationship with the woman sitting before her now.

Kristin recalled one particular incident about nine months after she'd won her first Wimbledon trophy. She and Max had been playing at the tournament in early spring at Indian Wells, California. She'd won her match and had gone searching for Max to share the news and perhaps hit some balls with him.

She'd found the handsome sixteen-year-old far from the crowd, smashing his tennis racquet against a bench near the practice courts. The frame was broken and the Wilson racquet head was bent almost in half.

"Hey," she'd said as she approached him. "You okay?"

When he looked up, she saw his eyes were red-rimmed. He'd swiped at them and said, "What's up, Princess?"

She felt thrilled at hearing the new nickname he'd given her the past fall at the U.S. Open, when he saw her posing for a publicity picture her dad had wanted taken with all her shiny gold and silver and crystal trophies around her.

Max had said she looked like an Arabian princess with a hoard of jewels. Except for her blue eyes and blond hair, of course. If she were truly an Arabian princess, her eyes and hair would have been black. "Make that a North American princess," he'd corrected with a laugh.

She'd laughed back at him. But he'd called her Princess as often as K after that. She wasn't sure which she liked better. She was just happy spending time with Max, secretly loving him.

If she'd been able to see into the future, she would have tried to kill that love. At the time, she'd been blissfully infatuated. She'd even tried thinking up a nickname for him. But Max was short and sweet.

In her head she called him "sweetheart" and "honey." But she was careful never to let on how she really felt. She knew the kind of woman he went for. Worldly. Sexually experienced. With a flashy figure.

Max might spend his nights with women like that, but he spent his free time during the day hanging around the tennis courts with her. She figured it was because he didn't have to be anyone but himself with her. She was the only one who saw him when he was feeling low. And he was usually feeling low because of something his mother had done.

Or hadn't done.

The duchess kept promising to come see him play. And making excuses why she hadn't shown up. She kept promising she'd get the family together. Then she'd tell him the family holiday in Tahiti or New York or on the Amalfi Coast had been canceled. She kept promising she'd call. And never did.

He'd told Kristin he didn't believe anything his mother

said anymore. But he kept waiting and hoping she'd change.

When Kristin found him smashing his racquet, she knew it had to be something the duchess had said. Or not done. "What did she do now?" she asked.

He examined the ruined racquet and said, "She was supposed to come see me play in the finals. I don't know why I thought she'd actually show up. She has some charity event in New York she forgot about. She's not coming."

"Why do you even care?" she said fiercely, hurting inside for the boy she loved. "She's a mean witch!"

He'd laughed, startled at her outburst, she supposed. "Princess, you're talking about my mother," he'd chided.

"I don't care. I'd call out anybody who treated you that way. Including that mean witch."

He'd grinned and ruffled her hair in a way that reminded her he saw her as a kid sister.

She slapped his hand away. "Stop that! You wouldn't do that to one of your girlfriends, would you?"

He eyed her askance. "Whoa, K. What's with the attitude?"

"I'm not five years old," she complained.

He studied her for a moment. She flushed because he seemed to notice she filled out her tennis togs better than she had the previous year at Wimbledon. "Point taken," he said at last. "Well, K, I'll say this for you. I'm not going to break any more racquets because of anything the Mean Witch does."

Kristin laughed as he parroted her expression.

From then on, that was how the two of them had referred to his mother. That was how she thought of the woman sitting before her now. The last thing Kristin wanted—or needed—was trouble from the Mean Witch.

She sank into the nearby chair, staring with wary eyes at the duchess. "How did you find out about Flick?"

"I employ a very good private investigator. Mr. Warren has been very helpful over the years. Please, let me start with the reason I'm here."

"I don't want anything from you," Kristin said.

"You may not want my assistance, my dear. But you need it."

"I've been taking care of my family just fine without help from anyone," Kristin flared.

"Yes, but you've just been suspended from your job, which seems to be in jeopardy. And you don't have the money to pay for your father's medical expenses or physical therapy. Or for after-school child care, or private school, for that matter, since Felicity has been thrown out of that Swiss boarding school where she had a scholarship. And you can't afford to pay a lawyer to defend you in the civil lawsuit that's been filed against you."

"How could you possibly know all that?" Kristin demanded, aghast. "I only found out twenty minutes ago that I'm on suspension. Flick's barely been home twenty-four hours. And a person's legal business and personal finances—"

"Can be examined without too much trouble. I

sponsored Felicity's scholarship, so the headmistress informed me immediately when she was dismissed for fighting.

"As for your suspension, I asked a friend in Washington if he thought you could get leave from the FBI to travel to London for a while. He said he'd check into it. I wonder now if he might have misconstrued my request. I didn't mean you should be put on suspension."

Kristin felt things shifting out of her control. "How dare you interfere in my life! I'm not going anywhere, especially not to London." Although she'd been considering exactly that half an hour ago.

"I understand you're scheduled to play an exhibition tennis match with Max against Elena Tarakova and Steffan Pavlovic on opening day at Wimbledon," the duchess said. "I couldn't have arranged it better myself."

Kristin felt her pulse pounding in her temples. How could the duchess possibly know about something the CIA had arranged with Scotland Yard? Then she remembered the duchess's "friend" in Washington. Had Bella suggested the exhibition match? Had Max been manipulated—without his knowledge—as well? Was there really an assassin after the president? Or had Bella and her friend in Washington made that up, too?

"Arranged?" she replied in as even a voice as she could manage.

"Well, I didn't arrange the match," Bella confessed. "I didn't have anything to do with that. But I must admit, it's an amazing coincidence that you've been asked to spend time with Max in London just when I decided to—"

"Even if I agreed to such a thing," Kristin interrupted, "I haven't played a professional match in ten years."

"It's only an exhibition, Ms. Lassiter. You and Max have plenty of time to practice before the match."

"I can't leave my father. Or my daughter."

"As I said, everything can easily be arranged. Felicity can come with you. I spoke with your father, and he agrees that you should play."

"My father doesn't run my life. And Flick goes nowhere without my say-so."

"The announcement of the match was made this morning in the *Times*. There's a great deal of excitement, actually, about having the four players who were the Wimbledon finalists ten years ago playing a mixed doubles exhibition match."

Kristin wondered if Max was hoping to force her hand by having the announcement made without her having consented to play. And if Bella had nothing to do with arranging the match, then it was likely the assassin existed and that Max's investigation of the tennis players at Wimbledon was necessary.

Which meant her participation in the match—and the investigation—might very well be important, as Rudy had suggested. Even if it dragged up a lot of unhappy history for her.

Ten years ago, Max had won the Wimbledon Boys' Singles Championship match against Steffan Pavlovic. Kristin had lost her Girls' Singles Championship match against Elena Tarakova. Kristin wasn't looking forward to seeing Elena again. The woman who'd stolen the Wimbledon prize from her had also ruined her life. With Max's cooperation, of course.

That was another story. One she'd tried to forget. Of love transcendent. And love betrayed.

"I've made arrangements for you and Felicity to fly to London on my private jet. Your father will be taken care of by a private nurse I've hired."

Kristin couldn't believe the duchess's gall. "What part of *no* don't you understand?"

"I hate to point out the obvious, my dear, but you're out of money. What other choice do you have?"

None. She was out of choices. And the duchess knew it.

"Why are you doing this?" she asked. It would be just like Bella Benedict to arrange for Kristin to go to London so that Max could take her to some British court and get custody of Flick. She suddenly wondered if Flick was in the room with her grandfather, or whether Bella might already have spirited her daughter out of the country.

"Have you seen Flick?" she asked anxiously. "Have you said anything to her about any of this?"

Kristin rose and was already headed down the hall when Bella said, "I don't want to take Felicity away from you, Ms. Lassiter. I only want to help you and my granddaughter."

Kristin marched back into the waiting room and confronted the older woman. "Why should you help me? What is it you want, really?"

"Happiness for my son with the woman he loves."

Kristin snorted. "You're barking up the wrong tree."

"By that, I presume you mean that my son isn't attracted to you."

"How about I'm not attracted to him," Kristin countered.

"I can see I'm ahead of myself again," the duchess murmured. "Will you sit down, please? This might take a while."

"Spit it out," Kristin said. "What is it you want?"

"I want you to marry my son."

Kristin would have laughed if she hadn't felt so near to tears. It seemed the Mean Witch was matchmaking. As crazy as it seemed, she'd apparently picked out Kristin for her youngest son.

Once upon a time, Kristin had loved—and trusted—Max Benedict enough to give him her virginity. He'd repaid her by treating what had been the most beautiful night of her life as though it were nothing. The next time she'd seen him, he'd been kissing her Wimbledon opponent—Elena Tarakova—a few moments before the start of their championship match.

Was it any wonder she'd lost? Kristin had been lucky she'd had enough composure to play at all.

Now fate had thrown the four of them—Max, Max's boyhood friend Steffan, Kristin and the woman who'd stolen Max away—back together for an exhibition match. With Max as her prize. Kristin wanted no part of it. Except…the duchess was right about one thing. She needed the woman's money. Kristin sat back down. "All right. I'm listening. How can you help me?"

"I'm ready and willing to pay all your debts and expenses. All I'm asking in return is that you play this exhibition match with my son."

"That's all?" Kristin said sarcastically. "That's plenty."

"I don't know what separated the two of you ten years ago, but I do know Max thought the world of you once upon a time."

Kristin didn't comment. In light of the events of the next morning, their one night of love felt more like a night of conquest, where Max took what was most precious from her and walked away. Kristin wasn't about to let Max back into her life, where he could break his daughter's heart by abandoning Flick the way he'd abandoned her mother.

"I'll never trust your son with my heart again."

"I'm not asking you to do that."

"You're not?" Kristin said. "I'm confused."

"I'm only asking that you play this exhibition match with Max. If you make up and he should propose marriage, well, whether you say yes is up to you."

Kristin laughed. "You want me to marry Max, but if he proposes, I don't have to say yes? Do I have that right?"

"That's right," the duchess said. "I'll give you all the financial support you require simply for going to England and playing the exhibition match."

"That's crazy."

"The two of you will need to spend a lot of time together on the tennis court to get ready for that match. Which will give you time to work out whatever issues separated you ten years ago. That doesn't sound so crazy to me."

"I'm not the least bit tempted by anything you've said so far."

"Maybe I have something that will tempt you," Bella said. The duchess took a black velvet bag from her purse. When she opened it, a waterfall of rubies and diamonds tumbled into her hands.

Kristin gasped when she recognized the beautiful stones. The duchess held out a ruby-and-diamond necklace, a ring, a bracelet and a pair of pendant earrings. Kristin could barely speak. "Are those…? I mean, I've heard of them, and I've seen pictures of you wearing them, but I never thought I'd see them in person. In a place like this. Are those…?"

"Yes, my dear," Bella confirmed as she held out the necklace, diamonds and rubies dripping over her fingertips. She held out the pendant earrings in her other hand. "These are the infamous Blackthorne Rubies.

"The largest ruby, the centerpiece of the necklace, was given to the first Duke of Blackthorne by Henry II in 1154, when Henry was crowned King of England and created the dukedom. It was a reward to Sir Philip Wharton for saving the king's life during one of his early battles to win control of the kingdom."

"They're…" Words deserted Kristin as she reached out to touch the breathtaking rubies.

"There's a legend attached to the rubies, that they bring the wearer courage. My husband gave the jewels to me as a love gift on the day my eldest son was born."

Kristin wondered if the duchess realized she'd said *my* eldest son, rather than *our* eldest son. She'd heard the rumors that Oliver wasn't Bull Benedict's son.

The duchess continued, "The jewels are yours if you play the exhibition match with Max."

The ruby-and-diamond jewelry the duchess had offered her was priceless. Kristin was suspicious. She sensed a trap. The duchess wasn't going to give away something so valuable without expecting something in return. "Why would you agree to part with something so precious in exchange for so little?"

"I want my son to be happy. Whatever the cost."

Kristin laughed. It wasn't a pleasant sound. "I don't believe you. You forget, I was Max's friend. I know how little time you spent with him when he was growing up. I know how little you really care."

She watched the duchess flinch at her accusations.

"It's true I sent my children away to school. And I didn't spend enough time with them when they were younger. But not because I didn't love them."

She didn't explain her reasons for keeping her children at a distance and Kristin didn't ask.

"You've wasted your time coming here," Kristin said, anxious to end the interview before Flick showed up. "You must know it's unlikely a playboy like Max would propose to anyone, let alone a woman who rejected him ten years ago. And even if, by some miracle, he did propose, I would refuse him."

"Then you have nothing to lose by agreeing to go to London," the duchess persisted.

Kristin tried to imagine what the duchess hoped to get in exchange for the priceless stones—especially if she didn't agree to marry Max. Maybe the duchess only wanted to provide for her granddaughter. But she'd chosen a strange way of doing it.

Kristin had just about decided she should go to London to participate in Max's investigation to uncover a potential assassin. So why not combine that logical reason for going with the duchess's illogical request?

All she had to do was play the exhibition match.

It was little enough for the reward she'd been promised. The truth was, she needed the financial assistance the duchess had offered. The Blackthorne Rubies… The rubies would provide security for her and her daughter until Flick was grown.

"All right," Kristin said at last. "I'll go to London. But Flick stays here."

"No!"

Kristin turned and saw her daughter leap up and out from her place of concealment at the entrance to the hallway.

"How long have you been hiding there?" Kristin demanded as she rose.

"Long enough to hear that my father isn't dead! Why did you lie to me, Mom?" she wailed.

"Sweetheart, I…" Kristin didn't know what to say.

She felt her heart squeeze at the look of betrayal in her daughter's Benedict-blue eyes.

"I can't believe I have a grandmother." Flick stared at the duchess. "You are my grandmother, aren't you?"

The duchess glanced at Kristin, who nodded, then turned to Flick and said, "Yes, my dear, I am."

Flick crossed the room until she stood face-to-face with the duchess. "What am I supposed to call you?"

"Grandmother?" the duchess proposed.

Flick made a face. "How about Gram?"

"Gram sounds fine," the duchess replied with a smile.

"Flick stays here," Kristin said emphatically.

"No." Flick turned to her mother and shook her head, her chin tilted mulishly. "I want to meet my father. Especially now that I know I have one." She crossed to the chair where Kristin was sitting and said, "You shouldn't have lied, Mom. You shouldn't have said he was dead, when he isn't."

He was dead to me. I thought you were better off without him. He couldn't abandon you if he was already dead.

She reached out for Flick's hand, but Flick jerked it away. "I know what's best, Flick. Staying here is best for you."

"If you leave me behind, I'll find a way to get to London on my own," Flick said, meeting her mother's gaze.

Kristin knew she shouldn't give in to her daughter's threat. The problem was, there was no one to take care of Flick if she left her behind. Her father needed to focus on his recovery. And Flick was resourceful enough to make good on her threat to find a way to get to London on her own.

"Felicity could stay with me at Blackthorne Abbey while you're in London," the duchess offered. "I could bring in a tutor so she doesn't get behind in her school work."

"What about Max? I want your assurance he doesn't see Flick—he doesn't even find out about Flick—until I say so."

She turned to Flick and said, "Do you understand what I'm saying, Flick. If you come to London, you don't have any contact with your father until I say so." She moved her gaze between the two, grandmother and granddaughter, and said, "That's the deal. Take it or leave it."

"I'll take it," the duchess and Flick said together.

"If it's any comfort to you," the duchess said, "Max never comes to the Abbey without prior notice. I suspect he's going to be too busy to come visit while you're in London."

"I don't want her 'accidentally' meeting Max," Kristin warned.

"I won't let that happen," the duchess promised.

"Then I can go?" Flick asked hopefully.

"You can go," Kristin replied. "I want your word you won't contact your father until I say it's all right."

Flick chewed on a hangnail a moment before she stuck out her hand to be shaken. "It's a deal."

The moment Flick let go of Kristin's hand, she said, "I can't believe I'm going to meet my father!"

Kristin closed her eyes and pressed her lips tight. In her daughter's mind, meeting her father was a foregone conclusion. Kristin wasn't at all sure she was going to allow it. She'd promised herself, from the moment she'd laid eyes on her daughter at birth, that she would never let Max hurt Flick. She had never imagined what she would do if Flick found out about her father and wanted to meet him.

The damage was done. She would take Flick to London now. And figure out whether to let Max into her daughter's life later.

9

"This meeting of the Castle Foundation is called to order. Good to see all of you."

"Good to see you, too, Oliver." Max wasn't crazy about Skype, but having a video computer conference from London with his siblings allowed him to see their faces every three months or so, no matter where in the world they were. He'd done his best not to miss any meetings, because it was just about the only contact he had these days with his siblings.

The Castle Foundation had been created by the four Benedict brothers with the money from their trust funds. It met once quarterly to decide how to invest and distribute the fortune they'd each received from their parents when they reached twenty-five.

It was impossible, when all his siblings were pictured on a computer screen at the same time, not to notice how different Oliver looked from the rest of them. His dark brown eyes and wavy chestnut hair were a far cry from everyone else's blue or gray eyes and straight black hair. Oliver was broader in the shoulders than his brothers, his nose thinner, his cheekbones sharper, his lips more full.

Their father had to have known from the first that Oliver wasn't his own flesh and blood. Max shuddered at the weight Oliver had borne his whole life of knowing he was technically—if not legally—a bastard. Max had never spoken to his brother about it. Oliver wouldn't have allowed it.

But it was Oliver he'd gone to when Kristin disappeared. Oliver who'd told him to forget about her and move on with his life. Oliver who'd first steered him toward the CIA, which had given his life the meaning it had now.

He'd never confirmed to Oliver, or to any of his siblings, that he was engaged in espionage. He'd been afraid his older brothers might laugh at him. And he couldn't trust Lydia to keep her mouth shut about it.

Interesting—fascinating?—that he'd told K exactly what he did for a living two minutes after he'd met her again. Especially when he continued to play the role of footloose playboy with his family. Of course, it had been necessary to tell K the truth, because they were going to be working together. But he could have made sure she was going to take the assignment before he'd peeled off his thin disguise.

The truth was, he'd wanted her to know he'd done something useful with his life. He'd wanted to impress her. He'd wanted her to regret throwing their friendship away. At one time she'd been closer to him than anyone else in his life, a substitute for the siblings from whom he was separated.

Because his middle brothers, Riley and Payne were close in age, they'd always been each other's best friends. Riley was older than Payne by a year and taller by an inch. Payne had a scar through his eyebrow where he'd had stitches after Riley had hit him in a teenage fight over a girl. They'd never gone after the same girl since.

Riley had light gray eyes. Payne's were sky blue, like their father's. Riley's straight black hair was shaggy. Payne kept his cropped. It was impossible to tell which of the two had a more cynical view of life in general and women in particular.

Max glanced at their younger sister's image and realized how stunningly beautiful their mother must have been when their father met her. Lydia's blue eyes looked almost as violet as their mother's. She had flawless ivory skin and long, silky hair, dark and shiny as an Egyptian scarab. No wonder Bull had forgiven the duchess's infidelity. No wonder he'd turned a blind eye to his eldest son's looks.

Lydia had recently turned twenty-five and thrown her trust fund into the pot. This was her first Castle Foundation meeting.

"Where are you, Lydia?" Max asked his sister.

"Venice," she replied. "What do we do at these meetings?"

"Mostly we listen to Oliver tell us what cause we're supporting with our money," Max said. "Well, Oliver?"

Oliver was president of the foundation and made the recommendations for which charitable organizations received their contributions and how their money was invested so it could grow. "We're giving a substantial amount for relief in Haiti, if that meets with your approval."

Max checked the actual amount on the documentation he'd received prior to the meeting. He whistled. "Nice."

"We need a vote," Oliver said. "All in favor."

They all cast their votes in the affirmative. Oliver would ultimately decide through which organization the money would be dispensed. When they'd finished their financial discussion, and confirmed the allowance each of them would receive for the coming quarter, Max said, "I couldn't get away to the States last week. I presume we all got the same invitation. Did any of you go see Mother on Mother's Day?"

"I was busy," Lydia said defensively. "I couldn't go."

"Hell no, I didn't go," Riley retorted. "I sent a card and a gift because that's the polite thing to do. Mother can never say I lack manners. Not that she ever notices one way or the other."

"I sent a gift but no card," Payne said. "It seemed easier to pretend I care than to make the point that I don't."

"I couldn't be there," Oliver said, making no explanation and giving no excuse. "But the fact that she summoned us at all was strange."

Trust Oliver to hit on the issue that had worried Max. He'd been called in to meet with Scotland Yard at the last minute and hadn't been able to make the trip. He'd been disappointed only because it meant he hadn't been able to slip down to Miami to see K. "Why do you suppose Mother invited us?" Max asked. "And to The Seasons, of all places?"

"It was Mother's Day," Lydia pointed out. "She wanted to see her children. Is that so strange?"

"It is for Mother," Oliver said bluntly.

"It's a little late for her to start pretending to be a loving parent," Riley said.

"Or for us to start pretending that we care," Payne added.

Max had always sided with his older siblings in their undeclared war against their mother, but he'd never been able to stop loving her. Even when she continued to disappoint him time after time. He was intrigued that she'd invited them. Especially when she might have expected the response—or rather, non-response—she'd gotten. "Why don't I try to find out what she had in mind?" he suggested.

"What's the point?" Riley asked. "I thought we gave up on her a long time ago."

"I'll tell you something you may not know," Oliver said. "None of us went, but Dad showed up. And Mother made an emergency trip to the hospital in Richmond."

"Is she okay?" Max felt a spurt of anxiety that he hid from his brothers. He wondered if his parents had gotten into another verbal fistfight that had left his mother reeling.

"According to Dad, it was only a panic attack," Oliver said.

"Panic over what?" Lydia asked.

"Probably over facing the husband she cheated on in a home that belongs to him but which she still has the right to enjoy," Payne muttered.

"More likely she was pissed off because nobody showed up," Riley said.

"Why don't I ask her?" Max said. "I have some engagements that will keep me in London for the next month or so."

"I read about one of your 'engagements' in the *Times* today," Lydia said with a laugh. "You're playing tennis at Wimbledon!"

"With Kristin of all people," Riley said with a grin.

Max grimaced. "Someone suggested it to the All England Lawn Tennis Club, and they thought it was a great idea. I'm going along for the ride."

"Don't tell me you aren't going to enjoy seeing Kristin again," Payne said. "You guys were best buds. Whatever happened with the two of you? How come you never talk about her anymore?"

Max shrugged away the question. It was easier than trying to explain. He hadn't realized how important his friendship with Kristin was until he'd lost it.

Kristin had understood what it meant to have parents who weren't together anymore. Hers were divorced. She'd understood why, as the youngest of four brothers, he'd wanted to be the very best at something, because she'd had an older sister who'd shown more promise on the tennis courts than she had. The sister had been killed in an auto accident. Kristin had spent hours on the tennis court trying to win her father's love by measuring up to that dead paragon.

Kristin had also understood how fame—she had a fair amount of it herself—made people want to be your friend for reasons that had nothing to do with liking you.

He still felt betrayed by the way she'd walked away without a word. He was the one who'd pushed to take their friendship to the next level. When they finally had, she'd bolted back to the States. He'd tried calling her and emailing her, but she wouldn't return any of his messages. Finally, he'd gotten mad enough—and sad enough—to give up.

"I haven't seen Kristin since she left the tennis circuit ten years ago," Max said straight-faced.

"Was that your choice or hers?" Lydia asked.

"It was mutual," he lied. Max didn't like to think of how badly he'd mismanaged things with K. He shouldn't have tried to make their friendship into something else. Friends like her were hard to replace. He hadn't managed to do it in the ten years since she'd walked out of his life.

It was far too late to do anything about it now. Their meeting in Miami had been worse than awkward. It was probably a good thing she'd nixed the tennis match. It would have been difficult practicing together. Speaking of which, he'd better start putting in some time on the court, if he didn't want to embarrass himself. He should contact Steffan and see if he wanted to hit some balls together.

And he'd better start thinking about a replacement for K.

"Are you going to meet with Mother in person?" Lydia asked.

"I guess so," Max said.

"Would you ask her if I can..." Lydia's voice trailed off.

"Ask her what?"

Lydia grimaced. "Never mind."

"Ask her what, Lydia?" Max persisted.

"I want to borrow the Ghost of Ali Pasha to wear at a charity ball I'm attending in Rome."

"You know how she feels about those stupid precious jewels of hers," Riley said. "That pearl necklace is more important to her than—"

"Any of us," Payne finished for his brother.

The Ghost of Ali Pasha was an enormous perfect teardrop pearl, the centerpiece of an exquisite diamond, emerald, ruby and sapphire necklace. The pearl had been owned by Ali Pasha of Yannina, an Albanian pasha from the western part of Rumelia, in the Ottoman Empire.

There was a legend attached to the pearl, which began when the pearl came into the possession of Ali Pasha. The pasha was notoriously cruel. He'd roasted rebels, flayed a man alive and executed another by having his bones broken with a sledge hammer. He seized control in 1788 and ruled most of Albania, western Greece and the Peloponnese for more than thirty years.

The pasha gave the pearl as a gift to his favorite concubine of the three hundred or so Christian, Muslim, Albanian and Circassian women in his harem. The pasha's favorite, a Circassian woman named Juba, was poisoned by a jealous woman in the harem. When the murderer wouldn't reveal herself, Ali Pasha ordered all of his concubines executed.

He wore the pearl in memory of Juba for the rest of his life. When Ali Pasha was finally defeated by his enemies and beheaded, he was wearing Juba's pearl. His head was sent to the Sultan Mahmud II, where it was presented on a silver plate, the pearl still around the pasha's throat.

The Sultan took the pearl as a prize of war—and was strangled by it in his bed.

That was the beginning of the legend that the pearl possessed the ghost of Ali Pasha, which had wreaked a terrible vengeance on his enemy. Thereafter, Juba's pearl was called the Ghost of Ali Pasha.

Somehow, the Ghost of Ali Pasha had ended up as part of the Spanish royal jewels. King Ferdinand VII was pictured wearing the pearl in 1806, in a painting by Goya, just before he was forced to abdicate the throne in favor of the Emperor Napoleon. The king hadn't lost his head while he owned the Ghost, but he'd lost his position as head of state.

In 1840, Queen Isabella II of Spain gave the Ghost to Queen Victoria of England as a wedding present.

The British queen disliked the legend that went along with the pearl and sent it as a gift to Frederick II when he became king of Prussia. The king died without ever having children, keeping the legend alive and well. The Ghost somehow found its way to France and was sold to Tiffany's in the late 19th century at an auction of French royal jewels.

Bull had bought the Ghost from a private owner and had it reset in a necklace with diamonds, emeralds, sapphires and rubies—all the jewels he'd previously given Bella—and presented it to her on the birth of their one and only daughter.

Max wasn't surprised Lydia wanted to borrow the necklace. It was exquisite. For some reason, his mother never wore it anymore. "Mother's not in London," Max pointed out to his sister. "How is she going to get the necklace to you?"

"She could have Smythe send it," Lydia said. "She trusts him with the keys to everything at the Abbey."

"He might have the key to the dungeon," Max said. "But I doubt he has the combination to the safe."

The Abbey had a dungeon belowstairs, where prisoners of past centuries had been tortured, with secret passages in the walls of the Abbey that could be used to reach it. The four brothers had played in those dark, musty, cobweb-laden passages as kids, even though it was strictly forbidden. His mother's priceless jewels were kept in an enormous safe in the dungeon, the outer door to which was kept locked.

"If you get permission from Mother, I'll make sure you get the Ghost of Ali Pasha," Oliver said to Lydia.

Max wondered whether that meant Oliver had the combination to the safe, or whether he knew someone besides Mother who did.

"I don't think she'll give it to me if I ask," Lydia said. "Would you ask for me, Oliver?"

"No. If you want it, Lydia, you need to ask for it yourself," Oliver said.

"All right," Lydia replied petulantly. "I'll ask."

But Max heard in her voice that she didn't think she had a snowball's chance in hell of getting it.

"Are we done?" Oliver asked.

Everyone nodded except Max, who added, "If I find out anything useful about why Mother invited us to The Seasons, I'll get back in touch with all of you."

"If there's nothing else," Oliver said, "this meeting of the Castle Foundation is adjourned."

10

"It's just like Sleeping Beauty's castle," Flick said, her arms spread wide as she turned in a circle within the stone walls of Blackthorne Abbey.

Kristin had to agree. Despite how much they'd shared about their lives, she'd had no idea Max had grown up in an actual castle. "Don't touch anything, Flick," she warned. Everything in the vast hall in which they were standing looked like an irreplaceable, not to mention priceless, antique.

"You're here at last," Bella said, smiling as she came down a wide stone staircase, trailed by a young woman, to meet them in the cavernous hall in which they were standing.

"Who are you?" Flick asked bluntly, staring at the plainly dressed young woman.

"My name is Emily Sheldon," the trim-looking young woman said as she joined them. "I'm going to be your tutor while you're here."

Flick grimaced. "Oh. You're a teacher."

"Emily has been with me for the past three years

as my assistant," Bella said to Flick. "However, she studied to be a teacher, which is fortunate, under the circumstances."

"I hope you and I will become good friends," Emily said to Flick.

Flick cocked her head, like a bird eyeing something strange, then said, "I've never had a teacher who was a friend before."

"There's a first time for everything," Emily replied with a smile.

Flick smiled back at her and said, "I like you."

"That's a good start," Emily replied.

Flick turned to her grandmother and asked, "Is this where my dad grew up?"

"Blackthorne Abbey was his home, yes," Bella said. "He was away at boarding school a great deal of the time, but this is where we gathered as a family on holidays."

Kristin realized their voices echoed in the domed entry to the Abbey. "How big is this place?" she asked.

"The castle could guest twenty knights and their retainers when it was first built," Bella said. "Which would have been more than a hundred souls. A lot of the smaller rooms have been turned into larger ones. Several wings were added in later years, which gives the castle its unusual shape."

"Can I see my dad's room?" Flick asked.

"Smythe is taking your luggage there as we speak," Bella said.

"Who's Smith?" Flick asked, using the same pronunciation the duchess had used.

"The butler. He met you at the door."

"Oh, the really old guy."

Kristin winced at Flick's frankness.

"Is this armor from a real knight?" Flick asked, crossing to a polished suit of armor and reaching out as though to shake the mailed hand that was posed in greeting.

"Don't touch!" Kristin warned.

"It's all right," Bella said. "Yes, it's real. I think my eldest son, Oliver, put it on once upon a time and scared the wits out of Smythe when he took a few steps in it."

"The knight who wore it wasn't very tall," Flick pointed out.

Kristin was surprised herself at how short the armored figure was. The knight couldn't have been more than five foot three or four.

"Men—and women—were smaller in the Middle Ages. Poor nutrition," Bella said.

"Oh, you mean they didn't eat the right foods to grow," Flick said, as she deciphered the meaning of *nutrition*.

"Exactly," Bella said.

"Who are all these guys?" Flick asked, pointing to several cracked and faded oil paintings hung around the stone walls of the circular entryway.

"Your ancestors," Bella said. When Flick appeared confused, she explained, "The lords and ladies who fought for these lands and lived at Blackthorne Abbey."

The idea of fighting apparently appealed to Flick, because she stepped up to take a closer look at a soldier on horseback, dressed in a blue uniform trimmed with red cuffs and gold lace, holding up a sword as though charging in battle. "The guy sitting on that black horse looks pretty big. He must have had better nutrition, huh?" Flick said with a grin.

"Oh, definitely," Bella agreed. "That is Captain Lord Marcus Wharton, wearing the uniform of the Prince of Wales's own 10th Royal Hussars. Lord Marcus was the younger brother of Alistair Wharton, the sixth Duke of Blackthorne."

"He looks brave," Flick said as she eyed the painting.

"Captain Lord Marcus was a war hero," Bella said. "He looks very handsome here, but he was wounded—half of his face was badly scarred and his hand was injured—during the Battle of Waterloo. He hid himself away in the north wing of the Abbey and never let anyone see him, so the village folk began to call him the Beast. But a beautiful woman fell in love with him, scars and all. They were married and lived happily ever after."

"Just like in the fairy tale," Flick said, clapping her hands. "'Beauty and the Beast.' I wish I'd known him. I wouldn't have been scared." She stepped up to the next painting, which featured a beautiful, dark-haired girl in an empire-waisted gown, a fashion which Kristin knew had been worn in the Regency era at the beginning of the 19th century.

One of the two children in the painting stood before an easel. She was painting an identical child who was sitting in a chair under an oak tree. An English spaniel lay near the seated child.

"That's cool," Flick said. "A painting of a girl painting herself. Who is she?"

"Twins run in the Blackthorne family," Bella said. "That's Lady Rebecca Wharton painting her elder twin sister, Lady Regina."

"Her Grace has a twin, as well," Emily said. "Her younger sister, Lady Alicia."

Kristin saw the sharp glance Bella shot her assistant. This was the first Kristin had heard about Bella having a twin sister. In all their talks, Max had never mentioned an Aunt Alicia. Was the twin sister supposed to be a secret? She wondered if Bella's twin was still alive, and if so, where she was.

Flick asked the questions for her. "Does your twin look like you, Gram? Can I meet her?"

"Yes, we're identical," Bella confirmed. "I'm afraid you can't meet Alicia. My sister left Blackthorne Abbey, oh, I don't know how many years ago."

"Where is she now?" Flick asked.

"I don't know."

Flick turned to Kristin and said, "Mom, you know how to do searches on the internet. Maybe we can help Gram find her sister."

Kristin glanced at the duchess and saw a brief, panicked look cross her face. Kristin looked to Emily for guidance.

The duchess's assistant said, "I've tried to find Alicia myself through the internet, but I haven't had any luck."

"You have?" Bella said, obviously surprised. "I didn't know that, Emily."

"I thought you might want to see her before—" She stopped herself and finished, "I thought you might want to find out how she's doing."

Bella didn't look happy with the prospect of seeing her younger sister anytime soon. Kristin thought there must be a story there. But she wasn't going to stay around to dig it out. She needed to get settled in her hotel, which was a long train ride north of the Abbey in London.

Kristin put a hand on her daughter's shoulder and said, "The last train to London is leaving soon. I have to go, Flick."

"I can arrange a car for you tomorrow morning if you'd like to spend the night," Bella offered.

"No, thank you," Kristin said. She didn't want to be any more indebted to the duchess than she already was.

"At least come upstairs and see where Flick will be staying," the duchess said.

Kristin glanced at her watch. "All right. But I can't stay long."

"Lead the way, Emily," Bella said.

Kristin watched Emily hesitate until Bella shooed her forward. The young woman took Flick's hand and said, "Come on, Flick. Let's go see your room."

"You mean my dad's room," Flick said. "Are there pictures of him there?"

Emily glanced at Kristin for guidance.

Kristin agonized for a moment before nodding.

Emily looked down at Flick and said, "Yes, I think there are a few pictures of your father."

Flick had already asked Kristin for a picture of Max, but she'd denied having one. Flick had tried to find a picture of him on the internet but in the very few pictures of him she found, his head was turned sideways, or the ball cap he wore playing tennis hid most of his face. It would have been odd if she hadn't wanted to know what her father looked like.

Flick pulled free of Emily's hand and ran up the stairs. Emily hurried after her. Kristin stayed with Bella, who climbed the narrow stone stairs more slowly, but steadily.

"Have you seen Max since you arrived in London?" Bella asked.

"I'm supposed to meet him at Wimbledon tomorrow morning," Kristin replied. By the time they traversed the upstairs hall to Max's childhood bedroom, Flick had already found a photograph of her father and was holding it in her hands.

The room was surprisingly tiny. It had a child's single bed along one wall and a desk along another. The drapes had been pulled back from tall windows to let in the afternoon sun, which had warmed the room. A chest sat at the foot of the bed. Flick had apparently already opened it to reveal tin soldiers and other boyhood toys. Emily was sitting in the chair at the adult-size desk.

Obviously, Max hadn't stayed in this room since he was a very young boy. So where did he sleep when he came to visit his mother? The answer Kristin came up with startled her. Most likely, Max hadn't stayed in his mother's home since he was a young boy. He'd been away at school. Or in hotels around the world, when he'd traveled on the road playing tennis. Kristin knew from her time with Max on the tour, that he'd bought a house in London where he lived when he wasn't on the road.

"Look, Mom," Flick said reverently as she held out a framed photograph and pointed to one face among many in what appeared to be a family portrait. "Emily says that boy is my dad." She pointed to a young boy pictured with his family around a beautifully decorated Christmas tree.

In the photo, Bella was holding an adorable baby girl on her lap. Max stood beside his mother holding an adult-size tennis racquet that dwarfed him. Bull stood with one hand on Bella's shoulder and the other hand on Max's shoulder. The tallest—oldest?—boy was standing beside an English racing bike. In front of him sat a grinning boy holding up a book about dinosaurs. A fourth boy sat cross-legged next to him, with a model sailboat in his lap.

"Max loved playing tennis," Bella mused. "We had a tennis court built on the grounds so he could practice."

Kristin wondered how much time Max had ever spent on it.

"I recognize you, Gram," Flick said. "Who are these other people?"

"Your aunt and uncles," Bella said. "And your other grandfather."

"I have another grandfather?" Flick said in wonder. "Where is he? Can I meet him?"

"He doesn't live in London," Bella said. "I'll let him know you'd like to meet him."

"How is that going to work out, exactly?" Kristin said, aware, as was the rest of the world, that Bull and Bella Benedict were separated, and not amicably.

Bella waved away her concerns. "Honestly, that's unlikely to happen on this visit."

Bella sat down in a wooden rocker in the corner of Max's bedroom, and called Flick over to stand beside her as she identified each of the boys in the photo. "Your uncle Oliver is standing beside the bicycle. Your uncle Riley is holding the book about dinosaurs. Your uncle Payne is sitting cross-legged with the boat. The little girl on my lap is your aunt Lydia."

"She's just as pretty as you are, Gram," Flick said.

Kristin saw the duchess was flustered by the compliment.

"Why, thank you, Flick," she said.

Flick surveyed her grandmother through narrowed eyes and said, "You have a lot more wrinkles now than you did then. But I still think you're beautiful."

Kristin saw tears well in Bella Benedict's eyes and watched her blink them away. Kristin saw something she couldn't have imagined happening, considering what she knew about the Mean Witch's behavior toward Max.

The duchess reached out and caressed Flick's head.

"That's the nicest thing anybody's said to me…in a while," the duchess said. "Thank you, Felicity."

To Kristin's further surprise, Flick brushed the duchess's skirt aside and edged her tiny fanny into the small space between her grandmother and the edge of the rocker.

"Tell me about my dad," she said.

Kristin would have given anything to stay and listen. She wanted to hear what sort of stories—fantasies—Bella concocted to describe the time she'd supposedly spent with Max growing up. During the years Kristin had known him, the Mean Witch had been a big black nothing in his life.

"I have to leave, Flick," Kristin said.

Instead of crossing the room to give her mother a good-bye hug and kiss, Flick nestled closer to her grandmother and said, "Will you bring Dad when you come back, Mom?"

Kristin did what mothers everywhere did when they didn't want to start an argument with their child by saying no. She smiled cheerfully, waved good-bye to her daughter, and said, "We'll see."

11

"Hello, Princess."

Kristin turned on the grass tennis court at Wimbledon and found Max standing before her. He was dressed in white shorts and a white sleeveless shirt, which revealed the powerful biceps she'd only suspected when he'd been wearing a suit. He'd obviously already been hitting balls for a while. His sweat-soaked shirt clung to his body, revealing impressive muscular abs.

Her throat ached at the sudden memory of the last time she'd seen him here at the All England Lawn Tennis Club when they were teenagers. She recalled the utter disbelief—and devastation—she'd felt at seeing Max kissing another woman the morning after he'd made love to her for the first time. How could she still feel so much pain?

She swallowed over the awful lump in her throat and said, "Hello, Max." It came out sounding wistful. She hardened her voice and said, "As I told you on the phone, I'm only here because my boss suggested it after I got suspended."

She'd called Rudy to tell him she was accepting the assignment from the CIA, so he'd know how to contact her when word came back from SIRT on how they planned to treat the second shooting incident. She was praying there would be no further disciplinary action required.

Before she'd left Miami, she'd also hired a lawyer to defend her in the civil suit. He'd told her nothing would be happening on the case until the SIRT recommendation came down. He'd also promised to find out whether the boy's family would be willing to settle out of court and if so, how much they wanted.

"I wish I could say I'm sorry you felt coerced into coming to London," Max said. "But I'm not. I need your help, K."

Could any words be more designed to appeal to everything feminine and nurturing inside her? For years she'd been so sure she was over Max, that she'd gotten him out of her head and her heart. But he'd been in her thoughts constantly since she'd seen him in Miami.

Especially after her meeting with the duchess. The mere idea of Max proposing to her was preposterous. Even the suggestion that the two of them might "kiss and make up" made her uncomfortable in her own skin.

Why hadn't she simply told the Mean Witch to take a flying leap off a steep cliff?

Desperation. Yes, she was desperate for money. But there was a more compelling reason she'd agreed to spend more time with Max. One that had kept her awake for too many nights over the past ten years. *Regret.*

What if she'd answered his phone calls ten years ago? What if there were some simple explanation for why he'd been kissing Elena? What might Max have done if he'd known she was carrying his child? Would he have asked her to love him and live with him forever? And the most wrenching question of all: Had he ever really loved her?

None of that mattered now, because she had turned him away. As she would turn Max away if he decided he wanted to pick up where they'd left off.

But she'd better watch her step. If she wasn't careful, the charming rogue would slip past her defenses. She didn't want to get hurt again.

She could feel Max's eyes on her, assessing her. Had he ever asked himself the same questions she'd been asking? Did he also wonder what would have happened if…?

When she turned and met his intent gaze, she felt off-kilter. It was unsettling to realize how attractive Max still was to her. How very blue his eyes were. Benedict blue. She remembered, during their one night of love, kissing his square chin, his sharp nose, his chiseled cheekbones. He'd made her blood heat and her body ache with need.

Funny how those feelings of love—and those first stirrings of teenage desire—were still so vivid after all these years. No wonder she was still alone, when she'd measured her response to every man she'd met since Max against the powerful passions evoked by her robust teenage hormones. What mortal man could compete with a perfect fantasy?

Except, Max wasn't a fairy-tale character. If only he had been she might have banished him. No, he'd been real, all right. Her feelings of love for Max had grown and ripened over the three years she'd known him, growing especially strong during the year after she'd dropped her robe and stood naked before him. She'd been more than ready, when the moment came, to go from being friends to lovers.

Strange, how the reality of physical intimacy with Max was so far from what she'd expected. The lovemaking had been awkward. Since she was a virgin and nervous—and Max was uninformed about the true state of things—the act itself had been physically painful. Still, she'd hugged the knowledge of their ultimate closeness to herself as she fell asleep alone in bed that night.

She'd wondered for years afterward if Max had felt the euphoric connection to her that she'd felt toward him. In retrospect, it seemed unlikely. Those three years she'd been secretly in love with him, he'd been dating—and bedding—a bevy of other women. Max had never revealed what it was that had finally caused him to take them from friends to lovers. Kristin would never have had the self-confidence, in light of Max's vast experience, to suggest sex herself. Strangely, she'd never asked him why he was physically attracted to her, when he had all those other, more experienced and fuller-bosomed women to choose from. She'd wondered if their night of love had fallen short of his expectations, too. Maybe she just hadn't pleased him in bed.

Since they'd parted ways after their single night of sex without speaking to each other again, she'd been left emotionally battered and bruised—and wondering—all these years.

The worst part of not knowing what had brought him to urge her to have sex was that, no matter how hard she'd tried, she couldn't forget him. Any chance she'd had to move on to a healthy and loving relationship with another man was stifled by leftover feelings for her first love.

Which was why she planned to use their time together now to kill those feelings once and for all. Unfortunately, she found herself fighting the temptation to be Max's friend again. That, she knew, was a slippery slope. Going from friend to lover could be a very short trip.

Kristin tightened her grip on her tennis racquet and focused on adjusting the strings with her other hand. She couldn't afford to fall in love with Max again. There was too much at stake. She planned to earn the Blackthorne Rubies, find the presidential assassin—if one existed—and go home.

At some point, she might be forced to introduce Max to his daughter. But not if she could help it. She felt sorry her daughter had grown up without a father, but Flick was better off without a man like Max in her life. That is, a man who put pleasure first and everything else far after.

Well, she could use that to her advantage.

The object was to play this match with Max without losing her heart. She had to make sure she didn't let her grown-up hormones rule her head. Which meant she had to guard against falling prey to his good looks. His very good looks. He appeared magnificently fit in tennis whites, his shoulders broad, his hips narrow, his belly flat. Her eyes followed the line of black down from his navel into the low-slung shorts.

Kristin realized what she was doing and jerked her gaze back up to meet his. She flushed when she realized Max was making a perusal of her every bit as thorough as the one she'd just done of him. She had on a fitted white tennis dress with a short, flirty skirt that showed off her trim waist and long legs. Her breasts were nothing to shout about, never had been.

Max seemed happy enough with the size of them when he held them in his palms, an insidious voice reminded her.

"You look good," he said at last. "Fit."

"You, too," she replied. Well, it was the truth.

"I've missed you, Princess."

She hadn't expected that. She didn't say she'd missed him, too. But Max had been a tough act to follow. She'd been engaged once but had called it off before the wedding. Frustrated in love, she'd focused on her daughter and her job. She'd put youthful things—tennis and Max Benedict—behind her.

"How do you want to do this?" she asked, swinging her racquet in a small circle over her shoulder to warm up her arm.

"We'll hit a few to warm up."

"The last time I played was with one of Harry's students," Kristin said.

"How is Harry?" Max asked.

Harry had been a good friend to Max—until she'd turned up pregnant. She hesitated, then admitted, "Dad had a stroke a few days after you came to Miami. His right side is paralyzed."

"That's too bad."

She had to admit Max looked truly concerned.

"What's his prognosis?" he asked.

"He's going to need a lot of physical and speech therapy. The doctors don't know yet how much use of his right arm and leg he'll recover."

Max was bouncing a tennis ball into the air from the face of his racquet, never missing even though his gaze was focused on her face. "Why didn't you let me know?"

"What could you have done? Besides, I didn't think you cared."

"I care," Max said sharply. "Harry was a good friend. I owe him a lot. He's the one responsible for—"

"We don't have the court for long," she interrupted, because she was starting to believe him. "Maybe we should practice first and reminisce later."

He seemed to be debating the point, then said, "All right. Let's just hit a few. Then we'll see how much work we need to do to get back into fighting shape."

During the past decade the racquets had gotten lighter and polyester strings such as Luxilon allowed players to take huge swings and generate enough spin to keep the ball on the court. Hardly anyone on the women's tour now used the one-handed backhand that had been Kristin's forte. Powerful two-handed backhands were the norm.

Kristin's FBI job had required her to be in good physical shape, and she'd played lots of weekend tennis, but instead of simply hitting crosscourt, Max ran her from one side of the baseline to the other. She was winded far sooner than she'd expected to be. She missed a bullet he hit down the line and trotted to the net to talk with him. "I guess I'm in worse shape than I thought."

"I was going to say the same thing about myself," he said as he huffed out a breath of air. "This game is harder than it looks."

"If you say so," a female voice said from behind Kristin.

Kristin turned and realized there was someone else besides Max she'd hoped never to see again. Elena Tarakova. She made herself smile and said, "Hello, Elena. I wasn't expecting to see you here today. The tournament isn't for a few more weeks."

"If we're going to play doubles, I thought the four of us ought to practice together," Max said. "After all, this isn't a competition, it's an exhibition."

Which made sense, if it had been any other two players they were matched against. But this was Elena, who'd beaten Kristin the last time she'd played at Wimbledon. And Steffan, who'd lost to Max the last time he'd played at Wimbledon.

As Kristin watched, Elena crossed to Max and gave him a continental greeting by kissing him on each cheek. Except Elena leaned in close, so her breasts brushed Max's chest. Kristin bristled at the other woman's impudence. She hadn't factored in Elena when she'd considered having to spend time with Max. Could the other woman possibly still be interested in him?

Kristin stood stiffly as Elena leaned across the net, her long black hair pulled back from her Slavic face in a pony tail that slid over her shoulder, and kissed Kristin on each cheek.

"How are you, darling?" Elena asked, her dark eyes searching Kristin's face for signs of age or dissipation or lord knew what.

Kristin kept her features neutral but said, "If you're asking if I'm in good enough shape to kick your butt on the tennis court, the answer is I'm fine."

Elena laughed. "You always were a feisty one." She turned her attention back to Max, flipped her ponytail down her back, and asked, "Where's Steffan?"

"Right here," Steffan Pavlovic said as he strode onto the practice court. He was tall and lean, his smile unbelievably brilliant against his tanned face. Sun-bleached chestnut hair crawled down his neck beneath a white ball cap that he'd tugged on backwards.

The two men grabbed hands, pulled each other close and bumped shoulders. "Good to see you, old friend," Max said. "How's Irina?"

"Mom is great. She wants to get together for supper sometime soon."

Steffan's mother, Irina, had been Max's coach, and a surrogate mother to him, for five years. The two boys had spent hours on and off the court together in their teens.

Steffan laughed and said, "I haven't missed you on the court. But I miss hunting with you."

"Hunting?" Kristin said.

"Girls," Steffan said with a sexy wink at her. "The man never missed his quarry."

Kristin flushed. *Including me.*

"When Max found out Elena and I were both in town early to meet with sponsors and do some publicity, he suggested we ought to practice together. I thought it sounded like a great idea. After all, it doesn't matter which team wins."

There it was again, the suggestion that who won didn't matter, that they just had to play the game. Kristin didn't agree. She had no intention of losing to Elena Tarakova at Wimbledon again, even in an exhibition match.

The problem was, Elena was the #1 ranked player on the women's tour. She'd been trading the top spot with Serena Williams for several years. Both of them were being challenged by Kim Clijsters, who'd successfully returned to tennis after a brief hiatus to get married and have a daughter.

Kristin hadn't played tennis professionally for a decade. In singles against Elena, she probably wouldn't have had a chance. But she was playing on a team with Max, who'd beaten Steffan at Wimbledon all those years ago. Of course, Steffan was still ranked in the top ten on the men's tour, while Max had left the game years ago.

"Let's play a little and see how it goes," Max suggested.

As he crossed around the net and joined Kristin she leaned close and said, "I want to beat them, Max."

"Me, too," he said with a grin. "Let's see how you serve."

It was clear from Elena's return of her opening serve that Kristin was no longer in the same league with her opponent. By the end of the "best two out of three sets" match, a set being six games, Kristin was gasping for air. What was worse, she and Max lost 6–2, 6–2.

"That's enough practice for today," Max announced. "See you guys tomorrow morning."

"Not so fast," Steffan said. "What about tonight? I thought we'd get together and hit some nightspots."

"That sounds good to me," Elena said, jogging to the net.

It irked Kristin to realize the other woman wasn't even breathing hard. "I can't," she said.

"Why not?" Max asked.

Because I have to take the train to Blackthorne Abbey to be with my daughter. "I have other plans."

"We'll miss you," Elena said.

Kristin could see the other woman was quite happy to have Max and Steffan to herself. Maybe Elena planned to make another play for Max. Kristin realized she didn't want Elena to win anything over the next couple of weeks. Not even Max.

Dire situations required difficult choices. If she wanted to run interference between Max and Elena, she was going to have to settle for a phone call to her daughter. "I guess I can rearrange my plans," she said.

"That's great!" Steffan said.

"We'll catch up with you two tonight," Max said. "I need to do some strategizing with my partner this afternoon."

Kristin watched as Elena and Steffan left the court. When they were out of earshot, she turned to Max, arched a brow and said, "Strategizing?"

He checked out the empty tennis courts around them, then said, "We have work to do, Princess."

"I don't think strategy is going to help," she said. "The pro game is faster than it was when I left. Me playing an exhibition match was a bad idea."

"You won't get an argument from me," Max said.

That stung. Kristin bristled, but before she could form a retort Max added insult to injury. "I was against this whole idea when it was suggested to me."

"Do you think I want to be here?" she shot back. "I'll be happy to plead an injury and go home." Except that wasn't really an option, was it? Not when she was in such deep financial trouble. To win the rubies, she had to stay here and play the match.

"The point is, we needed a female agent who's conducted investigations in the past and who can also play world-class tennis. Someone whose presence here at Wimbledon—and in the women's locker room—wouldn't stick out like a sore thumb. Your background was too perfect to pass up."

"I'm here," she said. "But in case you didn't know, I gave up my badge and my gun before I left the States. How am I supposed to help without them?"

"You couldn't use the gun here in England anyway, and you aren't going to need to flash your badge."

"Mind explaining how that works?"

"It's pretty simple, really. I'm here—we're here—at Wimbledon to evaluate whether the threat to the president might be coming from someone involved in tennis. That is, a player, a coach or someone in a player's family. Those folks will all sit in the family box at Flushing Meadows, near where the president sits to watch the final matches. Any player who's willing to sacrifice himself is also in a position to make an attack on the president from the court during the match."

"Why didn't my FBI boss simply assign me to this job in the first place? Why jump through these crazy hoops?"

"If an FBI agent started sniffing around, whoever we're looking for might close up shop until the heat is gone. The tennis exhibition gives you cover."

"Exactly what is it you expect me to do?" she asked.

"Most likely, the assassin is a male, but I want you to listen for chatter in the women's locker room."

"I suppose you'll be listening in the men's locker room."

He nodded. "I also plan to date as many of the female

players as I can. That won't work with the gay players. You're going to have to befriend them and find out what you can."

"What makes you think all these women will go out with you?" Kristin said sharply. She realized she was jealous. And was furious with herself for giving a damn.

He grinned. "I'm good-looking. I'm rich. I'm also the uncatchable catch. I should be able to wrangle at least a first date with the straight unmarried players. That's all I'll really need."

"You think someone helping to plot an assassination is going to blurt out her guilt on a date?"

His features hardened and she saw a man she didn't recognize. A man who could be a covert operative.

"I know what questions to ask," he said. "I know when someone's lying to me. I have resources that I can call on to find out more about a player if I think he or she's suspicious. Our job isn't to catch the assassin. It's to report our findings to the CIA—and the FBI—so they can take action."

"Then wouldn't it make sense if I date the male players?" she said.

"I didn't suggest it because I thought it would be awkward for you."

"Why would you say that?"

"You'd have to fend off a lot of oversexed males."

Kristin laughed. "You don't think I can do that?"

"I don't think you should have to do it," he said flatly.

That sounded distinctly like *Max* was jealous. "I think I can handle a bunch of tennis jocks. I don't intend to let them get me alone in the dark. I've come a long way since you seduced me, Max."

He eyed her askance. "I don't remember seducing you, Princess. I remember the two of us deciding we wanted to make love."

Max was shoving her into deep water. She quickly paddled her way back out. "Let's leave the past where it belongs. In the past."

"Fine by me," he snapped. "We're going to have to meet somewhere to exchange information. Where are you staying?"

"Park Plaza Victoria." The duchess had insisted on paying for a room in the four-star hotel near Victoria Station, so Kristin could easily catch the train to Blackthorne Abbey. She waited for Max to ask her why she was staying so far from Wimbledon, but he didn't.

"It'll be easier—more private—to meet at my flat."

"Where is that?" she asked.

He gave an upscale address near Regent's Park. "The fact we're playing this exhibition match gives us good cover to get together until we actually play the match on opening day. People on the tour know we were friends. That should be sufficient for us to spend time together. If worse comes to worst, we can always fake a romantic relationship."

"Like you did last time?" she blurted.

The barb apparently hit home, because he shot back,

"Sometimes we have to make sacrifices for the good of the nation. Don't push me, K."

She didn't apologize, although the urge was there. "Do you have anyone in particular you suspect? Is there somewhere I should start?"

"Let's start with Steffan and Elena."

Kristin's brows rose in surprise. "You suspect one of them? Or both of them?"

"Neither of them," he said. "But we can't afford to leave any stone unturned. Steffan's always had a crush on you. It should be easy to get him to talk."

"I never knew that."

He shrugged. "We were best friends. He knew I liked you, so he kept his distance."

He *liked* her. Had he ever *loved* her? "I'm pretty sure Elena had a crush on you."

He winced. "I'm going to be walking a fine line with her. She's made her interest known in the past."

Yeah. I saw the two of you kissing the morning after you made love to me. She had her tongue halfway down your throat. You weren't fighting too hard to get free.

He shrugged and said, "A man's gotta do what a man's gotta do."

"What does that mean?"

He shot her a grin and said, "I'm willing to kiss a few beautiful women in the service of my country."

Kristin growled low in her throat. Just let that hussy try to kiss Max tonight. She'd find an excuse to lay her out cold. Thanks to her FBI training, she knew exactly how to do it.

"See you tonight," Max said as he sauntered away.

Kristin felt unsettled. And frustrated. And unhappy. *I still want him. I still care. But I'll be damned if I ever let him get close enough to hurt me again.*

12

Max didn't like the way Steffan was looking at Kristin. Like he was a wolf and she was raw red meat. Kristin had been drinking champagne since the four of them—he, Elena, Kristin and Steffan—had arrived at the Black Kitty Kat, a popular hangout for pros playing at Wimbledon. Steffan and Kristin were huddled together on a red leather couch in a dark corner. Hell, she was practically sitting in his lap. Max expected Steffan to make his move any minute. He wondered how Kristin would react.

Max knew his friend the tennis pro had worked his way through a lot of beautiful women—models and actresses, waitresses and schoolteachers. But he couldn't very well warn him away from Kristin without looking ridiculous.

After all, he and Kristin weren't involved romantically. His chance with her had come and gone. They were merely friends. Or had been friends. He wasn't sure they were even that now, just colleagues on a job together. But didn't partners look out for each other?

He wished he knew more about the Kristin he'd met

this afternoon. Her figure hadn't changed much, but she was a woman now, not a sixteen-year-old girl. Her long, golden-blond curls were no longer in a flyaway ponytail but constrained in a tight bun at her nape. Enticing tendrils had escaped, suggesting that all he had to do was pull a few bobby pins free and the old, happy-go-lucky Kristin would escape along with her curls.

He remembered too well what she looked like under the tennis dress she'd been wearing on the court today, which left little to the imagination. She had a scar on her abdomen, where she'd had her appendix removed. Otherwise, her body was flawless. Her bosom was small, but a handful was plenty for him. And she was, by God, all legs. He would never forget having them wrapped around him.

At eighteen, sex was fun, a joyful experience he'd wanted to share with his best friend. The future never entered his mind. He'd never considered the possible consequences of taking their relationship from friends to lovers. He tried to remember now why he'd pushed her to have sex with him. Before that night, their relationship had consisted of simply hanging out and enjoying each other's company—except for that one, brief, enticing look at her naked body.

When she'd let that robe fall and he'd realized how beautiful she was, he'd wanted to make love to her then and there. The opportunity to take things further had been thwarted by her father's appearance. Later, she'd pretended like it had never happened. So despite how much he might have wanted to touch, he'd kept his hands off her.

But her beauty—and his desire—wasn't why he'd spent so much time with her. It was because K was the one person with whom he could let down his guard. She'd seen him in tears. She'd seen him raging after he'd lost a match. She'd seen him euphoric after he'd won and celebrated his victory with a night of great sex with another woman.

K never judged him. She was simply there for him. She'd been a solid sounding board for nearly three years, despite her youth.

When had he decided their relationship should include sex? He tried to remember what had happened to provoke such a decision. Had some other woman rejected him? He shook his head. He'd been shot down plenty of times before that night and never needed to find succor in K's body. Ah. That word, *succor,* was a clue.

Relief. From what had he needed relief?

Why hadn't he wondered sooner about this? Probably because he'd never needed to explain his behavior to the one person to whom it would have mattered. It had been enough to know he'd screwed everything up.

He'd never asked Kristin why she'd bolted after the night they'd spent together. He'd felt hurt and humiliated. He'd come up with a thousand reasons why she'd walked away. He'd finally decided she simply regretted what they'd done.

Had he pushed her into having sex before she was

ready? Maybe. A little. But she'd been willing. And eager. Until he'd hurt her.

He'd been surprisingly clumsy. He'd made love often enough to know that a woman needed more time to be ready for sex than a man. But he'd wanted her so badly, he'd rushed things. He hadn't known she was a virgin. He'd been taken off guard because he'd never encountered one before. She'd cried out in pain when he'd broached her. He remembered kissing the salty tears off her cheeks.

The timing had been terrible, too, because she had to play in the Girls' Singles Championship match at Wimbledon the next morning. Afterward, she'd asked him to leave her hotel room so she could get a decent night's sleep.

He'd walked out the door, never dreaming he wouldn't see her again for ten years. He'd tried to talk with her after she'd lost the championship match, but she'd avoided him like he was the British press. She'd left the country the same afternoon.

Maybe, if he'd been able to talk to her, he would have explained what had made him want to be closer to her than mere friendship allowed. Maybe, if he'd been able to talk to her, he would have told her the secret he'd discovered about his mother that had left him bewildered and afraid.

He'd pursued Kristin relentlessly after she'd left London. He'd wanted his best friend—and lover—back. She'd refused his calls. She hadn't answered his emails. He'd even flown to Miami to see her. Harry had met him at the door and told him to go away and stay away. Kristin didn't want to see him.

So he'd given up. He didn't need to be kicked in the balls more than once to learn his lesson. And he'd kept his secret to himself.

Max wasn't sure what he'd been expecting when he agreed to work with K on this job. That they'd be friends again, he supposed. And friends didn't let friends get seduced against their wills. In his experience, tipsy women rarely made intelligent decisions.

Don't make the mistake of sticking your nose in where it doesn't belong, a voice in his head warned. *Maybe she wants to be seduced. Or maybe it's all an act, and she's pretending to be into Steffan to get whatever information she can from him.*

Despite the shooting incidents—the second one coming a few days after Max had met with her—her boss had sworn Kristin was one of the best investigators he'd ever seen. Max already knew she was smart. Apparently she was also intuitive. So maybe he should leave well enough alone.

To be honest, he and Elena had been huddled as close, or closer to each other, at the mirrored bar, except they were on separate bar stools. Despite how things might look, he wasn't going to be spending the night with the female athlete. Not that she wasn't interested. He was the one who'd backed off.

Elena hadn't offered him much information about herself. Not that he'd asked her a whole lot of questions. To be honest, he'd gotten distracted watching Kristin.

Max jerked when Elena whispered in his ear, "If you want her, Max, go get her."

He pulled away and said, "It isn't like that between us."

Elena lifted a dark brow. "What is it like?"

He thrust a hand through his dark hair, shoving it off his forehead. "We're just friends."

"Friends?" Elena said, cocking her head to eye him more closely.

"Friends," Max repeated firmly. He'd been so busy keeping an eye on Kristin, he realized he'd forgotten entirely about Veronica. "I've been dating a reporter for the *Times*. For a couple of weeks, anyway."

Elena shot him a grin. "Isn't that about your limit?"

"Just about," Max replied in an effort to confirm his love-'em-and-leave-'em playboy image.

"If she's the flavor of the week, why isn't she here with you?" Elena said.

"She's on assignment in the United Arab Emirates."

Elena's eyes went wide. "She's a political reporter?"

Max chuckled. "Hardly. She's doing a feature on arranged marriages. She's been traveling a lot, to India, Pakistan and Africa, among other places, doing research."

"I'll choose my own spouse, thank you very much," Elena said. "If I ever decide to get married, that is. How about you? A reporter for the *Times* doesn't sound like your usual date. How serious are things between you? Will you invite me to the wedding?"

"Don't marry me off just yet. Veronica and I barely know one another."

"But you like her."

He took a swallow of Scotch before he said, "She's nice."

"So why can't you take your eyes off Kristin?"

He smirked to hide his uneasiness at her question. He couldn't deny he'd been watching her. Nor could he explain that they were partners in an investigation. He was beginning to feel like an idiot for suggesting that the two of them should date their way through the tennis world in search of an assassin.

"I guess I know how disposable women are to Steffan," he said at last. "I don't want K to get hurt."

Max was looking at Kristin as he spoke, so he was watching when Steffan made his move. He held his breath as the tanned athlete leaned in to kiss her.

Kristin accidentally—on purpose?—spilled her champagne on his silk shirt. She made a moue of distress and brushed at the stain with her free hand, accidentally spilling more champagne on his lap.

Steffan held his moss-green shirt out, shaking it off, then reached for a paper napkin and dabbed at his black slacks. He was obviously now more worried about the condition of his silk shirt and trousers than his seduction of Kristin.

"She looks like she can handle herself," Elena said with a laugh. She focused her dark eyes on him and said, "I'm more concerned about you."

Max frowned. "Concerned? Why is that?"

"I don't think you're over her."

The lines on Max's forehead deepened. "It's been ten years, Elena. Whatever might have been possible between us is a lost cause now."

"I wonder..." Her eyes narrowed as she perused his face. "How about if we do an experiment?"

"What did you have in mind?"

"This," she said.

Max didn't react quickly enough, and her lips were on his before he could turn away. Her kiss brought to mind the last time she'd kissed him, on her way to the Girls' Singles Championship match at Wimbledon.

"A kiss for luck," she'd begged.

He'd laughed and said, "I don't know what kind of luck you think I can bring, but sure."

In the few moments Max had been musing, she'd deepened the kiss at the bar. He put a gentle hand on her cheek and pulled away. "That was nice, Elena, but—"

She looked him right in the eye and said, "But you're in love with another woman."

He wondered if she meant Veronica. Or Kristin. He wasn't yet in love with Veronica. And he'd long since gotten over Kristin. He changed the subject by asking, "How's your father?"

Elena's father, Anton, had been her coach until she turned eighteen, at which point she'd fired him. It turned out he was almost as crazy as he was clever. He'd gone on to coach other top-ranked women players, so he was usually around when his daughter played.

"I ignore him when I'm on the court," she said. "When I'm off the court, he's not a part of my world."

"And your mother?"

"She still lives in Minsk. I see her when I can, which isn't often, considering the demands of the tour. I've become an American citizen, so visiting is more complicated."

Minsk was in Belarus, which became an independent republic in 1991 on the breakup of the Soviet Union. Belarus had ended up with 70 percent of the nuclear fallout from the 1986 Chernobyl power plant disaster across the border in Ukraine. A lot of farmland was still contaminated with radiation, although unscrupulous entrepreneurs were said to be using it anyway.

Max came up with a mental map of the place. Nestled between Latvia, Lithuania, Russia and Ukraine, the country was about the size of Kansas. The government was authoritarian. Max knew there had been some problems with the sale of weapons and weapons technology from Belarus to states known to engage in terrorism. He wasn't surprised that Elena had become an American citizen.

But her father hadn't. Anton might harbor some animosity toward the U.S., which had supported his daughter's declaration of her independence over his authority as a parent. Maybe something toxic had been brewing inside him for the past eight years. Max made a mental note to cross paths with Mr. Tarakova over the next couple of weeks.

He felt a tap on his shoulder and turned to find Kristin

standing behind him. He swiveled the bar stool around to face her. "Having fun?"

Her eyes looked troubled. Her voice was slightly slurred when she spoke. "I'm done in. I'm still not over my jet lag."

"I've got my car. I'll give you a ride back to your hotel."

"I can take the Underground," she said.

Max glanced at his watch and said, "It's pretty late for that."

"Oh. Well, if you don't mind."

Steffan was still brushing off his shirt as he approached them. "I can give her a ride back to her hotel, Max."

Max said, "I'll do it." He realized how curt he sounded and said, "It's no problem," in a friendlier voice.

"I'll take a ride, Steffan," Elena said.

Max realized that, once again, he'd been oblivious to Elena from the moment he laid eyes on Kristin. "I can give you a ride, too, Elena."

"The three of us might be a bit crowded in your Porsche, Max," Elena said with a laugh.

Max slapped his forehead. "I forgot which car I was driving."

She rose, retrieved her cashmere sweater from the back of her bar stool and slipped it over her bare shoulders. "You take care of Kristin, Max."

Steffan shot Max an aggrieved look behind Kristin's back, but Max refused to feel sorry for his friend. He'd had his chance. For whatever reason, Kristin had deflected Steffan's overture. He could try again another day. Or not.

Elena put her arm through Steffan's and led him toward the exit. "Come on, old boy. Time for bed."

Steffan turned back to wink at Max. Perhaps his friend was going to get lucky tonight, after all, Max thought.

Max turned to Kristin and asked, "Where's your jacket?"

"I forgot how cool the spring weather is here in London. I didn't bring one."

Max took off his navy blue sports coat and draped it around her shoulders. She pulled it close, apparently savoring the warmth that remained from his body, but at the same time shrugging off his arm, which had settled around her shoulder.

Max felt…sad. And…irritated. And damn it all… aroused. He bowed and gestured her toward the door. "Let's go, Princess."

13

"Did you find out anything from Steffan that might help us?" Max asked as revved his silver Porsche 911.

"He knows every woman on the tour," Kristin replied. She angled herself toward him in the bucket seat and said, "He's bedded most of them. I'd say he's been too busy having sex to plot an assassination."

Max noticed there was no slur in her voice, and when he met her gaze, her eyes were clear. Apparently she'd been pretending to be more tipsy than she was. "You got him to tell you that?"

"I couldn't stop him from telling me," she said with a rueful smile. "I think he wanted to convince me I'd be in for a delightful evening of carnal pleasure if I took him back to my hotel room."

"You weren't interested?" Max asked blandly.

"I thought I was coming here to…" She stopped herself, then continued, "Play a tennis match. You've changed that. I may not be an FBI agent for much longer, but so long as I am one, I intend to do a good job."

"When I talked to your boss, he didn't give me a lot of

details about the flap you're involved in. He just said you were a good agent. Want to tell me what happened?"

"No." She huffed out a breath and said, "I suppose you deserve to know. Several months ago, I shot a young man. I thought he had a gun. He was reaching for a cell phone. A few days after I met you in Miami, my partner and I were questioning some bank robbery suspects. The situation got hairy and I hesitated before drawing my gun. I didn't shoot when I should have. My partner was seriously wounded."

She grimaced and said, "Lucky for you, I don't have a gun strapped to my hip, so the problem isn't going to arise."

"About that. Check out the glove compartment."

She opened the tiny glove compartment. Inside was a Glock 27, the gun she normally carried. She left it where it was and turned to stare at him. "I thought we weren't authorized to carry weapons here in England."

"I don't want you defenseless in the event we uncover a plot and the assassin—and whoever he or she might be working with—decides to eliminate the pretty lady asking so many questions."

"You want me to carry an illegal firearm?"

"Yeah."

"Thanks, but no thanks," she said. "There's a small chance I'm going to get to keep my job. I don't want to blow it by creating an international incident. Besides, I usually carry at my waist under my jacket. There's no way to conceal a weapon when I'm wearing tennis clothes. It wouldn't do me much good in my tennis bag in the locker room—assuming I could get a gun past the soldiers doing personal searches at the gates during the tournament, which I doubt."

"Your choice," he said. "Let me know if you change your mind."

"Does this mean you're carrying a weapon?" she asked.

"Nope. I have other skills."

"Kung fu? Karate?"

He grinned at her. "Big fists. Long reach. Great footwork."

She laughed. "I remember you liked to box for exercise. You kept it up?"

He nodded. "I have to say, it's come in handy once or twice."

"I thought you were just a playboy, Max. Knowing you're working as a spy makes me wonder. What's your life really been like over the past ten years?"

It was the first personal question she'd asked. He was glad to hear it, because it was something a friend might ask. But it wasn't an easy question to answer. He deflected it by saying, "You first. What happened to you after that last Wimbledon match? Why didn't you stick around?"

They were passing under a streetlight and he noticed her face looked stricken. When they were in the dark again, she spoke.

"You made me believe I was invincible," she said quietly. "That I could beat anybody on the tennis court. Losing to Elena—when I should have won—was devastating."

"One loss and you quit tennis?" *And walked away from all your friends, including me?*

"It wasn't just the loss."

He waited for her to explain. When she didn't, he asked, "What happened, K? Why did you run away?"

They passed under another streetlight and he saw her eyes looked frightened now. What the hell had happened to her? The question had gnawed at him for ten years. He wanted an answer.

"Did someone hurt you?" Had she been physically attacked? Raped? The thought made his gut wrench, but he had to know.

"Yes," she whispered.

"Who was it? Did you report the attack? Did they ever find him?"

"It was you, Max," she said in a hoarse voice. "You hurt me."

The tires screeched as he braked the Porsche and swerved to the curb. He turned off the ignition and turned to face her in the enclosed space. His heart was beating hard in his chest, trying to get out, trying to get away. His throat was tight and he had trouble speaking, but he had to ask.

"Are you saying you weren't willing? That having sex with me left you traumatized so badly you quit tennis. That when we had sex…" He could hardly get the words out, but they had to be said. "That I raped you?"

"No!" She reached out to touch his arm, and when he flinched, pulled her hand back. "No, Max."

He frowned. "I remember you crying. I thought it was because it hurt when I...when we had sex, because it was your first time. Was it something else? Why were you crying?"

"Because of the pain. And because I was happy."

He shook his head in confusion. "That makes no sense. You just said I hurt you. But you were crying because you were *happy?*"

"Yes, I was happy. I liked you so much, Max. I wanted to be as close to you as I could possibly be, and sex seemed like the way to do that. Yes, it hurt. But I was glad we'd done it."

"Then why the hell did you run away the next day? Why did you refuse to see me? Why wouldn't you talk to me?"

She took a shuddering breath and let it out. He watched tears brim in her eyes and saw one slip onto her cheek.

"Talk to me, damn it!"

"I saw you kissing Elena the next morning," she said in a choked voice. "You made love to me and you kissed her—my rival in the match—the next morning right in front of me." Her voice rose and got angrier. "How do you think that made me feel?" Her face was a picture of agony. "I'll tell you, Max. It made me feel like a stupid idiot.

"I'd given you the most precious thing I had to give a man, and the next morning I found you kissing someone else. As though what had happened between us was... nothing."

Her eyes glistened with tears as she continued, "I was so hurt and angry I couldn't concentrate. I lost a match I should have won. I was furious with myself for letting you make me feel that way. And I was furious with myself for losing. I couldn't get away from you fast enough."

"You should have talked to me," he said quietly.

"I'm sure you would have come up with a good excuse for what you did. I didn't want to hear it."

"She asked for a kiss—for good luck. I gave it to her. That was all it was, K. A good-luck kiss."

She choked back a sob.

"Son of a bitch," he muttered. He shoved a frustrated hand through his hair. "Goddamn son of a bitch. All these years I spent wondering what the hell happened." He realized he was angry. Furious. "You should have said something to me. You should have given me a chance to explain."

It was too late to go back and undo what had happened. All these years he'd felt guilty, certain he'd done something wrong but never knowing what. And she'd run away because of a stupid misunderstanding.

"Your behavior after I left the tour convinced me I was right to cut you out of my life," she said defensively. "You didn't waste any time finding another bed partner."

He groaned and dropped his chin to his chest. He'd only stayed on the tour another year. But he'd done a lot of wild partying—with Elena, among others. He wasn't about to tell Kristin that he'd been trying to drown his pain and guilt—and the secret he carried about his mother—in booze and women.

"It's your turn, Max," she said. "Prove to me I was wrong. Have you ever had a serious relationship with a woman?"

"I'm a spy, Princess," he said in a mocking voice. "Spies don't do relationships. We have sex."

She winced. "I'm sorry for you, Max."

"What about you?" he shot back. "Where's your husband, Princess? Who's your boyfriend? What's your love life like?"

They were extremely personal questions. Things he would never have asked if he hadn't been so irritated by her attack on his life. Especially when it was his failure with her when he'd been a callow—and vulnerable—youth, and the terrible secret he'd never been allowed to share, that had made him so reluctant to commit himself to a woman.

"I was engaged once," she said. "It didn't work out."

"That's it? One engagement?" He realized he sounded snide. He wondered why he was still so angry. She'd explained. There was no big mystery. Just crossed wires. He should be relieved. He didn't understand why he couldn't let it go.

"I'm sorry, Max," she said, sounding genuinely contrite. "I should have let you explain."

For the past few minutes, he'd felt like a balloon filled so full of air it was ready to burst. Her apology was like a gentle pinprick that, instead of bursting the balloon, created a slow leak. He could feel the anger oozing out of him. Was that what he'd needed to hear? An apology for mistrusting him?

Without the anger to mask it, he realized what he really felt was grief. Something precious had been budding between them when they were kids. It had been snipped off before it could grow, and the plant itself had withered and died.

He reached for the key and started the car. "I'm sorry, too, K. At least now we both know what happened."

They were silent as he drove the last mile or so to her hotel, but he could feel the tension arcing between them.

As he pulled up in front of the Park Plaza Victoria, she said, "Would you like to come inside for a drink?"

"I'm done drinking for the night."

"Would you like to talk some more?"

"I'm done talking, too." He could see she was upset. So was he. He needed some time to process what he'd learned. "We have an early court time tomorrow. Get some rest."

She glanced at him once more, then reached for the door handle and let herself out of the car. She slid his jacket off her shoulders, then leaned in and laid it on the passenger seat.

"Thanks, Max," she said. And then, "I am so sorry."

He gritted his teeth to keep from saying something he would regret later. When she shut the car door, he gunned the engine and shot into oncoming traffic. A horn blared and he swerved, barely missing the shiny black fender of a London taxi. He kept his foot on the accelerator, forcing himself to focus on the road, while his heart beat heavy in his chest.

The problem was, the damned plant wasn't dead at all. The seeds of love had lain dormant in him, waiting for some nourishment to bring them back to life. Seeing her made him yearn for that innocent—yet powerful—love he'd felt all those years ago.

He had to kill the damned thing before it got a chance to take root again. He didn't trust her any more than he'd trusted any other woman in his life. He might once have been a fool for love. Not anymore. He wasn't going to let Kristin Lassiter anywhere near his heart again.

14

Kristin was fighting tears by the time she got to her hotel room. She kicked off her shoes, threw herself onto the bed and hugged a pillow to her chest.

I gave her a kiss for luck.

Why hadn't she asked Max to explain that kiss? How different things might have been! More to the point, why hadn't she contacted Max when she found out she was pregnant? If he'd known they were going to have a child, would he have asked her to marry him? Would he have stepped up and done his share of the parenting?

They'd been teenagers. Kids. Too young to marry. But still. They'd been good friends. He'd said he cared for her. She'd loved him. Maybe they could have made it. She would never know now. She'd never given him the chance.

Max had been so angry with her tonight. She didn't want to think what he might do if he found out she'd kept the existence of a daughter from him all these years. He wasn't a boy anymore. If he ever found out about Flick, she didn't think he would let her get away with running again.

Was that what she was going to do? Run again?

She'd worn the label *invincible* as a teen on the tennis court, but the truth was, she was a stronger person now than she'd been when those decisions were made. Of course, the self-confidence she'd gained raising a child on her own and pursuing a career that she loved had taken a battering over recent months. But she wasn't anywhere near down and out. She still had plenty of fight left in her.

Kristin swiped at her tears and headed into the bathroom to cleanse the makeup from her face with an inexpensive cold cream. After removing it with a tissue she rinsed with cold water. She looked at her face in the mirror, dripping with water, and didn't like what she saw in her eyes.

Defeat.

The duchess had been wrong. She and Max had discussed what had gone awry between them in the past, but it hadn't resolved anything. Except to make her feel like even more of a fool than she'd felt like ten years ago. Oh, how she wanted to pack her bags, collect her daughter and leave London!

She patted her face dry instead.

If she walked away, she would be leaving without the Blackthorne Rubies. She wanted—she needed—the financial security she would have if she stayed and played that stupid exhibition match.

She resisted the urge to grab her suitcase. She brushed

her teeth instead. Which left her staring at herself in the mirror again. And gave her far too much time to think.

It had occurred to her, when she saw Max this morning and realized the powerful physical attraction between them was still there, and tonight, when she'd realized that she wasn't the only one to be hurt by her childish behavior all those years ago, that she'd made a terrible mistake.

She felt wretched, wishing she didn't have to face Max again tomorrow. Especially knowing herself to be in the wrong.

There was something special between us a long time ago. I believe it's still there, beneath all the pain. Maybe Max and I could work through our differences. Maybe we could fall in love again. He could be a father to Flick and we could get married and live happily ever after.

She scoffed. Talk about fairy tales. She might still be attracted to Max, but he obviously didn't feel the same way. She'd seen him kiss Elena tonight. He might be a spy, but he was also still a playboy who used women like tissues and threw them away. She'd better settle for playing the damned exhibition match and not worry about living happily ever after. That special something—the spark between them—had been extinguished.

Liar, liar, pants on fire, a little voice said. *Max might be furious with you. And you might have ruined the possibility of ever living happily ever after with the decision you made to force him out of your life. But the sexual spark isn't gone. He wants you. And, admit it, you want him. So why not seduce him and see what happens. You know you can do it.*

That sounded manipulative. Cold and calculating. And very un-Kristin-like. It was also a plan that would work. But to what end? What was it she wanted from Max, really?

A commitment.

And how likely is that, considering who he is?

Kristin spit, rinsed her mouth and her toothbrush. It was time for a reality check. Getting back together with Max was a fantasy. Better to concentrate on searching for the assassin. And playing some good tennis. Then she could return to her life in Miami with Flick—and the Blackthorne Rubies.

Kristin reached for the hem of her short-sleeved cashmere sweater to pull it off but dropped her hands and slumped onto the bed instead. She put her feet up and grabbed the second pillow and hugged it tight to her chest.

Getting Max to commit was a stretch, no doubt about it. On the other hand, did she want to spend the rest of her life alone, like her father? She knew he was lonely without her mother. But he'd been too stubborn to fight to keep her. Was she going to make the same mistake? Why not fight for Max?

Kristin shook her head in disgust. Why couldn't she abandon the fantasy of happily ever after?

Face it. It's too late. Finish what you came here to do and get on with your life!

Kristin said a quick prayer for her father, hoping

he was doing well in rehab. She also said a prayer for Flick. She missed hugging her daughter and kissing her goodnight.

At least Flick was enjoying the time with her grandmother. When she'd spoken to her daughter on the phone earlier in the day, Flick had said, "Gram is really loquacious, Mom. I'm learning a lot about my ancestors, the Dukes and Duchesses of Blackthorne. Gram showed me lots of funny clothes she keeps in trunks in the attic. She says I can dress up in them if I want."

Kristin opened her mouth to say that sounded like fun, but Flick kept right on talking.

"Gram showed me more paintings of my ancestors in a room she called a gallery. Some of the duchesses are really pretty. And some of the dukes have noses like mine!"

Loquacious. It was great to hear her daughter being loquacious, too. *Full of excessive talk.* Yes, she could imagine Max's mother was doing her best to interest Flick in the Blackthorne family.

"And Mom," Flick had burbled, "there's a dungeon! I haven't seen it yet, because Gram says it's kind of dark and damp down there. But, Mom. A real, live dungeon!"

The next revelation from her daughter had given her pause.

"Dad's middle name is Hart. Smythe told me he's known my dad since he was in short pants. I didn't know what that meant, but Smythe told me it means he's known my dad since he was a little boy and wore pants that only came to his knees."

"I'm glad to hear you're getting along."

"Everybody's really nice," Flick said. "Smythe—his name is spelled with a *y*, not an *i*, and has an *e* on the end," Flick said, "Smythe has—" Flick paused and Kristin heard her asking, "What is it he's got, Gram?" Then Flick finished, "He's got arthritis, Mom. So he limps when he walks. Wait till you meet the cook, Mom! Everyone just calls her Cook, and she's got about a zillion wrinkles!"

Kristin had laughed. "A zillion?"

"Well, a lot, anyway," Flick said. "And she makes really good scones. Scones are like biscuits, sort of, and they're really good, especially when they're warm. You eat them with clotted cream, which is sort of like whipped cream, only thicker."

Kristin couldn't remember when in recent history she'd heard her daughter sounding so excited. Or so happy.

"Guess what, Mom?"

"What?"

"Dad is a *lord!* He's Lord Maxwell. Isn't that cool? That makes me Lady Felicity. Did you know that, Mom?"

Kristin felt a knot growing in her belly. If she'd been married to Max, her daughter would have been Lady Felicity. But the British peerage was a little prickly about legitimacy being necessary for the passing of titles.

"I'm glad you're having a good time, Flick. I'll try to

get down to the Abbey tomorrow to visit you. I need to talk with your grandmother for a moment. Would you please give her the phone?"

"Okay. I love you, Mom."

"I love you, too, Flick."

The duchess said, "Good afternoon, Kristin. How did your practice with Max go this morning?"

"The practice went fine. We're still going to lose."

"I wouldn't be so sure about that," the duchess said.

Kristin got to the point. "Please don't fill Flick's head with delusions of grandeur."

"I have no idea what you're talking about."

"For a start, she isn't *Lady* Felicity."

"Oh, that. She made the leap herself," the duchess explained. "She said some of the girls in her class at school had fathers who were lords, so that made them ladies. I didn't have the heart to correct her."

Kristin wouldn't have, either. "Flick was going on about a dungeon. She sounds determined to see it. Is it dangerous?"

"The dungeon is kept locked at all times. All of us here—myself and Emily and the servants—are enchanted with Flick. We won't let any harm come to her."

"Thank you. I appreciate you keeping her there."

"It's my pleasure, Kristin. I'm so glad to have the chance to get to know my granddaughter."

Kristin leaned back and hugged the pillow tighter to her chest. When she saw the duchess tomorrow, she was going to tell her that she and Max had discussed what had separated them ten years ago. Knowing it had been a simple misunderstanding had only made things worse. He blamed her for running away. And, she would tell the duchess, because there seemed no possibility of reconciliation, she had decided against introducing Flick to her father.

She closed her eyes a moment before getting up to change for bed. The next thing she knew someone was banging on the door.

15

Kristin sat bolt upright and stared at the door. The pounding continued, louder. She realized she'd fallen asleep on top of the covers, still wearing her clothes. The small lamp beside the bed left most of the room in darkness. Her heart was beating like a frightened bird against her rib cage as she grasped for the phone to call hotel security.

"K? I know you're in there. Open the door!"

Kristin lurched out of bed, relieved to hear a familiar voice. And then frightened at what Max's insistent banging might mean. "Max? What's wrong?" She yanked the door open, but the security chain caught. She saw a glimpse of Max looking agitated, his hair wild, his eyes gleaming like some jungle predator, before she slammed the door closed to release the chain.

"Hurry up!" he snarled.

She opened the door, terrified at the urgency—and anger—she heard in his voice. "What's wrong, Max? I—"

He captured her mouth with his, and when she gasped, he thrust his tongue inside.

She was rocked back on her heels and would have fallen, except he caught her at the waist and lifted her off her feet. He stepped inside, slammed the door closed, then turned and shoved her back against it. He imprisoned her body with his from breast to thighs, while his hands pulled at the pins that held her hair in a restricting bun.

As blond curls feathered around her face, he thrust both hands into her hair, angling her head for his kiss.

She yanked her head aside to say, "Max, what—"

"Don't talk," he said in a guttural voice. "Don't say anything. Just kiss me."

Because her body had already caught fire from the heat of his, because she'd imagined this moment for ten years, and because his eyes and his hands and his voice told her how badly he wanted her, Kristin did as he asked.

The moment their mouths met, she was swept up in a riptide of emotion. She felt so much. She wanted so much. She struggled to find her footing, but there was nothing but Max to grab onto. She grasped a handful of his hair with one hand, gripped his shoulder with the other and hung on for dear life.

He stopped kissing her long enough to tear off the sweater she was wearing, then reached behind her to expertly release her black push-up bra. He pulled it off her arms and threw it aside before reaching to undo the button and zipper on her pencil skirt. He shoved the skirt down and she shimmied her way out of it.

Leaving her wearing a black garter belt, black silk stockings and tiny black silk bikini panties.

"My God, Princess."

Kristin felt self-conscious as Max devoured her with his eyes. He grinned as he reached with a forefinger to snap one of the garters. The grin faded as his hand reverently cupped her naked breast. She held her breath as he leaned down to kiss the tip.

She felt a shiver of excitement roll down her spine as she laid her trembling hand on his head. "Why are you here, Max?" she asked in a quiet voice.

He lifted her into his arms and headed for the bed. "I thought my intentions were pretty clear."

She frowned at him and he smiled back.

"I want to make love to you, K."

"When I asked if you wanted to come upstairs for a drink, you refused. What changed your mind?" she asked as he leaned down to pull off the coverlet on the bed and then laid her down on the white sheets.

"I got halfway back to my place when I decided I got—we got—cheated," he said as he unbuttoned the top two buttons on his Egyptian cotton shirt and then yanked it off over his head.

Kristin thrilled at the sight of his broad chest covered in dark hair. She got up on her knees on the bed and reached for his belt. "Let me."

She realized her breathing wasn't quite even as she unbuckled his belt and pulled it out of the loops.

"Cheated?" she said, keying on the word that had motivated him to return.

"Cheated out of ten years of friendship," he said.

She let his belt drop on the floor and reached for the button and zipper on his slacks. His arousal was evident even before she shoved them down. He was wearing hip-length gray Calvin Klein underwear that bulged with the evidence of his desire. "Friendship?" she said with a mischievous smile.

"Yeah. That. And other things." He toed off his shoes and stepped out of his trousers before shoving off his socks.

She lay back and held out her arms. "Come to bed, Max."

He hesitated a moment, then reached for the Calvin Kleins and tugged them off.

She sat back up, her eyes wide. "My God, Max."

He shrugged and said, "I forgot we did all this under the covers the first time. You okay?"

She took a look at him and said, "It'll be a miracle if I live."

He laughed, then reached for her bikini panties, ripped them down the seam, and tossed them away. "The garter belt and black stockings are a nice touch, K. Makes me wonder who you put them on for."

"I put them on for myself, Max." She worked at a job where she had to be tough. The sexy underwear made her feel more feminine. And apparently pleased Max.

He grinned and said, "Thanks, anyway." He put a flat hand on her bare breasts to lay her back down, then shoved her legs apart and braced himself on his elbows as he leaned down to nuzzle her neck beneath her ear.

She put a hand on his cheek and turned his head so she could see his eyes, but they were closed. "Max?"

"Hmm."

"Why were you so angry at the door?"

"Do we have to talk about that now?" he said, never lifting his head as he kissed his way down to her breasts. He latched onto a nipple and suckled it.

Kristin decided talking could wait.

Making love to Max was a feast for the senses.

Touch. She indulged her need to touch his flesh, feeling the corded muscles in Max's arms and shoulders beneath the solid bone and enjoying the silkiness of the hair at his nape.

Taste. Max's skin tasted slightly salty when she kissed his throat. His mouth reminded her of the champagne she'd drunk at the bar, a mixture of flavors that weren't recognizable individually, but which tasted wonderful.

Smell. She inhaled, loving the masculine smell of him, filled with the pheromones that made her desire him.

Sound. She listened with joy to the sound of Max's murmuring voice, speaking words of desire. She relished his moans as she caressed him, and the guttural groan when she cupped him fed her desire. She heard her own sharp, uneven breaths, signaling her arousal.

Sight. And all the while, as he touched and she tasted and they reveled in their discovery of one another, Kristin focused on Max's heavy-lidded eyes, seeing desire and joy and a fierce need that matched her own.

"Are you protected?" he asked before he entered her.

It was a question the eighteen-year-old Max hadn't asked. A question she should have answered tonight before he'd inquired. "Yes," she said. She'd been taking the pill to reduce her periods. "STDs?" she asked.

"I'm clear," he said. "You?"

"I'm fine."

She marveled at how easily they were having a necessary discussion about a touchy subject. And how lucky they were that their answers allowed them to continue what they were doing.

It had been a year since she'd had sex, and Kristin felt tense, afraid that this joining of bodies, delayed for so long, might not meet her expectations. Or Max's, for that matter.

"Relax," he crooned. "We have all night."

This was a different Max, too. Patient and considerate. Willing to wait until she was ready for him. Willing to arouse her in a very different way.

As he kissed his way down her belly she felt adored. When he slid her legs over his shoulders and lifted her up for his intimate kisses, she felt an agony of delight.

"Max," she grated out. "Max!" She reached down and grabbed his hair.

He lifted his head to make sure she was okay and must have been satisfied with what he saw. "That's my name, don't wear it out," he teased before resuming what he'd been doing.

She laughed and then groaned as her body arched upward, seeking more of the unbearable pleasure he was providing with his lips and tongue.

She cried out as her body spasmed in climax, and Max held her until the powerful contractions eased. She was gasping for air, her chest heaving, as he slid up her body and pulled her close and held her tight.

She sought out his mouth to kiss him, tasting herself and him and wanting desperately to return the gift of pleasure he'd given her. But he resisted her attempts to leave his embrace.

"I want to be inside you, K."

"And I want you there," she replied.

He spread her thighs wide with his knees and she reached down to lead him inside, feeling the softness and heat of his flesh and the hardness that signaled his desire.

She was wet and ready and he filled her full.

"I need you, K," he muttered. He reached for her mouth and thrust deep with his tongue, mimicking the movements of his body below. He reached between them to touch her and Kristin cried out as her body came to climax for a second time.

Max's body tensed and he threw his head back as he spilled himself inside her.

She clutched him tight as he settled on top of her, wanting the weight of him for the few moments before he slid to her side and pulled her into his embrace.

This, also, was different. The eighteen-year-old Max hadn't wanted to be close after sex. He'd left her alone in the bed feeling bereft. Now she leaned her head against Max's chest, listening as his racketing heartbeat gradually slowed.

He reached over to turn out the light, then slid his arm around her and pulled her close. She waited for him to speak, or indicate that he was ready to listen to her speak. But her eyes drifted closed before that happened.

Kristin awoke sometime later with a start, expecting to find herself alone. She reached out and encountered a muscular arm. And smiled.

Max was asleep on the other side of the bed.

The room was still dark, but when she hit the luminous dial on her Timex, she saw it was nearly six. They were due on the tennis court at Wimbledon at nine.

She wanted to have the conversation Max had avoided last night. She wanted to know why he'd been so angry when he'd arrived. And why he'd changed his mind about making love to her.

"Max?" she whispered.

He turned to face her and said, "I'm awake."

She felt suddenly, ridiculously, shy. She lowered her gaze and felt his lips on hers.

"Sorry about the morning breath," he said.

She grinned and met his gaze as he leaned back onto his pillow. "Worth it to know you still feel like kissing me in the morning." She saw the brief frown between his brows, and suspected he was remembering the reason she'd given him for walking away ten years ago.

"Why were you so angry last night?" she said, wanting answers and afraid he might decide to bolt after all.

"I told you. I wanted what we lost ten years ago."

"What was that?" she asked. "Friendship?"

"The possibility of so much more than that." He crossed his arms behind his head and stared at the ceiling as he spoke. "I was in love with you, K."

Kristin sat up and shoved the pillow up behind her and pulled her knees to her chest, wrapping her arms around them. "I find that hard to believe."

He turned on his side, his head perched on his hand. "Why?"

"I can't even count the number of women who came in and out of your life over the years I knew you."

"The operative word there is *out* of my life," he said. "You remained the one constant."

"So when did you fall in love with me?" she demanded.

He shrugged. "I don't know. I didn't really know, until you were gone. I have to say, your reason for running was pretty lame."

"You underestimate the idiocy of a teenage girl in love," Kristin said quietly.

"Yeah. There is that."

"So what did you have in mind? An affair for the few weeks I'm here?" If he'd really loved her then, perhaps a proposal now wasn't beyond the realm of possibility.

What about Flick? He doesn't know he has a daughter.

For the very first time, Kristin felt guilty about keeping Flick a secret from Max. Now she was afraid to tell him, for fear that whatever feelings might have survived their ten-year separation would die a brutal death if he discovered the depth of her deceit regarding his daughter.

"There's something I've been waiting ten years to tell you," he said.

"What is that?" she said warily.

"A secret I discovered about my mother."

"Are you sure you want to tell me now?"

He sat up with his back to her, his feet on the floor. "I've been carrying this burden around with me because there's no one else but you I would trust with it."

"You couldn't tell Oliver?"

"Especially not Oliver," Max said.

"Is it something to do with him? Maybe you shouldn't tell me."

"I overheard my mother arguing with her twin sister. Did I ever tell you she has a twin? Anyway, Aunt Alicia showed up at the Abbey for Christmas. My mother wanted her gone. My aunt had a teenage boy with her she said was her son. But she wasn't married and never had been. She said Bull was the boy's father."

Kristin gasped. "No. Oh, no. Max, that's awful. What did your mother say? What did she do?"

"She turned white. Which made me think she believed my aunt was telling the truth."

"What did you do? What did you say?"

"I closed the door to my mother's sitting room and

walked away," Max said. "I didn't want to hear any more. I meant to tell you the night we had sex, but..." He smiled ruefully. "I got distracted. Later, I tried calling you, but you weren't talking to me. You wouldn't see me. You didn't want anything to do with me."

"I'm sorry I wasn't there for you, Max. What happened with your aunt? And her son?"

He shrugged. "I suppose my mother paid her off to stay away, because I've never seen either one of them again. It was just one more reason to distrust my parents. But I understood a little more about why my mother might have left my father. I mean, sleeping with his wife's sister..."

Kristin slid her arms around Max's waist from behind and held him tight. Little did he know how manipulative his mother could be. She'd bribed Kristin to get her to spend time with her son. Even knowing he might be hurt if he had feelings for Kristin that she didn't return.

Of course, the duchess might truly want her son to be happy and believe that Kristin was the woman for him. She might want even Max to have the chance to be a father to his daughter.

Kristin felt confused about what she should do. She was tempted to confess his mother's plot and her own part in it. But that would mean revealing the existence of Flick—and taking the chance that Max might be so angry about her deception that he would seek legal custody of their daughter.

She couldn't take that chance. She couldn't say anything. But she could tell the duchess she wanted no more part in her machinations. And she could enjoy the brief time she had with Max.

She glanced at the clock and saw they'd been talking for more than an hour. "We're going to be late."

Max smiled, reached around to pull her into his lap and said, "To hell with it."

16

For the past week, Max had felt like he was living in a dream. He and Kristin had been playing tennis every morning, dating other tennis players in the evenings, and returning to her hotel room late at night to exchange notes and make love. So far, they hadn't found anyone who stood out as a possible assassin. He'd even eliminated Elena's father as a suspect.

Kristin kept her afternoons to herself, pleading that she needed private time. He hadn't asked her what she did. He'd just been grateful for the time she was willing to spend with him.

Max wasn't sure why he found making love to her so satisfying. Maybe it was the enthusiastic way she responded to him. Maybe it was the way she looked at him with acceptance. And love. He didn't think he was mistaking what he saw in her eyes. Because it was the same thing he'd seen all those years ago without recognizing how rare and precious it was.

Tonight they were meeting up with Irina and Steffan for purely social reasons. He knocked on Kristin's hotel room door and heard her humming on the other side. His heart jumped when she opened the door and smiled at him.

"Hello, Max. I'll be ready in just a moment."

He stepped inside and pulled her into his arms as the door closed behind him. "How about a kiss?"

She laughed, kissed him quickly and wriggled to escape. "I'd love to stay here and play with you, Max, but we need to meet Irina and Steffan at that Indian restaurant near the British Museum in half an hour."

He'd left the choice of restaurant to her. "I like the taste of Indian food," he said. "But I like the taste of you better."

He slid his tongue along the seam of her lips and she opened to him. Her tongue dueled with his as he deepened the kiss. His hand sought out her breast, which was small enough to fit easily in his palm, and he used his thumb and forefinger to tease the nipple until it pebbled and he heard her moan.

She went up on tiptoe to fit them together where it would do the most good and rubbed herself against his arousal. Her hand came seeking between them, and he groaned as she traced the length of him behind the fly of his jeans.

"I want you," he rasped.

"We'll be late to dinner," she protested.

"I'll be quick."

She laughed and said, "That's what I'm afraid of."

He shot her a chagrined look and shoved her skirt up

to palm the heart and the heat of her. And discovered she wasn't wearing any panties.

"What did you expect?" she said when he raised his brows in surprise. "The way you keep tearing them off, I'm not going to have any left."

"I'll buy you more. Or not." He slid two fingers inside her as her mouth sought his. And discovered she was hot and wet and ready.

She unsnapped and unzipped his jeans and shoved them down as he turned and braced her against the closed door and lifted her to impale her. She gripped his hips with her legs as he drove himself to completion.

"I'm sorry," he gasped. "I should have waited—" He cut himself off as he looked into her dazed eyes and saw her sated expression.

She glanced up at him and said, "What?"

He chuckled. "Forget it."

She released her grip on his hips, but he had to hold her upright, since her legs wobbled like jelly.

"This door seems to be your favorite place to make love," she said.

He shot her an abashed look. He just never got very far into the room before he wanted to be inside her. The door made a handy vertical support for lovemaking.

"I'll see what I can do about making it into bed when we get back here tonight," he promised.

"Max, I don't think—"

He kissed her to keep her from protesting. He couldn't seem to get his fill of her. They often made love twice a day. Or three times, if they woke up in the middle of the night. But she was always willing. And he had a lot of years to make up for. Years when he'd yearned for someone who would look at him like K did when she made love to him.

Kristin shoved her curly hair away from her face as she headed for the bathroom. "Give me a few minutes," she said. "And I'll be ready to go again."

"Promise?"

She stared at him for a moment in disbelief. When he grinned and shrugged, she stuck out her tongue, ruffled her hands through her hair and shut the bathroom door in his face.

He liked that she hadn't put her hair up in a bun since he'd first taken out the bobby pins and let it fall free. Her ponytail had reappeared on the tennis court, sprouting through the back end of the ball cap she wore to keep the sun off her face.

Max realized he was falling in love with her all over again.

It wasn't just the sex. Although he had to admit that was pretty spectacular. K had always been a good listener. That hadn't changed. And she'd always supported him when he faced adversity. That hadn't changed either.

There was something new in their relationship that hadn't been there when they were teens. He'd been trying to put a finger on it for the past few days.

Perhaps it was that K stood on equal footing with him now. The age difference that had made him the more worldly one when they were kids, was insignificant now.

Perhaps it was that K understood and shared his interest in keeping the world a safe place. Interesting—almost odd—that they'd ended up in virtually the same line of work. Maybe it was finding all her good qualities combined in one person.

Along with the spectacular sex, of course.

For the first time in his life, he was thinking it might be nice to spend his life with one woman. And it wasn't Veronica, with whom he'd been trying to establish a relationship before K had shown up. He didn't know Veronica well enough to compare her in every way to K. But really, there was no comparison.

He wanted K back in his life.

Which was a problem, considering the realities of her life in America and his life in London and the travel required by his work for the CIA. Not that he had to keep his job, but it gave him something to do with his life that wasn't philanthropy or polo.

Would Kristin be willing to quit the FBI? He didn't think so. Although that might become a moot point, if she was fired. She still hadn't heard from SIRT. She lived every day on pins and needles, and he knew from how much she cared that she wanted to keep her job.

Max's brows furrowed in thought. Unfortunately, he didn't think his problem was going to be solved by her losing—or quitting—her job. He could tell from the reports K gave him about the men she interviewed on dates that she was too good an asset for the FBI to lose.

He wondered if she wanted kids. Would she leave

the FBI to be a full-time mother? That was a challenge worthy of her time.

He wanted a family. Two kids, maybe. Or four. Not three. That left an odd man out. But not right away. He wanted time to enjoy having K to himself.

Kristin reappeared looking so beautiful he wanted her again.

"I'm ready," she said with a smile.

"Me, too," he quipped. "But I think I can control myself till after dinner."

She laughed. And then blushed.

And he knew she wanted him as much as he wanted her. He headed straight for the hotel room door, knowing it would be too easy to get distracted again.

They had a short walk to the spot where Max had managed to find a parking spot for his Porsche. The weather had remained beautiful, sunny and warm, with no sign of the rain that made an umbrella a necessary addition to any outing in London.

The sidewalks were busy, and Max slid an arm around Kristin's waist and pulled her close to rescue her from a mother pushing an old-fashioned baby carriage through the crowd.

"I'm looking forward to catching up with Irina," he said.

"I'm surprised you haven't kept in closer touch with her," Kristin replied as she inched even closer to avoid two small children holding hands on either side of their mother. "It always seemed to me that Irina was more of a mother to you than your own mother while you were on the tour."

"She was," Max said. "I'm not sure why we lost touch. We were talking once a week. Then every couple of weeks. Then once or twice a year. And not at all for the past couple of years." Max shrugged. "My fault, I guess. I suppose I didn't need a mother as much once I got older."

"You always need your mother," Kristin said sharply. "And mothers never stop loving and caring for their children, no matter how grown-up and independent they are."

He laughed at her ferocity on the subject. "I'm not going to argue with you, K." He was reminded that Kristin had been without a mother most of her life. Maybe that was what made her so animated on the subject. "You must admit, my mother—"

"Worries about you," Kristin interjected.

His brows rose to his hairline. "I don't believe what I'm hearing. You really think the Mean Witch cares for me?"

She bit her lip and shot him a guilty look.

Which made him suspicious. He opened the passenger door of his Porsche, waited for her to get in and closed the door behind her, all the while watching her. He got into the car, started the engine and pulled out into traffic before he said, "What makes you think my mother cares for me?"

"All mothers—"

"I thought we'd established that my mother is the

exception to the rule," Max said. "Yours, too, for that matter."

"Maybe," Kristin conceded. "But Max, you must admit, she's had a difficult time—"

"Hold up just one minute," Max interrupted. "Now you're on her side? What is this, K?"

She chewed on her fingernail while she stared at him. "I'm wondering if perhaps you've misjudged her, Max."

"She sent me off to boarding school when I turned seven. We barely spoke during the holidays. She never showed up at a single match I played," he said. "Not once during my entire junior tennis career. That doesn't leave me with any warm and fuzzy feelings toward her."

"Maybe she had reasons—"

Max snorted. "Come on, K. You know better than that. You managed to be around for me for three years, despite all the traveling you had to do."

"She didn't have just one child," Kristin pointed out. "She had five. And a husband, who must have wanted some of her time."

Max had never thought of his siblings as taking any of his mother's time, because it didn't seem like she spent any more time with them than she had with him. Maybe he was wrong. And he knew at one time his father had loved his mother. Which would have made quite a few demands on her time.

"Maybe she wasn't able to be there for you because she was sad and unhappy about what was happening between her and your father."

He stared at her incredulously.

Kristin cried, "Watch out!"

A horn blared and he swerved the Porsche back into his lane. "What on earth has gotten into you? I don't believe what I'm hearing."

"I think you should give your mother another chance, Max. That's all."

"Why? What's different now? Has she been in touch with you? Is that what this is all about?"

He watched her face turn pale. Watched her open her mouth to speak and close it again before she finally said, "I talked with my father today on the phone. He's not doing well, Max." Tears brimmed in her eyes and she turned away, sniffing to hold them back. When she turned to look at him again, her eyes were filled with pain. "He said he wants to die."

"I'm sorry, K. I didn't know."

"I want to leave and go home and be with him, but he said he doesn't want me there. He doesn't want to see me. I think maybe I should go anyway."

Max pulled the Porsche to the curb in the shade of an oak and turned off the ignition. He turned to her and said, "What can I do to help?"

She sniffed and said, "Just listening is a help."

There wasn't room in the Porsche to pull her into his lap, so he settled an arm around her shoulder and pulled her toward him and kissed her gently on each cheek, catching a teardrop with the second kiss. "Take it easy, baby. Let me see what I can do about getting him flown here."

"He's in rehab."

"There are rehab facilities here. Let me do this for you, please. I need you here for this assignment." He made his plea professional, rather than personal, because he wasn't sure she was ready to hear how much he wanted her to stay in London for the rest of her life. Getting her father here would be a step in the right direction.

"All right, Max. I'll pay you back. I promise."

"When we get to the restaurant, I'll make a few phone calls. We should have your dad here before we play our exhibition match. If he's up to it, maybe he'll want to come."

She brightened and said, "What a good idea! That'll give him something to work toward over the next couple of weeks. Thank you, Max. You don't know how much this means to me."

He felt his throat swell with emotion. Pleasing her, making her happy, made him feel ten feet tall. Bloody hell. He had it bad. If only he could be sure she shared his feelings, he'd ask her to marry him tonight.

"K..."

"What is it, Max?"

"Nothing. We're here. We can talk about it later tonight."

17

Kristin wondered if she'd made a mistake accepting Max's offer to bring her father to London. But she'd been terribly worried when she'd talked to Harry. Surprisingly, the duchess had made the same offer earlier in the day. Which was what had motivated her to speak so kindly of the Mean Witch to Max.

Flick had phoned Kristin, crying because her grandfather didn't want her to call anymore. The duchess had suggested bringing Harry to London so Flick could be closer to him.

"It might keep your father—and Felicity—from feeling so low if she can visit with him every day," the duchess had said.

Kristin hadn't accepted Bella's offer because she didn't want to be indebted to the woman any more than she already was. But she'd been tempted. During her visits with Flick every afternoon, Kristin had been coincidentally getting to know Bella better. The more she knew about Flick's grandmother, the more she liked her. And the more she believed Bella only had Max's best interests at heart in her effort to get the two of them together.

Which was why, every time she'd had sex with Max over the past week—and they'd had a great deal of sex—Kristin had felt guilty. She had an ulterior motive in attaching Max's affection that he knew nothing about. It was uncomfortable to remember that she'd bargained with the duchess to spend time with Max in exchange for a few baubles.

Kristin laughed inwardly. The Blackthorne Rubies were hardly baubles. They were priceless gems. And they represented lifelong security for her and her daughter.

Unfortunately, as Max was getting physically attached to her, she'd been getting emotionally attached to him. She'd started wondering what it might be like to say yes if he actually did propose. Before she could possibly say yes, there were things she would have to confess that weren't going to present her in a very good light.

Her dilemma was twofold. First, how could she explain her agreement with his mother to play the exhibition match in order to spend more time with him? Second, how could she justify keeping his daughter a secret from him?

The first deception was certain to make him angry. The second might cause him to walk away from her—and try to take Flick with him. Kristin had been progressively torn between feelings of utter joy at the possibility of a life with Max and utter despair that her situation was hopeless.

She didn't want to hurt or humiliate Max with the

knowledge that she'd been willing to do whatever was necessary to earn the Blackthorne Rubies. And she felt sick in the pit of her stomach every time she imagined how duped and defrauded Max would feel when he learned he had a nine-year-old daughter.

But if they were going to have any hope of a future together, she was going to have to tell him everything. She dreaded seeing the look on his face when he learned that the goddess he adored had very human feet of clay.

Kristin realized she'd been lost in thought during the entire walk from the spot where Max had parked his Porsche to the Indian restaurant where they were meeting Irina and Steffan.

"Hello, beautiful," Steffan said, standing up from his seat at a table for four to kiss her on both cheeks. He caught Max's hand and bumped shoulders. "Good to see you, Max."

Kristin leaned over to kiss Irina on both cheeks before sitting in the chair across from Steffan. Max also kissed Irina before taking the chair across from the older woman.

"You should never have stopped playing tennis," Irina chided Max. "You're so good at it."

Kristin was starting to feel miffed that she hadn't been included in the compliment when Irina turned to her and said, "You have immense talent, Kristin, but not Max's love of the game."

Which was an assessment so close to the truth it was scary. "I suppose it's a good thing I quit," Kristin said with a smile.

"And too bad Max did," Irina said, reaching out to pat his hand, which lay on the table.

"What are we drinking?" Max asked, catching and squeezing her hand before releasing it.

Kristin had known Max liked Irina. She hadn't realized how much affection he felt for the older woman. It was clear Irina returned the feeling. She glanced at Steffan, wondering whether he'd ever been jealous of Max's place in his mother's heart. But Steffan's dark eyes were stone walls that kept emotions in and strangers out.

"I've ordered a bottle of cabernet," Steffan said. "Is that all right with everyone?"

Kristin nodded, although she needed something stronger. She had a lot of decisions to make. When to tell Max. What to tell Max. How to tell Max all the secrets she'd been keeping from him.

She was quiet through most of dinner, letting Max and Irina and Steffan reminisce. Which might have been why she noticed the number of times Irina made an uncomplimentary comment about the United States. She never went so far as to mention President Taylor. But not once during all the dates she'd had during the previous week had Kristin heard such anti-American sentiments.

When she looked at Max, he seemed oblivious. In fact, he was leaning his chin on his hand, listening raptly to Irina.

Kristin surreptitiously watched Steffan, wondering if he shared his mother's dislike of America. Steffan caught her looking at him and raised a brow. When she flushed, embarrassed at even considering Max's childhood friend as an assassin, he winked. She was more than willing to let him think her interest in him was personal.

But Max was not.

"That's my friend you're flirting with, Casanova," Max said, his voice like steel. "Leave her alone."

Steffan held both hands up like a man under arrest and said, "Sorry, old man. No harm, no foul."

Kristin didn't know whether to feel flattered by Max's protectiveness or insulted by it. She didn't belong to him. They'd merely been having sex—granted, a lot of really great sex—for a single week. Now that she thought about it, she was startled to realize that no words of love—or even affection—had been spoken between them.

It might be worth spending a little more time with Steffan to see whether he had feelings about America similar to his mother's. Unfortunately, she didn't have time to clear her brilliant plan with Max.

"Not so fast, Max," she said. She met his gaze and tried to tell him with a look that she had something besides a romantic interest in Steffan. But apparently Max couldn't see anything through the haze of green coloring his view. "You don't own me," she said at last.

"Well, well," Steffan said with a grin. "How about a nightcap, little lady?"

"K and I have plans later," Max said.

"I'd rather take a ride with Steffan," Kristin said. She watched Max squeeze his table napkin in his fist. She figured he was imagining it was Steffan's throat.

"Whatever you say, Princess," Max said through tight jaws.

"How about it, Irina? Want to go get a nightcap with Steffan and K?"

"You aren't invited, Max," Kristin said, staring him down.

"You heard her, Max," Steffan said, grinning broadly. "You had your chance, old man. Now it's my turn."

Kristin shuddered inwardly at the thought of what she might have to do to keep Steffan at arm's length. But if she could get confirmation of Steffan and Irina's attitude—positive or negative—toward America, it would be worth it.

"I'd love another cup of tea, Max," Irina said in an attempt to soothe the savage beast.

Kristin could see Max would rather pour the boiling brew over Steffan's head than drink it, but he said, "Of course."

"Shall we go?" Kristin said to Steffan as she stood.

"I'll see you later," Max muttered to her under his breath.

"I'll see you tomorrow, Max," she said firmly. She had no intention of having an argument with him later tonight at her hotel, when she'd be tired and perhaps have a drink or two in her. She could clear up any misunderstanding tomorrow morning on the tennis court. This trip wasn't just about the two of them. Max would forgive her when he realized she was just doing her job.

Without a second look, she turned her back on him and walked away.

18

"Good morning, Princess. Rough night?"

"Does it show?" Kristin hadn't slept well. She had a bit of a hangover. It had been necessary to have several drinks with Steffan to get him talking. Then she'd needed to fend off unwelcome advances while keeping a smile on her face. But she'd found out what she'd wanted to know.

She'd half expected Max to be waiting for her at the hotel, but her room was dark and quiet when she returned. She'd showered and gotten into bed around one. A frightening dream had woken her at three, and she hadn't been able to get back to sleep. She felt exhausted and the day had barely started.

The bad dream had concerned Max proposing. She'd been startled awake after seeing the horrified look on his face when she'd laughed and said getting him to propose was a game—with some pretty substantial prizes—devised by his mother.

Kristin swung her tennis racquet to warm up her arm,

then twisted at the waist. "How much time do we have before practice starts?"

"We've got a few minutes before Steffan and Elena show up. Why?"

"We need to talk about what I found out last night from Steffan."

"How is he as a lover?" Max asked, his eyes like blue ice.

She glared at him and said, "I went with Steffan because I noticed something last night at supper."

"How big his biceps are?" Max asked in a silky voice.

She resisted the urge to call him a jealous idiot and said, "I noticed how many anti-American sentiments Irina expressed during your conversation with her. I thought it was worth investigating Steffan's feelings a little further. There was no way I could tell you what I had in mind."

He stared at her as though deciding whether to believe her. "What did you find out?" he asked at last.

"They're possible suspects, Max. Both of them."

He laughed, but it wasn't a pleasant sound. "That's ridiculous. I don't have to tell you how close I am to Irina and Steffan."

"Which is why you didn't see or hear what I did last night," Kristin said. "You were so focused on entertaining Irina and enjoying her company that you ignored the negative things she said."

"Like what?" Max challenged.

"Paraphrasing, Irina said that Americans are using

up the world's resources without thinking of the consequences. That Americans think they have all the answers to the world's problems. That Americans stick their noses in where they don't belong. Which she followed with, and I quote, 'Someday someone is going to cut those long American noses off.'"

"Those statements are so general—"

"We're looking for an assassin in the tennis world, Max. Those statements, taken together, are enough to create suspicion. We need to mention Irina and Steffan Pavlovic as parties who should be investigated further by Homeland Security before they enter the States for the U.S. Open."

Plainly Max didn't like her conclusion, but she could see he didn't completely discount it, either.

"I'm sorry, Max," she said. "I wish things had turned out differently."

"We have a little while before our exhibition match," he said. "I'd like to wait to mention them as suspects until then. Maybe we'll get information that leads us in a different direction."

"All right, Max. I have no problem with waiting a little while." But even if they found other suspects, Max had to know Irina and Steffan would still have to be investigated. She wondered if he planned to say something to them. Surely not. He'd been a spy long enough to know how the game was played.

"I missed you last night, Princess," Max said as he took the few steps to bring him close enough to touch. "Can I see you this afternoon?"

Kristin flinched when he reached out to touch her arm. She saw his lips flatten before he said, "I'm trying not to act like a jealous fool, but—"

"Then don't!" she snapped. "Nothing happened, Max. Not that I should have to tell you that, or make any explanation at all. We aren't attached in any way. We've merely been having sex—"

"Is that what you think?" he said angrily.

She could see he was on the verge of declaring himself, of staking the claim that she'd denied. She wasn't ready to hear words of love, because she wasn't ready to tell him the truth. She was afraid if she spent any more time with him, especially time in bed with him, she would feel compelled to blurt out everything. She had to stop him from speaking.

"I'm sorry, Max." The apology kept him mute. For a moment. She hurried to say, "I can't see you this afternoon. I have some things I need to do. Personal business I need to attend to." Like visiting our daughter. About whom you know nothing. And who knows nothing about you.

She'd been wondering all week whether she was being selfish keeping Flick separated from her father. In fact, guilt over depriving Max from knowing Flick had kept her awake long after the proposal nightmare had woken her up. She'd wondered if she was being fair. Didn't Max deserve a chance to know Flick? Didn't Flick deserve a chance to know her father?

She was more confused than ever. More frightened than ever. Her greatest fear had always been that if Max knew about Flick, and was mad enough about her deception, he might try to take Flick away from her. His jealousy over Steffan had surprised her. In a million years she wouldn't have guessed that Max would be a possessive lover. While a little jealousy was flattering, she didn't think it was a particularly heroic quality in a man.

Now that she'd discovered one imperfect, unheroic flaw in the man she was starting to love, what other flaws might there be that she hadn't noticed? Keeping Max and Flick apart seemed like the prudent move right now.

Unfortunately, now that Flick had seen photos of Max, now that she'd slept in her father's bedroom, Kristin wasn't sure it was possible to keep her daughter from contacting Max on her own, even if Kristin decided not to introduce the two of them.

It wasn't realistic to think she could keep them separated indefinitely. Flick knew how to use the phone and the internet. At some point, probably sooner rather than later, Flick might very well contact Max on her own.

That thought was terrifying. Mostly because Kristin had no way of gauging Max's reaction to her deception. How ruthless would he be in pursuing custody, if he decided he wanted it?

She could feel the situation slipping out of her control.

She couldn't begin to fathom all the complications that might arise once Max and Flick were introduced.

Presuming she and Max didn't get married and live happily ever after, if Max became a part of Flick's life, her daughter would end up flying back and forth between continents in order to visit her father. That wasn't fair to Flick.

Not to mention the fact that she and Max had separate lives that were difficult to mesh, even presuming they fell in love and tried for the fairy-tale ending. He lived in London. She lived in Miami. One of them was going to have to give up her home and her job and her life.

She noticed she'd used the feminine pronoun in her hypothetical example, because she couldn't see Max making that sort of sacrifice. The problem was, she wasn't sure she could make it either.

Not even for love?

No one had said anything about love. Not her. And not Max.

"I'm sorry, Max," she said again. *For everything you don't know. For all the secrets I've kept from you.*

"It's too bad you're busy this afternoon," he said. "Because I can't see you tonight."

"Oh?"

"I have to pick up someone at the airport."

She raised a brow in question.

His lips twisted ruefully before he said, "A female friend."

"A girlfriend?" she said incredulously.

He shrugged and lowered his head and swiped a guilty palm across his nape. "Sort of."

"You have a *girlfriend* and you slept with me all week?" She fought back the bile that rose in her throat. Before he could respond to her accusation, she had an even more sickening thought. “You have a girlfriend, and you had the gall to be jealous that I was going to have a drink with Steffan?”

He opened his mouth to reply, but she cut him off by pointing her racquet at him. “I don’t want to hear an explanation. I don’t want to hear excuses. I feel like such an idiot! I should have known. I hope she finds out about me. And I hope she leaves you!”

He looked as unhappy as she felt. “Princess—”

“Don’t you *dare* call me Princess,” she snarled. “That’s the name my friend gave me when he treated me like one. Go away, Max. Get out of my sight.”

He stood where he was. “We have a practice scheduled in a few minutes.”

And an exhibition match to play. In which she didn’t want to embarrass herself. And for which she was going to receive the Blackthorne Rubies. “I might have to practice with you. I might have a job to do here. But I don’t have to talk to you. Or have sex with you. I’m going to be too busy for the rest of my time here to see you. Check that. Too busy for the rest of my life!”

She was glad she was about to play tennis, because she felt like hitting something.

“There’s something you need to know, Prin—” Max cut himself off and said, “I decided we need some help. So I got us some.”

“Help? What, you hired another spy?”

Max shook his head. “If we’re going to win this match,” he clarified, “we’re going to need some professional help." He pointed to a spot behind her and said, "Meet our new coach."

Kristin turned and saw Irina stepping onto the tennis court. She shot Max an incredulous look, then turned to the older woman, smiled and said, "Irina! What a nice surprise."

Irina's bushy gray hair was just long enough to stick out on all sides around the brimmed white fishing hat she wore to keep the sun off her tanned and wrinkled face. She looked like one of the sunbaked old women who sat on benches around Miami Beach. But Kristin no longer saw a benign old lady. She saw a potential assassin.

Before she'd come to London, Kristin had done background research on all the players and coaches. So she knew Irina had been a world-class cyclist before she became her son's tennis coach. She was short, with legs like oak tree trunks. She'd been born in Kosovo and had left the Balkan territory with her son after her husband was killed in a NATO bombing.

All that had happened so long ago, Kristin had dismissed Irina as a suspect, as she was sure Max had. Especially since Irina and Steffan had found asylum in America.

Irina's smile was famous—and contagious. When Kristin was on the tour, Irina had sat in the player's box during tennis matches and encouraged Steffan with that toothy grin. Kristin had always thought Irina was sending signals to her son—coaching wasn't allowed during the game—by the way she tugged at her hat, or her nose or her hair, like a baseball coach sending in the play. But no one could ever prove it.

Despite her misgivings, Kristin found herself smiling at their new coach. "How are you this morning, Irina?"

"You two need a lot of work," the woman said bluntly.

Kristin realized the smile on the coach's face took the sting out of her words. "Yes, we do," she admitted.

Irina turned to Max, her hands on her hips, and said, "Steffan isn't pleased about this."

Max snorted. "He only has himself to blame. He was the one who got himself a different coach a couple of years ago. Why shouldn't I take advantage of the chance to learn, from the person who knows Steffan best, where his game might be a little weak."

Kristin had unintentionally given Max even more reason to want to beat his friend on the tennis court.

"Let's focus on making your game stronger," Irina said. "Let me see how the two of you hit the ball before Steffan and Elena arrive."

Because Kristin had gotten so little sleep, her footwork was slow. Irina let her know it. Kristin felt her face flushing at the harsh comments. The criticism sparked her adrenaline, as it had so many years ago when she'd been coached by her father, and she began to play better.

"You two look like real tennis players," a male voice called out.

Max let the ball zing past him as he turned to greet

Steffan. "You didn't think we were going to let you win without a fight, did you?"

"Fight all you want," Elena said as she joined Steffan on the court. "You two are going down."

The tennis that followed was brutal. Kristin had forgotten how physically—and mentally—demanding it could be to play in a truly competitive world-class game of tennis. Today, Steffan and Max were hitting hard—at each other.

Perhaps Steffan was stinging from her rejection of him. As was Max. And they were taking it out on each other.

Balls whizzed past her. She couldn't seem to get her serve in the service box and double-faulted several times, losing points. Worst of all, near the end of the second set, she and Max hurtled into each other, both going for the same ball in the center of the court.

He knocked her sideways, and she landed on the grass with Max on top of her, their bodies aligned from breast to hip. Her tennis racquet was still in her hand, but his had gone flying. He levered himself up just enough with his palms to look down into her face.

She looked up into his eyes and saw regret. And love.

She wanted him. Right then. Right there. If they'd been alone she would have taken him inside her and loved him with all her might.

Thank God they weren't alone.

"You all right?" he asked in a gentle voice.

She was still too horrified by the discovery of how

much in love with him she was—despite hearing about the other woman—to speak. She soaked in every small detail of how it felt to have him so close, knowing that if they hadn't accidentally collided, she would never have let him touch her like this again.

She lay beneath the sweaty male weight of him, liking it. She breathed in and found his pungent male odor surprisingly pleasing. His legs were entwined with hers and she could feel his rough male hairs against her smooth skin.

A drop of sweat from his cheek fell onto her closed lips. She met his gaze as she reached out with her tongue and licked it away. Salty.

She saw the sudden flare of his nostrils and watched the black irises in his blue eyes grow with desire as he stared down at her. She felt the unmistakable tension in his body, saw the flex of muscles in his arms. And felt the hard length of him between the fragile pieces of cloth that separated their flesh and bone.

She forgot about everything but Max as his mouth lowered toward hers. His lips were full, his mouth slightly open, his breathing erratic.

She wanted his mouth on hers. Wanted to taste him, hold him, love him.

"Hey, you two! Everything all right?"

The question from Steffan, who'd apparently jumped the net, broke the spell. Kristin was horrified at what she'd been ready and willing to do.

He has a girlfriend. He kept her a secret from you.

How can you possibly forgive him so quickly? Or want him so soon? And so much?

A second later, Max was on his feet.

She felt bereft.

He leaned down, caught her by both wrists and pulled her to her feet. "You okay?"

She pulled her hands free and used the one not holding a tennis racquet to rub her suddenly aching hip. "I think so."

He looked deep into her eyes, searching for something. Maybe wondering, as she was, whether there was any hope that she would forgive him. There wasn't. She couldn't afford to fall in love with a rich playboy. She had responsibilities. And a daughter he knew nothing about.

"Are you sure you're okay?" he said. "We can stop if you're hurt."

Oh, she was hurt all right. But the pain Max had caused was more emotional than physical. She couldn't slap a bandage on it and expect it to heal anytime soon.

"Your match is in less than two weeks," Irina reminded them.

"I'm all right," Kristin said at last. Although that was far from the truth. She was still dazed, suffering from the shock of realizing how powerful her physical attraction was to a man she shouldn't trust. She'd better be careful. Even though she'd rejected him, she still wanted him.

"Let's keep going," she said. "We need the practice."

Practice wasn't the same after her fall. She couldn't concentrate. Apparently, neither could Max.

"That's enough for today," Irina said, calling the practice to a halt. "We'll try again tomorrow morning."

Kristin saw Max hold back as the other three left the court. He crossed to her and said, "Are you sure you're all right? That was quite a tumble."

"You don't need to worry about me, Max." *I can take care of myself. I've been doing it for years. I don't need you, or any man, to take care of me.*

But oh, how she yearned for someone to brush her off when she fell down—on the court and in her day-to-day life—and tell her everything would be all right.

Max pulled his ball cap off, shoved his sweaty hair back off his forehead with a towel, then tugged the cap back on. "K…I wish—"

"Forget it, Max," she interrupted. "It doesn't matter."

"Doesn't it? I'm sorry, K. For what it's worth."

"Apology accepted."

"We still have to work together, on and off the court. We can't afford to let this…glitch…keep us from doing what we have to do."

"Glitch?" she said sarcastically. "You having a girlfriend is a glitch?"

"She's not— I don't feel— She isn't—" He kept cutting himself off, looking more frustrated with each attempt to fit his absent girlfriend into the appropriate place in his life.

"Whatever she is to you, Max, she exists. If it's any

consolation, you've got your revenge for what I did to you ten years ago."

"I never intended to punish you, K. Veronica is—"

She held up a hand to cut him off. "I don't want to know her name, Max. Or anything else about her. I'll see you tomorrow morning."

She left the court without looking back.

When she'd accepted Bella's offer, she hadn't considered what Max might feel if he ever proposed and she told him she wanted nothing to do with him. She hadn't worried about wounding him, because it had seemed like just repayment for the way he'd made love to her and then kissed another woman the next morning.

But if she were honest with herself, she was every bit as much of a villain as Max. She was the one who'd refused to return his calls all those years ago. She was the one who hadn't allowed him to explain. She was the one who'd kept him from knowing his daughter. She could hardly blame him now for keeping secrets of his own.

Kristin wondered why she'd been so determined to cut Max off today, why she hadn't allowed him even to finish a sentence. She was fairly sure he'd been itching to explain away his girlfriend. Aching to ask for forgiveness. On the verge of declaring himself in love with her. She could have had the proposal his mother had been hoping would be the result of her machinations.

But Kristin no longer wanted to compete in the contest the duchess had devised. Love was just too dangerous a game to play. Because both she and Max were bound to be hurt by it.

Kristin gritted her teeth as she headed into the locker room. The moment she got to Blackthorne Abbey this afternoon, she was going to tell the duchess she wanted out.

19

Max was feeling rattled. He wasn't a jealous man. At least, he never had been in the past. Before last night, he would have said he didn't have a jealous bone in his body. But he'd gone nearly insane wondering what Kristin was doing with Steffan last night. He'd acted like a possessive fool when she'd shown up this morning.

Because he'd been afraid of losing her, he'd nearly proposed marriage. After what she'd done to him ten years ago. After all his vows to himself to watch his step. And despite having a brand-new girlfriend, about whom he'd completely forgotten.

His relationship with Veronica really was more about him wanting sex and conversation—and her wanting a powerful connection to a Benedict—than anything else. He hadn't broken up with her before he started sleeping with Kristin because, well, he hadn't expected what had happened between him and K to happen.

He'd gone to K's hotel room that first night on impulse, not knowing whether she would let him in or not.

Although, to be honest, he hadn't given her much choice in the matter.

No, that wasn't true. She was a trained agent. She could have stopped him at any time. She could have thrown him out if she hadn't wanted him there. But she had wanted him. She'd wanted him every bit as much as he'd wanted her.

He hadn't broken with up with Veronica in the week since he'd started having sex with K because the reporter was out of the country and he didn't want to do it by phone or text or email. He'd been taught better than that. Frankly, he hadn't expected to fall so deeply into… bed…with K.

Once again, he'd screwed up big-time. And once again, K hadn't given him a chance to explain. Which shouldn't have been a surprise, given her behavior ten years ago. Which didn't make it any less frustrating. Or make her less desirable.

Admit it. The woman gets to you.

Thank God Veronica was returning home today. He was picking her up at Heathrow this evening. He could break up with her then. Or not. Kristin wanted nothing to do with him. So why should he break up with Veronica? No reason. Except he no longer wanted to be with Veronica. He wanted Kristin. Whom he couldn't have.

Max realized he was thinking in circles. At least he had the whole afternoon free to figure it out.

During his shower in the locker room, he decided that this was a perfect day to go visit his mother. He'd been derelict in his promise to his siblings to investigate what her invitation to The Seasons was all about. He was more likely to get an honest answer from the duchess in person. And he could use the long drive from London to Blackthorne Abbey to think.

Max played "Boom Boom Pow" by the Black-Eyed Peas loud enough to rattle the dashboard as he raced his Porsche the whole way south to Blackthorne Abbey, but it didn't do much to drown out the memory of Kristin's body under his that morning. He could almost taste her lips. He could feel the heat of her. See the desire in her eyes.

"You're a fool, Max," he muttered to himself. "Get over her. You've got Veronica, who's crazy about you." *Or maybe crazy about the fact you're the Duchess of Blackthorne's son.* He wasn't really sure which, but at this point, he no longer cared. Veronica was the distraction he needed, the wedge he needed, to keep Kristin at bay. It was less than two weeks until their exhibition match. They'd be hanging around an additional two weeks while the matches were played leading up to the Wimbledon Championships.

Then K would leave and he could go back to living his life and forget about her.

Who are you kidding?

Max felt a pain behind his breastbone at the thought of a life without K. Funny, because he'd been living the past ten years just fine without her.

Have you been living just fine, Max? Think about it. No long-term relationships. No commitments. So, how great has life really been, Max?

They were uncomfortable questions to ask. And impossible to answer. Especially when the one woman he thought he might be able to love wanted nothing to do with him. Again.

Max was surprised at the rush of emotion he felt when he sighted the Abbey. He knew how privileged—how lucky—he was to have a home that had been lived in for centuries by his ancestors.

He could understand why his mother might have married his father for his money. Her family had been on the verge of losing their hereditary property for failure to pay taxes. They'd already been reduced to opening the Abbey to tourists. Even that additional income hadn't been enough for upkeep on the castle.

Now it was a showplace. The once-stagnant moat was filled with sparkling water. The extensive grounds were manicured and emerald green near the castle and growing gloriously wild in the acres beyond it. Blackthorne Abbey, which had been named by the first Duke of Blackthorne for the monks who'd once inhabited it, had been updated inside. The original stone walls of the castle, complete with turrets—towers raised above the castle wall to give a view of the valley below, and crenels—the gaps between the stonework at the top of the castle through which defenders would have fought, had been carefully preserved.

Max drove over the drawbridge and under the portcullis, a strong oak grille that had once protected the gate against attack, and then through another gateway to the middle bailey. Beyond this courtyard stood the stone keep itself, several stories high and large enough to house twenty knights and their retainers. The eight-foot-thick walls kept the Abbey cool inside but also moist. Even with modern air-conditioning, his mother fought a constant battle against mold.

The castle had provided endless possibilities for growing boys, home on holiday, to explore and play. Ancient shields adorned the walls, along with armor, swords and pikes. Oliver had always been lord of the manor. Max's two older brothers, Riley and Payne, had been Oliver's knights. As the youngest boy, Max had been relegated to playing a *villein*, a lowly peasant working on the lord's land, not to be confused with a *villain*, which was a bad guy. He usually had to be rescued by the lord and his knights.

When Lydia was little, she'd insisted on being a princess in the tower. Her role consisted of dressing in a child's faded blue silk dress—still encrusted with tiny pearls across the bodice—that she'd found in a trunk in the topmost tower and waiting for a knight to come and carry her away on a white horse.

Max had been the best rider among them, and willing to do the deed, but he never got to play a knight, so her fantasy was always left unfulfilled.

As Max parked in front of the keep, he realized he had only one happy memory of being at the Abbey with his mother and father. He had a picture in his childhood room at the Abbey of that perfect Christmas. He was standing beside his mother, as his family gathered around the tree showing off their presents and laughing, the fifth Christmas after Lydia was born. He would have been seven or eight. Everything before that—and after that—he'd wiped clean.

Because he knew Smythe would answer the door, and he wanted to see how the old man was doing, Max used the metal knocker in the shape of a lion's head, rather than walking right in.

Smythe's bushy white eyebrows rose to his missing hairline at the sight of Max, but he didn't verbally acknowledge his surprise at finding Max at the door. Instead, in good butler fashion, he simply said, "Welcome home, your lordship."

"I've come to see Mother," Max said as he stepped inside.

"The duchess is upstairs in the sitting room," the butler said as he closed the door behind Max.

"How are you, Smythe?"

"Tolerably well, milord."

As a boy, Max and his brothers had tried to ruffle Smythe, to get him to lose his stoic composure. They'd never succeeded. Max didn't even try now. "I can find my own way, Smythe," he said.

"Very well, my lord."

Max wondered at the worried look he saw in the butler's eyes an instant before he turned away. It was more sentiment than he could ever remember finding there. He wondered if the butler's concern had anything to do with his mother's strange invitation to The Seasons. If it did, he would find out in a few moments.

Max found the duchess sitting in a flower-patterned

brocade wing chair, one of two that faced a crackling fire in an oversize stone fireplace. The room was toasty warm. He noticed Emily sitting on the opposite side of the room at a table containing a chess board. A young girl sat across from Emily, apparently playing chess with her. Max thought the girl must be one of Emily's numerous poor relations.

He crossed directly to his mother and settled into the chair next to her with his back to Emily and her opponent. "Hello, Mother."

His mother put a hand to her mouth as though he'd scared the life out of her and made a gasping sound.

He chuckled. "You look like you just saw a ghost. It's only me."

"Oh, my goodness." Her eyes darted toward Emily and back to him. "What are you doing here?"

Max felt stung by her reaction. He started to rise as he said, "I can take myself out of here—"

She reached out and caught his arm. "Please, stay. I'm just—I'm so surprised to see you." And then, because he must have looked ready to bolt again, she said, "And I'm so glad to see you."

"Are you, Mother?" She wasn't acting like it. He thought she rather wished him to Hades.

"Yes, Max, I am glad," she said, her face a picture of distress. "It's just—"

He stood. "Look, I know when I'm not welcome."

When he stood, he heard the girl at the chessboard make a strangled sound. When he turned toward her, she stood so abruptly her chair fell over backward. She was gawking at him as though he had two heads and neither was human.

"Oh, my goodness!" Emily cried, as she rose to her feet, also staring at him.

When he turned back to his mother, he found her standing, her hand against her heart, taking laborious, shallow breaths.

The startled—fearful?—reactions of the three females raised gooseflesh on his arms. "What the hell is going on?" he said in a harsh voice.

"Dad?" the girl said.

Max whirled and looked behind him toward the doorway, expecting to find someone standing there. From the three females' anxious behavior, the girl's father posed some kind of threat.

The doorway was empty. The door, in fact, was closed.

He quickly turned back to his mother. She edged around the wing chair, holding onto the back of it for support.

"Max," she said, her voice slightly breathless. "There's someone I'd like you to meet."

Since there was only one person in the room Max didn't know, he turned back to the girl. While his back was turned, she'd crossed the room and was standing right in front of him. She peered up at him, her blue eyes wide. Her heart-shaped face was so pale a sprinkling of freckles stood out across her nose.

"Hello," he said. It wasn't a particularly pleasant

greeting because adrenaline was still flowing from his fight-or-flight response to the girl's missing father.

When the girl didn't speak, he turned back to his mother for direction.

She cleared her throat and said, "Max, this is your daughter, Felicity."

"Flick," the girl corrected.

Max's heart stopped for a second as he turned to stare at the girl, then began to gallop. His daughter? The girl was nine or ten, if she was a day. He turned back to his mother and said in a hard voice, "If this is a joke, Mother, it isn't funny. Where did you find this kid? What makes you think she's mine?"

"She's your daughter, Max," his mother said firmly.

He turned back to the girl and demanded, "Who's your mother, kid?"

The girl lifted her chin and said, "My name is Flick, not kid. My mother's name is Kristin Lassiter. And I don't care if you are my father. I don't like you!"

She punctuated that statement by sticking out her tongue, then raced from the room, slamming the door behind her.

"Don't worry, Your Grace," Emily said to his clearly agitated mother as she ran after the girl. "I'll take care of her. She's just had a shock. She'll be fine."

"*She's* had a shock?" Max said sarcastically. He still hadn't quite processed the fact that the girl's mother was Kristin Lassiter. Ten years ago he'd spent a single night with Kristin. They'd had sex one time. He rubbed a hand over his face. Apparently, once was enough.

Good God! Was it possible the girl was his daughter? He turned to his mother, jaw agape, shaking his head in disbelief.

"Close your mouth, Max. You're going to catch a lot of flies that way."

He snapped his mouth shut, then opened it to say, "What's going on, Mother? If that child is Kristin's daughter, what's she doing here with you? How do you know she's mine?"

"Let's sit down where we can talk comfortably," his mother said, crossing back around to take her seat in the wing chair.

Max paced the carpeted stone floor in front of her, too upset to sit. "I'm waiting, Mother."

"I knew how upset you were when Kristin left the tour and wouldn't return your calls."

He tried to remember whether he'd ever said anything to his mother about his friendship with Kristin. Anything at all. He remembered his mother asking once if he had any close friends on the tour. He might have mentioned Kristin. "How did you know about that? I mean, about Kristin not returning my calls?"

His mother sighed. "I hired someone, a private investigator, actually, to keep me informed about—"

He stopped pacing and turned on her. "You spied on me?"

"It wasn't spying, exactly, Max. You boys never returned my calls. I was worried. I needed some way to make sure you were all right. So I—"

"Hired someone to spy on me," he said angrily.

"That's one way to put it," she said. "My investigator turned up an interesting piece of information. Very soon after Kristin lost at Wimbledon, she sought out an ob-gyn. I thought she might have some female problem, that she might be sick. I thought it might give you some comfort to know that Kristin had turned you away because she didn't want you to worry about her being ill.

"It turned out she was pregnant. I couldn't be sure the baby was yours. My investigator took measures to confirm the fact with DNA. Felicity *is* your daughter."

"You've known all these years that I had a daughter, and you never said a word?"

"It wasn't my secret to tell."

Max wanted to get away, but there was no escaping the truth. He crossed to the mullioned windows draped with red velvet and looked out at the green hills that stretched as far as the eye could see. But his gaze was turned inward. Too many emotions were rioting through him. Anger was first and foremost. Somewhere, trying to get out, was awe. *I have a daughter.* And joy. *I have a daughter!*

A spunky daughter, he thought. A grin teased at the corners of his lips as he recalled Flick's response to his uncivil behavior. The grin was never born, killed by more anger.

He stalked back to his mother and confronted her. "What is Flick doing here, Mother? I've spent the past week in Kristin's company." *That was an understatement!* "And she never said a word about having a daughter. Much less that her daughter was staying with you."

He saw the panic flicker in his mother's eyes before she said, "I thought it was time you settled your differences with Kristin—and met your daughter. I simply arranged it so Kristin would play that exhibition match with you at Wimbledon."

"You what?" Max said.

"I wanted to help."

"Why didn't you just tell me I had a daughter?" he demanded.

"What would you have done?"

"What do you mean?"

"I have a better question," she said. "What do you plan to do now that you know about Felicity?"

"Do? About what?"

She made an exasperated sound. "Are you going to be a father to your daughter? Are you going to spend time with her?"

"Doing what?"

She made a frustrated sound in her throat.

"I have no idea what a father does," he said, exasperated now himself. "Except send his children away to school," he said bitterly. "What is it you expect me to do?"

"I'm sure Felicity could come up with a few ideas," his mother said. "She's a very bright child."

"She doesn't like me," Max said irritably.

"What do you expect? You talked down to her and insulted her mother."

Someone knocked at the door. Max had his mouth

open to say "Go away!" when the duchess called, "Come."

The door opened and Emily stepped inside. Felicity was right behind her. Emily urged Felicity forward. The girl took several more steps into the room, then looked back at Emily, who nodded.

Felicity faced Max and said, "I'm sorry I stuck out my tongue at you."

"And?" Emily coaxed.

Felicity made a face, then said, "I'm sorry I said I don't like you. But you were so malicious, what did you expect?"

Max was surprised by the apology. And offended by the word his child—apparently she *was* his child—had chosen to describe his behavior. "Malicious?"

"Yes," Felicity confirmed with the quick nod of a chin that was the spitting image of her mother's. Her blue eyes—eyes the same color as his—were liquid with tears. "That means you hurt me on purpose," the girl said. "It means you tried to be mean. And you were!"

Max felt his neck heating. It had been a long time since anyone had made him feel ashamed. "I owe you an apology," he said. "I never knew I had a daughter. I was a little…surprised. I took it out on you."

"I could see your disapprobation," she said seriously.

He was startled into laughter by her use of a word he'd only heard in stuffy conference rooms. But knowing she thought he *disapproved* of her was no laughing matter. He could see he'd hurt her feelings again. "I'm not laughing at you, Flick," he said, using the nickname she apparently preferred. "I'm simply delighted by your vocabulary."

She looked up at him earnestly, sighed and said, "It's the bane of my mother's existence."

He laughed again. "Your mom never was much of a student. She probably has to look everything up in the dictionary."

Flick smiled shyly and said, "I don't mean to confuse her, I just think it's fun using the new words I'm learning."

Max was over his shock enough to take a closer look at his daughter. Flick was tall for a nine-year-old, which she was if she'd been conceived the day before the Girls' Singles Championship match at Wimbledon ten years ago. She had his eyes and nose and his black hair. She had her mother's chin and cheekbones. And she was smart as a whip. Which she'd probably gotten from her grandmother.

"Your grandmother said you might have some ideas about things we could do together while you're here in England," he said.

Flick brightened. "Do you have any horses?"

Max shook his head. "No." She looked so crestfallen he said, "But we could go riding in Hyde Park. They have horses for rent there."

"Could I?" she said in an awed voice.

Max was delighted that his daughter wanted to ride. He'd been riding horseback since before he could walk and had spent a lot of hours on fast, sleek horses playing polo. Riding horseback was something he loved that he could share with his newly found daughter. He smiled and said, "I don't see why we couldn't go riding."

"I'll tell you why not," a sharp voice said behind him.

Max turned and found Kristin standing in the doorway like an avenging fury. Her anger wasn't addressed at him. It was aimed at his mother.

"How could you!" she said to the duchess. "You promised!"

The duchess laid a protective hand across her breast and said, "I'm so sorry, my dear. Max showed up without warning. There was nothing I could do."

Apparently, that was enough to excuse the duchess, because Kristin turned her wrath on Max. "You don't go near Flick without my permission!"

"Flick is my daughter," he replied in a quiet voice. "As I have belatedly found out. I have the right—"

"You have *no* rights," Kristin said, crossing to stand nose to nose with him, her voice low and furious. "She's *mine!*"

Max would never have questioned Kristin's right to make the decisions about Flick's life if she hadn't thrown down the gauntlet. But she was wrong about one thing. "Flick isn't just yours. She's *ours,*" he corrected. "I'm her father, as my mother has been at pains to point out. A fact I've barely had time to process. I believe I'm entitled—"

"Stay out of her life!" she hissed. "Stay away. Stay far away."

"Mom!" Flick cried. "Why are you so mad?"

Kristin turned away as though he no longer existed and enfolded her daughter in her arms. "I'm sorry, Flick. I wasn't expecting to find your father here."

"Dad says he's going to take me horseback riding," Flick said.

"I'm sorry, sweetheart. That isn't going to be possible."

"Why not?" both Flick and Max asked at the same time.

She left Flick and crossed to snarl at him under her breath, "Because I say so!"

Max felt a ball of anger growing inside him. Along with the fact he had a daughter, he was belatedly realizing that he'd been robbed of the chance of knowing Flick the first nine years of her life. Robbed. "How about we let the courts decide how much time I get to spend with my daughter."

He watched her face blanch at the threat.

"You wouldn't do that."

"Watch me."

She glared at him, but she said, "Fine. You win."

He raised a brow. She'd conceded without much of a fight. Without any fight at all. Which meant she already knew he'd get some sort of custody if he took her to court. Maybe *full* custody? Was that what she feared? That he wanted to take Flick away from her?

The thought hadn't occurred to him. It might have at some point, he conceded. But he'd spent enough time separated from his own parents to know that that was no life for a kid. "I just want to take my daughter riding in Hyde Park," he said. "You're welcome to come along."

Why had he said that? Kristin probably wouldn't come. But if she did, it was going to be an uncomfortable hour for both of them. He glanced at Flick, whose anxious glance shot from one parent to the other and back again. Damned uncomfortable, and not just for the two of them. For the *three* of them.

"Flick has never been on a horse," Kristin said.

"They have gentle mounts," he said. "And I'll be with her." He corrected himself, "We'll be with her."

"I don't know how to ride, either," she said.

"As I said, they have gentle mounts. I can teach you both. We'll walk the horses. You'll be safe as houses."

"Please, Mom?" Felicity said. "I've always wanted to go horseback riding, but you never let me."

So she'd appealed to a brand-new father. Smart girl, Max thought. He could see Kristin wavering and said, "I'd like to spend some time with Flick. We might as well do something she's always wanted to do."

"All right," Kristin said. "But we'll have to wait until after the exhibition match to—"

Max shook his head. "The match is too far off. Tomorrow's Saturday. We can go in the afternoon. After practice."

"How is Flick going to get to London?" Kristin said.

"You can take her back to London with you tonight. She can stay in your hotel room and come watch us practice tomorrow morning. I can drive both of you back here tomorrow after we go riding."

"In your Porsche?" she said skeptically.

"I've got a Range Rover," he said. "It's got plenty of room."

"Then I can go?" Flick asked her mother, bouncing on her toes, she was so excited.

"Yes, you can go," Kristin said.

Flick lurched the few steps to grab her mother around the waist and hug her.

Max barely had time to envy Kristin before Flick whirled and slammed her frail body against his. She grabbed him around the waist and hugged him tight. Before he could react, she'd pulled free and was running for the door.

"I've got to tell Smythe," she yelled over her shoulder. "He said you might take me horseback riding, Dad, if only I would ask."

Dad. Max marveled at the word and everything it involved. He had a child. Who'd been without a father for nine years. He only knew one thing for sure. He wanted to be a part of her life.

He turned to Kristin and said, "We need to talk." When he saw his mother opening her mouth to speak, he added, "Alone."

20

Kristin followed Max across the hall to the Blue Room like a condemned woman heading to the gallows. No fire burned in the blackened stone fireplace, and the high-ceilinged room—decorated in shades of blue, of course—was chilly. She wrapped her arms around herself, to quiet her trembling body, but she still felt cold inside and out.

This was her worst nightmare come to life. Max seemed determined to insinuate himself into Flick's life. She was going to be left to deal with the aftermath of tears and loneliness when he was gone. Maybe there was a way to convince him to keep his distance after their horseback ride tomorrow. Or perhaps not to take the ride at all.

Max walked to the tall windows, shoving aside the royal-blue damask curtains that concealed the view, to look outside. Kristin saw the morning sun was gone, replaced by gray skies and threatening rain clouds. She remained near the door, keeping a low Victorian sofa between them. Max must have driven here. She'd taken the train, which had gotten her here too late to stop him from meeting Flick.

When Max turned to her, he had his hands behind his back in a pose she'd seen used by his father, the billionaire financier. It was a pose that spoke of power and privilege. It was a pose meant to intimidate a lesser mortal.

You're invincible, Kristin. The words immediately played in her head, the way they had a lifetime ago when she'd found herself facing an opponent she feared. She squared her shoulders, loosened her grip on the back of the sofa and slid her weight to the balls of her feet, an instinctive fight-or-flight response to danger.

Max met her gaze and said through tight jaws, "I'm resisting the urge to choke the life out of you."

She wasn't sure how to reply to a statement like that. She thought it was hyperbole, but she wasn't entirely sure. *Hyperbole* was one of Flick's first big words. Kristin had looked it up but never used it. Until now. It meant *an extravagant exaggeration.* If that was the case, there was no need to respond—or to run. So she held her tongue.

His eyes never left hers. She saw murder in them.

Her heart began to race, speeding adrenaline into her veins. He was angrier than she'd thought. Dangerously angry. She understood why he'd linked his powerful hands behind his back. She remained poised to flee.

"A week past, I found out how little you trusted me ten years ago," he said. "Today I found out how fully you betrayed my trust in you."

Kristin felt her cheeks heating with shame. It was an awful condemnation of what she'd done—keeping him from his daughter. And an accurate one.

"How could you not tell me I had a daughter? How could you keep her existence a secret from me all these years?"

The agonized accusations stung. What she'd done had seemed perfectly logical at the time. In hindsight, and fully aware now of the false brush with which she'd tarred Max's character, she could understand why he judged her actions so harshly.

But she didn't think she'd been wrong. "Would you have wanted to be a father at eighteen?" she demanded. "I can tell you, Max, it wasn't easy being a mother at sixteen. You don't go to parties. You don't travel the world. You have someone making demands on your time every single moment of every day and all through the night. You have to think of someone else first and foremost and of yourself a long way after that."

She crossed around the sofa, stepping into the space he'd claimed as his own. "Be honest, Max. Would you have been ready for that kind of responsibility at eighteen?"

"We'll never know now, will we?" he raged.

"Think back, Max. Where did you go after Wimbledon? What did you do?"

She watched his forehead furrow. And waited for him to remember.

"Bloody hell. That's not fair, K."

"What did you do, Max?" she persisted.

"After a year on the pro tour, I tried sailing around Cape Horn alone in a too-small craft, to prove it could be done," he said quietly.

"Your sailboat sank in a storm, Max. You were missing for eighteen hours after you radioed to say your mast had snapped and your boat was going down. Before you left, you told the press you weren't taking a life preserver, because you'd rather drown than get eaten by sharks if you ran into trouble. You were given up for lost, presumed dead."

The story of Max's sail around Cape Horn, on the extreme southern tip of Chile, famous for its monstrous waves, terrifying winds and frigid temperatures, hadn't made the national news. But her father was a sailor when he could find time for it, and he'd heard scuttlebutt at his yacht club about Max's adventure—and its apparently tragic ending.

She remembered how she'd mourned a love that had died before it was really born. How she'd grieved for a man who'd betrayed her. "Then I heard about you on the BBC news channel, that you were alive and well. They said you laughed away the danger. As though it had all been a lark."

"I had an inflatable raft on board," he said sullenly. "I was wearing protective clothing against the cold. I was fine."

"You could have floated around in that ocean until you died of thirst. Or been thrown out of that flimsy raft by a monster wave and eaten by sharks or drowned. You were only rescued by the grace of God," she said.

"You've always been a risk-taker, Max. Look at what you're doing with your life now. You're a *spy,* for heaven's sake."

"It's a job, Princess, nothing more or less."

"It's a *risky* job, Max. I don't want Flick to start loving you if you aren't going to be there for her because you're dead."

"What about you?" he countered. "You're an FBI agent. You've shot at the bad guys, and they've shot back. Doesn't that make you as much of a risk-taker—maybe even more of one—as I am?"

Kristin realized she hadn't thought through her argument before she'd started it. "Maybe that's true," she conceded. "But most FBI agents never draw their weapons during an entire career."

"Most spies don't get caught and killed, either."

"All right, Max, I wasn't going to go there, but let's get to it. The real reason I don't want you involved in Flick's life is because I don't think you'll stick around for the long haul. Having a child is a novelty to you right now, but I wasn't kidding when I said it's a 24/7, 365 days a year job. And it doesn't end when she finishes high school or graduates college."

"I know that," he said. "I had parents."

"Forgive me for saying so, but not good ones."

"Your father wasn't a paragon, either," Max retorted. "And your mother abandoned you."

She met his gaze and saw remorse in his eyes for pointing it out, though he didn't apologize. She'd more than once complained to Max about her father's heartless behavior and his ruthless teaching tactics. "Harry has been a wonderful grandfather. A better grandfather than he was a father," Kristin said. "He's been a steady rock in Flick's life, someone besides me she could always count on."

"And I'm what, sand under her feet?" Max asked.

She could hear the resentment in his voice. She was less willing to believe the hurt she heard, as well. She continued inexorably, "I don't want Flick to end up pining for a father who's never there."

"I can't very well be there all the time if we live on different continents," he snapped.

"My point exactly."

"What is it you expect me to do?"

"Stay out of her life. Make some excuse not to take her horseback riding tomorrow."

"No."

"Just no?"

"You may think it doesn't mean anything to me to know I have a daughter who's lived without a father since birth. You're wrong. I never asked to have a child. Given a choice, I'm not sure I would ever have had any children."

"Then why—"

"Shut up, K, and let me explain. I never wanted to be a parent because I know firsthand how much a child can miss a parent who isn't there. I never wanted to do that to a child of mine. Thanks to you, I've committed that sin in spades. That ends now. I'm not going to spend another day separated from my daughter."

"Max, you can't—"

"Marry me, Princess."

Kristin might have laughed, except she couldn't get enough air into her lungs to make any sound at all. He looked as shocked by what he'd said as she felt hearing his abrupt proposal.

"It's not a bad solution to the problem," Max said when she remained silent. "We were friends once. We can be again. That's more than most couples can say."

We were lovers, too, Max, she thought. *Does that mean love is off the table?*

"What about your girlfriend?"

He avoided the question. "Are you saying yes?"

It occurred to her that she had the proposal his mother had been hoping for. But now that she had it, she wasn't sure she wanted it.

"What if I say no?" she said.

"I wouldn't do that if I were you."

She heard the threat in his voice and saw it in his ice-blue eyes. "I'm not really being given a choice, am I, Max?"

"No, K. You're not."

"I'd want a prenup."

Max snorted. "There's nothing you have that I want, Princess."

"What I'd want is financial security for Flick if you walk away."

"I'm not going anywhere," Max said with finality.

Kristin wasn't so sure.

"I'll have my lawyer put together a prenup for you to

look at on Monday. We can be married as soon as your lawyer approves it."

Kristin felt a frisson of fear race down her spine. Why was Max in such a hurry? "What's the rush?"

"My home is here in England. I want us married so you and Flick can stay here from now on."

"No, Max. My job is in the States." If she still had a job. There had been no word from SIRT.

"There's no need for you to work once we're married."

"What if I want to work?"

"You're being ridiculous, K. You just got through telling me your job is dangerous. In fact, you may not even have a job to go back to when you get home. What's the big deal?"

"I don't like being manipulated, Max. That's the big deal. And I don't want to be dependent on you." Which meant, she supposed, that she didn't think a marriage between them was going to have much chance of succeeding.

She added another argument against marrying Max and staying in England. "Flick won't want to be separated from her grandfather. And Harry needs me right now."

"That problem has been taken care of. I've already made arrangements for Harry to be transported here. He should be arriving early tomorrow morning."

She was stunned at how quickly he'd acted to get her father to London. Flick would be over the moon. She wondered what he'd said to Harry to get him to agree to come. Most likely, he hadn't asked. He hadn't persuaded. He'd simply issued orders and expected them to be obeyed. Like he was doing now.

"From what you've said, it's doubtful Harry's going to be going back to work as a tennis coach anytime soon," Max said. "I'll be glad to make arrangements for him to live somewhere close to us."

It was unfortunate Max was so rich. Money could solve so many problems.

"What if Harry won't agree to stay?" she argued.

"From what you've said, he won't want to be separated from Flick. If Flick is living here, Harry will stay."

He was probably right. Damn it.

"Then it's all settled," he said.

"I haven't said yes."

"But you will."

The smugness of his smile caused her to blurt, "My answer is no."

The smile disappeared. "You don't have any choice about this, K."

"You're wrong, Max."

"All right, spill it. What's your real objection to my suggestion?"

Kristin's heart ached. It had since Max had first proposed this arranged, loveless marriage. She had nothing to lose by telling him how she felt. "I want to care for the man I marry, Max. I want to love him, and I want him to love me and my daughter. You know nothing about the woman I am now. You know nothing about our daughter. You've proposed marriage as an easy solution to a difficult problem. Marriage isn't easy, Max. No more than parenting is easy. You're just not a good risk."

She turned and headed for the door. When she got there she turned and said, "I refuse your generous proposal, Max. I'd rather figure out some other way for Flick to see her father, if you insist on becoming a part of her life.

"I'd hoped to spare her the pain of having a father who might abandon her if something—or someone—more exciting came along. Since that isn't possible, I'm not going to compound the problem by marrying you."

As she closed the door quietly behind her, Kristin wondered if she'd done the right thing. She'd loved Max once upon a time. That love had been reborn during the past week. Now she knew he'd had feelings for her then, which she believed had been growing over the past week.

But she hadn't trusted him then, not after what she'd seen the next morning. And after hearing about Veronica, she still didn't trust him.

Oh, he'd said all the right things about wanting to be a good father. She just couldn't be sure he meant them. And agreeing to a marriage of convenience was asking for heartache. She would rather not reach for a nebulous happy ending at all, than endure the pain of a fairy-tale ending that never came true.

21

The moment Bella saw Kristin's face, she knew things had not gone well between Kristin and her son.

"Where's Flick?" the agitated young woman asked as she entered the sitting room and found her daughter missing.

"I sent her to the kitchen with Emily to ask Cook for some scones with clotted cream." Bella gestured toward the chair beside her and said, "Come here, my dear, and tell me what happened with Max."

"He proposed," she said flatly. "I refused."

"I feared as much," Bella said. "The rubies will still be yours when—"

"Keep them. I'd hate myself if I took them." Instead of sitting, Kristin headed straight to the fireplace. She reached her hands out, seeking heat from the fiery coals.

"Before you refuse the rubies, I wish you'd let me tell you a little bit more about them." When Kristin didn't object, she said, "The air is chilly in here. There's a knitted quilt on the back of the chair beside me. Why don't you sit down and get comfortable?"

For a moment Bella thought Kristin was too upset to sit, but the agitated young woman grabbed the colorful quilt and dropped into the chair, spreading it over her lap before pulling it all the way up to her neck.

"I've already told you the Blackthorne Rubies—the diamond and ruby necklace, pendant earrings, bracelet and ruby ring—were given to Philip Wharton, the first Duke of Blackthorne, as a gift from Henry II for saving his life. When Philip fought for the young king, he earned himself a bride as a prize of war—along with the dukedom.

"Unfortunately, as the Blackthorne family fortunes rose and fell, the rubies were lost, a piece at a time."

"I had no idea," Kristin said. She frowned and added, "If that's true, how is it you have all of them now?"

"Ah. That is a story worth telling. Bull found them, every one. He tracked down their current owners and made each of them an offer they couldn't refuse."

"How on earth did he find them all?" Kristin asked. "I mean, if they were lost over time."

"The recovery of the jewels is a fascinating story. But first, you need to know how the Blackthorne Rubies were lost."

"Lost? As in, misplaced?" Kristin asked.

Bella chuckled. "Nothing so simple as that. Each piece has a history of its own. For instance, the pendant earrings were used during the French Revolution to buy the freedom of a French aristocrat, a beautiful woman condemned to the guillotine. One of my Blackthorne ancestors had fallen in love with her. He rescued her. And married her. I showed Flick a painting of her in the gallery. Flick pointed out that she looks like me."

"That sounds romantic."

"It is. It was," Bella said. "It would be nice if all the rubies had been lost for such noble causes."

"They weren't?" Kristin said.

"The ruby-and-diamond necklace was used to pay a gambling debt during the Regency period, around 1812, I think. The duke wagered the rubies on a horse race. And lost."

Kristin made a clucking sound. "It seems criminal to wager something with so much family history on something so risky."

"Especially when the rubies weren't his to wager," Bella said. "The duke had already promised them to another creditor for another debt."

"Couldn't his gambling debt have been paid some other way?"

Bella shook her head. "The American who made the wager with the duke insisted on having the necklace. It seemed there was bad blood between the two men. The duke gave up the rubies rather than taking a chance on being shot and killed in a duel. The American took the rubies—and the duke's fiancée, with whom he'd fallen in love—and disappeared."

"That's a love story, too," Kristin pointed out.

When Bella raised a questioning brow, Kristin explained, "The American fell in love with the duke's fiancée."

"Yes, he did, didn't he?" Bella said. "When the duke later tried to retrieve the necklace, the gambler had disappeared. It seemed he'd lied about who he really was."

"He was never found?" Kristin asked.

"Never," Bella said. "The necklace was never recovered."

"How sad," Kristin murmured.

"The bracelet and ring were stolen by a Southern privateer during the American Civil War," Bella said. "They were in the possession of the Duke of Blackthorne, who was traveling to meet his affianced bride, the daughter of a wealthy munitions manufacturer in Boston."

"The duke was going to marry an American? Not someone with a title?"

"That was the plan. Of course, without the jewels, the duke was essentially penniless. He didn't want to come to his bride without the rubies he'd intended as a bride gift, so he set out to find them. Of course, he found a new love along the way. He married a Southern bride, a woman from Texas, instead."

"So the rubies led to love again," Kristin said. "Did the duke ever recover the stolen jewels?"

Bella shook her head. "An English merchant's daughter showed up at a steeplechase in London wearing them, along with an atrocious hat."

Kristin laughed.

"It's good to see you smiling again," Bella said. "So

you see, the Blackthorne Rubies seem to inspire love, or perhaps, the courage to find love, in their owner. Which is why I wanted you—want you—to have them. I thought they might work their magic on you and Max."

Kristin sobered. "Max only proposed as a way of getting custody of Flick."

"Yes, of course he did. A marriage is expedient and convenient. When you sort out what went wrong between you in the past, the situation between the two of you could improve markedly. Is there any hope you might reconsider?"

The distraught young woman stood, dropping the quilt on the chair as she once more sought out the fire, reaching for the warmth that seemed to have deserted her. "We've already discussed what happened between us ten years ago. As you suspected, it was a simple misunderstanding. I was mistaken in what I thought I saw. It's all water under the bridge."

"Then there's no reason why the two of you can't start over," Bella said.

Tears brimmed in the young woman's eyes. "There's nothing left between us on which to build a relationship," she said simply.

"Nothing? You have a daughter together. What about Felicity?"

Bella saw an anguished look flicker across Kristin's face before the young woman said, "I'm not going to allow Flick to end up in a tug-of-war between us. It's over."

"Does this mean you're not going to play the exhibition match with Max?" Bella asked.

Kristin shook her head. "I'll stay for the match and perhaps for the tournament as well, to see old friends. Then I'm heading home. With Flick. And my father. Max has arranged for him to come here."

Bella raised a brow. If Max had exerted himself so far as to make that sort of arrangement for Harry Lassiter, there was far more going on between the two young people than Kristin was admitting.

"I'm sorry to hear you've refused Max," Bella said. "I will, of course, be taking care of all your expenses, as I promised."

Kristin met her gaze and said, "I'll pay you back. Every penny."

Bella had seen how Max looked at the mother of his child. And how desolate Kristin seemed at the thought of a life without Bella's youngest son. Bella was more and more certain this woman belonged with Max. Her son had handled things badly. It hadn't helped that he'd had that abrupt introduction to Felicity. She should have planned that better. "I presume you and Max have worked out some sort of visitation schedule."

"We didn't get that far," Kristin admitted.

"Don't you think that might be a good idea?"

"I'm not sure I want Max visiting Flick."

"That doesn't sound fair to Felicity," Bella said, careful not to mention how very unfair it also seemed to her son. "Doesn't she deserve a father?"

"It would be worse if she had a father who only showed up half the time. Or never showed up at all."

Bella frowned. "You believe Max would be that kind of father?"

"I've always thought so."

"Based on what, may I ask?" Bella said, indignant on her son's behalf.

"Based on how badly he treated me ten years ago."

Bella met Kristin's troubled gaze and said, "I thought you said you were mistaken about Max's behavior in the past. Doesn't he deserve a chance to prove what kind of father he would be?"

"Not if it means Flick gets hurt."

"Forgive me if I'm wrong, but it appears you're the one who fears getting hurt if Max stays a part of your life," Bella said quietly.

"So what if I am?" Kristin retorted. "No one wants to be hurt a second time by the same person."

"If you and Max have unfinished business, perhaps you should take advantage of the time you have together here in London to work it out," Bella said.

Kristin reached up to tuck a stray curl that had slipped from her ponytail back behind her ear. "Flick and I need to leave if we're going to catch the next train back to London. I should go pack a bag for her."

"You know where her room is. If you don't mind spending the night here at the Abbey, I can arrange a ride into London for you tomorrow morning so you can meet your father at the airport."

"I don't want to spend any more time in Max's company than I have to."

"Max is leaving." She'd make sure he did, after she gave him a good talking-to. "I'd enjoy your company if you'd like to stay."

Kristin sighed. "I didn't bring anything with me to wear. I don't even have a toothbrush."

"That's no problem," Bella said. "Check with the housekeeper. Mrs. Tennyson can get you anything you need. And I'm sure Emily will have something you can wear."

"Thank you. It's been a long day. I'd like to spend time with Flick."

"I'm so glad you're staying," Bella said. "Dinner is at seven."

"I think I'll find Flick and let her know I'll be here overnight," Kristin said.

Bella waited only until Kristin had left the room before she rose and headed across the hall, hoping Max hadn't yet left the Abbey. She found him slumped in a comfortable overstuffed chair, his stocking feet up on a petit-pointed footstool. As she crossed to him, he clumsily rose and shoved his feet back into his tasseled leather shoes.

"Mother. What brings you here?"

"I just spoke with Kristin," she said. "Sit down, Max. I'll join you," she said, settling on the less comfortable Victorian sofa across from him.

He dropped back into the chair but kept his shoes on. His feet stayed on the floor. "Kristin doesn't want anything to do with me," he announced. "The three of us are still going horseback riding, but she wants me to stay away from Flick in the future."

"What did you say to that?" Bella asked.

"I told her I knew what it felt like to want a parent who isn't there," Max said. "And I wasn't about to do that to my daughter."

She wondered if Max knew how it pierced her heart to hear about his pain. He must know. It seemed the gloves had come off. She knew the example she and Bull had set for her children had left lasting scars. It seemed Max's wounds were still seeping. It made her more determined than ever to do what she could to keep him from living unhappily ever after.

She was convinced that Max cared for the mother of his child. She'd done her best to get Kristin here to England so the two of them could fall in love again. But her plan had been ill-considered.

Or maybe not. Maybe she'd challenged the wrong person to make peace with the other.

"Kristin told me you proposed," Bella said. "And that she refused you."

"Being married makes the most sense," he said. "It's the most logical solution to the problem of how I can be a part of Flick's life."

"Did you discuss whether it was going to be a real marriage?" Bella asked. "I mean, were you each going to be allowed to carry on your separate affairs—romantic affairs, that is—as usual?"

He snorted. "I've had enough experience with what

happens when one party isn't faithful to the other to know fidelity is important in a marriage."

Another shot, right to the heart. She met his gaze and realized he was fully aware of the verbal slap he'd taken at her. And didn't care if she was injured by it.

No, that wasn't precisely true. She saw a flush in his cheeks that revealed he wasn't as nonchalant about his ruthless condemnation of her as he wanted her to believe. She didn't have time to pretend anymore that she hadn't caused damage to her children. Max had suffered, and he blamed her for it.

All she could do now was try to make amends.

The best way to do that was by giving Max the nudge he needed to woo Kristin. He'd fallen in love with her once before. As far as Bella had been able to determine, it was the first—and last—time he'd given his heart to a woman. It seemed he'd been hurt, or felt betrayed, as badly all those years ago as Kristin had. Bella could only hope it wasn't too late for him to find his way back to loving her again.

"Kristin told me the two of you discussed the misunderstanding that separated you."

He cocked his head, apparently surprised that she'd spoken to Kristin. Or perhaps that Kristin had been so frank with her.

"We did."

"Do you still love her?"

"Still?" he said. "Did I ever?"

Bella ignored his attempt at denial and said, "If you want her, why don't you go after her? Woo her. Pursue her. Convince her you'd make a good husband as well as a good father."

He scoffed. "Why should I?"

"I've never known you to take no for an answer when no wasn't the answer you wanted," Bella persisted. "Do you want to be a part of your daughter's life, or not? Because without Kristin's approval, it's going to be a nasty uphill battle."

"When you put it that way, wooing her makes sense," Max mused. "But K's no dummy. If I start making calf's eyes at her now, she's going to suspect my motives."

"So what if she does? Convince her you care. Convince her you'll take care of her *and* Flick. That you want to be a father *and* a husband."

His lip curled in a sneer. "What makes you think I want to be a husband? That I'm willing to give my heart to any woman, let alone one who's crushed it before?"

Bella's heart ached for her son. Her hands were trembling with fatigue. But she couldn't rest until she'd convinced Max to give love one more try.

"I've never spoken about the mistakes I made that caused your father to leave me," she began.

Max lurched to his feet. "I don't want to know—"

"I'm not going to do so now," she continued over his interruption. She met his anxious gaze and said, "I think it's important for you to know that the happiest days of my life were the ones I spent loving Bull—and being loved by him. You don't have to make the mistakes we made. You and Kristin can have a long, loving life together."

"Why are you so determined to see us together?" he demanded.

"I only want to see you happy, Max." *Before I die.*

"I was a lot happier before I found out my daughter has lived the first nine years of her life without a father. Something you could have remedied, if you'd only taken the time to speak."

"I've told you why I made the choice I did. There's no going back, Max. We can only move forward. Are you going to let Kristin take Flick and walk out of your life?"

"When you put it that way, Mother, the answer seems obvious." He glanced at his watch, then smirked. "Time to go. I have to pick up my girlfriend at Heathrow."

Bella sat where she was until after Max had left the room. She wondered if her arguments had held any sway at all with him. A girlfriend? Oh, yes, the reporter from the *Times*. Their relationship wasn't serious. Yet. Kristin had arrived in England in the nick of time. She had the added enticement of being the mother of Max's child.

Bella was simply going to have to wait and see if Max picked up the gauntlet she'd thrown down.

22

was halfway back to London, fighting to see road in the pouring rain, glad he was in his road-ging Porsche, when he realized he hadn't questioned mother about her invitation to The Seasons. She'd cted him with the suggestion he ought to pursue n in earnest.

He still couldn't quite believe he'd offered to marry K. ce the words were out of his mouth, it had seemed like illiant solution to their problem. He'd been shocked n she refused him. And, if he were honest, a little ted. Or perhaps mortified was a better description ow he was feeling. It was humbling to be rejected of hand.

Vith an arrogance that arose from being born into althy and titled family, he'd believed any woman uld consider herself lucky to get a catch like him. His h alone was a narcotic to most women, and thanks two attractive parents, he'd been born with good looks. His mother had pointed out exactly how unthinking his proposal had been.

Kristin had wanted more than an easy solution to a custody dilemma. She'd wanted love.

He'd figured sex and fidelity and friendship, and the chance to be parents to Flick, would make a pretty good marriage. Love had never crossed his mind.

I want to care for the man I marry. I want to love him and I want him to love me and my daughter.

Loving Flick was no problem. Loving Kristin was another matter altogether. Max shook his head. Enduring love was a fairy tale. Ten years ago, he'd enjoyed one night of love before love had ended. Recently, his fairy tale had lasted an entire week. He snickered. At this rate, lifelong happiness was an unattainable dream.

Max thought back to the night he and K had created their daughter. Who would have thought a child so precious—and precocious—could have come from that awkward encounter?

He remembered lying beside K in the hotel room she'd booked in London while on the tour and thinking how beautiful her face was in the moonlight. He could still hear her voice in his ear, soft and hesitant, as she lay naked in his embrace for the first time.

"I've never felt this way about anyone before, Max. And what you're doing to me feels so good it hurts."

"Is this where it hurts?" he'd asked, brushing his knuckles across her breast near her heart. "Shall I kiss it better?" He'd leaned down and kissed the slope of her ivory breast, then turned his head to listen to her racing heartbeat. He'd felt so much love for her, he'd thought his chest might burst from the force of it.

He didn't know exactly when friendship had turned to love. He'd simply realized one day that the sex he had with other women was simply that—sex. The relationship he had with K was something special. She understood him. She liked him. She tolerated his moods. She made him feel good about himself. She listened to him and commiserated with him. She cared. She made him feel loved—and lovable, something he'd doubted all his life.

He'd raised his head so he could look into her eyes and said, "I like you, too, Princess. A lot." He'd meant to say *love*. But the word had stuck on his tongue. It was too scary to be that vulnerable. What if she didn't love him back? After all, she hadn't admitted to loving him, just to loving the time she spent with him.

He'd kept his feelings close to his vest all his life. Which made it all the more difficult to speak of them when it meant the most. He only knew he wanted to hold her and love her. And be loved by her.

He'd watched the tears well in her eyes as she smiled up at him and said, "Oh, Max. I'm so glad—"

He'd kissed her because his throat had swollen closed and it was no longer possible to profess his love in words. He took possession of her mouth, sliding his tongue inside. He felt a surge of arousal when she returned the favor with enthusiasm.

He twined two fistfuls of her long blond curls in his hands and arched her head back on the pillow so he could kiss her throat. Her hands roamed his back, tracing his shoulder blades, the crease down the center of his back, the rise of his buttocks, then returned to settle around his neck, playing in the hair at his nape.

"Max," she whispered, kissing his ear. "Max. I feel so much. It feels so good."

Her words, and the whispery kisses, created an inferno of desire, a fire that couldn't be quenched with mere kisses or touches. He needed to be inside her. Couldn't wait another moment to be inside her, to be joined with her as close as two souls could possibly be.

He released her hair and rose to his knees. He caught her legs behind her thighs, spreading them wide around his own thighs as he yanked her farther down the bed toward him.

"Max?"

He heard the hesitation in her voice, but he was too focused on his great need to consider what it might mean. She offered no resistance as he slid his hands beneath her and lifted her. He was almost mindless with desire when he thrust himself inside her.

Almost mindless. From a deep erotic well he heard her cry, "Max! I'm—" He cut off her protest with a deep kiss.

Max checked the speedometer in his Porsche and saw it had sneaked up to a hundred and fifty-five. Even if he translated kilometers into miles, ninety-five was too fast. He brushed a hand across a forehead that was dotted with sweat from remembering what he'd done. Stupid, thoughtless teenage boy.

In hindsight he knew Kristin had been nowhere near

ready to be entered. At the time, he'd only been aware of her willingness. And her great desire to please him.

And she had pleased him greatly. She'd been so tight. Once he was inside her, there had been blood to lubricate the way. His satisfaction had been immense. He'd heard her making noise, but he was too far gone—his eyes closed and his head thrown back—to identify the sounds.

He'd quickly climaxed. Faster than he'd wanted. A brash kid who couldn't control himself.

Max focused on the narrow, curving road in front of him when what he wanted to do was close his eyes. He would give a great deal to erase the image that rose in his mind's eye of K's face when he'd looked down at her after he'd taken his pleasure.

He would never forget the tear tracks that had stained her cheeks. Or the first sound she'd made. That whimper of pain had created a knot in his gut.

Too late he'd been full of concern for her. But the damage had been done. He'd seen the blood on the sheets and frantically asked, "What's wrong? What happened?"

"I've never done this before," she said, her eyes lowered in embarrassment. "You hurt me."

He'd been too chagrined to ask anything else. Too humiliated even to apologize. He'd just wanted to get away.

He remembered rising from the bed and crossing into the bathroom. He'd grabbed a towel and wiped the blood off himself, then grabbed a towel for Kristin. He'd decided a warm washcloth was a good idea and remembered it had taken forever for the water to get hot.

When he'd returned to the bedroom, she was sitting hunched over in bed with her knees pulled to her chest and the covers pulled up all the way up to her neck.

He'd sat down beside her and met her shy gaze and said, "Let's get you cleaned up, Princess."

She'd taken the warm washcloth from him and slid it under the covers. She'd closed her eyes and he'd seen the relief on her face as the warm cloth soothed the pain he'd caused. He'd handed her the towel next, and she'd slid that under the covers, too. He'd watched her lift her bottom and slide it under her. The washcloth never came back out, and he presumed she'd left it where it would do the most good.

"I'm sorry, baby," he'd said, tucking handfuls of curls behind both her ears so he could see her face better. "I didn't mean to hurt you."

"I know," she said. "I should have warned you sooner that I hadn't done this before."

"Yeah," he mumbled. "About that..."

"It's all right, Max," she said, reaching out a hand to touch his cheek. "I wanted you to be the first."

Max swiped at his blurry eyes and grabbed the wheel with both hands when the Porsche slid on the dirt at the side of the road. He'd never thought about birth control, because the girls he had sex with took care of that sort of thing. He'd only used condoms when the girl suggested it.

The possibility that he'd gotten K pregnant had been

no part of his thoughts when he'd put his hand over hers and said, "I'm sorry, Princess."

"Don't be sorry," she'd said. "I'm not."

He hadn't believed her. The tears and the blood and the winces when she'd slid that washcloth under the sheet made a liar out of her. But he'd asked, "Really? Are you sure you're okay?"

"I'm sure. You should go. I need to get some sleep before my match tomorrow. Besides, my dad's liable to check on me before he goes to bed. I don't want him to find you here."

"Lord, no!" he'd said, jumping up from the bed. He'd looked down at her and felt a wave of love wash over him. She'd looked so beautiful. And vulnerable. He'd vowed never, ever to hurt her again.

Of course, he was the one who'd ended up getting hurt. Her tender feelings hadn't lasted beyond a single night. If she'd really loved him, if she'd really cared, she should have trusted him. She should have given him a chance to explain that kiss he'd given Elena. She shouldn't have run away.

In hindsight, he should have persisted until she let him explain. He should have followed up to make sure she wasn't pregnant. He'd assumed she must be on the pill, since she hadn't said a word about protection. Most of the girls on the tour were, because they wanted to control their periods. It was a pretty big assumption, he realized now.

It wasn't just his experience with Kristin that had convinced him love was fleeting. His parents had supposedly been in love. Not at first, of course. He knew about their tumultuous courtship and their even more turbulent marriage. But there wouldn't have been so much hate between them after they'd separated if there hadn't been so much love between them somewhere along the way.

So when Kristin had said this afternoon that she wanted love as a prerequisite to marriage, he was naturally a little sour on the subject.

It was fortunate he and Kristin had to work together both on court and off. Otherwise, he was sure she would have packed up their daughter and headed back to the States. He didn't have much time to bond with his daughter, so he planned to make good use of it.

It occurred to him that he might make equal use of the time to convince K that she ought to marry him—love be damned. He still believed living together was the easiest way to co-parent Flick.

The attraction he'd always felt to K was still there. He loved making love to her. He loved talking to her. He loved the way she listened to him. He mentally compared his one-week relationship with K with what he'd felt over the past month with Veronica. It wasn't a comfortable comparison to make. He and K had a history together that he thought might be coloring his feelings toward her—making them brighter, more sensual.

It was more than a little disconcerting to think he'd completely forgotten about Veronica when he'd proposed to K a couple of hours ago. He shuddered to imagine how he would have explained his sudden engagement when he picked up the girl he'd been dating for the past month at Heathrow.

So was he going to stick with Veronica? Or pursue K?

He wasn't in love with Veronica, but he was halfway to being there with K. He hadn't allowed himself to fall for her further than that. He tried to imagine what marriage to K might be like. And remembered all the problems that had to be solved before they could even think of heading to the altar.

Where would they live? Should K keep her job? Was there something else she could do in England? Would Harry be willing to stay in England if they ended up living here? If he asked Kristin to quit her job, should he keep spying for living?

His job wasn't always dangerous, but at least once in the past he'd been a breath away from being shot dead. He'd talked his way out of it, but he knew he was lucky to be alive.

Max rotated his shoulders against the Porsche seat to ease the tension gathering there. All he knew for sure was that he wanted his daughter to become a part of his life. Getting along with K was important to that result. He wasn't sure himself whether he could—or even wanted to—fall in love with her again.

At least he had horseback riding in Hyde Park with Flick to look forward to tomorrow. It felt good to be able to do one thing for his child that her mother hadn't already done. He wondered for a moment why K hadn't wanted Flick to go riding. There were hazards, but it was a great sport. He'd have to ask her. If they were going to be parenting together, he needed to know what K was thinking.

Parenting together. The idea was mind-boggling. He tried to imagine the response he would get when he told his brothers and sister that he was a father. He grinned when he envisioned Lydia's smile and lilting laughter. And grimaced when he thought of what snide comment Oliver might make. He raised a rueful brow when he imagined Payne and Riley's joking ripostes.

In the end, he didn't contact any of them, because he knew they'd all have questions for which he had no answers. It would be better to wait until after he'd resolved his differences with K. The tennis court would be a good place to talk with her. Because he didn't want to discuss custody around Flick.

It dawned on him that neither Kristin nor Flick were likely to have brought proper riding attire with them. He would have to do something about that.

Max's cell phone rang and when he answered it, Veronica was on the line.

"I'm back, Max."

"I thought you were getting home later tonight," he said. "Where are you?"

"I managed to get a ride back on someone's private jet."

He wondered who the someone was, but he didn't ask. "I was visiting at the Abbey and I'm still an hour from the airport. You might want to catch a cab to your place. I can meet you there."

"I'm not going home. I've gotten an invitation to a reception at the British Embassy. I'm going shopping at Harrods and then straight to the party."

Max realized he felt relieved. He wasn't going to have to do any explaining tonight. He would have the evening free to do a lot of soul-searching. He wondered if he was going to lose Veronica to another man. Maybe he'd already lost her. "Who gave you the ride home, Veronica?"

She laughed. "Oh, Max, you aren't jealous, are you?"

"Not at all. Just curious." And he wasn't, he realized.

"The British ambassador to the UAE has a personal jet. He offered to bring me home."

"Nice guy, is he?" Max said.

"Very nice. I'll probably be up late tonight. I'm sorry I won't get to see you practice tomorrow morning. We can catch up later in the day."

"I've already made plans for tomorrow afternoon."

"Plans that include me?" she said coyly.

He was still stinging from K's rejection of him. And a little irked with Veronica, if the truth were known. Why not get the two women together and let them see—and size up—the competition? "How do you feel about horseback riding in Hyde Park?"

"That sounds positively inspired. Did I tell you I used to be a junior dressage champion?"

"No, but it doesn't surprise me. By the way, we're going to have some company."

"Oh? Who's joining us?"

"My tennis partner, Kristin Lassiter. And her daughter."

Max didn't know why he hadn't said *my* daughter. Or even *our* daughter. He'd chickened out at the last moment. He realized if he didn't tell Veronica now, it was going to make things awkward tomorrow.

Get a grip, Max. Just tell her.

"Look, Veronica. There's something I need to tell you."

"Not now, Max. The ambassador's limo is here. *Ciao,* baby. See you tomorrow."

She hung up before Max could say another word.

He could call her back. But he didn't feel like sharing his business with the British ambassador to the UAE. Who happened to be a good friend of his mother.

Max had a horrifying thought. Could his mother possibly have called her friend, the British ambassador, and asked him to give Veronica a ride home on his jet? Had the duchess arranged for Veronica to be invited to the embassy reception by the handsome elder statesman? Was the duchess manipulating his girlfriend to test her feelings toward Max?

His imagination was working overtime. His mother had never cared enough about any of them to get involved in their lives.

She knew about your teenage friendship with Kristin. She knew about Flick. She encouraged Kristin to participate in that exhibition match, so the two of you would be forced into each other's company. She kept Flick at the Abbey. She urged you to go after Kristin.

His mother's invitation to The Seasons was looking more and more suspicious in light of her current involvement in his personal life. What did she want from him? From all of them? Was she trying to make up for all the years she hadn't been a part of his life? Of their lives?

Making amends at this point was impossible. He was a grown man. He didn't need a mother anymore. Especially not one who interfered in his love life.

Max wasn't going to be tricked by his mother into starting a romance with K. It made a lot more sense to spend his time convincing her that a marriage of convenience was the smart choice for both of them.

He was sure of just one thing. Love was off the table.

23

Kristin backed up to hit an overhead smash and heard enthusiastic clapping from the stands.

"Yay, Mom!" Flick shouted from a green bench along the sidelines.

Kristin shot a quick glance at her daughter, who was grinning ear to ear, and found herself smiling back. Flick had tennis genes on both sides, and at nine, she was already an accomplished player. She simply had too many other interests to focus on the game. And, unlike Kristin, Flick had never felt like she needed to be good at tennis to earn Harry's love. She was as happy to watch others play as she was to play herself.

"Great shot!" Max said as he crossed to give Kristin a high five. "We got a set off them today. We're making progress."

Elena and Steffan came to the net, and Max and Kristin met them there.

"Good match," Elena said to Kristin as they shook hands.

"Great serve," Steffan said to Max as they shook hands.

By the time they'd switched places, and the ladies were shaking hands with the gentlemen, Flick was on the grass court.

"Great game, Mom. You, too, Dad."

Kristin had made Flick promise to stay off the court during their practice. She hadn't warned her not to mention that Max was her father.

Steffan looked from Flick to Kristin to Max and said, "Max? Is there something you haven't told us?"

"This is my daughter, Flick," Max said. "She's been living in Florida with her mother."

Irina had been sitting in the stands near Flick so she could offer coaching advice. Kristin saw the surprise on her face at Max's announcement. She frowned at Kristin, then said, "This is a surprise. You never said a word, Max."

Kristin saw his discomfort as he admitted, "I didn't know. Flick, this is Miss Irina, who coached me when I was learning to play."

"Hello, Miss Irina," Flick said politely.

"Congratulations, old man," Steffan said, hopping the net to give Max a bear hug. He crossed to Flick and held out his hand, "Good to meet you, Flick."

"Your backhand down the line needs work," Flick said.

Steffan turned to Max and laughed. "You've got a budding coach here, Max."

"She's right," Irina said, eyeing Flick. "You have a good tennis eye, young lady."

Flick grinned and said, "My grandpa taught me everything I know."

Kristin put her hands on Flick's shoulders, when what she really wanted to do was put a hand over her daughter's mouth. "I'm afraid he's also encouraged her to say what she thinks," she said to Steffan. She brushed her daughter's bangs aside and said, "Flick, be nice."

"I was being nice," Flick said. "His second serve is pitiful."

Kristin was horrified and turned to apologize for her daughter.

Steffan waved her off with a laugh. "Unfortunately, she's right." He pointed his racquet at Flick and said, "That's how your dad beat me at Wimbledon."

Irina added, "And why you can't beat the top five players on the tour."

Steffan shot Max an aggrieved look and said, "Help! I'm getting it from all sides."

Max laughed and said, "I warned you about that second serve ten years ago. I thought you'd have it fixed by now."

Elena eyed Flick, then turned to Kristin and said, "I guess you and Max were better friends in the old days than any of us knew."

To Kristin's surprise, Max leapt into the breach.

"We made a beautiful daughter together, that's for sure," he said as he slid an arm around Flick's narrow shoulders.

Flick stared up at him with adoring eyes.

Kristin felt her heart squeeze. It was too late to keep Flick from being hurt if—when—Max walkcd out of her life. Her daughter had been ready to love any man in the role of father. For many years, Harry had been that man. Max had finally taken his proper place. Kristin had never seen Flick look happier. Or Max, for that matter.

"Be sure to stretch," Irina called to Elena and Steffan as they headed off the court.

Steffan waved his racquet over his shoulder to acknowledge her orders.

Irina put her hands on Max's cheeks, looked into his eyes and said, "A daughter is a blessing. Enjoy her."

"I will," Max said.

"I've got to catch Elena before she's gone," Irina said. "I'll see you both on Monday."

"No practice tomorrow?" Kristin asked.

Irina shook her head. "Steffan and I have plans."

As she walked away, Kristin whispered to Max, "Doesn't that sound suspicious to you?"

"They're probably spending time with other players who are arriving for Wimbledon," Max said.

"Others might mean there's a conspiracy, Max."

He stared after Irina. "I don't like what you're suggesting, K. But I'll see what I can find out from Steffan in the locker room."

"I'll do the same with Irina before heading to the hotel," she said.

"I thought we could go straight from here to Hyde Park Stables," Max said.

"Flick and I need to go back to the hotel to change."

Max shot Flick a mischievous look Kristin had last seen on his face when he was eighteen. "That won't be necessary. Your riding clothes are waiting for both of you in the ladies' locker room."

"Riding clothes?" Flick said in an awed voice. "Like jodhpurs and a helmet and everything?"

"And everything," Max confirmed, turning her toward the locker room and giving her a tiny swat on the rump to get her moving in that direction.

Flick took off at a run. "Mom, come on. Let's go see!"

"What have you done?" Kristin asked, not bothering to hide her dismay.

"I bought my daughter some riding clothes. You have a problem with that?"

"You said you have clothes for both of us."

"You have a problem with that?" he repeated.

"I can buy my own clothes."

"Do you have riding gear at the hotel?" he asked.

"We planned to wear jeans and shoes with leather heels. Which is perfectly fine. I checked with the stables."

"I bought riding boots and the best protective hat I could find for Flick. I want my daughter to be safe. I thought it would be nice for her—more comfortable for her—if you were dressed the same way."

Kristin knew he was right. "Fine. Flick and I will wear your riding clothes. But I'm going to pay for mine."

"Don't be absurd!" Max snapped.

She didn't stay to argue with him. She marched off toward the locker room. By the time she got there, Flick already had her jodhpurs on, together with a beautiful white blouse with a frill across the bodice. "Look at the jacket, Mom," she said as she slid her arms into a beautifully tailored jacket and smoothed her hands over the tweed fabric. "And I've got real boots!"

Kristin admired the expensive jacket and the tall black riding boots with leather so supple she felt sure they were the best that could be found in London. Somehow, Max had acquired their entire ensembles overnight and arranged for their delivery here at Wimbledon.

"Hurry up, Mom. Get your shower so we can go!" Flick urged.

Kristin had just turned off the shower when she heard a voice in one of the toilet stalls. Someone was whispering, which made her voice echo. It took a moment for Kristin to remember she was here to spy. She was shivering but couldn't grab a towel without exposing herself. She stayed where she was and listened.

She only caught a word or two.

Those few words left her feeling cold to the bone. She heard "Kill her." And "Too late." And "I can do that."

That sounded ominous, considering the fact the American president was a woman.

Kristin heard the toilet stall door open and close and peeked out, but she couldn't see who it was. She grabbed a towel and, teeth chattering, headed into the main locker room quickly and quietly to see who was there.

The door to the outside hall was just sliding closed. Elena was still dressing after her shower. She and Irina were talking, their heads close, as though they were sharing private information. That wouldn't have been unusual if the room were full of other tennis players, and Irina wanted to keep her coaching advice discreet. But the locker room was empty except for Flick. So why were they talking so secretively?

Kristin put her back to the other two women and asked Flick, "Did you see who just left?"

"Some lady. She was dressed nice."

Kristin didn't like the idea of involving Flick in espionage by asking her to look at a bunch of pictures of players. But she wanted to know who'd spoken those words in the bathroom stall.

Whoever had come into the locker room had to have had an ID to get in. Which made her a tennis player or a coach or a member of the All England Lawn Tennis Club. Or a member of the press. Or some staff member or cleaning lady. The suspect list grew longer the more Kristin thought about it.

"What did she look like?" Kristin asked her daughter.

"Why don't you ask Miss Irina who it was? She talked to her when she first came in," Flick said.

Kristin debated whether to do that and decided against it. There was no reason for her to be asking Irina about some stranger. It was as unbelievable to her as it was to

Max that Irina or Elena could be part of some assassination plot. She needed information, but she didn't want to make them wary of her by asking questions. Her usefulness as a spy depended on her remaining a simple tennis player.

"Come on, Mom. Get dressed," Flick said.

While Kristin examined her riding clothes, which were hanging near her locker, she tried eavesdropping on Elena and Irina's conversation. But it seemed whatever conversation they'd been having was over. Irina left before she heard anything.

Kristin wondered what Max would think when she told him that Irina had spoken with the woman she'd heard whispering when she was in the shower. He wasn't going to like it, that was for sure. Irina was looking more and more guilty.

Once Kristin had on her blouse and jodhpurs, she sat down to pull on a pair of luxurious leather riding boots similar to Flick's. She paled at the thought of how much Max must have spent. She probably couldn't afford the protective, velvet-covered riding hat, let alone the breeches, jacket, blouse and boots.

To her amazement, everything fit her perfectly, just as Flick's clothing had fit perfectly. How had Max known their sizes?

"Probably sent a spy to the hotel to check our clothes and shoes in the middle of the night," she said to herself.

"What's that, Mom?" Flick said.

"I was just saying how nicely everything fits."

"Come on, Mom. I want to show Dad how I look."

When they met Max outside, Kristin found him outfitted in a tailored male version of their riding gear. He handed Flick a small leather riding crop and said, "This was my crop when I learned to ride."

Flick took the short leather riding crop as though it were a scepter and she were being crowned Queen of England. She flicked the whip a couple of times, then slid the leather band on one end around her wrist and, with the crop dangling, threw her arms around Max's waist. "Thanks, Dad!"

Once they were in the limo, Max said, "Flick, I want you to meet Freddy."

The limo driver turned to face Flick and said, "Nice to meet you, Miss Flick."

"Freddy's also a connoisseur of big words," Max said.

"Connoisseur," Flick said, scrambling across the seats in the back of the limo until she was draped over the front seat where she could easily talk to the limo driver. "That means you're an *expert,*" Flick said. "I'm only *adept* with words."

Freddy grinned and said, "That means you're as *facile* with words as I am. Good on ya, Miss Flick."

Flick laughed. "I'm able to use big words with ease, all right. But I don't know what 'good on ya' means."

While Freddy explained to Flick that "Good on ya" was an Australian expression that meant "Good for you," Kristin asked Max, "Why did you arrange for a limo?"

"I figured we needed time to talk without Flick around. Freddy will keep her entertained up front while we do."

"I'm glad you thought ahead," Kristin said. "I overheard something in the locker room we need to discuss."

"What?" he said.

"Someone was talking in one of the bathroom stalls—I presume on a phone. I couldn't see her because I was in the shower. She said, 'Kill her.' And 'Too late.' And 'I can do that.' She left the locker room before I got a look at her. But Flick saw her. She said the woman spoke to Irina when she came in."

"Flick saw her? Did you ask her what she looked like?"

"She said she was dressed nicely. So maybe not a tennis player," Kristin said.

His eyes were troubled when he asked, "You're sure she spoke to Irina?"

Kristin nodded. "That's what Flick said. When I came into the locker room Irina and Elena had their heads together. They were speaking quietly enough that I couldn't hear what they were saying."

"I'm having a hard time believing Irina and Elena are terrorists plotting an assassination," he said flatly.

"How well do you know Elena, Max?"

"You know Elena as well as I do. Which is to say, not at all."

"We don't really *know* any of these people anymore,

Max. It's been ten years since Irina coached you. How much contact have you had with her since then?"

Max made a face. "You've made your point. But Irina? And Steffan? And Elena?"

"Maybe I misunderstood what I overheard. You know how people use expressions like, 'I'm going to kill her,' when what they mean is they're mad at someone. Maybe it was something like that."

"Maybe it wasn't," Max said grimly. "What bothers me is that if Irina is involved, then Steffan probably is, too."

"Should we try to follow them tomorrow?"

Max shook his head. "Too dangerous. Especially if there are more people involved. Too easy for someone else to spot a tail on Steffan or Irina. But it might not be a bad idea to see if we can have drinks with Steffan tomorrow evening. Maybe we can get him to tell us how he and Irina spent the day."

"He isn't going to admit he's part of a conspiracy, Max."

"No. But what he does tell us can be confirmed—or not. Which will tell us whether he was lying."

"Oh, I see. Should we invite Elena, too?"

"Why not? It'll make it seem more like a social occasion. Come to think of it, maybe Steffan will want to invite Elena. That would be even better."

"I never thought we'd find any substance to this threat," Kristin said quietly.

"Maybe we haven't," Max said.

Kristin realized he was still hoping they hadn't. She

couldn't imagine being forced to report that someone she loved and cared about was a terrorist.

Kristin listened to the vocabulary contest going on between Freddy and Flick in the front of the limo. "Flick was impressed with the clothes," she said to Max. "She loves the riding crop." She hesitated, then added, "And she thinks you're wonderful."

"The feeling is mutual. She's a great kid," Max said.

"I know."

"I wish I'd been a part of her life from the start."

"I can't undo the decisions I made, Max," she said defensively. "I'm not going to apologize for them, either."

"You can make sure I get to spend the rest of Flick's life being her father."

"By joining you in a loveless marriage? No thanks."

"It doesn't have to be loveless," Max said.

"You don't love me. I don't love you. That sounds loveless to me."

"Keep your voice down," he warned.

Kristin looked to make sure Flick was still engrossed in her conversation with the limo driver before she said, "What are you suggesting?"

He rubbed a hand across his nape, beneath the collar of his tweed riding jacket. "I don't know."

"Your mother asked me if we'd discussed visitation rights."

She watched a muscle flex in Max's jaw before he said, "I don't want to visit my daughter. I want to live with her."

"What if that isn't possible?"

"There has to be some way to make it possible."

Kristin shook her head. "It's too late, Max. Flick and I have our lives in America. You live here."

"I'll move."

"What?"

"You want to live in America? Fine, that's where we'll live."

"Where *we'll* live?"

"I'll get a house nearby. Flick can move back and forth between your house and mine."

"No."

"Now you're being unreasonable."

"I'm trying to protect my daughter—"

"Get this through your head," Max interrupted angrily. "Flick has two parents. She's not just your daughter. She's mine, too!"

"Dad? Mom? What's wrong?"

Max swore under his breath.

"Nothing's wrong, sweetheart," Kristin said. "Your dad and I were discussing—"

"Me," Flick finished as she scooted back across the black leather seats to join them at the back of the limo. "You were arguing about me. I've been wondering if we're going to be living together from now on. Are we?"

Kristin's heart hurt when she heard the hope in her daughter's voice. She didn't want to dash those hopes. But she didn't want to encourage them, either. "Your father and I are trying to work that out."

"You sounded mad, Mom. Don't you like Dad?"

"Yes, Flick, but..." She met Max's stony gaze. She waited for him to say something, anything, to take the awful, fearful look from Flick's eyes.

"Your mother and I were friends a long time ago," Max said. "We're learning to be friends again, but we don't agree on everything. So sometimes we argue."

"Oh, okay," Flick said. "Sometimes I fight with Jane. She was my friend at school in Switzerland. But we always made up." She turned to Kristin and asked, "Are you and Dad going to make up?"

Kristin nodded, because that was easier than trying to speak past the lump in her throat.

"Are you going to *kiss* and make up?" Flick asked Max with an impish smile.

He glanced at Kristin and raised a brow. "How about it, Princess? You want to kiss and make up?"

Kristin met Flick's anxious gaze and realized a kiss was a small price to pay for her daughter's peace of mind. "Why not?"

She leaned toward Max, expecting a peck on the cheek.

Max caught her chin and angled her face so his mouth pressed lightly against hers. His mouth was soft, his kiss gentle. And she melted inside like ice cream on a hot sidewalk.

"That wasn't so bad, was it?" Max asked.

"Not bad at all," Kristin croaked. Her throat was still swollen with emotion, but she managed to smile for Flick.

Flick clapped. "Now you're friends again!" She clambered back to the front of the limo and said, "Freddy, my mom and dad kissed and made up." And then, "Are we there yet?"

24

Max deeply regretted inviting Veronica to meet him at Hyde Park. He dreaded the confrontation he could see coming. Flick might not understand the implications of having another woman along for the ride. Kristin would.

He was relieved to discover, when they arrived at Hyde Park Stables, that Veronica wasn't there. Maybe she'd slept in longer than she'd planned.

When Flick saw the small chestnut horse with a white blaze that had been selected as her mount, she was so excited she seemed ready to jump out of her skin. "He's pretty big, Dad," she said, backed up against him, staring warily up at the horse.

"But gentle, miss," the hostler said as he finished saddling her mount.

Flick asked Max, "Can I pet him?"

Max put a hand on her shoulder and walked her to the horse's side. The horse turned his head to look at the little girl. Before she could jump back, Max said, "No sudden moves, Flick. You'll frighten him. Just reach out and stroke his neck slowly and gently."

His daughter reached out a small, tentative hand. When she touched the animal, his shoulder muscles rippled as though to shake off a fly. Max held on to Flick to keep her from running.

"Touch him a little more firmly," he instructed. This time he took her hand and stroked the horse's neck along with her, then its throat, and finally its nose.

"His nose is so soft," Flick said in wonder. "Like... velvet."

When Max sought out Kristin's gaze to share his enjoyment of Flick's delight, he saw that she looked anything but happy. He raised a questioning brow and watched her attempt a smile. She didn't make it.

Before he could ask what was wrong, the hostler said, "Are you ready to mount, miss?"

Flick looked anxiously at Max.

He smiled down at her and said, "When I lift you up, Flick, just slide your leg over the horse's back and you'll be sitting in the saddle."

Flick did as he instructed. She looked worried for a moment, but he had a hand on her hip to steady her. He kept a reassuring smile on his face and announced, "You're up."

She grinned down at him, turned to her mother and said, "I'm sitting on a horse, Mom!"

"I see, baby," Kristin said.

Max arranged the reins, one in each of Flick's hands

and said, “Pull this rein if you want him to go left, and this one if you want him to go right.”

“Just like turning my bicycle,” Flick said.

“Right,” he replied. “Now let’s get these stirrups adjusted.” He settled her booted foot in one stirrup with her knee slightly bent, then adjusted the buckle underneath to shorten the length. The hostler did the same with her other foot.

“How does that feel?” Max asked.

“Good, I guess,” Flick said. “Now what?”

“You get to practice walking your horse in the ring until your mother and I get mounted.”

The hostler led Flick to a fenced-in riding arena and gave her instructions on how to use her heels to urge the horse to walk, while Max checked to see what was delaying Kristin.

“What’s wrong, K?” he asked quietly.

“I’m scared, that’s what’s wrong,” she said, refusing to look at him.

“Of the horse?” he asked skeptically. The placid animal was tied to a hitching post.

“Of falling off the horse.”

“I’ve never known you to be scared of anything,” he said. “What happened to make you frightened of horses?”

“I got thrown from a horse when I was about Flick’s age.”

“I wondered why you never let Flick go riding.”

“I’ve never gotten back on a horse since.”

"You didn't get right back on after you were thrown?"

She shook her head. "I dislocated my shoulder."

"Would you rather not ride?" he asked.

"I don't want to spoil Flick's day."

"It'll spoil Flick's day a lot worse to see her mother in a panic," Max said sardonically.

"I can do this," Kristin said. "I want to do this."

Max could see she was trembling. "Are you sure?"

She nodded her head jerkily.

"Okay. Let's think about this a minute." He stood in front of her, wrapped his arms around her and gently pressed her face against his chest. "Think about yourself sitting on that horse and walking along the beautiful, oak-lined trails in Hyde Park with me and Flick riding beside you."

He waited until he felt her trembling stop. Then he released her and took a step back. He lifted her chin with a forefinger and said, "No ordinary horse is going to get the better of the girl I know."

He took Kristin by the hand and led her to the pretty bay mare that had been saddled for her. He took that same hand and reached out with it to stroke the horse's neck, much as he'd done with Flick. He ran Kristin's hand along the horse's forehead, moving the animal's forelock out of the way.

On her own, Kristin ran her hand down the front of the mare's face and across her nose. "I forgot how soft a horse's nose is," she murmured.

The horse's ears pricked back and forth as she spoke.

"Why is she doing that?" she asked nervously.

"She's checking you out, just like you're checking her out. Come on, time to get on."

She grabbed for his hand and said, "I'm not sure I can do this, Max."

"Sure you can." He freed himself from her grip, made a cup of his hands and said, "Put your left hand on the front of the saddle, face me and put your left foot in my hands, and I'll boost you up. Once you're up, slip your leg over the horse's back and you'll be in the saddle.

Because she was so lithe, Kristin had no problem doing as he instructed.

"Now breathe," he said.

She exhaled loudly before drawing enough breath to say in wonder, "I'm sitting on a horse."

He constrained the grin that was trying to break free and merely said, "Yes, you are. Now put your feet in the stirrups."

When she looked down to locate the stirrups, she said, "It's not as far down as I remember."

"You're more grown-up," he reminded her as he adjusted the stirrups one at a time.

"How do you know so much about all this?" she asked.

"I spent a lot of time on horseback at one of the boarding schools my brothers and I attended. As I recall, it was an incident with a horse that got us thrown out."

He mounted his horse and instructed her how to turn

her horse left and right, how to stop her mount and how to make her go. He distracted Kristin from her fear with the story of how he'd let the headmaster's stallion out of his stall, how the stallion had gotten friendly with the Latin instructor's mare and how he and his brothers had been kicked out of school long before the resulting foal had been born.

Kristin was laughing when they joined Flick at the riding ring.

"Are you ready to go, Flick?" Max called.

"Ready, Dad."

"I'm ready, too," a voice called from behind him.

Max turned his horse and found Veronica sitting on a prime piece of horseflesh—not a rented hack, but her own dainty Arabian mare—wearing a faultless hunter-green velvet riding habit.

Kristin took one look at the other woman and said, "Come on, Flick. We'll take the lead."

The woman who was supposedly afraid of riding horseback urged her mount onto the trail with their daughter beside her. He was left to deal with Veronica.

"I didn't think you were coming," he said.

"I thought you were kidding about having company for the ride," she said, eyeing Kristin and Flick down the bridge of her very pert nose. "Who are those people again?"

"The woman is Kristin Lassiter. I'm playing an exhibition match at Wimbledon with her. The child with her is her daughter." There it was again. The reluctance to say *my* daughter. Or even *our* daughter. He'd created his very own drama by inviting Veronica to come along on this ride. He might as well get the worst over with.

"Come on," he said. "I'll introduce you."

They trotted to catch up with Kristin and Flick. "Hold up," he called to the two of them. "There's someone I want you to meet."

Kristin ignored him, but Flick held up her mount until Veronica, posting with perfect posture in her English saddle, caught up to her.

"I've always wanted a white horse," Flick said, eyeing Veronica's mount.

"Actually, Blanca is dapple gray."

"Her name means *white* in Spanish," Flick pointed out. "And she's mostly white."

Veronica smiled indulgently. "Yes, it does. And yes, she is."

"Can I ride with you for a while?" Flick asked.

"Of course," Veronica replied.

"That way my mom can ride with my dad," Flick added.

"Your *dad?*" Veronica turned to Max, her brows raised in patent disbelief, and said, "This is your *daughter?*"

"Veronica Granville, I'd like you to meet Kristin Lassiter and her daughter—our daughter—Felicity, who goes by the nickname Flick."

"Is this woman your wife?" Veronica asked.

Max choked, but Kristin said, "No. We're not married."

"I see," Veronica said, looking from one to the other. "Well, Flick. Shall we ride ahead?"

"Okay," Flick said. "But I can't ride very fast."

"Walking will be fine," Veronica said. "I'm in no hurry at all."

Max had to hand it to the reporter. She'd taken the news better than he'd expected. Of course, she'd also gotten herself a scoop. Max Benedict had just admitted to having a daughter, and that he and the girl's mother weren't married.

Max exchanged a glance with Kristin, who shrugged and shook her head in equal disbelief at Flick's maneuvering and Veronica's savoir faire.

As Veronica and Flick rode ahead together, Max joined Kristin behind them. He'd just opened his mouth to ask how she was enjoying the ride when Flick asked Veronica in a loud voice, "Are you my dad's girlfriend?"

"That's a very good question, young lady," Veronica said, glancing at Max over her shoulder. "One I think you should ask your father."

Max bit his tongue. The pain kept him from blurting an answer.

Flick turned her horse around to face Max, while Veronica pulled her mount to a halt and turned to join her. Max and Kristin caught up to Flick, and the four of them sat on their horses facing each other.

"Dad? Is Veronica your girlfriend?"

There he was, on the spot, with no safe answer to Flick's question.

"Well, Max?" Veronica said with a sardonic smile. "I'd like to hear the answer to that question myself."

Max realized he was going to have to make a choice,

one from which there was no turning back. He might have given a different answer yesterday, before he'd known he had a daughter. And before Veronica had chosen to abandon him last night in favor of a stately ambassador.

He was slowly but surely realizing that his days as a carefree bachelor were over, even if he didn't end up marrying Kristin. Being a father to his daughter was going to require some sacrifices. Sleeping his way across several continents was sure to be one of them.

He met the reporter's gaze and answered, "Veronica is my friend, Flick. Not my girlfriend."

He watched Veronica's back stiffen and saw her mouth flatten into a hyphen.

He'd made his choice. He wasn't too sure just how deeply his rejection had cut. Maybe not as much this morning as it might have before the ambassador had come into her life. He didn't think he'd done more than bruise Veronica's ego. "How was the reception last night, Veronica?"

"The ambassador is a man of many talents, Max," she said. "If you know what I mean."

He did. She deserved the chance to remind him that she was a desirable woman, and that he was going to regret letting her get away. But he didn't feel sorry. Except for having invited her in the first place.

"I think I'll ride ahead," Veronica said. "I'd like to give Blanca a little more exercise than she's gotten on this family ride of yours."

"We'll see you back at the stables," Max said.

"I'm afraid I'll be gone before you get back, Max. I've got other plans this afternoon. It was nice meeting you, Kristin. And you, Flick."

"Nice meeting you, too, Miss Veronica," Flick said. "You have a really pretty horse."

"Thank you, dear." Veronica rode over and kissed Max on the cheek. She leaned close and said, "Goodbye, Max. Thanks for the scoop."

Max watched Veronica canter her horse away, her form perfect in the saddle. He might have been able to bring pressure to bear to keep her from selling what she knew to some gossip rag. But he wasn't ashamed of Flick. And maybe the publicity would push Kristin into his arms.

"I think she likes you, Dad," Flick said when Veronica was out of hearing. "Do you like her more than Mom?"

"Flick!" Kristin said.

"No, Flick," he replied. "I like your mom the best of anyone I know."

Kristin shot him a surprised look. Quietly enough so Flick couldn't hear she said, "Then why did you invite Veronica to come today?"

"Let's say it was a mistake and leave it at that."

"Can we trot now, Dad?"

"I need to teach you how to post first." He showed Flick how to lift her body off the saddle when the horse was jogging by standing slightly in the stirrups and then sitting in the saddle again in concert with the horse's up and down stride, allowing for a smooth ride.

"Got it!" Flick said. "This is neat, Dad," she said, posting as she trotted ahead.

Max turned to Kristin and asked, "How about you? You okay with trotting?"

Kristin nodded. "I think I've got it, too."

They jogged along infamous Rotten Row, where Regency-era lords and ladies had driven their curricles in the afternoon to see and be seen, now a wide dirt path running along the outer edge of the park. Max corrected Flick's form as she posted in the English saddle. When their horses slowed again, he nudged his horse close to Kristin and said, "You're doing great."

She laughed nervously. "I wouldn't dare fall off and ruin this outfit."

He eyed her up and down appreciatively. "You look amazing in it."

"Thank you. I've been wondering about something all afternoon."

"I'll be glad to satisfy your curiosity." He was glad to be talking to her at all, considering her threat yesterday not to speak to him for the rest of her life. "What is it?"

"How did you know what sizes to buy for the two of us?"

He chuckled. "That's easy. I called my mother. She had Flick's measurements because she planned to buy her a few things."

Kristin nodded in understanding. "And she had mine because I borrowed some clothing from Emily, and we're the same size." She met his gaze and said, "It was a thoughtful thing to do, Max. Flick is over the moon—with her outfit and with the chance to ride horseback."

"Thanks."

"I'm still going to pay you back."

"Look, K," he said, trying to keep his voice from sounding as aggrieved as he felt, "you're going to have to get used to me spending money on Flick. Sometimes, like today, it's going to mean spending money on you, too."

"I'm used to taking care of Flick and myself by myself."

"You've got me now." He didn't say she would have had him from the start if she'd only told him she was pregnant. Mostly because he thought her fears about how he would have reacted at eighteen probably had some foundation. He had no idea what he would have done. She was right about one thing. It would have been hard to give up being a heedless teenager to be a father.

He was older and wiser now, ready to shoulder the responsibility of being a father.

And a husband? That, too. If he could get her to agree to marriage on his terms.

While Flick rode ahead, Max said, "I wish you'd reconsider marrying me, Princess."

"You asked your girlfriend to go horseback riding with us, Max."

"If you were listening, you heard she isn't my girlfriend."

She shot him a severe look.

"Not anymore," he added.

"How many more girlfriends are waiting in the wings?"

"None."

She cocked her head and said, "I'm supposed to believe you?"

"It's the truth."

"I'd rather focus on the job we have to do, if it's all the same to you."

"Obviously we're not going to be dating our way through the player roster anymore," he said.

She lifted a brow. "Why not? We're both still single adults."

"The word is going to get out that we're parents."

"So? We're still *single* parents."

"Not for long, if I can help it," Max muttered.

"Have you figured out what excuse we're going to use to get together with Elena and Steffan tomorrow?"

"How about having a drink with us?" Max said.

"You're suggesting we invite potential coconspirators in an assassination to dinner?"

"Why not?"

"It doesn't sound like you're taking this threat seriously, Max."

"This is how I do my job, Princess. And I'm good at what I do. People say far more in social situations, when they've got a few drinks in them, than they realize."

"Well, this isn't what I do. I'm relying on you to make sure we don't foul up this investigation."

"Keep your chin up, Princess. There's always the possibility they've sent us on a wild-goose chase. All the

CIA had to go on was a couple of emails intercepted by Interpol. Someone could have had an idea to do the bad thing but never figured out how to make it happen."

"I hope it is a false alarm. I don't want Irina and Steffan to be the bad guys. I wish I could take Flick and go home, but I've got to stay for the exhibition match. And Harry's plane arrived early this morning. We helped him settle in at the rehab center before practice and he's expecting Flick and me to come and visit him again later today."

"May I come, too?"

"I can't very well keep you away when you're paying for everything," she said.

"I won't go if you don't want me there," Max said.

"I think Harry would like to see you."

"We have two weeks of Wimbledon competition after our exhibition match until the final matches," Max said. "Will you stay until then?"

"I signed up for the whole job, plus I don't want to move Harry again too soon. So, yes, we'll stay until the Gentlemen's Singles Championship match on July 4."

July 4. America's Independence Day. That meant he only had a few weeks to work out some sort of compromise on custody, if she wouldn't marry him.

Flick slowed her mount and said, "Can I ride with you, Dad?"

"Sure."

"I have a question."

"Go ahead and ask," Max said.

"Are you and Mom going to get married?"

Max's glance slid to Kristin, who shook her head, apparently used to Flick's candid questions. "I don't know," he said at last.

"I like having a dad and a mom."

"I'm still going to be your dad, even if your mom and I aren't married," he pointed out.

"Yeah, but if you and Mom get married, we can do more things together, like this."

"I can't make your mom marry me, Flick," he said.

Flick stared at him with her mouth open in surprise. "You mean you've asked her?"

Max couldn't see the harm in admitting he'd proposed. "Yes, I've asked your mom to marry me. She wasn't too keen on the idea."

He saw Kristin roll her eyes.

"Why didn't she want to marry you?" Flick asked.

"You'll have to ask her," Max said.

"Mom, why don't you want to marry Dad?"

Kristin glared at him over Flick's head. Then she met her daughter's gaze and said, "A man and a woman who get married should love each other, Flick. Your father and I aren't in love. That's why I said no."

"Oh," Flick said. "I see."

Max watched her forehead furrow in thought. Then she lifted her chin, smiled at Max and said, "Well, Dad, you're just going to have to convince Mom to fall in love with you."

25

"Gramps!" Flick cried.

Max stood back as his daughter barreled past him into her grandfather's room. The rehabilitation center he had chosen for Harry was situated near the small village of Wimbledon, where the grass tennis courts of the All England Lawn Tennis Club were located, to make it easier for Kristin and Flick to visit him every day.

Max watched as Flick climbed onto Harry's bed, easy as you please, and hugged him tight around the neck. He was glad Kristin had warned him about her father's appearance after his stroke. Harry's face sagged badly on the right side. When he talked to Flick, Harry's features contorted so he looked like some kind of made-up movie monster, but she didn't seem to notice.

"I rode a horse, Gramps!" Flick told Harry. "And I have a father!" she added.

Max realized the horse had come first. He'd been an afterthought. He had a lot to learn about the priorities of nine-year-old girls. "Hello, Harry," Max said as he approached the bed. He turned to look for Kristin and realized she'd hung back by the door.

Max noticed Harry reached with his left hand to shake the right hand Max extended to him.

"Ih uh oo ee oo," Harry said laboriously.

"He says it's good to see you," Flick translated.

"Aow ime."

"He says—" Flick began.

"Never mind," Max said. *About time.* He could decipher that for himself. Kristin had told him that Harry had known all these years that Max was Flick's father. The old man must have resented the extra responsibility, although it was clear he adored his granddaughter. It seemed he was happy the secret was out.

Max shot a look over his shoulder at Kristin and saw she'd moved into the room and was leaning against the side wall. He'd known about Harry's paralysis. He hadn't realized Harry's speech was so bad.

"They've got a great speech therapy program here," he said to Harry.

"Own ee ih."

"He says he doesn't need it," Flick translated.

Max glanced back at Kristin and saw the despair on her face as she slumped back against the wall. No wonder she'd looked so distressed during the trip here. Harry might not want speech therapy, but he needed it. He saw her dilemma. How could you argue with a man who'd had a stroke? Especially when you couldn't be sure whether upsetting him would cause another one?

"I think your speech could use a little work," Max said.

"Max," Kristin said in a warning voice, stepping away from the wall. "I don't think—"

"Because I can't understand a thing you say until Flick translates for you," Max finished.

Max watched as Harry's face got red. His glare blazed from one eye while the other drooped at half-mast.

"Oo un itch!" Harry huffed out.

"He said—" Flick began.

"Don't repeat what he said!" K said as she stepped between the two men. "That's enough from both of you. Dad, you need speech therapy."

"No!" Harry barked.

"You're pretty good with the negatives, Harry."

"Shut up, Max," K said without looking at him. She kept her eyes focused on her father as she said, "I'm not going to argue with you, Dad. I'm going to the speech therapist tomorrow morning, and if she tells me you've scheduled a therapy session, Flick and I will come visit you. If you haven't, we won't."

"Mom, that's coercion!" Flick complained.

Max hadn't known his nine-year-old was familiar with the word. But he personally applauded Kristin's willingness to compel Harry to choose speech therapy by threatening to withhold his granddaughter's visits.

"I'd believe her, Harry," Max said. "She means it."

"Eez a uffff irl," he mumbled.

"What's that, Gramps?" Flick asked, for once not able to understand him.

"He says your mom's a tough girl," Max said. He turned to see what Kristin thought about her father's remark and felt his heart squeeze when he saw the tears brimming in her eyes. She blinked them back—like the tough girl she was—but Max was beginning to realize just how much Kristin had been dealing with on her own in recent months.

He wanted to help. He was determined to help, whether the "tough girl" liked it or not. Better late than never, he supposed.

His mother and her assistant, Emily Whatever, had moved to the Blackthorne residence in Berkeley Square on the West End of London, so Emily would be available every day to tutor Flick until she finished her class work for the current year. But he wanted his daughter in a good London public—which was England's version of a private—school in the fall. Not necessarily a boarding school.

Max had spent too much time separated from his parents growing up to be a big fan of sending kids away. He could understand it might have been the best choice when Kristin was on her own. But if he could convince her to marry him, he wanted them to live together like a family.

Convincing her to marry him seemed impossible at the moment. Kristin wanted not just someone who loved her, but someone she could love. And he had no idea how to accomplish that feat.

No woman he'd dated had ever loved him. Not for himself, anyway. Kristin had come closest to caring. But he'd ruined all that ten years ago. He wasn't sure what he could do to make her start to care again. But he was going to do his damnedest to figure it out.

"Time to go, Flick," Kristin said. "Say good-bye to Gramps."

Max watched as Flick clung to her grandfather's neck. "Get well, Gramps," she said. "So we can go home."

Home. If Max got his way, she was already home. He suddenly realized that, while he'd worried how Kristin would make the transition from living in Miami to living in London, he'd never considered Flick's feelings on the subject. He was going to have to readjust his thinking to keep her in the loop.

Max was jolted from his reverie when he felt a small hand grasp his. He looked down and found his daughter looking up at him expectantly.

"Ready to go, Dad?"

"Sure," he said. "K?" he said, glancing in her direction. "You ready?"

She was brushing her father's hair back from his brow. Both of them looked embarrassed to be caught in such a tender pose. "Yes, I'm ready," she said, dropping her hand. "Remember what I said, Dad."

He made a face but didn't reply. Max would have put money on the fact the old man would be in speech therapy starting tomorrow.

"Where to now?" Max asked as they left the rehabilitation center.

"Your mother invited Flick and me to stay at the

Blackthorne mansion in Berkeley Square, and I've accepted. We've already been there to see our rooms."

Max barely kept his mouth from dropping open in surprise. Kristin voluntarily accepting the hospitality of the Mean Witch? The world was turning on its ear.

She flushed, so he knew she was aware of how peculiar her decision seemed.

"If we stay with the duchess, Flick can have her own room and I'm still close enough to get to her if she wakes during the night," Kristin explained.

He shot a worried look at Flick, then looked back at Kristin and asked, "Does that happen often? Her waking up, I mean?"

"She sometimes has nightmares."

Max imagined his child having nightmares. And him not being there to hold and comfort her. "I think I'll ask my mother if I can stay with you in Berkeley Square."

"I don't think that's a good idea," Kristin said.

"Why not, Mom?" Flick asked plaintively.

Kristin made a face at Max.

Max realized he'd better start recognizing the fact that his daughter was listening whenever he spoke and wasn't shy about sharing her opinions of whatever he said. In this case, her sentiments helped him, but that might not always be the case.

"I want to spend as much time as I can with Flick," he said. *And you.* "There's plenty of room in that huge old place."

"That 'huge old place' is a magnificent home," Kristin said.

"And really, really old," Flick added.

Max laughed. "The Blackthorne mansion dates back to the mid-eighteenth century, I think around 1754."

"When we visited Gram there, Mom and I got really good scones at a place around the corner," Flick said.

"Don't forget the delicious tea," Kristin said.

Max frowned, trying to think of which place they might be talking about, then said, "Oh, yeah. Now I remember. The Gunter Tea Shop. It was originally called Gunter's."

"It's really old, too," Flick said.

"You're right about that," Max said with a laugh. He couldn't believe how much he was enjoying this simple conversation with Flick and Kristin. But he could already feel both of them slipping away. His exhibition match was just around the corner. Two weeks after that, Kristin and Flick would be returning to the States.

It didn't seem like nearly long enough to make Kristin fall in love with him. Especially considering how long it had taken him to fall in love with her. Of course, there had been the age difference back then. He tried to think what it was about Kristin that had made him start to care for her. Maybe he could emulate that behavior with the same result.

Listening. Helping. Caring. Simple things that had made him love her. All easier to do if he was staying with Kristin and Flick at his parents' Berkeley Square mansion.

It was time he got started.

26

Kristin couldn't believe how easily Max had gotten himself invited to stay at his mother's residence in Berkeley Square. The impressive, three-story house, which faced the park at the center of the square, had been designed by the distinguished eighteenth-century architect, Robert Adam. It had been owned by many famous personages as it passed in and out of the possession of various Dukes of Blackthorne through the years.

"What a wonderful idea, Max!" the duchess exclaimed. "It makes perfect sense for you to stay here."

Kristin shouldn't have been surprised that Max's request to stay at the mansion had been received so well. She knew Bella was desperately hoping for a fairy-tale ending to their love story.

"You can stay in your old room," the duchess said. "I don't believe it's changed much since you were a boy. The original bed is large enough to accommodate you, as I recall."

The "original bed," Kristin discovered, was a monstrosity with an eight-foot high headboard and a gruesome scene carved in the footboard. The first thing Max would have seen when he woke up each morning was a knight cleaving another knight in half with an ax. Kristin couldn't imagine letting a child sleep there. Max said it had been his bed since he was five and had gotten a room of his own, and he obviously loved it.

"That bed was slept in by Henry II," he told Flick proudly.

"Who was he?" she asked.

"A famous king of England."

Kristin figured the duchess must be positively salivating at the idea of her and Max sleeping in that royal bed. But nothing was going to happen. Kristin would make sure of that.

She planned to keep her distance from Max while he was staying under the same roof. She didn't want to end up hurt any worse than she already had been. It had been awkward, to say the least, when Max's girlfriend showed up at Hyde Park this morning. Kristin considered the whole episode a wake-up call, to remind her who she was dealing with.

A rogue. A man who never followed the rules. A man who took what he wanted when he wanted it. A man incapable of deep emotional relationships. Although, she didn't really blame Max for his inability to love.

Kristin knew how often he'd reached out to his mother in his teens and been rejected. It had never occurred to her until this very moment, but his relationship with his father must have been even worse. Max had never even had an expectation of seeing Bull show up at a match.

Kristin wondered just how many of the women Max had dated had considered him to be a deep pocket and a great lover, rather than a man in need of love and succor? No wonder he had no idea how to give or accept love.

Yet he'd offered friendship—and support—to a lonely girl. And he'd been faithful to that friendship until she'd pushed him out of her life. All because she hadn't been willing to believe that he truly cared for her.

Max might not be able to love, but you're unable to trust. Maybe you should take a look at the pot before you start calling the kettle black, a voice inside her head chided.

She missed Max's friendship. If they were going to have to parent together, and it seemed they probably would, maybe that was the place to start. Kristin had to admit, it had been nice to have Max's help to cajole—or coerce, to use Flick's word—her father into attending speech therapy sessions.

Flick loved having her father around. She clung to his hand when they were walking or to his neck whenever he sat in a chair, as though she expected him to disappear if she didn't have hold of him.

Kristin knew she was going to have a great deal of trouble with Flick when they left London—and Max—behind and headed back to Miami. Her daughter was becoming more and more emotionally attached to her father. It was easy to see why.

Max listened raptly when Flick spoke. He catered to her every whim, something no parent could afford to do for long without spoiling a child. Kristin hadn't said anything to Max so far, because she didn't think he was going to be around for long. But if he were ever to share custody of Flick with her, she would need to deal with the problem.

Meanwhile, Max and Flick were basking in each other's company. And in each other's adoration.

Kristin didn't think the word was too strong for what Flick felt for Max. It was only tonight, when he was tucking Flick into bed for the first time, that Kristin saw what could only be described as adoration for his daughter on Max's face.

"This is the neatest bed ever," Flick said, gazing up at the blue silk canopy that covered the bed she was lying in.

"Do you want me to read you a bedtime story?" Max asked as he sat down beside her on the bed.

"Daddy," Flick said in a reproving, singsong voice. "I've been reading since I was four."

"Too bad for me, I guess," Max said.

Kristin could see he was disappointed.

"Have you read *Winnie-the-Pooh*?" he asked Flick.

"A long time ago."

"How about the Harry Potter books?"

"I read them all last year."

"What are you reading now?" Max asked.

"I just finished *Treasure Island*."

"How did you like it?"

"It was kind of boring in the beginning. Then it was okay."

Max laughed. "I think I had the same reaction when I read it. What are you going to read next?"

She glanced at her mother and said, "I want to read the Stephenie Meyer books. You know, the ones about the vampires and the werewolves. Mom says I'm too young and that I might have more nightmares." She leaned in close to Max and said in a voice she didn't think Kristin could hear, "I've read Mom's Stephen King books, and they didn't give me nightmares, so I don't think Stephenie Meyer is going to be so bad."

Max had shot a look of admiration for his daughter at Kristin, who'd simply shaken her head in an attempt to keep him from encouraging Flick to flout her mother's rules.

The mixture of Flick's intelligence and her youth was something else Max was going to have to learn to balance.

He'd responded to Flick's admission with pride in her ability to read, when it also deserved concern that Flick might be reading about subjects that could confuse or frighten her, long before she was old enough to understand them.

Max listened with patience as Flick said the brief prayer Kristin had taught her, ending with, "God bless Mom and Gramps and—"

Flick stopped herself and asked earnestly, "Do you mind if I ask God to bless you, Dad?"

Kristin watched Max swallow hard before he said, "That's fine with me, Flick."

"Okay. God bless Dad and Sissy and Rita and Ralph. Sissy is my cat," she explained, "And Rita and Ralph are my goldfish. They're staying with my friend, Sally. Oh, and God bless Gram and Emily and Smythe and Cook and Mrs. Tennyson." She glanced over at Kristin and asked, "Have I forgotten anyone, Mom?"

"I think that's everyone, sweetheart," Kristin said.

"Then Amen," Flick finished.

"Amen," Kristin and Max said together.

"Can you tuck me in, Dad?" Flick asked.

Max pulled the blankets up under Flick's arms. When he rose, she instructed, "You have to go all the way around."

Max tucked the blanket around her small body, down one side, around her toes, and back up the other side, then said, "How's that?"

"I feel safe now," she said.

Max shot Kristin a look, but he didn't ask the question she saw in his eyes: *Safe from what?*

"Goodnight, baby," Max said.

"I'm not a baby," Flick admonished.

"Right. Goodnight, Flick." He leaned over, hesitating as though waiting to be reproved by his daughter, before he kissed her gently on the forehead.

She grabbed his cheeks with her hands and pulled him down to her, turned his face in her hands and flicked her eyelashes against his cheek. When she let him go, she grinned and said, "They're butterfly kisses, Dad."

Max cleared his throat before he said, "Thanks, ba—Flick."

"Can I have the light on, Mom?" Flick said anxiously.

"Sure. I'll turn it out after you're asleep."

"Would you check the closet again, Mom?"

Kristin went to the closet and opened it and moved aside the clothes to make sure nothing was hiding there.

"And under the bed?"

"I'll check for you," Max said.

"I want Mom to do it," Flick said quickly.

Kristin saw that he was hurt that Flick didn't trust him. Apparently, Flick's fear was greater than her desire to please her new father.

"Are the windows locked?" Flick asked.

"We're on the second floor," Kristin reminded her.

"Would you check anyway, Mom?"

Kristin crossed to the windows, shoved the curtains aside and struggled to open each one without success. "They're locked tight." She crossed back to Flick and leaned down to kiss her. "Goodnight, Flick."

"Don't close the door all the way when you leave," Flick reminded her.

"I won't," Kristin promised.

After they left the room, Max turned to her, his voice hard and accusatory and said, "What is she so afraid of, K? Checking the closets and under the bed not once, but twice? Why does she have to be tucked in to be *safe?* Why is she afraid of the dark? What happened?"

"Let's go somewhere to talk," she said. "I don't want Flick to hear us."

Max shot a glance at Flick's open bedroom door down the hall. Then he gestured Kristin into his bedroom. And closed the door.

27

Max was feeling rage and helplessness. Something bad had happened to his child. And he hadn't been there to stop it. He was almost afraid to hear what Kristin had come into his bedroom to tell him. "I'm listening," he said. "What happened?"

Kristin wandered around the room touching things. She traced the shape of a porcelain shepherd with his collie and studied the face of a Regency-era ormolu clock. He wondered if she wasn't able to speak or whether she just wasn't sure how to tell him whatever horrible thing it was that had made his daughter so fearful of the night.

"K? I have to know."

She settled on the edge of the bed, near the violent carvings on the footboard. He wished for a sword or an ax like the ones held by those long-ago knights—any weapon that could make a bloody pulp of whoever had frightened his child.

With her back still to him she began, "Since she was seven, Flick has been attending a Swiss boarding school, but she always comes home for holidays. She was home this past Christmas and wanted to spend the night with a new friend she'd met at Sunday school."

She looked at him, her eyes liquid with emotion. "I couldn't see the harm in it."

Max felt his gut tightening with fear. He wasn't sure he wanted to hear the rest. But he had to know. "What happened?"

"The weather was beautiful. It almost always is in Miami," she said with a sigh. "Last Christmas it was almost too warm. Flick and her friend were camping out in the family room in sleeping bags. The family left their jalousie windows open overnight to take advantage of the cool air."

Max held his breath, waiting to hear what came next.

"A burglar came in through the window."

"Bloody hell."

"He accidentally stepped on Flick. She woke up and made a noise and he grabbed her to shut her up."

Max could feel his heart squeezing with pain and fear for his daughter. "He didn't—"

She reached out to him and said, "No, Max. He didn't. But he covered her nose and mouth with his hand to keep her quiet."

She looked at him, her eyes agonized and said, "She couldn't breathe. She thought she was going to suffocate."

"Bloody, bloody hell."

"The family's dog started barking and growling to wake the dead. Flick's friend woke up and screamed and her father came running with a baseball bat. The burglar threw Flick down and slid back out through the space he'd made by removing a few of the glass louvers in the window."

Max's hands bunched into fists so tight his knuckles turned white. "Did they catch the son of a bitch?"

Kristin shook her head. "He disappeared into the night. Ever since, Flick has been…anxious at bedtime."

Max had only seen Flick in the daylight, when she was a vivacious and effervescent and *normal* child. Who, it turned out, was terrified of demons in the dark.

"I should have been with her."

"I've told myself that a thousand times," Kristin said. "There was nothing you—or I—could have done to keep what happened from happening. Because of what I do for a living, I'm a nut for security at home. But I can't very well demand equal care from every friend of Flick's. What happened to Flick…" she shrugged helplessly and said "…just happened. The chances of it ever happening again are astronomical. But the incident left her scarred."

"Permanently scarred?" Max asked. Was his beautiful daughter going to spend the rest of her life expecting a bogeyman to jump out of the closet or out from under the bed.

"She got a lot of good counseling at school. She seemed to be fine. Until we came here. Staying at Blackthorne Abbey and then at my hotel and now here. I guess it's just too many strange places."

"What can I do?" Max asked. "How can I help?"

"She'll be fine, Max. With love. And time."

He crossed around the foot of the bed and sat beside her. "I want to be there to protect her, K. I want to be a father to her. What can we do to make this work?"

"The crisis is past, Max. There's no need for you to do anything."

"What I *need* is to be there for my daughter," he shot back. He shouldn't be surprised by the protective instincts he felt. It was how the human species had survived. "I intend to be there for her from now on. Whatever it takes."

"Meaning what?" Kristin said, lifting a worried brow.

"Meaning that if we can't work out some sort of shared custody—"

"Don't try taking Flick from me, Max," she warned, jumping up from her perch on the edge of the bed. She faced him like a lioness protecting her cub, her hands curved into dangerous claws and her teeth bared. "I'll fight you. With everything I am. With everything I have."

He rose, towering six inches over her head, a dark avenging angel with broad, muscular shoulders and powerful arms. But physical strength wasn't his only—or even his greatest—advantage. "Whatever you do, it won't be enough, K. I have more money, more time, more resources."

"I'm her mother!"

"And I'm her father."

"What do you want, Max?"

"Marry me, K."

"You're not a good bet, Max," she said bluntly.

"Maybe I wasn't in the past. I can change."

"Not fast enough," she said even more brusquely.

"We're good together, K. Admit it."

He saw she didn't want to. At last she said, "Yes, we're good together. In bed—"

"And out," he finished for her.

"I think I could love you," she continued inexorably.

The words were a balm to his heart, but when he took a step toward her, she held out a flattened hand to keep him at bay. Tears were streaming down her face, but her eyes looked fierce and her jaw was clenched.

"This isn't just about us, Max," she said ruthlessly. "Not anymore."

He couldn't believe what he was hearing. She was going to give him up to save her—their—daughter from him. "I can be a good father to Flick," he argued.

"You think being a father is wielding a baseball bat at one of the bad guys. You think it's taking a child on a horseback ride. You think it's buying her clothes—"

"It *is* all those things," Max protested.

"It's also holding a sick child's head while she vomits in the toilet, or cleaning vomit off the carpet, when she doesn't make it to the bathroom. It's listening to her whine when she's tired and having the fortitude to send her away to boarding school when it's the best thing for her."

"How is boarding school the best thing for Flick?"

he asked angrily. “How is being away from her mother for months at a time best for our daughter?”

“I had to work to support us. A lot of times it meant being away nights and weekends. My father was busy eighteen hours a day with his tennis academy. Flick was left alone with babysitters and housekeepers. I got off work so late the only interaction I had with Flick was to kiss her forehead after she was sound asleep.”

“So quit.”

She glared at him. “You haven’t heard a word I said. I have bills to pay! I need my job! I can’t be home for Flick. At least at boarding school she gets to spend her days and nights with girls her own age. Girls in her same situation. When she comes home on holiday, I take my vacation days and spend every minute with her.”

“Quality time?” he said sarcastically.

“Make fun of me if you will,” she said. “It’s worked for us. I’m not saying the situation is perfect. But you can see Flick is happy and well-adjusted. I did the best I could.”

“I can do better,” he said, his voice rough with emotion. “I can arrange to be there when Flick comes home for dinner every night.”

“Can you?” she demanded. “Are you willing to give up a challenging and rewarding job? Willing to give up traveling the world, at least during the school year? What, exactly, are you planning to do during the day while your daughter is away at school? The dishes? I doubt it!” she snapped.

“You’re being ridiculous.”

"Am I? As time goes by, and Flick goes off to college, where will you be? Home, without a life of your own, that's where!"

Max had to admit she was asking questions he'd never had to consider. Raising issues that had never crossed his mind. He was rich enough never to have needed to work. He'd done a great deal of gambling and sailing and playing polo and riding around in flashy cars with fast women in his teens and early twenties. He'd quickly gotten bored. He'd wanted to lead a life that mattered.

The CIA had been delighted to have him. He'd worked for his country for the past four years—and done some good, he thought. The undercover investigation he was involved in right now might save the president of the United States from being assassinated. If he did quit, what would he do with his life?

Being a parent was a big job, but Kristin was right. The job changed dramatically when Flick turned eighteen and left home for college and began to lead her own life.

That was only nine years from now.

He was reminded again of how much of his daughter's life he'd missed. And more determined than ever not to miss another minute of it.

"What if we just live together, without being married?"

"Live together where?" she asked. "Miami?"

"You don't have to work, K. You can come to London and—"

"My life needs purpose, too," she said simply. "I work for the FBI. In the United States."

"Maybe not for much longer," he couldn't help pointing out.

She paled. "Maybe not. But until I'm forced to quit, I'm not going to quit."

"I can support you."

"Yes, but will you? What happens if you get bored with us, Max? What happens if another woman catches your fancy?"

"We can write a contract—"

"That your lawyers can fight in court," she pointed out.

"I can put money in a bank account for you and Flick."

"If we have your money, why do we need you?"

Max had never felt so frustrated. "Is that all you think I have to offer? Financial security?"

"It's the only thing I'd be willing to count on you providing."

"You can trust me, K."

"Based on what?"

"Give me a chance, K. Please." He couldn't believe he was begging.

She shook her head. "I'm sorry, Max. I can't take the risk."

"You can't keep me out of Flick's life."

"I don't think that's going to be a problem, Max. You'll get an assignment from the CIA that takes you to Argentina or Morocco or Belarus, and we won't see you again. Until then, the less you see of Flick, the better. I don't want her to spend her life waiting and hoping that you'll come back someday."

"That's not fair, K," he said quietly. "You were the one who shut me out of your life."

She pressed her palms against her damp eyes. "Point taken."

There was no sense arguing anymore. They weren't going to agree. Instead he said, "I'd like to play tennis tomorrow with Flick."

She opened her mouth to deny him, he was sure, but changed her mind. "All right. What time?"

"No objection?"

"I'm sure Flick will enjoy it."

"How about ten?"

"Fine."

"Will you come with us?" he asked.

"You and Flick on opposite sides of a tennis court? I wouldn't miss it," she said with a Cheshire grin.

"Why is that?"

"I expect to see your daughter kick your ass."

28

Max couldn't believe his nine-year-old daughter was handing his ass to him on the tennis court. He could see Kristin laughing behind her hand in the stands.

He should have paid more attention to the fact that Flick's grandfather was one of the best coaches in tennis. And the fact that Flick herself was the daughter of two world-class tennis players. Which meant she'd been born with great eye-hand coordination and stunning reflexes.

"Forty-love, Dad," Flick said, announcing the score.

She'd already won the first set six games to four. She was up five games to three in the second set. And she had three of the four points she needed to win the sixth game.

He was proud of his daughter but flabbergasted at how easily she was beating the pants off him. They'd only been playing an hour. He was about to lose the match.

When they'd arrived at the court, they'd spun a racquet to decide who served first. Flick had called "Up" and the W on her Wilson tennis racquet had been right-side-up when the racquet landed on the ground.

"I choose this side, Dad. That means you can serve first."

Max realized he'd ended up on the side of the court that required him to look directly into the sun during his first service game. Nevertheless, he'd taken it easy on Flick. He didn't want a hundred-and-twenty-mile-an-hour tennis ball to hit Flick and injure her.

She returned his half-baked serve short and at such a sharp angle that the ball was off the court before he could reach it to return it. She did it four times in a row. He lost the first game love-forty.

It was her turn next. They had to change sides of the court between the first and second game. Max figured Flick would have the sun in her eyes, too. Then he realized she played tennis left-handed. Which meant she would serve with the sun at her back. Clever girl!

While he waited for Flick's first serve, Max wondered just how hard—how many miles-per-hour—a nine-year-old could hit a tennis ball. As it turned out, it didn't matter how hard she hit the ball, because she could place her serve wherever she wanted it.

She hit her first serve directly at his body. He couldn't get out of the way and returned the ball straight up in the air. She sent the second serve down the T in the middle and curving away. He never got a racquet on it. An ace.

She hit her third serve short and out wide. He got to that one and returned it crosscourt. She came in to the net and returned the ball down the line on the opposite side of the court. He couldn't get across the court fast enough to reach it.

When Flick got ready to serve for the fourth time, Max glanced at Kristin and saw her beaming at their daughter. She grinned at him. Gloating. He was *not* going to lose a game forty-love to a nine-year-old.

Flick's fourth serve was so short—barely over the net—that he never got to it before it died.

Flick shot her mother a grin and announced, "That's game, Dad."

He'd grabbed his towel and wiped his face to hide his chagrin.

Other than restricting the force of his serve, Max had played Flick as he would any other opponent. She'd shoved every serve right back down his throat and made her own serves impossible to return. He'd lost game after game after game.

Until he found himself in the spot he was in now. Which was to say, about to lose. He had one more chance to save this game. He bounced on his toes, then crouched down, ready to spring for the ball when it came at him.

Her serve went straight up the T. He never got a racquet on it. Another ace.

Flick came trotting to the net, her hand outstretched to shake his. "That's game, set and match."

Max dropped his racquet on the grass, reached over the net and caught his daughter under the arms and lifted her up into his embrace. "Brilliant game, Flick. You're bloody marvelous!"

Her arms circled his neck, tennis racquet still in hand. She stuck her nose against his sweaty throat and whispered in his ear, "Don't say *bloody,* Dad. It's a bad word in England. It'll make Mom mad."

He laughed and swung her in a circle, making her giggle, and set her back on her feet. He caught her shoulders as he went down on one knee, so he could look into her sparkling blue eyes. "How the hell did you get so good?"

She grinned and looked back over her shoulder at her mother, who was making her way onto the court to join them. "I used to practice with the students at the Lassiter Tennis Academy. And with Mom, of course. And I played at school. After a while, no one wanted to play with me, though, because I beat them all."

He was amazed she was so good, considering she'd been at boarding school since she was seven. And considering no one would play against her. He wondered why Kristin wasn't nurturing her talent. That was something he could help with for sure.

"Would you like to play competitive tennis?" he asked Flick.

She wrinkled her nose. "I don't think so, Dad."

"Why not? You're really good."

"It wouldn't be fun if it mattered whether or not I win."

Kristin laid a hand on Flick's shoulder and said, "You did great, sweetheart!"

"I beat Dad, Mom!"

"You sure did!" Kristin said.

"Of course, he didn't serve hard, like Harry does," Flick said.

"Your grandfather serves hard?" Max said.

Flick's brow furrowed. "He used to. Before his stroke, I mean. Usually ninety or a hundred miles an hour. No more than that," Flick said.

"To a kid?" Max said incredulously.

Flick shrugged. "Like you said, Dad. I'm good. Thanks to Gramps."

Max laughed. There was no false modesty in his daughter.

Her young brow furrowed and she said, "I wonder who's teaching all of Gramps's students until he gets well."

Max turned to Kristin and asked, "Do you have any idea who's running your dad's academy while he's recuperating?"

"He has a few assistants keeping his classes going," Kristin said. "That's all I know."

"Who's going to take his place?" Max asked.

"As soon as Gramps is well, he's going back to work," Flick replied. "He told me so himself."

Max exchanged a look with Kristin. "Have you heard about this?"

Kristin looked appalled. "I had no idea, Max. I can't believe Harry thinks—" She cut herself off.

Max didn't need Kristin to tell him Harry wasn't going to be back on the tennis court—unless he was in a wheelchair—anytime soon. He also knew why she'd cut herself off. Apparently, Flick had no idea her grandfather might very well be spending the rest of his life in a wheelchair or a walker.

"Flick, why don't you run ahead to the locker room," Kristin said. "I need to talk to your dad."

"Sure, Mom. I'm sorry I beat you, Dad. Promise you aren't mad?"

"I'm not mad," Max promised. "I loved that you beat me."

"You won't mind playing with me again?" Flick asked apprehensively.

"I look forward to playing with you anytime you like as often as you like," he assured Flick.

The smile that appeared on her face made his heart leap.

She took off for the locker room at a run and shouted back over her shoulder, "I had a really good time, Dad! Thanks!"

As soon as Flick was out of earshot, Max said, "She's amazing."

"Yes, she is," Kristin agreed.

"I had no idea she had so much talent. It's too bad she doesn't want to compete."

"You know what life on the tour is like, Max. All those weeks on the road, living in motel rooms, sitting on airplanes, the friction and competition between players. Would you really want her to live like that?"

"I guess not." He toweled off his face and the

back of his neck. "Speaking of living lives of quiet desperation—"

"Is that what we did all those years ago?" she interrupted with a rueful smile.

He continued as though she hadn't interrupted. "Maybe you should have a conversation with Harry the next time you see him about what he wants to do with his academy. He's living in fantasyland if he thinks he's going to be on the court anytime soon. Unless he plans to show up in a wheelchair."

"I don't want to discourage him, Max, by forcing him to acknowledge that his career may be over. He's having enough trouble dealing with his condition as it is."

"How about a reality check?"

She looked pained. "I just can't. I think the hope of getting back on his feet is all that's keeping him going. As of this morning he's agreed to go to speech therapy, and I want to encourage him as much as I can to do as much as he can. Flick and I are going to see him later this afternoon."

He smiled. "So your threat worked?"

She nodded. "I never thanked you for your support yesterday, getting Harry to agree to therapy. I appreciated it."

"So I'm good for something," Max said.

"Something," she agreed.

Max recovered his tennis racquet from the ground and stuffed it in his tennis bag. "How about going out with me tonight?"

"All right."

"Where would you like to go?" he asked.

She smiled and said, "You're the one who asked me out. What did you have in mind?"

He laughed and admitted, "I didn't expect you to say yes."

Her smile disappeared. "I thought we could talk some more about…everything."

He started to say "I'd rather not" but bit his tongue. The more time he spent with Kristin, the more time he had to convince her he was a man worthy of her trust. And her love.

"Sure," he said at last. "We can leave the house around eight. I want to say goodnight to Flick before we go."

"Flick would like that," she said.

"Maybe tonight she'll let me check the closets and the windows and under the bed for her," he said.

"After the solid trouncing she gave you this morning, I think that's the least she can do," Kristin said with a laugh. "I'm going to go check on Flick in the locker room."

Max watched her walk away. He realized there was a whole day ahead of him that they were going to spend apart, unless he did something about it. "Hey, Princess, wait up," he called out.

Kristin paused and turned to wait for him.

He wondered at the tension he saw in her shoulders and the worry he saw in her eyes. What was it she feared? He was no threat to her. Except maybe to her peace of mind. But he couldn't walk away. Not if he wanted a life with her and their child.

He put a smile on his face and asked, "What are you and Flick doing for lunch?"

29

Bella was sitting up in bed with several pillows stacked behind her, engrossed in a Stephen King novel Flick had recommended to her, reading glasses perched on the end of her nose, when a soft tap came at the door. "Who is it?" she called.

The door opened and a small voice whispered, "Gram, it's me."

"Come in, Flick." Bella set her book aside and pulled her glasses off and laid them on the bedside table, so her arms would be free to hold her grandchild.

Flick climbed up onto the bed and right into her arms. The strange thing was, Bella had never done this sort of thing with her own children. She wasn't quite sure why. Maybe because her parents—and her aunt, once her parents were both dead—hadn't done this sort of thing with her. It had simply never occurred to her that children could, or should, climb into their parents' bed in order to cuddle with them.

"I thought I heard your parents putting you to bed," Bella said.

Flick grinned. "You did. I had Dad check all the windows and look under the bed and in the closets twice. And I said my prayers with him and let him tuck me in, as though I were a baby."

Bella chuckled. "You naughty girl. Making your parents worry that you're still traumatized by that burglary, when you've been sleeping like—dare I say it?—a baby for months without a single nightmare."

Flick looked up at her with hope in her eyes and said, "It's working, Gram. Our plan is working!"

"I don't deserve any credit, Flick. It was your plan."

"Mom and Dad have gone out. I think they're on a date," the child said.

"I think you might be right. I can hardly believe you spent the entire day together."

"After we visited Gramps, we had lunch at the fish counter at Harrods," Flick said. "Then we went sightseeing to Buckingham Palace and the Tower of London and Westminster Abbey, where one of the Blackthorne dukes is buried. Then we went to the British Museum and saw the dinosaurs. They were pretty neat. Then we went to dinner at an Indian restaurant near the museum. I *love* Indian food," Flick gushed.

Bella thought what Flick *loved* was enjoying a wonderful day in London with both of her parents. It had been Bella's goal since the day she'd left the hospital in Richmond to get her son together with the mother of his child. She'd been surprised to get so much help from Flick.

During the time she and Flick had spent together

when Flick first arrived at the Abbey, Bella had discovered how much her granddaughter missed living at home. And how much she dreamed of having a father. Bella had been as delighted as Flick when Max had shown up at the Abbey uninvited and met his daughter. Flick was nothing short of ecstatic when Max insisted on spending time with her.

Bella had felt vindicated in her efforts to arrange a marriage between her son and the mother of his child. But it was also clear that Kristin and Max had significant issues they were going to have to work out in order to make a halfway normal marriage possible. And plenty of pitfalls threatening to keep them apart.

This morning, the *Times* had broken the story that Max Benedict, youngest son of Bella and Bull, had a love child. The tabloids were having a field day betting whether Max would acknowledge the child or marry her mother. Max had made paper airplanes out of the lurid articles and sent them flying out the dining room window. But Kristin had been obviously unsettled by the vicious nature of the attacks on her good name.

Fortunately, Kristin had gotten some good news during this past week. The Shooting Incident Review Team had recommended no further disciplinary action. Her suspension was over. Her job with the FBI was secure. Which created as many problems as it solved, as far as Bella was concerned. How were two people with demanding careers on different continents going to manage to live together in the same house?

It was Flick who'd come up with the perfect solution.

"I dropped a lot of hints today," Flick said. "I'm sure they'll figure it out soon."

"Do you really think they'll go for it?" Bella asked.

"I could tell Dad loves tennis. I know Mom does. It's the one thing she always finds time to do, even when she's busy."

"Do you think your grandfather will go for it?" Bella asked worriedly.

"I had a talk with Gramps today while Mom and Dad were talking to the doctors," Flick said. "I suggested maybe Mom and Dad could help him out at the academy. I think he knows he's not going to be able to work as hard as he used to. I just hope Mom and Dad realize it's the perfect solution. If they helped Gramps with the academy, we could all live together in Miami and be a normal family."

Bella hoped Flick would get her wish. She had her fingers crossed that Max and Kristin would discover for themselves the "perfect" solution to their problems that Flick had seen so clearly.

"Can I sleep with you, Gram?" Flick asked.

Bella realized the child might be more prone to nightmares than she was admitting to anyone. The bogeyman might have come into her room while she'd been gone.

"Of course, my dear." The bed was large. It had been slept in by royalty, once upon a time. But Bella was sure her granddaughter was the most precious thing that had ever deigned to curl up in this old bed.

Flick turned onto her side facing away from Bella, then scooted around until her tiny rump was pressed firmly against Bella's hip.

Bella put her glasses back on and picked up her book.

Flick glanced over her shoulder and said, "Watch out for the dog, Gram. He's kind of scary."

"Thanks for the warning, Flick." Personally, Bella thought the situation between Flick's parents was scarier. She had five children to get married off before her heart failed. But she didn't dare leave London until she was sure Max and Kristin had resolved their problems. Maybe Emily could help. She would have to think on it.

She set her book and glasses aside for the second time and focused on her dozing granddaughter. She'd never expected, when she'd set out to help her children find love, that she would find herself wanting it for herself, as well.

Where are you, Bull? she wondered. *What are you doing tonight?* She wondered if there were some perfect solution to their differences like the one Flick had found for her parents. She fell asleep trying to work one out.

30

Kristin had butterflies in her stomach, fluttering violently. The reason was simple. The day of the exhibition match had arrived.

She shouldn't be nervous. She and Max had practiced long and hard for the match. Yesterday, when they'd played Elena and Steffan, they'd beaten them soundly. However, Kristin knew that in the actual competition, Elena and Steffan would play harder to win. And nerves might cause her to choke.

"Worried?" Max murmured from his place beside her in the corridor leading out to Centre Court.

"Terrified," she admitted.

"Me, too."

She shot him a surprised look. "You have nerves of steel."

"And a herd of zebras in my stomach."

She laughed. "Sounds painful."

"Nice to see you laughing," he said. "Don't worry, K. We're going to beat the socks off them."

Kristin continued to smile after the laughter had

faded. She'd spent an amazing week with Max. They'd practiced in the mornings, then eaten lunch in the Players Lounge and spent the early afternoons in the Wimbledon locker rooms, talking and listening for any hint of an assassination conspiracy.

They'd frolicked—that was the word that came to mind—in the late afternoons with Flick and enjoyed the long, languid evenings with each other. Kristin didn't think she'd enjoyed a week more in her entire life. She was sorry their time together was coming to an end.

It doesn't have to end. You and Flick can have a life that includes Max. You just have to reach for it.

Was she willing to make the sacrifices necessary to be with Max? It would mean leaving her job. It would mean taking the risk that he would stay with her through adversity. It would mean trusting him with her heart. In her mind, that was more perilous than any work she'd done for the FBI.

Max had spent the past week showing her what life with him could be like. He'd driven the Range Rover, rather than the Porsche. He'd cooked dinner for her in his home in the West End, near his parents' mansion in Berkeley Square. She'd been impressed by his menu—the green salad, leeks and potatoes with salmon and the mangoes with pound cake and Britain's amazing heavy cream for dessert.

Max lived in a surprisingly modest, three-story flat that a decorator had furnished for him. "It could use a few personal touches," he'd admitted. "Any suggestions?"

She'd suggested a more comfortable chair in his study.

"There's nowhere in here for you to relax." Lighter curtains on his bedroom windows. "It's too dark in here. Like a bear's den."

He'd waggled his eyebrows and agreed he'd done a great deal of hibernating there.

She'd also suggested two chairs for the outdoor balcony. "So we can sit and enjoy the sunset."

"That sounds pretty damned wonderful to me, K," he'd said.

They were standing on the balcony when she'd made her suggestion, and she'd seen he wanted to kiss her. Since she'd wanted it, too, she'd stood still and waited. He'd drawn close enough that she could feel his breath on her face. Then he'd waited, ever so patiently, for her to bring their mouths together.

The kiss had been a mere touch of lips. Sweeter than sweet. For about five seconds. Then Max had opened his mouth over hers and his tongue had come seeking the honey within. A streak of desire had raced through her breasts and down her belly to settle between her legs. She'd pressed her body against his, wanting to feel hard male flesh.

Max didn't disappoint.

She'd wanted him, and she hadn't seen one good reason not to have sex with him. This week together was a brief moment in time. She wanted to enjoy it while it lasted.

Max had backed her into his bedroom from the balcony, and she'd realized why he had dark curtains on the bedroom windows. The bedroom became a dark cave in which the savage beast could claim its mate.

The liaison had been brief. She'd come as fast as he had. Her orgasm had been as powerful as his.

It was only later, lying in bed alone at Bella's Berkeley mansion, that Kristin regretted what she'd done. Because the prospect of spending the rest of her life without Max suddenly seemed a tragedy of vast proportions. All she saw ahead of her were long, endless years alone.

Kristin felt a tug on her tennis skirt, pulling her away from her thoughts. She looked down to find Flick standing beside her.

"Mom," Flick whispered. She gestured Kristin down to her level.

Kristin bent down and asked, "What is it, Flick?"

"I just wanted to say good luck."

"Where's your grandmother?" Kristin asked, looking around the hallway. Bella was supposed to be taking care of Flick. Kristin didn't see her anywhere.

"She's waiting in the box for players' coaches and families, where we're sitting."

When Kristin narrowed her eyes, Flick admitted, "I snuck away. But I'm going right back."

Kristin gave her daughter a quick, hard hug and said, "Thanks for coming, Flick. Now hurry back. Your grandmother will be worried about where you are. You know you need to be seated before the match starts, or you'll have to wait for a break to get inside."

"I'm going. As soon as I wish Dad luck."

Kristin let go of her daughter and watched as Flick

tugged on Max's short white sleeve. He'd been talking with Steffan and seemed as surprised to see Flick as she'd been.

"What are you doing here, young lady?" he said, his voice showing his disapproval of her appearance. "Where's your grandmother?"

Flick shot Kristin a chagrined look before she said, "Mom asked the same thing! I came to wish you and Mom luck. I'm going right back to the box where Gram and I are sitting."

He flipped her bangs, then said, "Thanks for coming. Now get out of here!"

"Good luck, Dad. Good luck, Mom," Flick called as she hurried away. She was looking back over her shoulder when she spoke, so she ran smack into someone coming down the hall, who wasn't watching where she was going, either.

Flick went sprawling.

"Flick!" Kristin dropped the tennis bag she had over her shoulder and ran to aid her daughter.

Flick was already on her feet by the time Kristin reached her, swiping at the liquid that had spilled on her blouse from the cup the woman was holding, and apologizing profusely to the lady she'd run into.

"I'm sorry, Miss Veronica," Flick said. "I wasn't watching where I was going."

"I'll say!" Veronica was swiping at her skirt, which was covered with what Kristin could see was the remnants of a plastic cup of Pimm's, Wimbledon's version of the Kentucky Derby's mint julep. Pimm's drink dated back to 1840 and consisted of cut-up citrus fruit, cucumbers and crushed mint with iced soda and alcoholic spirits. "Next time, watch where you're going!"

"She told you she's sorry," Kristin said curtly.

"She should be," Veronica retorted. "Look at me! I'm a mess." The reporter's white skirt was stained with the brown liquid. "What is she doing here, anyway?" she demanded.

"She's here to wish her parents luck. What are *you* doing here?" Kristin shot back.

"Mom," Flick said, tugging on her skirt. "Mom."

"Just a minute, Flick." Kristin had been anxious about the match and Veronica's attack on Flick gave her a place to vent her high-strung emotions.

"What's going on?" Max asked, joining them.

"Your daughter ran into me and I ended up spilling Pimm's all over my skirt," Veronica said.

"And all over Flick," Kristin pointed out, holding out her daughter's white blouse, which was wet from the drink.

"Mom," Flick said urgently, tugging on her mother's tennis skirt.

"What, Flick?" Kristin said, irritated at the interruption.

Flick held a hand up to hide her mouth, as though she wanted to speak to Kristin privately and tugged on Kristin's arm.

When Kristin had taken a couple of steps away from Veronica, Flick tugged her down so she could whisper something in her ear. "What is it, Flick?" Kristin asked, irritated at being drawn away from the other woman.

"I didn't think of it till I saw her in that white skirt again," Flick said, still holding her hand up to hide her mouth from Veronica. "Miss Veronica is the lady who came into the locker room and talked to Miss Irina."

Kristin nearly turned to stare at Max's old girlfriend but managed to resist the urge. She kept her face level with Flick's and said, "Thank you, sweetheart."

She stood upright and took Flick's hand and said to Max, "I'm going to take Flick into the locker room and rinse her off. I'll be right back."

The moment she got Flick away from Veronica she said, "Are you sure Miss Veronica is the woman you saw with Miss Irina in the locker room, Flick?"

Flick nodded vigorously. "Uh-huh."

"Why didn't you say something when you saw her in the park?"

"I guess I didn't think about it," Flick said. "I was kind of excited about riding."

"You're *sure* she's the one."

"Uh-huh."

At that moment, Veronica slammed open the locker room door and headed for one of the sinks. She turned on the water, wet a white towel and began brushing at the brown stain on her skirt.

"I'm really sorry, Miss Veronica," Flick said.

"I heard you the first time," Veronica said ungraciously.

Kristin was afraid Flick would blurt out something

about her mother's inquiries and hurried her daughter out of the bathroom. At the last moment, she turned back to the reporter and said, "You deserve that—and more—for printing that article about Max."

Veronica shot her a sour look without replying.

Kristin took her daughter by the arms and hurried her down the hall as she instructed, "Go back to the box and sit down beside your grandmother and *don't move* until your father and I come to get you. Do you understand?"

"Is Miss Veronica the one who wants to assassinate President Taylor?" Flick asked.

Kristin stopped dead in her tracks, staring at her daughter. "What are you talking about?"

"Come on, Mom. I'm not stupid. I've heard you and Dad talking."

Kristin couldn't believe she and Max had been that indiscreet. "When did you hear us?" she demanded. "Where?"

Flick looked guilty. "I snuck into Gram's sitting room after you put me to bed one night. I heard you discussing all the tennis players and who might be suspected in an assassination plot. I had to look up *suspected* and *assassination* and *plot* in the dictionary. Jeez, Mom. What are you guys, anyway, some kind of secret agents?"

"Hey, Princess," Max called to Kristin from down the hall. "What's holding you up? They've announced our names. It's time to go!"

Kristin didn't want to let her daughter out of her sight. But she was going to cause a scandal if she failed to show up for the doubles match. She took her daughter by the arms again, to make sure she had her attention, and said in her severest voice, "I want you to forget what you think you heard. I want you to go back to your seat beside your grandmother and be quiet and not say a word. To anyone. Your father and I will come get you when our match is completed."

"All right, Mom. But if Miss Veronica is planning to kill the—"

Kristin put a hand over her daughter's mouth and looked around to see if she'd been overheard. "That's enough, Flick. You heard what I said. Not another word. I mean it!"

Flick made a face. "Okay. But—"

"No buts!"

"K! Come on!" Max yelled.

"Go find your grandmother. Now!" Kristin waited until Flick was started on her journey before she turned back to Max. She hurried down the hall, glancing at the closed locker room door, wondering if the reporter inside was a potential assassin. And whether Veronica was involved in a conspiracy with Irina, and perhaps her son.

"Max, I have something—"

He shushed her and grabbed her hand. "Come on. We need to get out on the court."

"But, Max—"

He pulled her along behind him, lifting his free hand to wave at the polite but enthusiastic fifteen-thousand-strong Centre Court crowd.

It seemed to Kristin that now that Centre Court had a

retractable roof, it never rained on days when important tennis matches were being played. Today the retractable roof was open, letting in the hot sunlight and the occasional pigeon or English sparrow, who found a roost on the white roof struts.

Kristin sought out the family box, to the left of the royal box at the far end of the stadium, looking for Flick. She searched each row and found Bella but not her daughter. She was ready to leave the court—scandal or no scandal—when she saw Flick come running out of a tunnel and scoot up the stairs to a seat beside Bella.

Kristin was so focused on her daughter that she was oblivious to what was happening on the court. She only realized they'd won the serve when Max said. "Your serve, Princess."

"Max, there's something I need to tell you."

"Not now, Princess. Time to play tennis."

Kristin hit her first two balls into the net, double-faulting and losing the first point.

"You okay?" Max asked as he met her in the middle of the court.

"Veronica is the woman Flick saw talking to Irina in the bathroom," she blurted before moving to the other side of the court, so she could serve the next point.

Max was as stunned as she'd been when she'd first heard the news. The umpire calling the match said, "Time."

Kristin only had twenty seconds between each point. Telling Max what was troubling her had released enough tension that she was able to get her next serve into the box. But Elena returned it down the line, and Max was apparently still so distracted that when he swung at the ball he missed.

They met again in the middle of the court as Kristin headed back to the deuce side to serve for the third time.

"Why didn't you say something to me sooner?" Max demanded.

"Flick just told me in the hall."

"Did you see where Veronica went?"

"I left her in the locker room cleaning herself up."

"Time," the umpire warned again.

Kristin hurried to the ad court. They were already down love-thirty. She managed to gather her wits enough to hit an ace down the T for fifteen-thirty.

As she and Max crossed paths again, changing from the deuce to the ad court, she cupped her hand over her mouth so no one could read her lips and said, "Flick knows we suspect Irina and Steffan are plotting to assassinate the president."

"She what!" Max exclaimed.

"I told Flick not to say anything to anyone about what she knows. But now she knows I also suspect Veronica. I'm worried she's going to let something slip."

They both glanced up at the family box, where Flick, who was sitting beside Bella, waved back excitedly. "Serve," he said brusquely. "Let's get this damned match over with. Then we'll figure out where to go from here."

Once she and Max committed themselves to finishing

the match as quickly as possible, they began to play amazingly well. They took risks to shorten points. And won gamcs. And then the first set.

Between sets, Kristin saw Flick hanging over the rail at the front of the box waving at them. Irina sat at the back of the box alone. Kristin waved back at her daughter and said, “Max, Flick’s waving at you.”

Max waved back, but he said, “I’m going to have a serious talk with that young lady. She has no business eavesdropping. She might have jeopardized this entire investigation.”

“She promised not to say anything.”

Max shot Kristin a piercing look. “You believe a nine-year-old can keep a secret like this?”

Kristin shrugged helplessly. “We’ll just have to impress on her—”

“Time!” the chair umpire called.

Halfway through the second set, Kristin glanced up and felt her heart stop. Irina had been sitting in the family box throughout the match, but several rows back. Now she was sitting beside Flick. And Flick was talking animatedly to her.

“Oh, no,” she said to Max as she changed sides of the court for Max’s serve. “Look at the box.”

Max glanced up and said, “Brilliant. Do you suppose Flick’s spilling everything she knows?”

Kristin didn’t have time to consider the question. But when the point was over, her eyes went automatically to the family box. Irina had moved back to her original seat several rows behind Bella and Flick. But she was no longer alone.

"Max!" she said, elbowing him in the ribs. "Veronica's joined Irina in the family box."

"That can't be good," he said, eyeing the two of them.

"Should we just quit now and go get Flick?" she asked.

"On what pretext?"

"I can fake an injury."

He eyed the box and said, "Let's just finish. I don't want to create a scene that provokes a lot of questions."

They won the second set. And the match.

When Kristin knew they'd won, she looked up into the box where Flick was waving enthusiastically back at them. Bella was beside her, exhibiting the calm decorum befitting an English duchess. Veronica and Irina were still sitting several rows behind them. Relieved to see that Flick and Bella were safe, she threw herself into Max's open arms.

"We won, Max!" She turned with him to look back toward the box and saw that Flick and Bella were leaving the box—with Irina and Veronica.

"Oh, no!" she cried. "Max!"

Max let go of her and looked where she pointed. "Let's go!"

"Stop them!" she shouted, pointing toward the box. But the crowd was cheering so loud, no one heard her. "Someone stop them!"

Max didn't call for help. He didn't hesitate. He headed straight across the grass court at a run and climbed upstairs and across seats, right into the family box, then headed for the closest tunnel leading into the hallway, where the four females had disappeared.

Kristin dropped her racquet and ran after him.

31

Bella's heart was racing. She and Flick were being kidnapped. The unlikely kidnappers were Max and Kristin's coach, Irina Pavlovic, and Veronica Granville, the reporter for the *Times* whom Max had been briefly dating. They were being forced to exit the stadium to an unknown destination.

"Don't worry, Gram," Flick said. "They won't dare hurt us."

"You seem pretty sure of that, kid," Veronica said.

"My mom's an FBI agent and my dad's a spy and when they catch you, they're going to shoot you dead!" Flick said with relish.

Bella was both astonished and horrified at Flick's announcement. "Flick, don't incite them."

"Incite?" Flick said, focusing on the word she didn't know rather than the warning Bella was trying to give her.

"Don't encourage them," Bella said. "These people are dangerous."

"I see you understand the gravity of the situation," Veronica said.

"The gravity of the situation?" Flick said curiously.

"Do what I say or you die," Veronica hissed into her ear, hurrying them down a hallway that had British soldiers at every entrance back to Centre Court.

Bella couldn't believe what was happening. She would never have guessed when she'd woken up this morning that she would find herself in the middle of an intrigue.

When Flick had returned to her seat after disappearing for a short while, she'd asked if she could tell her grandmother a secret she wasn't supposed to tell anyone. Bella had told her that secrets were best kept to oneself. The girl hadn't been happy, but she'd remained silent.

They'd had room to spread out in the box, because there were so few family members to be seated for this exhibition match and Irina was the only coach. Flick had moved one seat over, then two, then down a row, then up two rows.

Bella finally said, "Flick, come sit here beside me."

"I have to tell someone," Flick said.

"All right. I'll listen to what you have to say. Just so you know I don't approve of telling other people's secrets."

She'd been sure Flick was about to tell her something about her parents' courtship. Bella had been watching Max and Kristin, and she thought the possibility of them ending up together looked much more promising by the end of the week than it had at the beginning.

She'd turned to her granddaughter and said, "I'm listening, Flick. What is it?"

"Miss Veronica is planning to kill the president of the United States."

Flick had spoken loudly enough that Irina apparently overheard what she'd said. Irina leaned forward across the two rows of seats that separated her from Flick and asked, "Where did you hear that?"

Flick had glanced over her shoulder, apparently surprised that Irina had heard her. She suddenly looked wary. "From my mom and dad."

"How could they possibly know a thing like that?" Irina asked.

Flick shrugged in response to Irina's question, then leaned close to Bella and whispered in her ear, "They're spies."

Bella thought the child was making it all up. Kristin worked for the FBI. But Max? A spy? She'd chuckled. She hadn't thought anything of it when Irina left her seat during one of the ninety-second breaks between odd-numbered games.

Until Irina returned with Veronica. Who'd threatened to hurt Flick if Bella and Flick didn't leave with her and Irina as soon as play stopped.

"My mom told me to stay right here till she comes to get me," Flick protested.

"If you don't come with me—and keep your mouth

shut—I'm going to hurt your grandmother," Veronica threatened.

Flick had grabbed Bella's hand protectively and said, "Don't worry, Gram. They're going to be in big trouble."

"Keep your mouth shut, kid."

"I won't!" Flick said.

Bella had urged Flick not to resist. But Flick was her mother's daughter. Fearless. And this lion cub had claws and teeth and wasn't afraid to use them.

When Veronica slid her hand across Bella's seat to squeeze her neck, Flick had bitten her.

Veronica had strangled a yelp as she pulled her hand free. Then she'd leaned close to Flick and said, "You do anything like that again, and I'll kill your mother."

That threat had been sufficient to turn Flick into a statue. The nine-year-old had sat frozen in her seat, her eyes wide and frightened.

As they were ushered out of the family box, Bella felt terrified. Her heart was thumping hard in her chest. She put a hand against it in a futile attempt to calm herself. The last thing she wanted was to have a heart attack. That possibility seemed almost irrelevant right now. She had no doubt that if Veronica truly was planning an assassination, she and Flick would not survive their encounter.

Bella felt frustrated because she'd left so much undone. She'd counted on the two or three years of good health she had left to get her children settled down with loving partners. It seemed that timeline might be cut considerably short.

Because of the soldiers guarding the entrances during play, to make sure people stayed in their seats, they hadn't been able to exit until play stopped. Play hadn't stopped until Max and Kristin won.

Bella hadn't waved back at Kristin when she sent her a victory wave, hoping she would notice something was wrong.

Veronica hissed from behind her, "Wave. And smile. Then both of you, get up and come with us."

Once they were in the hallway, Flick said, "What if I just yell for help?"

"I'll push your grandmother down the stairs," Veronica threatened.

"Don't you dare!" Flick said, grasping Bella's hand and hanging on tight.

"Is that sort of threat really necessary?" Irina asked.

"I'll decide what's necessary," Veronica snapped.

The two women were so engrossed with each other, that Bella didn't think they saw Max running down the narrow corridor toward them. Kristin was twenty steps behind him.

"Dad!" Flick cried. "Mom!" She turned to Veronica and said, "I told you so!"

Bella saw the indecision on Veronica's face before she turned and ran for the stairs. Irina headed back out through one of the tunnels to the stadium.

As though they'd agreed on a course of action ahead

of time, Kristin raced after Veronica, while Max headed into the tunnel to cut off Irina's escape.

"Get her, Mom!" Flick shouted.

As Bella watched, Kristin launched herself into the air, caught Veronica by the shoulders and brought her down. Veronica rolled over to fight and Kristin hit her with her fist in the chin, stunning her.

As Veronica lifted her head, Kristin straddled her, fist cocked and said, "Go ahead. Get up. Give me an excuse to hit you again."

Veronica lay where she was.

"Mom! You got her!" Flick shouted.

Bella grabbed for Flick, but she tore free and ran to her mother. Bella followed as quickly as she could. Fortunately, Max reappeared in the tunnel holding Irina's arm in his grip and marched her down the hall to join them.

Several soldiers who'd been guarding the entrances to the tunnels into Centre Court seating appeared in the corridor, apparently summoned by Max. Max helped Kristin up as the soldiers took custody of Veronica and Irina.

Before the two women could be led away, Max focused his gaze on Irina and said one word. "Why?"

Bella heard a wealth of pain in his voice. She gasped at the hatred she saw in Irina's eyes when the older woman spoke.

"I sat across the dinner table from you, Max, and told you every reason I have for hating America. President Taylor is a woman without conscience. She encourages the United States to take what it wants without thought for the rest of the world."

"There are legal ways to protest," Max said.

"But no better way to end this woman's foreign policy than to kill her!" Irina snarled.

Max turned to confront Veronica and demanded, "How did you get involved in this?"

Veronica's eyes narrowed as she spat, "It's time we women took back our power. Getting rid of that foul female in the White House is the first step toward a better world. My aunt and I are of like minds."

"Your aunt?" Max exclaimed. His glance darted between the two women. "Irina, you never said anything about a sister."

"I thought my sister was dead," Irina said. "It turned out she escaped to England when I brought Steffan to America. She thought I was dead, as well. It wasn't until my sister died and Veronica went through her mother's jewelry box and found a picture that showed her mother with me that she realized the connection between us and contacted me."

"I don't understand," Max said to Irina. "America gave you asylum. You and Steffan became citizens."

"America helped create the havoc that ruined Kosovo and killed most of my family. America is still interfering where it has no business interfering."

"Is Steffan involved in this?" Max asked.

"No," Irina said with a sneer. "Steffan is a fool. He *loves* America."

Max shook his head. Then he turned to the soldiers and said, "Take them away."

When Veronica and Irina were gone, Max said, "Steffan will still have to be arrested. I don't know whether he's involved, but we can't take the chance he is. I'm betting—hoping—that he's innocent, but he'll have to prove it."

Bella watched as Kristin put a hand on Max's arm and asked, "Are you all right?"

He grimaced and said, "Yeah. Just disappointed."

And sad, Bella thought. What a shame that the person who'd been a surrogate mother to her son had betrayed him. What must he be thinking now? She wished she knew what to say or do to comfort him. But she wasn't sure he would even accept comfort from her. She reached out a hand to her son, but let it drop before she touched him.

"Are you all right, Flick?" Kristin asked. She ran her hands over her daughter as though she were blind and needed to feel flesh and bones to know Flick was unhurt.

"I'm fine, Mom. I knew you'd come. I told Veronica so."

"How do you suppose Veronica found out we suspected her?" Max asked Kristin.

Kristin looked down at Flick and said, "Flick?"

"I didn't tell her! I just told Gram."

"Irina was sitting close enough to hear," Bella said, filling in the missing piece. "I had no idea there was any danger. I thought Flick was kidding when she said you were a spy, Max. Are you? Really?"

His lips quirked. "Yes, Mother, I am."

"Oh, my."

"But not for much longer," he added.

Bella felt like a patron at a play as she watched Max and Kristin exchanging significant looks. "You're quitting, Max?" she asked.

Max put an arm around Kristin's waist and a hand on Flick's head and said, "Yes, I am. I want to settle down in one place and be a father. And a husband, if K will have me."

Bella saw the anguished look Kristin shot at Max. Clearly, Max was forcing the issue. She felt sure her son loved this woman. But it seemed Kristin hadn't yet made up her mind whether to accept him. Bella could see Max ready to open his mouth and perhaps cause her to reject his proposal, when she might only need a little more time to consider it.

So she fainted.

"Mother!" Max cried, catching her on the way down.

Flick broke into tears. "Gram!"

She almost opened her eyes, Flick sounded so frightened and unhappy. But she kept them closed as Max eased her onto the floor.

"I guess the strain was too much for her," Kristin said.

"We'd better get her to the hospital."

"Should we call an ambulance?" Kristin asked.

"Maybe we'd better," Max said worriedly.

Bella couldn't afford to have doctors examine her. They would discover her secret and perhaps tell Max. She fluttered her eyelashes and moaned. And slowly opened her eyes.

"Mother?" Max said.

"What happened?"

"You fainted," Kristin said. "How are you feeling?"

"I guess I fainted with relief that the danger was over. I'm feeling better now. Can you help me up, Max?"

"Mother, I think—"

"I'm fine, Max," she said in a voice forceful enough to prove she was fine. "Please take me home."

She would make a point of taking Flick out of the way when they arrived at the mansion on Berkeley Square, so Kristin and Max would have time—and privacy—to discuss Max's long overdue proposal.

32

When they arrived back at Berkeley Square, Bella said, "Max, would you please help me up to my room."

She could see he wanted to go with Kristin, to make another plea to her to marry him. She wanted a chance to talk to him first. "Please, Max."

She watched him hesitate before duty—she was sure it was duty and not love—caused him to put an arm around her to assist her upstairs. "Come along, Flick," she said. "Give your mother a chance to relax and change her clothes."

Emily was waiting in Bella's room when she got there. "Would you wait just a moment, while I change?" she said to Max.

He looked longingly at the door but said, "All right, Mother."

She headed into the adjoining dressing room with Flick and Emily and changed out of the Chanel suit she'd worn to Wimbledon into a fashionable blue silk robe.

"I heard what happened at Wimbledon, Your Grace," Emily said. "It's all over the telly."

"I'm fine. We're all fine. There's no need to worry."

"You should rest, Your Grace," Emily admonished.

Bella was going to refuse, but she realized she was trembling with fatigue. She had to take care of herself. Her heart was strong enough to keep her alive only if she took care of it. "Very well. You may help me into bed."

Max was standing by the windows when Bella came out of the dressing room. She allowed Emily to help her into bed while Flick plumped up the pillows behind her.

When she was settled, Emily asked, "Is there anything else you need, Your Grace?"

"No, thank you, Emily. That will be all." As Emily turned to leave, Bella called Flick to her side and said, "Would you mind checking on your mother? Then come back and tell me how she is?"

"Sure, Gram," Flick said, loping out the door on Emily's heels.

Once they were alone, Bella adjusted the covers around her robe, waiting for Max to give her his attention. But he never did. Finally she said, "I have a confession to make, Max."

He turned to her at last and said, "I already know you didn't really faint, Mother."

She looked surprised. "How did you know?"

"I've held unconscious bodies before. You weren't anywhere near a dead weight. And you hesitated just long enough before falling to be sure I'd catch you before you hit the ground."

"Fascinating. That sort of discourse suggests you really are a spy."

"Was a spy," he corrected. "I'm quitting, as soon as I'm sure Veronica and Irina have been delivered to the proper authorities, and I know whether Steffan was involved in their plot to assassinate the president."

Bella didn't know where to start. She was silent so long Max asked, "Is that all, Mother?"

Bella wanted to paint her actions in the best light. But she was pretty sure no matter how she explained herself, Max was going to be upset. Finally, she just met his gaze and said, "I'm afraid I've interfered terribly in your life."

"I doubt it," Max said with the beginning of a smile.

"I need to talk to you about Kristin."

"I'd rather you stay out of my personal business, Mother."

"I'm afraid it's a bit too late for that."

"What have you done?"

"I was only trying to help," she said, excusing herself before she explained herself.

"Right. I asked what you've done."

Bella saw in his eyes a look that would not be denied. So she laid her confession before him. "I offered Kristin the Blackthorne Rubies if she would come to London and play in the exhibition match with you."

Max looked like he'd been poleaxed. "You did *what?*"

"She accepted my offer. And won the rubies."

"What on earth would possess you to do such a thing?"

Bella gave a small shrug. "I thought if you two spent time together you'd work out whatever differences separated you ten years ago. I wanted you to meet your daughter. And I hoped you would want to propose to Kristin and—"

"I did propose. She refused!" Max said indignantly. "Sorry you wasted your precious jewels trying to get me a wife," he added sarcastically.

"She refused them."

"What?"

"Kristin only accepted my proposition in the first place because she needed money. She wouldn't accept the rubies. And she promised to pay me back every penny I'd promised to loan her."

Max frowned. "Why wouldn't she take the rubies?"

"You'll have to ask her that." Bella reached into the pocket of her robe and took out the black velvet bag that contained the priceless jewels. She held the bag out to Max and said, "Since Kristin wouldn't take these, I'm giving them to you. Maybe you can get her to accept them."

"Why do you think she'd take them from me, when she wouldn't take them from you?"

"Perhaps because you'll be offering them as a gift to your bride, whom you love," Bella said. Her hand was starting to tremble again. She managed to hold the velvet bag steady as Max crossed the room and sat on the edge of her bed. She dropped it into his outstretched hand. "I hope you and Kristin have a long and happy life together."

"She hasn't accepted me, Mother."

"She will, Max. Because she loves you." Then she did what she hadn't done in the hallway at Wimbledon. She reached out and touched her fingertips to his cheek. It was the closest she'd come to a gesture of love to one of her children in many a year. "Now go and find her."

Max remained frozen like a wild thing under her hand for another moment, as though savoring the love she was bestowing with this simple caress, then jerked free and rose, as though he were breaking chains to escape. But he didn't leave. Instead, he shot her a piercing look with Benedict-blue eyes. And slowly sat back down on the bed.

"What were you doing at The Seasons, Mother? What was that invitation to the five of us all about?"

For an instant, Bella was terrified. Had Max somehow found out about her heart specialist in Virginia? Did he know she was dying? She would never be able to continue her matchmaking if her children knew the truth. And if Max had found out, he would tell the rest of them.

Bella's heart was racing so hard it hurt. "It's been so long since we were all together, I thought…it would be nice."

Such a simple answer. Absolutely true. And yet, not the entire truth. Would her son accept it?

Max hesitated so long that she thought perhaps her secret had been discovered. Then he shifted the rubies from one hand to the other and stood again. "I just wondered," he said, looking down at her. "We all wondered why…"

"It was nothing nefarious. I had no evil intentions," she said, defining the word as Flick might have done. "Just a desire to see my children. Is that so strange?"

"Yes, Mother, it was," Max said. "But it was still a good idea. I miss seeing my siblings all in one place."

"Well," she said, revealing a wealth of emotion in the single word. "Maybe I'll try again next year."

He grinned. "If you do, I'll come."

Bella felt a sudden ache in her throat, felt the sting of tears in her eyes. "I'll be looking forward to it. Now, get out of here. You have a lovely woman waiting for you."

Max left the room without looking back, closing the door silently behind him.

She'd done her best. She believed Max and Kristin loved each other. Hopefully, her son would find the right words to woo her to be his wife.

33

Kristin had just sent Flick from the room and gone into the bathroom to check on her bath when she heard a knock on the door. As she opened it, she said, "Flick, I told you—"

"It's me," Max said.

He was still wearing his sweaty, grass-stained tennis clothes. She'd changed out of her tennis dress into a white terry-cloth robe. But the curls on her neck were still damp with sweat. And she smelled like she'd just played two athletic sets of tennis. "What do you want, Max? I've got the water running in the tub for a bath."

"I want to talk."

She hesitated, then stood back to let him in and closed the door behind him. "I guess we're done now with everything we needed to do," she said. "The match is over, and our most likely suspects are in custody."

"We never had a chance to celebrate our win," he said as he held out his hand.

She put her hand in his and he drew her into his arms for a hug. "Congratulations, K. We won."

"And scandalized the tennis world by taking off without our honorary trophy," she said with a wan smile.

He looked into her eyes and said, "That isn't why I came in here."

"Oh? Why did you come, Max?"

He looked into her eyes and said, "I love you, K. I want to spend my life with you. Will you marry me?"

Kristin laid her head on his shoulder, her face turned away from his to give herself time to think. She supposed she was saying something simply by staying close to him, rather than pulling herself free. But she really hadn't yet made up her mind, and she wanted to be held by him, in case this was the very last time she was ever going to find herself in his embrace.

"What can I say to convince you to marry me?" His voice was hoarse and she could hear the emotion in it.

"I do love you, Max," she said. "So much it hurts."

He stepped back, separating them, and held her head between his large hands. "Then what's holding you back?"

"You can't quit your job, Max. You love it. Someday you'd hate me because you'd miss it. And I can't quit mine for the same reason. There's just no compromise that works for us."

"Oh, for heaven's sake," a child's voice interrupted.

"Flick?" both adults said at the same time.

Flick came crawling out from under Kristin's bed.

Kristin gawked at her. "What on earth are you doing under there?"

"I thought you were afraid of bogeymen under the bed," Max said.

"I'm not afraid of bogeymen," Flick said as her father took her arms and pulled her upright and set her on her feet. "Or demons in closets or outside the windows."

"Then what in the world—"

"I had to do something to get the two of you together," she said disgustedly. "I can't believe you didn't figure out the solution to your insoluble problem," she said crossly. "*Insoluble* means there *is no solution*. But there's a perfectly good solution to your dilemma staring you right in the face."

She balled her small hands into fists and stuck them on her hips. "A *dilemma* is a problem with difficult or undesirable choices," she explained, as though they were ignorant of the word.

She turned to Kristin and said, "Gramps and I figured it out together a million years ago. I've been giving you all the hints I can, but I guess the two of you are too dense to work it out on your own."

Flick turned to Max and said, "I mean the two of you are *thickheaded or extremely ignorant* as opposed to *having a high mass per unit volume*. So I'm going to tell you the answer."

"Listen, young lady—" Max began.

"You can both teach at the Lassiter Tennis Academy," Flick said. "That way, I can go to Miami Country *Day* School and come home every night for dinner."

She looked expectantly from one parent to the other. "Well?" she said, suddenly unsure, both hope and fear staring out at them from her Benedict-blue eyes. "What do you think?"

Kristin turned to look at Max, feeling suddenly buoyant. What a simple solution to their insoluble dilemma. "Well, Max?"

His lips slowly curved into a smile. "Sounds like a good idea to me."

"Me, too," Kristin agreed.

Max went down on one knee in front of Kristin. "K, I love you. Will you marry me?"

From the corner of her eye, Kristin saw Flick with her lower lip clamped in her teeth. She smiled down at Max and said, "Yes, I will."

He reached into his pocket and came out with a ruby ring with a square-cut stone so large it made her gasp.

"Max, what is that?"

His lips quirked. "Would you believe one of the Blackthorne Rubies? Give me your hand, Princess."

When Kristin held out her left hand, it was shaking.

Max slid the ring onto her finger, then stood and pulled her into his arms.

"Hey," Flick said, "Don't forget about me!"

They opened the circle to include Flick, who hugged them both tight as they leaned in to kiss each other.

"Wait until Gram hears about this," Flick said, grinning up at them. "She's going to be really glad."

Max and Kristin both laughed.

Kristin didn't think life could be any better, didn't think the future could look any rosier.

"Hey, Mom," Flick said. "Aren't you forgetting something?"

Kristin frowned. "No, I don't think so."

"Dad, do you want to tell her, or should I?"

"Tell her what, Flick?" Max said, now looking as worried as Kristin felt.

Flick put her hands on her hips and said, "If Mom doesn't turn off the water in the bathroom pretty soon, the tub is going to overflow."

Kristin took one look at Max's stunned face and felt a giggle escape. Max took one look at her and guffawed. The two of them fell into each other's arms, laughing so hard they had to hang on tight to stay on their feet.

Flick shook her head at her *incomprehensible* parents. She just didn't understand their behavior sometimes. At least, with her help—and Gram's, of course—they'd managed to find their way to each other.

Her parents were kissing now, completely oblivious to her. And kissing. And kissing. With no end in sight.

"Well," she said at last. "If nobody else is going to do it, I will."

Neither of them responded. They just kept on kissing.

Lacking mindful attention to me and everything around them, she thought. Completely *oblivious*. Although *abstracted* fit just as well. They were totally *preoccupied* with each other. She walked completely around them and they didn't even notice her.

Yep. That's what they were all right. Obliviously distracted.

Flick grinned, then headed for the bathroom to turn off the overflowing bath water.

Epilogue

She should never have doubted the duchess could do what she'd set out to do, Emily thought as she viewed the tableau before her from her seat high up in the stands. There sat Harry Lassiter in his wheelchair on the sidelines of a Har-Tru tennis court at the Lassiter Academy. Flick stood by his side, talking animatedly—no doubt using big words—to her grandfather.

Kristin and Max had been husband and wife since a ceremony in London the day after the Gentlemen's Singles Championship match at Wimbledon. Steffan had been Max's best man, having been cleared of all involvement in his mother's plot with Veronica to assassinate the president. The plot had been confirmed by emails exchanged between Irina and Veronica which they'd attempted to erase—unsuccessfully—from the hard drives of their computers.

The newlyweds stood at the back of opposite ends of the court. Each was shouting instructions to a student as the youths slammed a ball back and forth with amazing speed and accuracy.

"Down the line," Kristin instructed her student.

"Crosscourt!" Max advised his. And then, "Too short."

"Move in! Move! Drop shot!" Kristin said.

Kristin's player hit the ball with perfect touch, so it stopped dead on Max's side of the net before the player Max was coaching got anywhere near it. Emily could hear Max saying to his player, "You have to push off with that back foot. And finish your swing! He couldn't have hit that shot if you hadn't left your ball so short. It's all about footwork and follow-through."

Emily would have thought Kristin would be complimenting her player for his terrific shot. Which she did, for the first five seconds. Then she said, "You can't drop the ball and stand there like a stone. You need to get yourself positioned for whatever return might come back at you. Everyone isn't going to miss. Follow the ball toward the net."

"They look happy, don't they?" the duchess said from her seat beside Emily. "I know Flick is happy." The duchess smiled and said, "She told me so this morning. In fact, she's *deliriously* happy. She was quick to inform me she didn't mean the first definition of the word—*mentally disturbed*. She meant the second—*frenzied excitement*."

Emily smiled. The child was a delight. She viewed the scene below them and agreed, "Yes, Your Grace, they do look happy." But people weren't puppets. They couldn't be made to do anything they didn't want to do. In this case, Kristin and Max had a previous relationship and a child together. It made sense that they would end up living happily ever after.

However, later today, she and the duchess were taking a plane from Miami to Hong Kong, where Her Grace planned to try out her matchmaking skills with a son who had no known attachments with a specific woman. How was the duchess going to succeed with Riley, when there was no woman waiting in the wings with whom he had a previous relationship and a child?

Emily thought the trip was ill-conceived, and dangerous, considering how taxing it would be to fly, even first class, from Miami to Hong Kong. But she'd had no success trying to talk the duchess out of her plan.

Emily's phone rang and she was immediately the focus of all eyes on the court. She'd been warned ahead of time that cell phones weren't allowed. But she was waiting for a report from Warren & Warren Investigations about exactly where Riley was in Hong Kong, so she'd left it on.

Emily rose and said to everyone on the court, "I'm so sorry." She answered the phone to stop it ringing, said, "I'll be with you in a moment," into the phone, then held it against her chest as she said, "Please excuse me, Your Grace. I've been waiting for a call—"

"Of course, Emily," the duchess said. "No need to explain. Go."

Emily left the stands, moving so hurriedly she was afraid she'd trip and go sprawling. She stopped away from the court, in the shade of a palm tree, and said breathlessly, "Emily Sheldon speaking."

"Emily?"

The voice sounded familiar. But the phone number wasn't. "Lydia? Is that you?"

The girl on the other end of the line sobbed. "I'm in trouble, Emily."

"Where are you, Lydia? Are you all right? Do you need help?"

"No one can help."

Emily felt a shiver run down her spine. She looked back at Her Grace, who would be devastated if anything happened to her youngest child. Then she thought of the one person she was certain could help, if anyone could. "I'll call Oliver and—"

"Not Oliver!" Lydia cried. "I don't want him to know."

"Calm down," Emily said. "I won't contact Oliver, if you don't want me to. Tell me where you are."

"Rome," Lydia said.

"Are you in danger?"

"Not exactly," Lydia said.

"What does that mean?" Emily asked. She had only a few hours left before their flight to Hong Kong to resolve Lydia's problem, whatever it was. She didn't want to involve—and upset—the duchess. Despite the feelings she knew Her Grace's children had toward their mother, Emily loved her employer. And it was her job to keep the duchess's life as stress-free as possible.

Emily's British accent was clipped as she asked, "Are you in danger, Lydia? Or aren't you?"

Lydia half sobbed, half laughed and said, "Only from Mother. She's going to kill me when she finds out what I've done."

"The duchess loves you, Lydia. There's nothing you can do that she won't forgive."

"Really?" Lydia said. "What do you think she'll say when she finds out I've lost the Ghost of Ali Pasha."

Emily felt all the breath leave her in a whoosh. She couldn't draw another breath for a moment, in order to speak, so she remained mute.

"Emily? Are you still there?"

"What happened?" Emily managed to say at last.

"I lied to Oliver and told him I had Mother's permission to borrow the Ghost of Ali Pasha, so he arranged to have it delivered to me. I wore it to a charity ball last evening. During the night, someone stole the necklace from my hotel room."

"You didn't have it in a safe?" Emily asked, not believing how irresponsibly Lydia had acted with what was a priceless piece of jewelry.

"I got back to my hotel room late. I thought—"

"Never mind," Emily said, her mind racing. The loss was incalculable. Far worse was the pain Lydia was going to cause Her Grace, because of her deceit. "How long has the necklace been missing?" The longer the necklace was gone, the harder it would be to recover.

"I'm not quite sure. I didn't wake up until almost noon Rome time. I don't know what woke me up. I looked for the necklace on the table beside the bed, but it wasn't there, or around my neck—or anywhere! I couldn't believe it at first. I've looked for what feels like hours," she said in a distraught voice. "It isn't here."

"I wish you'd called me sooner," Emily said. "Maybe, if the search for the thief began immediately, there might be some hope of recovering the necklace before its loss was discovered by Her Grace. Please let me call Oliver—"

"No!" Lydia cried. "Please, please, Emily. Don't tell Oliver. He thought I had Mother's permission to borrow the necklace. He's the one who arranged to have it sent to me from the vault at Blackthorne Abbey. He'll get in trouble, too. I don't want him to know I lost it like this. Once I find it, I can apologize to Mother—and to Oliver—for being so careless. But not until then."

Emily made a command decision. "All right. I'm going to call someone to come and help you find the necklace. His name is Sam Warren. He's a private investigator from Dallas. He's the very best, Lydia. He should be there early tomorrow morning. You can stop worrying, Lydia. If Sam can't find the Ghost of Ali Pasha, it can't be found."

Lydia moaned.

Emily gave a shaky laugh. "What I meant to say is that Sam will find it. He's never failed on a mission yet."

"Thanks, Emily. Let me know when his flight is arriving and I'll go meet it."

"Oh, I don't think Sam will want your help, Lydia." Or accept it, she thought.

"He doesn't have a choice," Lydia said. "I lost the necklace. And I intend to be there when it's found."

* * * * *

Dear Reader,

Welcome to the world of the Benedict Brothers! You met the American branch of the Benedicts in *Outcast.* In *Invincible* I've introduced the British branch of the family. I hope you come along for the ride as I explore the adventures of both families. Next up is Lydia's story, *Unforgettable.* I can't wait to see what kind of trouble the youngest Benedict gets into as she tries to find the stolen Ghost of Ali Pasha!

Meanwhile, if you'd like to read more about the historical Dukes of Blackthorne, look for my Captive Hearts series, *Captive, After the Kiss, The Bodyguard* and *The Bridegroom,* already in stores. If you want to read more about the modern-day Blackthornes in Texas, check out *The Cowboy, The Texan* and *The Loner.* There are fifty Joan Johnston novels and novellas out there to choose from, so have fun!

Be sure to sign up on the mailing list at my website, *www.joanjohnston.com,* if you'd like to receive a postcard or enewsletter when the next book is in stores. As always, I appreciate hearing your comments and suggestions.

Take care and happy reading,

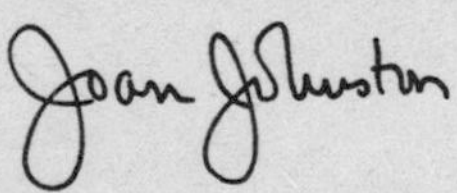

ACKNOWLEDGMENTS

I want to thank Angela Bell, public affairs specialist in the Office of Public Affairs, Federal Bureau of Investigation, for her invaluable help with information relating to the FBI. If Kristin Lassiter seemed like the real thing, it's all due to Angela. Any mistakes are mine.

I owe a great debt of gratitude to my friend Sally Schoeneweiss, who is always there to talk me through the hard parts. She keeps my books front and center through her public relations firm, Talk Ink, Inc. You can find her work on my website, *www.joanjohnston.com.*

Thanks to Caroline Applegate, whom I met on a plane on the way back from the Kentucky Derby. Caroline lost her husband to heart failure and shared facts about his illness that helped me to make Bella's heart failure more believable.

Last, but by no means least, I want to thank the team at Harlequin Books and MIRA Books, who take such good care of all their authors while making each one feel special, including Donna Hayes, Loriana Sacilotto, Craig Swinwood, Valerie Gray, Margie Miller, Margaret O'Neill Marbury and Linda McFall (my fabulous editor). Thank you all for the "just flat gorgeous" cover you created for *Invincible!*

JOAN JOHNSTON

32829	SHATTERED	___$7.99 U.S.	___$9.99 CAN.
32574	OUTCAST	___$7.99 U.S.	___$8.99 CAN.

(limited quantities available)

TOTAL AMOUNT $______
POSTAGE & HANDLING $______
($1.00 for 1 book, 50¢ for each additional)
APPLICABLE TAXES* $______
TOTAL PAYABLE $______
(check or money order—please do not send cash)

To order, complete this form and send it, along with a check or money order for the total above, payable to MIRA Books, to: **In the U.S.:** 3010 Walden Avenue, P.O. Box 9077, Buffalo, NY 14269-9077; **In Canada:** P.O. Box 636, Fort Erie, Ontario, L2A 5X3.

Name: ______________________
Address: ______________________ City: ______________________
State/Prov.: ______________________ Zip/Postal Code: ______________________
Account Number (if applicable): ______________________

075 CSAS

*New York residents remit applicable sales taxes.
*Canadian residents remit applicable GST and provincial taxes.

MIRA®

www.MIRABooks.com

MJJ1110BL